Edgar Allan Poe

and the

Jewel of Peru

ALSO BY KAREN LEE STREET

Edgar Allan Poe and the London Monster

Edgar Allan Poe

and the

Jewel of Peru

KAREN LEE STREET

PEGASUS BOOKS
NEW YORK LONDON

EDGAR ALLAN POE AND THE JEWEL OF PERU

Pegasus Books Ltd
148 West 37th Street, 13th Fl.
New York, NY 10018

ISBN: 978-1-68177-667-5

10 9 8 7 6 5 4 3 2 1

Printed in the United States of America
Distributed by W. W. Norton & Company, Inc.

For my father
and for Milo

No one knows better than a bird of the air
where treasures are concealed.

(Aristophanes, *The Birds*)

PHILADELPHIA
FRIDAY, 12 JANUARY 1844

It had been left by the front door after night had fallen. I was working on a tale by the kitchen fire when I heard a soft noise—the wind or perhaps sleet upon the glass. The sound was almost imperceptible, yet something in its nature disturbed me and I peered from the window. The darkness was too complete, so I made my way to the door and eased it open. Cold air charged in like an angry spirit, but there was no one to be seen or heard, no footprints in the soft white snow to mark an intruder's presence. Yet on the step was a box, round in shape, wrapped up tidily in brown paper, its folded edges sealed with wax and tied with string. My skin prickled with unease as I brought it inside and placed it on the kitchen table.

I held the lamp above it. My name and "Philadelphia" were written upon the parcel in ink that had bled into the paper. I cut the string, broke the wax seals and discovered a tin hatbox. Disquietude gave way to pleasure. My hat was increasingly shabby, an embarrassment on close inspection, and my wife and her mother must have contrived to buy me a new one. How like them!

It was a full week before my birthday, and yet I could not resist—the wrappings were undone after all. My fingers greedily unlatched the lid. But when I looked inside, several pairs of obsidian eyes stared up at me—*demon* eyes. I leapt back, hands protecting my face, for crouched in that hatbox were three crows, beaks agape in their desire for flesh. I grabbed the fire iron to fend off the explosion of wings, yet the room remained silent, except for the ragged sound of my own breath. Cautiously I approached the box again and held the lamp over it. There was no doubt—the birds were dead.

My relief was fleeting, though, for as I lifted one of the creatures from its peculiar tomb, I found its head was severed from its body, as were its wings and legs. What cruelty was this? So gruesome was the effect, I near retched as I placed the parts of all three birds onto the brown paper, searching in vain for some message. Oddly there was no smell of death or decay— the creatures had surely been mummified, like favored pets of an Egyptian pharaoh or perhaps the Emperor of Death himself. These wild fancies subsided, but my horror did not, for I knew with absolute certainty who had delivered the trio of ebony birds. It was my foe, my nemesis, the man who wished me dead: George Rhynwick Williams had returned to torment me.

FRIDAY, 19 JANUARY 1844

The world was a ghost of itself. All color had been muted to white and an eerie stillness prevailed. Trees glistered in the rising sun, their limbs frozen by the ice storm that had come in the night, and the river was a sleek ribbon unfurled through the heavy cloak of snow. It appeared as solid as the ground surrounding it, but I kept to its banks, following my memory of the now invisible footpath that I walked daily. In the warmer months, it was my habit to rise early to swim in the Schuylkill River, and when it was too cold to swim, I walked along its edge to revivify myself with the exuberance of nature. As I made my way along my customary route, the deep snow hushed my footsteps and the sun danced wildly upon the ice. I seemed to be the only living thing in that crystalline world, entirely alone amidst its unearthly beauty.

"*Kee-rah!*" A screech tore through the implacable quiet—it was a hawk of some kind. I scanned the heavens above me, but there was nothing to be seen, until a piece of sky hurtled down, skimmed over me and landed on the frozen branch of an oak tree. "*Kee-rah!*" A deceitful blue jay called out with the voice of a hawk as it skittered pugnaciously back and forth along the branch.

"Kee-rah!" A call in response—or perhaps in challenge—as a red-shouldered hawk soared across the frozen river and, talons extended, approached the large oak where the blue jay waited. It appeared to have badly miscalculated its attack, for it crashed through the oak's uppermost branches high above the lively jay. But the hawk had keener eyes than mine; it set a large bird into flight, a bird I had not noticed, so perfectly had it merged with the tree. The great horned owl left its refuge and glided up into the early morning sky, its wings rippling through the air in slow, undulating movements. The hawk followed, its own wings beating vigorously, and in moments it was upon the owl, talons piercing flesh, dislodging feathers. The owl wheeled mid-air and retaliated, slashing at the hawk's reddish belly, then the two raptors locked talons and began to plummet earthwards, necks craning, beaks thrusting. Their vicious flapping stirred the snow into a whirlwind as they tumbled into it, still grappling. The pristine whiteness was soon spattered with red, and the air reverberated with the birds' shrieks. I hastily packed a snowball, hoping to startle the enemies into a temporary truce, but before I could meddle in the forces of nature, the fighting birds rose up from the snow and thrashed their way into the sky together, like some ancient demon from hell, then broke apart, one flying north and one south.

"Kee-rah!" The blue jay mimicked the hawk one final time before it too took wing and sailed across the Schuylkill, leaving me shivering on the river's bank, the cold from the snowball numbing my hands and the vision of that avian battle filling me with disquiet.

Later, as I approached our brick house on North Seventh Street, the first person I encountered was my mother-in-law, who was busily scraping ice from the footpath. She was a study in perpetual motion, ceaselessly working at household tasks and refusing all offers of assistance or entreaties to rest herself, with the words, "Industry pleases God", or "Diligence is its own reward". "Muddy", as my wife and I called her, did not enjoy idleness and we had learned to appreciate rather than protest the fact that she made our lives much more comfortable. Despite my best efforts, I still had not managed to earn enough through my work as an editor, or in selling my tales and poems to support my family in the manner that I wished—that they *deserved*—and I was ever grateful to my industrious and canny mother-in-law. She had rescued us from the brink of penury far too often, whether through taking in washing and sewing, gathering edible wild plants to supplement our meals or her tenacious bartering at the market.

"Beautiful, isn't it?" I said, indicating the thick coat of ice that sparkled on the tree limbs, the roof of the house and the snow itself.

"That tree branch is likely to come down," Muddy observed, nodding at a large elm, "and we'll lose some of the smaller trees when the thaw comes."

I looked at the lithe trees that were elegantly stooped with the weight of the ice and could see that Muddy's dour presumptions were probably correct, but my heart fell a little with her words. Moments later my wife Virginia, my darling Sissy, appeared in the door and my joy was revived.

"Oh, Eddy, isn't is glorious? It's like a fairy-world." She stood on the front step, wrapped in the paisley woolen shawl I had bought her in London, the beauty of which could not rival hers as sunlight fell on her chestnut hair and revealed hues of copper, like the hidden sheen of color in a bird's feathers.

"That is just what I thought to myself during my walk. Magical, isn't it?" I hurried up to the porch and put my arms around her.

"You are half-frozen." She pulled me by the hand into the warmth of the kitchen, where a fired roared and there was coffee and porridge on the stove. "Tell me what you saw at the river," she said, as she set breakfast before me. "I so miss our walks! I have cabin fever, truly I do."

"The river is beautiful, fully frozen and glistening, with every tree around it sheathed in ice. But it is treacherous out," I added, as longing crept over her face. "I tumbled half a dozen times despite my boots. My dignity was quite defeated."

"I suspect you are exaggerating to bring me comfort."

"Not at all. Spring will be here soon enough. It would not do to fracture a limb and be confined to your cabin for weeks."

"I am not so fragile as you and Mother believe. I am certain I could navigate a snowy riverbank."

"It is the ice that is treacherous more than the snow, for it is difficult to see on the ground and one would need crampons to resist its slipperiness. And you are not so hardy as you declare yourself." I kissed her cheek to take the sting from the truth of my words. My wife had a frail constitution, but heartily disliked it when her mother or I tried to "cosset" her, as she put it. "I did witness a peculiar spectacle at the river," I added. "A battle of the birds, in fact." I recounted what I had seen, and Sissy was entranced.

"How strange and marvelous! I am not certain whether I would have wished the hawk or the owl to prevail. The owl, I think. They are such uncanny night creatures—what a rare thrill to see one in daylight."

"But what of the red-shouldered hawk?" I said. "Such a bold, brave fellow and so elegant with his mottled feathers, yellow beak and talons. It is glorious to watch him soar on the sky's currents."

"But the great horned owl is equally handsome with his golden eyes and tiger-striped feathers. And he does seem so very wise. I think it is the feathery eyebrows."

"You will soon have him sporting a waistcoat and monocle, and smoking a meerschaum pipe, like some creature from a child's fairy tale." I smiled. "And what of the blue rapscallion? What do you think his motive might have been, for surely he stirred up the enmity between them?"

Sissy pondered this. "Self-preservation. The jay knew that he might become breakfast for either the hawk or the owl and so he pitted them against each other. And if he is lucky, neither will return to that spot on the Schuylkill; each fearing the presence of its nemesis, and so the blue jay will be safe to nest in that oak tree."

My wife's explanation seemed plausible, which filled me with good cheer. So strange and intense had the spectacle been, I half-feared the battle to be an omen connected to the dreadful package that had been left outside our door the week before.

Sissy pulled her shawl tighter around her shoulders with a shiver. "Come, let us go sit in the parlor. Muddy has laid the fire and there is a piece I'd like to play for you."

"Of course, my darling."

I followed her from the kitchen to the parlor and when she opened the door, Catterina looked up from my chair, where she was curled in a neat circle. She arched up, then stretched her back legs, but did not relinquish her seat, merely allowed me to settle in before rearranging herself on my lap. She slowly blinked her green eyes at me twice, then retreated back to her dreams, purring her satisfaction as my fingers ran across her tortoise-shell coat and the first notes rose up from the strings deftly plucked by Virginia's fingers.

> As I was a walking one morning in spring,
> For to hear the birds whistle and the nightingales sing,
> I saw a young damsel, so sweetly sang she:
> Down by the green bushes he thinks to meet me.

I smiled as I recognized the folk song and leaned back in my chair, eyes closed to take in her words, which were accompanied by Catterina's purr. As wonderfully as my wife played the piano, there was something in the sound of her harp music that had the effect of truly elevating my spirits.

> *I want none of your petticoats and your fine silken shows:*
> *I never was so poor as to marry for clothes,*
> *But if you will prove loyal and constant to me,*
> *I'll forsake my own true love and get married to thee.*

I silently accompanied my wife as she sang, enjoying the lyric without ruining the beauty of her voice by mixing in my own. A patter of applause came with the end of the song, and I opened my eyes to see my mother-in-law seated in her chair, clapping. Such was my concentration, I had not heard her enter the room, nor deposit the two parcels wrapped in brown paper and the envelope that were now lying on the table next to me.

"You thought we had forgotten," Sissy said, laughing. "Mother did not believe you would fall for our ruse, but I can tell from your expression that we managed to surprise you."

"You did indeed, my love. And I am as delighted with your cruelty as you are." I did not spoil her joke by telling her that I had forgotten my own birthday. My twenty-one-year-old wife viewed all such anniversaries and holidays as joyful occasions to celebrate with loved ones, whereas turning thirty-five merely made me anxious about all I had yet to achieve.

"Are you trying to guess the contents of your packages or have you left us again to worry at some new story like a dog with a bone?"

"Attempting to guess, of course, applying every principle of ratiocination known to me."

"And your verdict, sir?" my wife asked.

I scrutinized the packages on the table with mock concentration. "I believe this one is a magical purse that will never be emptied of gold. And this one a fount of ideas that is ever full. And this last packet is the most valuable of all, for it contains the vessel of your love for me, which can never be diminished, despite all the trials I put you through."

"Correct! How ever did you guess?"

Muddy looked from her daughter to me and back again, shaking her head in amiable confusion, as she inevitably did when our fancies got the better of us.

"Well, let's take a look at these wonderful gifts." I picked up the package from Muddy and undid the paper to reveal a muffler and a pair of thick socks, both knitted from ivory-colored wool. "How perfect," I said, wrapping the scarf around my neck three times. "Long enough to remain secure on my rambles. And the socks—I fear you wearied of my complaints about my frozen toes in this icy weather."

"Indeed we have." My wife smiled. "And Mother pledged to solve the problem." She handed me the other package and watched with anticipation as I unfolded the paper to reveal a black silk neckcloth, elegant and beautifully made, hemmed with tiny stitches that attested to the patience of its maker.

"It could not be more perfect," I said. "When did you manage to sew this without my knowledge? It must have taken quite some time."

"When you were on your walks and at your desk, I was busy stitching. I hope you will wear it tonight." She slid the envelope toward me.

"An entertainment also? I am more than spoiled."

"Yes, you are," my wife agreed.

I opened the envelope to find two tickets for a play at the Walnut Street Theater that night. *The Vengeful Specter*? I would not have thought a play with such a title would appeal to you."

"I know little about the play itself, but Mrs. Reynolds is the lead. She is quite the toast of Charleston, Richmond and now Philadelphia."

"Indeed she is. I wonder if her skills as an actress match her reputation, and if the play itself is any good."

"I do hope you won't mutter whenever something displeases you. It can be very wearing for all around you."

"Not as wearing as a terrible play."

Before my wife could contradict me, there was a knock at the door. Muddy hurried out and returned a few moments later with a tall, broad-shouldered gentleman close to fifty years of age. His silvery hair was wavy and thick, his eyes a piercing blue, and he was dressed in a black habit with a scapular. I rose to my feet to shake his hand.

"Father Keane, what a pleasure. Do sit."

"How lovely to see you, Father Keane," my wife said. "Did you miss your walk along the Schuylkill this morning? Eddy has tried to convince me that it is dangerously icy out there."

"I'm afraid I did," he replied as he lowered himself onto the sofa. "And your husband is not wrong about the ice. It would be safer to travel with skates on."

I had made the priest's acquaintance almost a year ago, soon after we took up residence in the Seventh Street house. Our paths had crossed at the riverbank—he went there most mornings to watch the birds and record his sightings. Father Keane was a highly cultivated Augustinian friar, born near the banks of the Shannon River in the west of Ireland and washed up in the port of Philadelphia, as he put it. He was also an amateur ornithologist and taught natural philosophy to the students at St. Augustine Academy. We quickly became friends as he was knowledgeable about an array of subjects, never pressed his religion on me and was not averse to the occasional card game.

Father Keane removed a wooden cigar box from the folds of his cassock and held it toward me. When he noticed my look of anticipation and my wife's consternation, he said, "It is not what you might presume."

My brief disappointment turned to pleasure when I saw what was inside: a bottle of ink, some pounce and three feathers that had been neatly fashioned into quill pens. The first was pure black, the second soft gray and the third, brown with delicate white markings.

I examined them carefully, then made my guess: "Crow, goose, turkey?"

"Correct. All found along the river, a true gift from our avian neighbors."

Muddy leaned in to peer more closely at the quill pens. "Very fine. You made them?"

"I did. A useful hobby," he said.

My wife held the turkey feather up to the light and admired its markings. "They are beautiful. And the perfect gift for my husband, of course."

"Perfect indeed. I will both treasure them and use them often, for they are bound to add some mysterious otherness to my work. Thank you truly, sir."

"My pleasure. I hope you have many happy returns of the day." Father Keane rose to his feet briskly. "And now forgive me, for I must make haste. I am due in the classroom in thirty minutes. Perhaps we will see each other at the Schuylkill tomorrow." He reached out to shake my hand, then bowed to the ladies. Muddy began to rise, but Father Keane said, "Please don't get up, madam. I will show myself out. Enjoy your day." And he was gone, like a bird on the wing.

We were seated near the back of the Walnut Street Theater, not an ideal position, but the stage was visible enough. Sissy drank in the ambience: the shimmer of golden embellishments under gaslight, the luxuriant scarlet stage curtain and the audience itself—Philadelphians in their best attire, giddy with anticipation of the night's entertainment. My wife was not dressed in the most recent fashions or bedecked in costly jewels, but she had cunningly altered a champagne-colored silk dress from three seasons ago by adding lace to the sleeves and bodice and a flounce, embroidered with scarlet roses, to the hem. In my eyes she outshone all around us.

When at last the show commenced, my assumptions regarding its quality were quickly proved accurate. *The Vengeful Specter* was written by one of the company and had recently debuted in Richmond, where it was highly popular with audiences but derided by critics. It featured the usual characters one might expect from a melodrama of its ilk: the saintly maiden, her elderly father, the dastardly villain and the hero. It began in an unsurprising manner: the villain robbed the maiden's father of both his life savings and his reputation, but pledged to restore the fellow's good name in exchange for the saintly maiden's hand in marriage. The elderly father refused the odious demand and consequently was taken away to prison, where he confided his plight to a young and handsome debtor before mysteriously expiring that very first night in his cell. He was not content to remain in the grave, however, and reappeared as the vengeful specter of the title to plague the villain with his silent, accusing presence. Sadly, his ghostly efforts were ineffectual as the villain persuaded the saintly maiden to marry him by promising to clear her father's name (an obvious hoax if ever there were one). Just as the two were about to be joined in holy matrimony, the hero (conveniently released from prison) arrived at the church under the guidance of the insipid specter and shot the would-be groom dead. Surprisingly, the wedding guests were overjoyed by the groom's violent demise and joined in the chorus of a lively little song, performed by the saintly maiden herself, who married the hero moments later. All but the villain lived happily ever after, any traces of cold-blooded murder swept under the carpet. It was utter drivel, but my wife extinguished my whispered commentary of the play's flaws with a ferocious frown and muttered, "Hush now."

When the maiden stepped out onto the stage for a curtain call, Sissy clapped along with the crowd and said to me: "The story might be ridiculous, but Mrs. Reynolds is utterly convincing, just as reviews from Richmond said."

It was clear from the actress's extravagant modesty in accepting the rapturous applause that she fully cherished her own histrionic talents.

"I cannot deny that Mrs. Reynolds is a talented performer and rises far above the play itself, but it would be in her interests to find a better dramatic vehicle if she wishes to rival Mrs. Burke and Mrs. French."

"You are being too harsh, my dear. We might agree that justice triumphed far too conveniently, but the happy ending has had the desired effect on the audience. The playwright did his job well enough."

"I cannot argue with you, for the chatter shows me that you are correct," I murmured. "Alas, we are the only ones here able to distinguish Art from mere entertainment."

"Do not be so certain of that," Sissy countered. "A night of undemanding entertainment is a very fine remedy for a long, cold winter spent locked up indoors. I cannot be the only one who was in need of a light *divertissement*."

When the applause finally died down, we stood and followed the crowd from the theater into a foyer, where admirers were clustered, waiting for the actress to bestow her presence upon them. I made my way toward the theater door, but Sissy clutched at my arm.

"I would like to congratulate Mrs. Reynolds," she said.

"Truly?"

"Her talents gave me an enjoyable evening. Consider how your mother must have appreciated praise from her audiences."

Sissy did not wait for my response and joined the mob of disciples. I reluctantly followed, swayed by my wife's words rather than any wish to meet the Fair Maiden. As Virginia well knew, it was a pleasure for me when I attended the theater to imagine my own mother on the stage, where she had spent most of her short life, from her debut at only nine years old until her untimely death at twenty-four, when I was but an infant.

"Mrs. Reynolds, your performance was magnificent." A booming voice drew my attention to the throng of admirers, now dominated by a tall man holding a basket of red roses so large it was ostentatious rather than elegant, not unlike his appearance. He had a quantity of tawny hair, and his clothing was dandified, cut with too much flair and set off with a deep-purple silk waistcoat embroidered in a fashion more suitable for a Chinese emperor's robes. "We Friends of the theater lobbied heavily to bring you to Philadelphia and the show did not disappoint." The man bestowed the floral basket on the actress, who was quite obscured by it.

"Thank you, sir." Mrs. Reynold's voice cut through the babble of the crowd. "Mrs. Laird, would you put these in my room," she directed. The flowers were whisked away and a figure dressed entirely in bright green was revealed.

"You were wonderful, Mrs. Reynolds," an admirer exclaimed.

"Extraordinary," others chorused.

"How kind. Pleasing the audience makes it all worthwhile," the actress said with great sincerity, as she deftly turned her back on the man who had presented the flowers. His haughty, thin-lipped smile shifted to an offended scowl as the lady directed her full attention to the platitudes that rained down upon her. He stood there awkwardly for a few moments, then strode off, his ornate silver walking stick tapping out his anger on the floor. There seemed to be a story hidden in the awkward exchange I had witnessed; I wondered what it was.

"Congratulations, Mrs. Reynolds." It was my wife's clear, soft voice. I moved forward through the thinning crowd to join her and to see better the object of her praise. What immediately struck me was that the thick white theater paint covering Mrs. Reynolds's face made it a ghoulish mask at close quarters; but I was startled from my idle scrutiny when I noticed that the actress's kohl-lined violet-colored eyes were fixed upon me.

"Thank you. How kind, Mrs. Poe," the lady said to my wife, her eyes never leaving my face. Sissy was startled by her words, but did her best to hide it. "And how are you, Mr. Poe? It has been a long while since we last met." Mrs. Reynolds offered the ghost of a mocking curtsey and in that instant I understood at last who she really was.

"Mrs. Fontaine?" I stammered. "I am sorry that—"

"I am afraid you are mistaken," the lady said haughtily. "It is Mrs. *Reynolds*. Much has altered since we met in London."

"Yes, I see," I responded, while I did not see at all. "My wife and I greatly admired your performance," I added, hoping to steer the conversation away from London and the nefarious things that had occurred there under the direction of the lady's paramour.

"Thank you. The play was written by my husband, George Reynolds. Did you enjoy it?" The note of challenge in her voice tempted me to discard tact for honesty, but my wife intervened.

"The play enraptured your audience, of course. I have rarely heard such lengthy applause," she said with an earnest and pleasing smile.

The lady I knew as Mrs. Fontaine, the inamorata of my greatest enemy, George Rhynwick Williams, turned to look at Sissy, as if seeing her for the very first time. "That is not quite what I asked, Mrs. Poe, but thank you for the admirably delicate answer. My husband has a certain skill—quite recently discovered in this fine new world—for penning melodramas that tug the heartstrings, and our collaborations have been highly successful. The critics have not always been so kind, but they are not the ones who pay for our suppers." She smiled, and the effect upon the paint that coated her face was startling, the smooth surface erupting into an array of crevasses that added twenty years to her age. The lady then staggered slightly and appeared to become faint; I hurriedly gripped her elbow to steady her. "I really must sit down for a moment," she murmured.

"Of course," my wife said. "You must be exceedingly weary, and we are making you more so."

Mrs. Reynolds shook her head as if to clear it, then returned her gaze to mine. "Please join me in my dressing room—both of you. Some tea will set me right, and there are a few things that must be said." She did not wait for my response but merely retreated back into the room from which she had emerged, and I followed after my eager wife, not without some trepidation.

The small dressing room had been cleverly transformed into a place of refuge specific to "Mrs. Reynolds, Thespian and Undisputed Queen of the Theater Boards", as one theater bill affixed to the wall put it. Other notices had illustrations of the lady in dramatic poses and elaborate costumes. A mirror was hung on the wall under a gas lamp and above a table upon which stood a very large chest filled with the concoctions that comprise an actress's toilette. Mrs. Reynolds took a seat in front of the mirror, and I jumped as a small, rotund lady of middling years emerged from the shadows.

"Are you ready for me now, my dear?" the lady asked.

"Give us a moment, Mrs. Laird."

"Your engagement is in one hour, and we must allow thirty minutes to repaint," the woman argued. "Let me remove the paint and arrange your hair while you speak to your admirers."

"Very well," Mrs. Reynolds said with irritation. "Do what you must."

Mrs. Laird nodded and stationed herself by the table. She tipped various potions onto soft sponges and began the apparently laborious process of removing the white cream from the actress's face.

"Forgive the inelegance, but I wish to unburden myself while you are before me, Mr. Poe."

My wife gave me a sideward glance, but said nothing.

"And do sit. There are two chairs just there—bring them closer."

I did as the lady bid, and we positioned ourselves so she was able to peer at our reflections in the mirror.

"I shall come straight to the point as it is unlikely we'll meet again without my husband present, and I will not repeat what I will tell you in front of him."

If Mrs. Laird had any interest in what was to be revealed, she did not show it, but kept rubbing steadily at her mistress's face, removing the thick white mask.

"Please, I am more than interested to hear what you have to say," I offered.

"I have told my husband it is time to lay the past to rest. The bitterness was consuming him and, through that, eroding our bond. We now have the life we wished for and my feeling is that the business between your families is finished."

Certainly I had every desire for that to be the case, but I did not believe her husband felt the same. Was the lady not cognizant of the hideous package he had left on my doorstep?

"You are aware of the injustices committed," she said, "and surely you cannot fault his actions—*our* actions—for they are negligible when compared to what George and his father were forced to endure."

She spoke those astonishing words as if they were an inarguable truth, and such was my shock that I was rendered mute. Sissy was equally quiet and carefully concealed her bewilderment.

"If this war between you continues, all that we hold dear will be destroyed," the actress declared, and for once I had little doubt that her words were true.

Mrs. Laird removed the last of the face paint, and I saw Mrs. Reynolds's unembellished face with a sense of horror I did my best to hide. Her unadorned skin was the color of rancid butter and had the texture of a child's worn-out leather boot. When Mrs. Laird removed her mistress's luxuriant wig to reveal a recessed hairline and gray locks that were considerably thinned, my shock was palpable, and must have been visible, judging by the jab I felt in my side from Sissy's elbow.

Mrs. Reynolds flinched when she saw her own reflection. "These past three years have not been as kind to my looks as they have to my career, Mr. Poe. I do my best to conceal that fact from my admirers and trust you will aid me in my efforts."

"Of course." I could not think of another thing to say.

"Hold still, my darling," Mrs. Laird said as she began to smooth fresh white paint over her mistress's face, throat and décolletage. I watched, fascinated, as the lotion settled over her features like a layer of white enamel, obscuring much of the ravaged palette beneath it.

"Then let us pledge that while we are both on this earth, our husbands will not further shame us with enmity and the desire for revenge." Mrs. Reynolds's violet eyes were fixed on Sissy.

"Any quarrels between your husband and mine are forgotten, I assure you, Mrs. Reynolds. Fate has brought us together today to make that clear." My wife's expression was perfectly composed as if she understood all that the lady was saying, which truly was not possible. "I give you my word." Sissy took the hand of my enemy's wife into her own. "And I wish you better health."

"And I, you," Mrs. Reynolds said in return.

The two women exchanged an inscrutable look that seemed to penetrate each other's soul, then my wife squeezed the actress's hand before standing up and making her way from the little dressing room, her face heavy with compassion. As Mrs. Laird began the delicate task of drawing blue veins onto Mrs. Reynolds's snow-white skin, I wrenched my gaze away from her macabre artistry and murmured "Farewell", then hurried after my wife.

We debated the merits of the play during our journey home, but did not speak of the actress herself. When we were in the parlor, cups of mulled cider in hand to banish the night's chill, Sissy fixed her eyes upon me and waited. I had thought hard about what I might say during the coach ride and decided I would not sully the truth, but equally I would not reveal the whole of it.

"I met Mrs. Reynolds and her husband in London, where they went by the names Mrs. Rowena Fontaine and Mr. George Williams. I believe that she was married to another at the time, but she had an understanding with Williams."

Sissy pursed her lips as she contemplated this. "You mean that they were lovers and were deceiving her husband?"

"Yes," I agreed, happy to cast a tarnished patina on them. "She wore a brooch that was a painted replica of his eye and he wore one that was a facsimile of hers to declare their alliance. I do not know why they have changed their names. Perhaps Mr. Fontaine is still alive, and they absconded to these shores or felt the shadow of divorce would interfere with their chance of success in the theater."

Sissy nodded at this. "But it's quite the coincidence that Mrs. Fontaine arrived in Philadelphia just after you returned home from London." She took a sip of her drink, eyes never leaving mine. "And the portrait of her that Mr. Street exhibited at the Artists' Fund Hall—how odd for her or her paramour to commission such a work when so recently in the city."

It was over three years since we had seen the portrait of Mrs. Fontaine at that exhibition, and I'd hoped Sissy had forgotten about it, for I did not wish to worry her with the truth of Mrs. Fontaine and George Williams—that they had done their best to murder me in London.

"It does seem odd, dearest, but do remember that Mr. Street claims to have a nose for the talent of others and declared it an honor to paint my portrait as he knew my artistry would stand the test of time. I would wager his nose sniffed out the lady's vanity, as well as her fragrant talent, when she first arrived in this city and offered to capture her likeness for a nominal fee."

Sissy smiled as she gazed up at the portrait of me she had hung upon the parlor wall. In protest, I had positioned my chair under the thing so I would not need to look at it. I had steadfastly refused Robert Street's entreaties to let him paint me for posterity (and a fee), but then he offered to do the job gratis and I could not refuse my wife when she asked for the portrait as a birthday gift. It was a competent work, but there was something in the expression I did not much care for, and the notion to depict a pen clutched in my fingers, hovering over a sheet of paper, seemed far too obvious.

"Well, I remember his striking portrait very well," Sissy declared, turning back to me. "Indeed, I believe that image of Mrs. Reynolds was reproduced for *The Vengeful Specter* playbills."

"The lady must take bittersweet pleasure in that painting now, for it captured her beauty before it was so mightily diminished. I believe the paint she wears must contain some noxious element. Arsenic, perhaps. And that green costume is probably colored with arsenic dye. Truly vanity is the vengeful specter that haunts the lady's decline."

"It is very sad," my wife said. "I believe she knows her health is severely compromised and wishes to banish all vengeful specters as a way to make peace within herself."

"You are both astute and kind."

"But I am none the wiser as to why there is enmity between you and Mrs. Reynolds's husband." Sissy's gaze was a challenge; I would not be able to dance away from her question any longer.

"George Williams thinks my grandparents were responsible for his father's confinement at Newgate prison for six years and believes that, as their descendent, I too am guilty for their perceived crimes."

" 'The son shall not suffer for the iniquity of the father, nor the father suffer for the iniquity of the son. The righteousness of the righteous shall be upon himself, and the wickedness of the wicked shall be upon himself,' " Sissy recited.

"A truer thing has rarely been said, but I fear Williams is thoroughly embittered. I can only hope that in taking on a new identity, he has also adopted a new character. Or that his wife successfully persuades him to."

"I believe she will," Sissy murmured, "from my very heart. Death has whispered to her, and she does not want the time she has left to be tainted or wasted. Surely that is why her performances are so compelling. She lets her spirit fly when on the stage so she may be remembered for her best gifts not her lowest thoughts."

Was it possible that I had nothing more to fear from that creeping, malevolent imp called Revenge? Perhaps success had indeed changed the pair for the better. I could not help but wonder, though, if in truth it was the festering of the actress's ill intentions that had corrupted her beauty so mercilessly.

WEDNESDAY, 14 FEBRUARY 1844

It is uncanny how much the fabric of one's life can be altered by an unforeseen event, how its quiet weave is disrupted by dread. Two years previously we were enjoying an evening, as we often did, listening to Virginia sing as she played the piano, when blood began to seep from her mouth and fall like the Devil's rain upon her dress. As much as I declared the episode a ruptured blood vessel that rest would cure, that moment was a scar on my memory and every subtle shift in my wife's constitution, whether a vague discomfort of the throat, increased pallor or mere fatigue, would plunge me into despair, and when she improved my heart would dance with relief.

My oscillation between hope and fear aggravated my wife, as did the way Muddy and I hovered over her, as she put it, like vultures watching for any sign of weakness. And so I had done my best to live in the moment, to enjoy each day in her company and to pretend that she was perfectly well. More often than I would like to say, this sent me on a spree to drown my fears.

But the arrival of the ghastly package of dismembered birds had jarred me into sobriety. I was determined to protect my family from this more tangible threat and so I took the hatbox with its grim contents to St. Augustine Church, knowing that Father Keane would understand my need to conceal the gruesome birds from my family and yet keep them as evidence. And he did the same when another strange package arrived for me at the post office almost a full month later on the sixth of February. It contained a carefully packed rectangular glass box with a hinged lid, about two feet long, eighteen inches wide and a foot high. This Wardian case was filled with several inches of soil that was covered in verdant moss. A painted backdrop was affixed to its interior back panel, an amateur work of what appeared to be green mountains tall enough to reach the clouds. There was a rectangular hole dug in the mossy earth near the front right corner of the container, like an open grave.

When I asked the postmaster about the origin of the package, he had no information for me. No message had accompanied it, but I felt in my soul that only Williams, who had tormented me with his delivery of letters four years ago, would do such an insidious thing.

A third parcel, left at the post office on the twelfth of February, was even more disconcerting. It contained a small wooden table, no more than four inches by three inches. A collection of miniature knives and sharp implements was neatly arranged at one end of it and glued in place. I had wanted to believe Mrs. Reynolds when she said that she and her husband had reinvented themselves and that, truly, they had put the past to rest, but how could it not seem like a false pledge when the table, with its array of blades, so blatantly recalled the crimes of the London Monster?

Of course I made no mention of the threatening items to my wife and maintained a wary composure, which abruptly ended when my mother-in-law rapped on my study door two days after the third package arrived, and stepped inside with another.

"I was on Market Street and called into the post office. They had this for you." She handed me a small parcel.

"Thank you," I managed to whisper.

Muddy squinted at me, attuned to my disquiet, but I offered no explanation and she left without another word.

I stared at the package for a time, filled half with dread and half with anger, for it was the fourteenth of February, a day that was meant to be filled with joy and declarations of love. I took a pair of scissors from my desk, cut the twine and immediately removed the brown paper that covered the box, which was about twelve inches long, eight inches wide and six inches deep. I took a deep breath to steel myself, lifted the lid and removed the strips of soft paper that concealed the contents. There, nestled in that makeshift coffin, was a small dead man, or more precisely, the effigy of one. The manikin was dressed in the type of clothing one might wear for an arduous ramble: knee-high leather boots, a wide-brimmed hat, and fawn-colored breeches and a jacket of a heavy cotton. A large hessian bag was slung over his shoulder and a cross fashioned from wood, roughly half the figure's height, was next to him in the box. The figure was modeled from wax, and hair—dark in color—had been affixed to his head. When I lifted him from the box, I saw that a knife was buried in his back.

Fifteen minutes later I was on my way to see Father Keane, the rewrapped parcel tucked under my arm.

I waited in the library, where the quiet industry of the students from St. Augustine Academy helped to soothe my disquiet. The boys were aged from about six to twelve; some had previously attended Philadelphia primary schools, others were newly arrived from Ireland: all attended mass at St. Augustine Church. I had sent a note with a thin, studious-looking boy, and it was not long before a shadow fell over me.

"Mr. Poe," said a soft voice with a mellifluous Irish accent. "It is good to see you."

"And you, Father Keane."

He raised his brows at the package on the table. "Shall we?"

I nodded, and we left the silence of the library to make our way down a long hallway. Father Keane opened a door near the end of the corridor and revealed his sanctuary, a small study where he kept his personal library and a number of scholarly curios: an antique globe, a microscope, binoculars, small creatures preserved in jars and a collection of bird eggs, with a large teal-blue emu's egg in pride of place within a glass display box.

"When did it arrive?" he asked.

"This morning. Again, there was no message with it, no information regarding the sender."

"May I?" Father Keane indicated the hastily rewrapped package.

"Of course."

He untied the string and the brown paper fell away. When he saw what the box contained, he did his best to hide his shock.

"A threat, you must agree," I said gravely. There was no doubt in my mind that the figure was meant to be me.

Father Keane frowned. "Surely this is all too complex to be a mere threat."

"You do not know my nemesis."

"That is true," Father Keane said, "but whether a threat or a more complex message, we have failed to solve the riddle presented so far." He took the gruesome little doll from the box and examined it carefully. "The clothing is neatly made by someone possessing great facility with a needle and thread, that is obvious." He tugged open the hessian sack and huffed with surprise. He produced a pair of long tweezers from his desk and gently retrieved something from the sack—it was a black crow, perfectly constructed in miniature. Father Keane extracted two more birds from the little bag.

"Quite marvelous," he declared. "The feathers are genuine, the proportions perfect. They look as if they might take flight."

"Indeed, for they are all in one piece, unlike the dismembered creatures delivered to me," I said.

Father Keane nodded, unperturbed. "You are meant to see that connection and understand that the same person sent both packages."

"I would hardly presume otherwise, given the peculiar—nay, sinister—contents of each," I muttered.

My friend did not seem to hear my words, so engrossed was he in the construction of the miniature bird. He had been equally intrigued by the ominous creatures that were first delivered to me, and had, back in mid-January, arranged the bird parts on his desk with large, gentle hands.

"Very neatly done," he had commented.

"The . . . dissection?" I had not known what else to call it.

"The taxidermy work. One would hardly know the creatures to be dead if they were not left unassembled."

"Indeed, I had feared them to be alive when I first opened the bag."

"An unusual thing for an experienced taxidermist to do, to leave his work so patently unfinished." He had looked to me as if expecting an explanation.

"I can only surmise that my nemesis instructed the taxidermist to finish the birds in this manner to torment me, for truly it is a hideous design that threatens death."

"Crows are associated with death, it is true," Father Keane had said, "but to hire a taxidermist to do this work is very odd—an extreme way to make a threat."

"It is not beyond the man. George Williams's stated goal in life is to take revenge on my family for some imagined injustice. He is undeniably unbalanced."

I made no mention of the fact that Williams's father had been imprisoned in London's Newgate Gaol for crimes that my grandparents had truly committed or that Williams had followed me from London three and a half years ago, pledging revenge upon me and my family.

"Perhaps this is the clue we need." Father Keane's voice broke my anxious recollections. He was triumphantly holding the tweezers aloft, a folded piece of paper held between their tips. "At the bottom of the miniature bird collecting bag," he said, answering my unspoken question as he handed the paper to me.

It was very fine, thin stationery sealed shut with a tiny dot of red wax that resembled a droplet of blood. I prized it open and examined the paper. It seemed to be a diagram and I presumed it referred to the Wardian case. A rectangle was drawn on the paper with numbers written inside it and a basic key to the diagram in the lower left-hand corner interpreted what each number represented.

"I believe it's a diagram that shows how to transform the Wardian case into a diorama." We moved over to the Wardian case, which was situated on a table near the window, and I gave the diagram to Father Keane, who quickly studied it.

"The painted mountains are annotated as 'Chachapoyas' and this hole in the earth is labeled 'J.M.' The wooden cross is meant to go here." He situated it at one end of the rectangular hole, which immediately confirmed my initial impression that it represented an open grave. I placed the wax figure of the dead man into the sepulcher and there was no doubt that it had been fashioned to accommodate him.

"Very strange. But is it a threat, a warning or some other message?" Father Keane tapped at the diagram key. "J.M.—someone's initials, perhaps."

"The victim's or the killer's? Or perhaps they are not initials at all, but an abbreviation of some sort."

Father Keane ignored my suggestion and placed the killing table near the left front corner of the Wardian case. "The diagram shows that the table is to be placed here, yet the key labels it as 'H.L.' Given the scene before us, perhaps these are the initials of the would-be murderer of J.M." he concluded.

It was a logical interpretation that held no meaning for me. H.L.? The initials did not fit anyone I might suspect capable of murder, not George Williams, his father, Rhynwick, his accomplice, Rowena Fontaine, nor indeed their aliases. I could think of no one with the initials J.M. either.

"I am bewildered. If these are initials, they mean nothing to me."

Father Keane nodded. "Then we must consider the other clue: Chachapoyas."

I shook my head.

"The Chachapoyas is a region in Peru. We Augustinians have a connection with the place. In the mid-sixteenth century, Father Juan Ramírez traveled there and brought many of the natives to our faith," Father Keane said.

"Do you think the diorama has some relation to St. Augustine's? Or is it a threat to someone here?" As I said the words, I did not quite believe them.

"It seems unlikely. Do you have any connections with Peru yourself?"

"Peru? I have never been there nor anywhere at all in that region." The question seemed absurd until a flash of a memory came to me of a day spent in the Regent's Park, London, with my good friend C. Auguste Dupin during that terrible summer of 1840. As we ventured through the zoological gardens there, Dupin noticed some llamas and revealed that he had travelled to Peru. I was still unable to imagine the urbane Dupin in such a location, but if his words were true, might the diorama suggest a threat to him?

"Has something occurred to you, Mr. Poe?"

"Indeed it has. My friend the Chevalier C. Auguste Dupin travelled to Peru in his youth. He rescued me on several occasions from my nemesis. I wonder if this diorama suggests that he might be in danger."

"You must of course warn him," Father Keane advised. "His link with Peru may be only a coincidence, but there is no harm in taking precautions."

"Unfortunately, he lives in Paris and it will take two weeks for my letter to reach him by steam packet, and several weeks longer if it goes by sail packet."

"We must pray then that anyone who may wish him harm is on these shores as opposed to the other side of the Atlantic."

His words filled me with dread. We had not discovered the origin of the packages—they might have been sent from within Philadelphia or indeed from Paris. My friend picked up the metal hatbox and carried it to his desk, where the miniature crows were arranged in a neat line. He retrieved the mummified bird parts and laid them out on the desk top also.

"What does it mean?" he said softly. "Three crows in miniature—constructed—and three real birds, killed and dismembered but preserved with the art of taxidermy. And this scene of a man's death . . . Six crows . . . A *murder* of crows. Of course. Somehow we must put the pieces together"—he looked down at the dissevered birds—"and prevent the murder."

"Assuming it has not already occurred," I said grimly.

"I don't think so. Your enemy has gone to much effort to send you these items. We might think of it as a ransom note in puzzle form," Father Keane suggested.

"I hope you are correct. Indeed, I pray it."

But I could not get Dupin's oft-spoken pledge from my mind: *Amicis semper fidelis*. Of course that promise was reciprocated, but how was it possible to stand by my friend in the face of danger when we were on opposite sides of the Atlantic? And how would I ever forgive myself if Dupin were murdered by the man who wished me dead?

6

A sense of foreboding would not let me sleep, so I made my way to my desk as quietly as a thief. Catterina wrapped herself around my shoulders like a feline shawl and purred contentedly as I penned my warning to Dupin, then immediately rewrote it, trying to strike a calmer tone. I knew he would pay little heed to a letter of caution that was, in his opinion, a product of my overwrought imagination. I described in detail the strange items that had been sent to me, the diagram with its key for constructing the morbid diorama, and how the clues within it suggested that Dupin was the target.

"I fear you are in danger," I wrote. "And that my enemy intends to harm you simply because you are my friend. Please take every precaution and write immediately to tell me that you are safe." I sealed my letter with wax and knew there was nothing more I could do except perhaps pray, or entreat Father Keane to do so on Dupin's behalf.

And yet a morbid restlessness would not let me return to my bed, and before truly cognizant of my actions, I was crouched down levering up the floorboards next to my desk. My hands seemed to move of their own accord, scrabbling and searching, until they held the mahogany box that was hidden in that makeshift crypt. I had not looked at it since we had moved home to Seventh Street, and I had interred it under my study floor, for I knew that its malignant power was taking too great a toll on me. But now that it was before me and the key that had been in my desk drawer was in my grasp, I could not resist unlocking it and opening up the lid. As I leaned to look inside, I was half-expecting to see only emptiness—the result of some dark magic—but to my relief, or perhaps truly it was terror, the bundle of letters lay there like a corpse and the malevolent violet eye stared back at me.

Did you truly believe you might escape by entombing me? That my gaze would not find you from this crypt? I see everything, I know everything. I am the testament to truth and to securing justice.

Terror had found me again. Or perhaps it had merely risen up like a half-dead thing that had never truly succumbed to the conqueror worm.

7

SUNDAY, 10 MARCH 1844

There was an odd sound, a rhythmic tap-tap-tapping, which I took to be nothing more than the wind, until Sissy cried out: "How curious!" She left the breakfast table and crept to the kitchen window, where there was a flittering shadow. When I peered over her shoulder, I saw a robin perched on the sill, tapping at the glass.

"Does it wish to come inside?" she asked. And as she spoke those words, the robin whirled away with a flutter of wings.

"We will have a visitor today," Muddy announced.

"Really? And whom are we expecting?" I asked.

"You must ask that of the robin," she said, shrugging. "It's an old country saying: 'See a robin red-breast in the morning and you will have a guest later that day.'"

Sissy laughed. "How clever of the robin to warn us in advance. Now we will have the chance to prepare for our mysterious guest."

"There is little to do, surely," I said. "For there is not a speck of dirt within the house."

Muddy offered half a smile, but her pleasure at my words was clear.

"We might prepare some tidbit to serve with tea. We have blackberry conserves, walnuts and dried apple," my wife suggested.

Muddy nodded as if creating something delicious from those ingredients was the simplest thing in the world.

"I would dearly love a visitor," Sissy mused. "Truly February is the longest month, and while March promises spring, it seems a false promise when we are already a third of the way through it and the icy weather still holds me prisoner indoors."

"Spring will be here soon, dearest. And I think tea is quite enough for any visitor who is but a figment conjured from an old wives' tale." The sight of Sissy's downcast expression made me regret my words. "But I will go out in search of some small delicacy for the person your robin has promised us." And I kissed her cheek in pledge.

* * *

The air was brisk and the footpath slick with islands of ice, but it was a bright morning, which imbued fellow pedestrians with an optimistic air, judging from the friendly greetings I received as I walked down Seventh Street. The cupola and clock of the market shed soon came into view and I made my way toward them, hoping to find some treat for Sissy there. The market shed was surrounded by a flotilla of wagons, where solemn farmers and fishermen were selling a variety of produce. A large country woman stood behind an artful display of fruit conserves; their glass jars were topped with pretty circles of fabric and tied with ribbon. If I could not find the shortbread that my wife was particularly fond of, I would return for a jar or two of peach preserves.

The market normally held an amiable chattering crowd, but there was a murk of unease inside. Men and women roughly pushed by me, moving toward the doorway with uncommon speed. Near the market's center there was a group of people hovering near a table where a woman who appeared to be Muddy's age was selling fine linen handkerchiefs. Two brutes were planted in front of the lady's stand, facing each other like fighting dogs in a tavern yard.

"Get back to Kensington Market with your own kind," the larger of the two men growled, his hands curling into fists.

"She has every right to be here, as do we all," the other man retorted. His voice had a clear Irish inflection, and I had no doubt the grey-haired woman selling handkerchiefs had left that same homeland.

"This is our market. We've been selling our goods here for years," the red-faced man said, jabbing his finger into the Irishman's chest. "Your kind is taking the food from our mouths." He shoved the man to emphasize his words.

The woman fearfully gathered her wares with speed. If her table were knocked over, the snowy linen would be spoiled under the boots of the men before her. I wished I had the money to buy all her handkerchiefs. There was scuffling as two opposing camps formed, and I followed the crowd that hurried toward the exit, leaving behind the angry mob.

As I headed away from the market, I was saddened to witness yet more conflict incited by those who called themselves "Nativists"—Philadelphia-born and of the Protestant faith— against immigrants to the city. I could not help but think of my own grandmother—an actress—who emigrated from London to join a theater in Boston, bringing my mother to a new and transient home with traveling players when she was just a young girl. When I myself was a child, my adoptive father took my adoptive mother and I to live in London, where we spent five unsettling years as he tried his fortunes in that city and brought us close to ruin. I knew, therefore, what it was to be newly arrived somewhere, to never fully belong. I understood how not being "native" or naturally born to a place or a family might bring unmerited suffering.

My reverie was cut short when I found myself in front of a familiar red-brick building. Surely the imp of the perverse had drawn me to the post office for it was too soon to receive the return correspondence I awaited from Dupin. If there were a package waiting for me inside, it was one that would only cause me anxiety and grief.

"Yes, I do have something for you, Mr. Poe," the jolly postmaster told me. "Arrived this morning." He handed a small package over the counter. My "Thank you" was an utterly false sentiment, and I carried the thing gingerly, as if it were infectious, to the first tavern I spied.

After a large sip of brandy to steady my nerves, I unknotted the string and opened the brown paper that was wrapped around a small, rough wooden box. Inside, cushioned by strips of soft paper, was a figure—female this time—dressed in a plain black frock with ebony boots, gloves and a veil like the bride of Death. Her waxen face was very pale, and her tiny hand clutched a black feather. *A murder of crows*, I thought. There was no doubt in my mind that the figure was a miniature of my wife, Virginia, cloaked in funereal garb. I wanted to crush the loathsome manikin, but feared that if I did so, the infernal magic that had shaped it would steal her life away.

8

I hurried back home, my promises of finding some confection purely forgotten. How could I defend my family or myself from my aggressor when I did not know where he was or how he had discovered where I now lived? Was he stalking me, dogging my footsteps, secretly watching me as he had in London?

When I reached our house at last, I found a fire burning merrily in the kitchen but neither my wife nor her mother in the room. Anxiety rose up in me, provoked by the evil doll I was carrying, and I rushed up the stairs hoping to find Sissy napping; but the bedroom was empty. My fear increased, and I dashed to my study and threw the poppet into a desk drawer to escape its malign influence, then I stumbled back down the stairs, puffing air until at last my constricted breath turned to words.

"Sissy!" A raven might have croaked her name. "Sissy!" I called out again.

"Yes, my dear?" Her calm voice came from the parlor.

The dread that had surged into me ebbed away, and I opened the door with a relieved smile, but froze at the threshold, astonished at the sight before me. There, nestled in my armchair, was a creature from some dark fairy tale. She was very small of stature, petite of frame, with a chalky complexion and round green eyes that did not seem to blink. Her age was not easily determined, for while she in many ways resembled a child dressed in adult clothing, her demeanor was that of an elderly, world-weary person, and her peculiar garments added to this veneer of the ancient. The dress appeared black at first glance, but as sunlight dappled over it, dark green and purple hues were visible, like an English starling's plumage. The full skirts were curiously layered and the voluminous sleeves were unexpectedly tight at the forearms; a large pelerine of black lace decorated with feathers gave its wearer the semblance of wings. The adornments she wore gleamed emerald and sapphire with a flash of ruby and topaz, but they were not fashioned from gems—hummingbird heads were mounted onto gold and hung from her ears and around her neck, while three of the tiny birds were left whole to nest in the twists of her pinned-up thicket of auburn hair. I would have appreciated the lady's finery more had I not known that the wondrous birds that had once sipped flower nectar had been stilled by a taxidermist's knife, indeed *her* knife.

"It is a pleasure to see you again, Mr. Poe," my visitor said in a whisper of a voice.

Etiquette at last prevailed, and I managed to hide my shock with a welcoming bow. "And may I say the same, Miss Loddiges. A pleasure and a most unexpected surprise. What brings you to Philadelphia?"

"A message from Grip."

Her words made no sense to me and that was clear from my expression.

"Grip—Mr. Dickens's raven," Miss Loddiges said.

Again, the lady managed to take me utterly by surprise, and I fear I stood there slack-jawed, unable to say a word. Dickens's pet raven, Grip? Surely she was jesting. Dupin and I had

encountered the creature at Dickens's house and while it chattered incessantly, it spoke nothing but nonsense. Sissy noticed
my discomfiture and intervened.

"I was just telling Miss Loddiges about our other visitor this
morning," she said. "The robin is indeed a prescient fellow, and
in future we must have more faith in his promises."

"Yes, we must," I admitted. "For I am afraid I did not bring
back any sweetmeats."

Sissy smiled, not in the least surprised by my negligence.
"No matter, for Miss Loddiges does not wish for anything but
some tea. I'll just put the kettle on. Please sit and entertain our
guest."

My wife left for the kitchen, leaving me alone with Miss
Helena Loddiges, a woman I thought of as my benefactress due
to the very generous fee she once paid me to edit her ornithological treatise. It was this fee that had allowed me to undertake
my trip to London in the summer of 1840 to investigate a
mystery regarding my family, and as I had not met Miss Loddiges
before, I paid the reclusive young woman a brief courtesy visit
at her home in Paradise Fields while I was there. It was more
than a surprise to see this unusual lady outside the boundaries
of the Loddiges's estate, much less on the other side of the
Atlantic or, most improbably of all, in my home. Miss Loddiges
stared at me with her round, green eyes as I sat down in Muddy's
favorite chair.

"You mentioned Grip, Mr. Dickens's raven. I did meet the
irksome fellow, but truly cannot fathom how he might have
given you a message other than pure nonsense. I was not aware
that you were acquainted with Mr. Dickens," I said.

"We are acquainted through my work. Grip expired three
years ago, and Mr. Dickens asked me to immortalize his friend.
He had seen my father's hummingbird collection and felt I
would preserve the raven with best regard to his spirit."

"What a pity for Mr. Dickens, for he was terribly fond of the creature, but I am certain you made him very happy with your work."

"I did my best."

"But, please, if the raven has expired, how did you receive a message from it?"

Miss Loddiges tilted her head to one side and scrutinized me, much as a robin might stare at the ground before plucking an earthworm from it. "The boundary between life and death is but a shadow—who may say for certain where one ends and the other begins? Somehow the birds communicate to me, whether alive or gone to the other side." She shrugged as if her pronouncement were the most natural thing in the world.

"I see. And if I may be so bold, what was the message Grip delivered?"

She paused for a moment, as if deciding how best to convey it. "It was regarding your skills of ratiocination. You see, Mr. Poe, I need your assistance in solving a terrible mystery—a *murder*. Do you recollect my father's bird collector, Andrew Mathews, and his son Jeremiah?"

"Yes, I had the pleasure of meeting them at Paradise Fields."

"Both are dead," Miss Loddiges announced. "Andrew crossed over not long after Grip in 1841, while on an expedition. The cause was said to be a fall to his death, but Jeremiah did not believe the fall was accidental. And now I know for certain that he was correct and truly it was murder, for now Jeremiah has died—he was murdered this past October here in Philadelphia, directly after a bird-collecting trip for my father. We were informed that he had fallen from the ship and drowned the night before he was due to sail to London with all he had gathered during the expedition; but it is a lie. I need your skills to find the culprit who took his life."

Once again I was left slack-jawed and speechless. I had told her nothing of my family mystery or of meeting with Mr. Dickens's irksome pet raven. Certainly I had no idea how she had come to the notion that I was skilled in the art of ratiocination, an accolade that was undoubtedly reserved for my friend C. Auguste Dupin, who seemed able to divine a man's soul through mere observation and came to his solutions with a degree of acumen that appeared preternatural.

"Perhaps you could tell me a bit more?" I muttered.

"At first I had dreams of Grip. I would see him come alive again within the bell jar, and he would tap upon the glass, attempting to tell me something."

"What a terrible nightmare."

"Not at all. It was clear he was a friend, but I was frustrated not to understand his message. And when the birds began to move within the house, I knew it was vital that I fathom the auspices."

"How do you mean?" I asked, becoming increasingly certain that my benefactress was more than merely eccentric.

"It was the birds on display in the parlor. My mother had set them out in a manner she found pleasing to the eye, utterly disregarding any scientific principle, but one morning all the birds from South America were gathered together upon the hummingbird cabinet, as if in a conference. My mother accused the maid of undoing her handiwork, but both my father and I knew that to be impossible given how the birds were grouped. He chastised me later for it and was dismissive when I told him it was a message from Grip."

"He does not believe in ornithomancy," I suggested.

Miss Loddiges shook her head. "Of course he does, which is why his reaction was peculiar. And the following night, when a person managed to enter one of the glasshouses, my father refused to report the crime."

"Was anything stolen?"

"No, but the padlock on the glasshouse door had been removed and Enfys, our little hummingbird, had been released from her enclosure and was flying freely throughout the glasshouse. I feared the shock might kill her."

"Perhaps your father thought it merely an accident, that someone forgot the padlock and the enclosure door was not shut properly."

"Not possible," she declared. "I checked on Enfys myself before I retired for the night."

I understood why her father might hesitate to bother the police with something so easily explained by human error.

"The following night all was made clear to me when I awoke to see Jeremiah," she continued. "The draperies were parted, the room dimly lit with moonlight—and there he was, standing in the doorway to my room.

"'Jeremiah!' I cried out. 'We were told you had drowned!' When I spoke, shadow seemed to envelope him, and I realized with an aching heart that it was him in spirit only. 'Don't go,' I said. 'Do you have something to tell me? Some message?' The moonlight seemed to grow stronger, dispelling the shadow, and he was there again.

"'*La Joya*,' he whispered. 'Where is the Jewel?'

"'What jewel? What do you mean?' But the moonlight faded, and I could not see him. I left my bed and made my way to the corridor, hoping to find him there, but it was empty. I went through the entire house calling his name, but Jeremiah had vanished," Miss Loddiges concluded, her green eyes fixed upon me.

"How disturbing," I said. "Were you very frightened?"

"Frightened? Of course not. It was *Jeremiah*. But when I woke my parents to tell them what had occurred, my father insisted it was but a dream and sent me back to bed with a calmative."

Her expression suggested that I should share her disgust at this injustice, but I could not help wondering if she had imbibed something rather stronger than a calmative before her vision. Fortunately, I was saved from expressing such thoughts when my wife entered with tea and thin slices of cake. She smiled brightly at our guest as she filled her teacup, and their proximity reminded me with a start that Miss Loddiges was but four years older than Sissy.

"I never believed I would have the chance to meet you, Miss Loddiges. I greatly admire your book on ornithology. My husband so enjoyed working with you in London."

I flinched inwardly, for I had told Sissy that the reason for my journey to London was to work with Miss Loddiges, as I could not bring myself to divulge the awful mystery I had inherited. How could a woman as good as my Virginia love a man descended from criminals or remain with a husband whose grandparents should have hanged for their crimes? I waited for Miss Loddiges to reveal my fabrication, but the lady's expression did not alter as she quietly took a sip of her tea.

"Your husband's work on my book was excellent," she finally said, "and I am hoping he will do me the honor of a further collaboration."

"How wonderful!" Sissy exclaimed.

There was no doubt to me that Miss Loddiges was referring to her unexpected request that I solve a murder, a task I had no desire to undertake, particularly when I was embroiled in my own mystery.

"Of course I would like to be of assistance," I said carefully, "but I fear I am not suitable for this particular work. It is quite different to our last collaboration."

"I will pay the same fee and any expenses," Miss Loddiges announced as she retrieved a thick, sealed envelope from a reticule attached to her dress and handed it to me.

Sissy's smile brightened even more and her eyes met mine. I turned the envelope over several times. From the heft of it, the full amount was inside. The handsome fee that Miss Loddiges was offering would help us enormously, and to refuse her would invite questions that I did not wish to answer.

"Miss Loddiges, if you truly believe I might be of assistance, then of course I am at your service."

"Thank you, Mr. Poe. I am so very grateful. Is it possible to begin tomorrow? I am staying at the Bartram estate with my acquaintance Mrs. Carr. If you could visit me there, we might go through all the details of the work."

"Yes, I am free tomorrow. Perhaps at noon?"

"That would be ideal," she said in her whispering voice.

Sissy could barely contain her delight. And so, it seemed that I was to be Miss Helena Loddiges's accomplice in tracking down a phantom murderer, whether I wished to be or not.

9

I should have understood at supper that something was amiss when my wife simply told her mother that the robin's premonition was correct, that a visitor had indeed arrived. She did not describe our unusual guest or her strange attire, nor did she mention the offer of paid work, which would have greatly pleased Muddy. But I did not notice any of this at the time, so great was my relief that Miss Loddiges did not compromise the tale I had told my family about my sojourn in London.

Muddy retired early as was her wont and my wife and I settled ourselves in the parlor, she with some needlework and I with a book that remained closed as I stared at the fire, which crackled and hissed, sparks floating up the chimney like fireflies from the grass in summer. The atmosphere was one of precarious rather than companionable silence.

"Miss Loddiges is an intriguing woman," Sissy finally said.

"Yes, one might call her eccentric given her sense of fashion and occupation. Much could be attributed to her upbringing. Her father positively encouraged her taxidermy work, a useful service to him given his hobby of bird collecting."

Sissy nodded and continued to ply her embroidery needle through the hooped muslin, fashioning a bouquet of flowers on it stitch by patient stitch. "In your letter from London, you described her more than perfectly. Muddy and I could not imagine her ornaments fashioned from mummified birds, as you put it. To see them for myself was both fascinating and a little horrifying"

"I hope our guest did not terrify you too much. She is much more a scientist than the exotic witch she looks."

My wife smiled. "Miss Loddiges is charming, not terrifying at all. Indeed, I find it difficult to comprehend how such an unworldly creature got herself from London all the way to Philadelphia unassisted. You mentioned in your letter that she seems to live in an imaginary kingdom populated solely by birds and rarely leaves the house, so I am puzzled as to why she did not write to you about this new endeavor, but instead made such an unpleasant, frightening journey alone and arrived in Philadelphia unannounced." Sissy looked up from her needle-work and waited calmly for the truth.

I knew that my face had been the picture of surprise when I first saw Miss Loddiges, so it was no good fabricating a forgotten letter in which she had announced to me her intention to travel to Philadelphia. Furthermore, my wife had clearly committed my letters to memory, whereas I had very little recollection of what I had written to her during my fearful adventure in London. There seemed no point in trying to protect Sissy from Miss Loddiges's peculiar request. I could only hope that my benefactress would continue to pretend that I had worked on her ornithology book while in London—I was not willing to compromise all that I held dear in life by telling the truth about the life my grandparents had led or the harm my nemesis wished to me and my family.

"Miss Loddiges's journey from London surely was an ordeal for her," I said, "and honestly I do not know why she failed to write to me about her intended arrival in Philadelphia."

"One can only assume that her family did not wish her to make the journey."

I had met Mr. George Loddiges very briefly, but Sissy's hypothesis seemed accurate.

"Perhaps Miss Loddiges persuaded her father to allow her to conduct some business on the estate's behalf," I said, thinking aloud. "She does know a great deal about botany as well as ornithology, and the Bartram and Loddiges families have business connections through trade in plants and seeds and the like."

Sissy shook her head. "No, I think not. If Miss Loddiges were here on family business, there would have been an announcement in the newspaper of her arrival, particularly if she were visiting with the Carrs at Bartram's estate, and I would have noticed her name in the newspaper—I've read her book, after all. Miss Loddiges has undoubtedly come here without her father's permission to undertake some task that he does not wish her to pursue. She may have used the Bartram connection to her advantage, but her real purpose was to see you, and it was not to do with editing another ornithology book." She waited, needle dipping in and out of the cloth, her mild and patient gaze more potent than any violent inquisition.

"Miss Loddiges asked for my assistance in solving a mystery," I confessed. "Quite why I do not know. Her father's bird collector, a man named Andrew Mathews, died while on an expedition for Mr. Loddiges in 1841. They were told he was killed in a fall, but Miss Loddiges believes that Mr. Mathews was in fact murdered. His son Jeremiah died by drowning here in Philadelphia last October. She believes that he too was murdered. She is also convinced that she has seen his ghost," I added, signaling my skepticism with raised eyebrows and a worried shake of the head.

Sissy absorbed this for a moment. "You met Mr. Mathews and his son?"

"Yes, I met them both at Miss Loddiges's home."

"Tell me about the day you met him. I do not recall any mention of him in your letters."

"It was but a brief meeting during my first trip to Paradise Fields—and my initial impression of Miss Loddiges greatly overshadowed that of both gentlemen," I said truthfully. I remembered the charismatic Andrew Mathews, but could not fix his quiet son as clearly in my mind. There was mention that Jeremiah's mother was Peruvian, and I had presumed the young man favored her with his dark good looks and shorter stature. I tried to take myself back to the very beginning of my journey, hoping more details would spring to mind as I recounted them to Sissy.

"It was a bright morning, and I set off at nine o'clock in a hackney cab. As we travelled east, my journey seemed guided by saints: Dunstan, Bride, Martin, Paul, Mary and Leonard—it seemed fitting that some of London's most venerable ecclesiastical structures marked my path from Piccadilly to Paradise Fields in East London. The vast fields surrounding my destination were a welcome relief from the city's grime, and the famous Loddiges hothouses—I am certain I told you about them in my letters—were as impressive as their reputation suggested. When I arrived, quite a number of day-trippers were assembled to tour the great glass structures with their array of exotic plants."

As I described the start of my visit, I became immersed in my memory of Helena Loddiges's peculiar home. The details of that morning sharpened in my mind until I was *within* them, as if in a dream, and I described what I saw to Sissy.

"A young maidservant invited me into the house and led me along a dark corridor to the sitting room, where the girl abandoned me with a cheerful grin, saying that Miss Loddiges would be down to meet me presently and I should take a seat. I did as she suggested and observed my surroundings. While the room was spacious, it was made to seem a quarter of its size by the number of articles crammed into it. Ferns pressed against the glass of enormous Wardian cases, as if intent on creeping into the very room. Etchings of tropical birds and plants decorated the walls, obscuring the dark green paint. Books dedicated to botany and ornithology filled the shelves, which were topped with a heterogeneous flock of bird-life. I flinched when I spied a raven perched right above me, remembering the antics of Mr. Dickens's infernal pet, but soon realized that the ebony bird with its tilted head and glistening eye was perpetually captured in quizzical repose. All the other birds were equally inanimate, but posed so convincingly I felt that I had entered some ancient avian kingdom.

"The rattle of china made me turn to the door just as the maid-servant arrived with a wooden trolley carrying tea paraphernalia, cakes and a bowl of some exotic fruit. I nearly jumped from my skin when I noticed that the armchair nearest to mine was now occupied by a creature that could have been half woman, half bird—our whimsical Miss Helena Loddiges, of course."

"I am picturing it perfectly," Sissy said, crumpling up her embroidery in her pleasure. "What a curious place. So perfect for Miss Loddiges."

"Her natural habitat, no doubt. But her maidservant is less at home in that environment. She rebuffed my efforts to assist with laying out the tea things, despite her struggles to move a magnificent scarlet macaw and a collection of smaller brightly colored birds that filled the occasional table placed between our two armchairs."

"Dusting Miss Loddiges's flock must present the girl with awful problems," Sissy said, shaking her head with mock grav-ity. "Mother would find some way to cook them up for dinner if she were forced to deal with them."

I smiled to imagine that very likely scenario. "Perhaps that was what the girl meant when she nearly dropped the macaw and grumbled, 'I'll cook your goose, you wretch.'"

Sissy giggled. "And did you manage to hide your astonishment at Miss Loddiges's appearance?" she asked. "I suspect you did not, and hope you didn't ruffle the dear lady's feathers too much. Miss Loddiges is much more astute than one might presume from her eccentric garb."

Just as my wife was much more astute than her charmingly light-hearted manner suggested, I thought.

"I believe I managed initially, but fear I gawped in an ungentlemanly fashion when I noticed her adornments, which are gruesome in my opinion. In fact, that is something I found interesting about Mr. Andrew Mathews and his son. Neither was in the least discomfited by Miss Loddiges's attire or demeanor or her peculiar sitting room. Perhaps they were merely accustomed to the lady and her surroundings, or perhaps such adornments are pleasing to those who collect and skin birds."

"That is a horrible thought," my wife shivered. "Were Mr. Mathews and his son also assisting with Miss Loddiges's ornithology book?"

"In a sense. Obviously *père* Mathews provided birds for Mr. Loddiges's collection, which our dear lady studied and preserved. And of course he described the exotic places he visited to Miss Loddiges. Mr. Mathews was a jovial character, not at all how I imagined an explorer of the most remote parts of South America to be."

"Not a fearsome pirate or a grizzled fellow with uncombed hair, dressed all in animal skins?"

"I'm afraid not. But my first encounter with Mr. Mathews was quite remarkable all the same. After tea, Miss Loddiges took me to see the great glasshouses where they keep exotic orchids and ferns and the like. The heat made me feel quite drowsy, and I thought I was dreaming when a fairy creature appeared before me, darting to and fro inside a diaphanous bubble." The memory of that improbable creature drew me back to Paradise Fields, as if a mesmerist had directed me there . . .

"May I present Mr. Edgar Poe, writer and literary editor," my hostess had said to a dark-haired man, small in stature, who looked like a tropical woodland satyr in his dark green suit, and a young man who surely was no more than eighteen. "This is Mr. Andrew Mathews, botanist and bird collector. He has captured all the finest birds in my father's collection. And this is his son Jeremiah, who is studying ornithology."

"A pleasure to meet you, Mr. Poe," the bird collector said and grasped my hand enthusiastically.

"And you, Mr. Mathews," I muttered, with my attention utterly fixed on the tiny fairy that hovered in front of him.

Andrew Mathews noticed where my gaze was directed and laughed. "This is Enfys," he said. "*Trochilus colubris*. I have at last succeeded in bringing one of its species back alive. I hope it might prove possible to establish a small colony of them in one of the glasshouses. What a fine thing that would be."

I bent closer to the gauzy bubble with its flittering prisoner and saw that it was indeed a tiny emerald hummingbird, its throat decorated with red.

"The bag is kept distended by a rod of whalebone. She is quite content inside." Mr. Mathews pulled a small bottle from his pocket and held it up to the thin gauze. "Saccharine water – they are partial to it."

I watched with disbelief as the tiny creature thrust its long bill through the fabric and supped from the sweet nectar. When it finished feeding, the hummingbird nestled down at the bottom of its cage, which was attached to Mr. Mathews's jacket button. If I had not witnessed his unusual pet myself, I would have condemned the tale as a hoax. It was some time before I noticed that our hostess was also staring at the hummingbird, an anxious expression upon her face.

"Are you quite all right, Miss Loddiges?" I asked.

She nodded unconvincingly.

"Have you spied a message, Helena?" Jeremiah Mathews asked softly.

She closed her eyes and shook her head, but it was clear her denial was a polite fabrication.

"Helena believes in ornithomancy, a useful art when in the wilds of South America, where the actions of birds may alert the traveler to danger, but rather less helpful when it makes the practitioner afraid to go outdoors," Andrew Mathews explained. His words might have been insulting, but they were delivered with the tenderness of an elder brother to a beloved sister with no offense intended.

None seemed to be taken, for Miss Loddiges merely said, "I feel the need for more tea. Will you join me?" Without waiting for a response, she led us to her sitting room.

Before we could take our seats, Andrew Mathews said, "You must see Helena's most impressive work."

He led us to a large box draped with a cloth that dominated one corner of the room and unveiled it to reveal a humming-bird cabinet, truly the largest I had ever seen. It was as if a host of miniature angels was captured within its glass walls, so perfect were those winged creatures, so myriad their vivid hues. The tiny birds were perched upon tree branches or crouched in petite nests, while some were suspended by gossamer threads and appeared to hover mid-air. It was a vision of the sublime rather than the mundane, for there looked to be over one hundred species of hummingbirds displayed inside the cabinet . . .

"How lovely," Sissy whispered, waking me from my vision.

"Yes, it was. And at the center of the cabinet was a pair of the most elusive birds in their collection: *Loddigesia mirabilis*—the marvelous spatuletail—named after Miss Loddiges's father. Andrew Mathews had collected them, and Miss Loddiges had preserved them forever in the midst of their courtship ritual."

"What an uncommon thing to see, but how sad to kill such beautiful creatures," my wife said.

"Precisely what I thought, my dear. But it is the passion of her father and of many other collectors. Mr. Mathews seemed to have a paradoxical love of the birds; he delighted in observing them in their natural habitat, but did not flinch at extinguishing them in the name of science, as he put it. And he had a treasure trove of tales about his many hazardous expeditions through South America—Andrew Mathews was a most charismatic fellow. Conversely, his son was clearly intelligent but less gifted in the art of conversation. It was a delightful interlude to our working day, and Miss Loddiges seemed to wilt like a cut flower when they took their leave."

"And that is when you realized that Miss Helena Loddiges was in love with the bird collector's son."

In truth I had not realized that at all, but I knew then that Sissy was absolutely right. Helena Loddiges was in love with the recently deceased Jeremiah Mathews, who, in her view, succumbed to the ill will of another human being just before he sailed back to England.

"And so of course you must assist Miss Loddiges, for she is heartsick with grief. It was her affection for Mr. Mathews that made her find a way to Philadelphia against all odds. We cannot send her home disappointed and still grieving for her lost love. You must discover whether Jeremiah Mathews died by drowning, as was reported, or if truly he was murdered here in Philadelphia, as she believes," Sissy declared. "And if he was, the specifics of the terrible crime might indicate whether his father too was murdered."

"But, my dear, how do I even begin such an impossible task? Truly I cannot see how I can help the woman, as much as I would like to."

"You meet with Miss Loddiges at Bartram's estate tomorrow and you listen to all she has to say. I do not doubt that you will hear something in her full story that gives you an idea as to how to begin solving her mystery. And if you find that you truly cannot help her or her instincts regarding Mr. Mathews's death are wrong, then you will at least have comforted her in her grief, which is a noble thing in itself."

"All right. I will do as you suggest."

"And invite her to spend the day with us on Tuesday. She is lonely and grieving and I like her very much." My wife got up from her chair and leaned over to kiss me. "And now I must go to dream of a Peruvian forest filled with hummingbirds. Please do not stay up half the night reading, my love." She kissed me again.

For the second time that day, I was charged with finding the perpetrator of a murder that I was not convinced had truly occurred, for there was no body, no murder suspect nor any weapon—no concrete evidence at all that the likable Andrew Mathews had been sent to an early grave by human malevolence rather than an unfortunate whim of nature, or that his son had suffered the same terrible fate.

10

MONDAY, 11 MARCH 1844

The journey to Bartram's estate might have been a pleasantly refreshing one if it were not for the malevolent pixie that crouched in my pocket. With each bump and twist of the carriage I felt it shift and flex its limbs as if it were a live thing, not merely a doll constructed from wax and cloth. I had decided that the best course of action was to pay my respects to Miss Loddiges, see precisely what she wanted from me, and then journey on to St. Augustine's to reveal the new poppet to Father Keane.

When we arrived at last, I made my way up a path through a garden that was dormant but impressive in size and would produce quite a display of roses, daffodils and other flowers when they sprang from the earth in the next few months. The house itself was rather plain at first glance, constructed from local Wissahickon schist, gray in color but flecked with mica that glinted when the sun's rays glanced upon it. Three imposing Ionic columns gave it a quiet grandeur and curved embellishments carved around the main front windows added a certain prettiness. The house appeared to have three floors, with dormer windows—a trio—arising from the roof. I stepped onto the covered entranceway and let the knocker fall several times. The door opened moments later and there was a handsome woman, three score years or more, dressed in the severe clothing of a Quaker.

"Please come inside, Mr. Poe," she said, ushering me into the hall. "I am Mrs. Ann Carr, as you must have gathered."

"It is a great pleasure to meet you, Mrs. Carr."

She led me toward a crackling fire. "Helena is expecting you. She sends her apologies for her tardiness. She lost all sense of time while setting up her work table. Please, take off your coat and warm yourself." Mrs. Carr indicated a chair and I happily sank into it while she took my overcoat. The house was decorated simply but comfortably. A painting of an elderly man—no doubt a Bartram—was hanging above the fireplace, and I wondered briefly if it was by the same peculiar artist responsible for the portrait I so detested in our own parlor. Hanging opposite the window was a more appealing still life of blossoms arranged in a turquoise bowl. The flowers were very striking, white with vivid yellow stamens and long oval leaves of claret.

As Mrs. Carr settled herself into another armchair, she said, "*Franklinia alatamaha*. We cultivate them. The leaves change from green to scarlet in autumn, when occasionally they will also blossom."

"Quite the spectacle," I said.

"Have you visited our gardens previously, Mr. Poe?"

"We came last June. My wife was captivated by the peonies in particular."

Mrs. Carr smiled. "You must bring her again. The gardens are ever-changing through the year. We have many exotics in the glasshouses and a very extensive collection of native plants."

A serving girl came in with a tea tray and a lovely aroma suffused the air as she poured. When she handed me my cup, I greedily drank down the warming beverage.

"Good afternoon, Mr. Poe."

I looked up to see Helena Loddiges swathed in a large pinafore. "Miss Loddiges." I jumped up and the cup rattled as I placed it back on the tray. "I am so sorry. I did not hear you enter."

"She speaks and walks as quietly as a mouse," Mrs. Carr said. "She would make a fine bird collector herself, for she can creep up on man or beast unnoticed."

Miss Loddiges frowned slightly. "Except that I would find it impossible to kill the birds."

I found this declaration more than odd given her work as a taxidermist and her penchant for wearing adornments made from creatures that had once soared the skies.

"To extinguish the life of an animal is quite different to *reviving* a dead creature through my art," she said as if she had read my mind.

"Indeed it is." Mrs. Carr rose to her feet. "It was a pleasure to meet you, Mr. Poe. I will let you two get on with your business while I attend to my own." She nodded her head and left the room.

Miss Loddiges perched on her chair and picked up the tea that had been poured for her. She sipped and waited as if expecting me to speak.

"Have you been at work?" I asked, nodding at the pinafore.

She glanced down at her attire and seemed surprised for a moment. "Yes. I should have left the pinafore at my work table," she said ruefully. "But it seems quite clean."

"Yes, very. Fear not." I was certain that a pinafore stained with bird entrails was not polite attire for any Philadelphia drawing room, even one owned by scientists, but Mrs. Carr had not seemed affronted by her guest's clothing. "Is your project something for the Carrs?"

"For Colonel Carr. He rescued an injured *Trochilus colubris*, and kept it for several months in a heated glasshouse, but it succumbed when the temperature dropped one night, just before I arrived."

"Quite the coincidence."

Miss Loddiges's eyes flashed with indignation. "Not a coincidence. It is much more than that."

I remembered the light-hearted remark Andrew Mathews had made about her belief in ornithomancy. "You think it to be a sign?"

Miss Loddiges stared as if I were profoundly slow-witted. "A *Trochilus colubris* is attacked by a *Falco sparverius*—most uncommon—but is rescued by Colonel Carr. He keeps the creature alive in the simulacrum of a jungle paradise for several months, but it expires a day before I arrive in Philadelphia?" She said it as if delivering a lecture.

"You believe the uncommon attack on the hummingbird is some kind of message regarding Jeremiah Mathews's death?"

"*Murder.*"

"Murder," I echoed. "And was Jeremiah's expedition to Peru conducted on behalf of your father?"

"Yes," she said mournfully. "He was to bring back bird skins for me to mount for my father's collection."

I could not think what words might console her, so said nothing. She finished her tea and abruptly stood up. "Perhaps it would help your investigation if you understood the process?"

As first I was baffled, then realized with some horror what she meant, but could not politely refuse the lady.

"Yes, it would be illuminating to see your work."

Miss Loddiges led me down a hall to the back of the house. We exited the door into a garden area with scattered heaps of stubborn snow and entered the door to a large glasshouse, which was kept warmer than the Carr family home. It was filled with exotic plants and the winter light gleamed with a sharp,

blue brilliance through the glass. Miss Loddiges made her way
to a table stationed under a palm, and I followed.

On the table was an open box which contained a needle and
thread, some cotton wool, a pot of some mixture, a jar of white
powder and a variety of delicate scissors, knives and pliers all
neatly arranged with their tips pointing upwards, ends aligned
with precision. Somehow this looked oddly familiar to me,
although I had not seen the lady's work station at Paradise
Fields.

To the right of the glinting implements was a small cone of
paper. Miss Loddiges unfurled it with long fingers made ugly by
savaged cuticles and nails, and despite my knowledge of what
that delicate paper would hold, my heart still jittered. The luminous corpse, with its emerald back and wings, its pearly-white
breast slashed with scarlet at the throat, looked so forlorn, so
very *dead*.

"The *Trochilus colubris*. Colonel Carr named it Ruby," she said
softly. "Although of course the bird is a male." She placed the
hummingbird onto a piece of clean paper and then pointed out
each of the implements on the table. "Tow, preservative
mixture, scissors, a skinning knife, French cutting nippers, two
pliers—bell-hangers' and feather—tow forceps and stuffing
iron. All essential."

And then it occurred to me where I had seen such a table
before—I had been sent one, in miniature, as part of the
macabre diorama. But why? Was Miss Loddiges included in
the threat against me?

Fierce concentration overtook my benefactress, and she
began to work quickly and confidently, despite the minuscule
proportions of her subject, explaining in her whispering voice
each of her actions.

"First I must renew the cotton in the mouth, nose holes, ear
cavities, vent and shot hole, if there is one," she said, as her

fingers executed the delicate task. "One must not disarrange the feathers or stretch the neck." She sprinkled the tiny carcass with cornmeal. "To absorb any blood or grease that might soil the feathers." Miss Loddiges then measured and recorded every aspect of the hummingbird before she fastened its beak together with a tiny piece of bee's wax. I had the most terrible vision of the poor creature swallowing down its shrills of fear.

"Now we may begin properly." She pointed at the humming-bird's tiny wing. "I leave the humerus intact—to break the humerus in any wing is to cripple the most spiritual part of a bird. It is never truly necessary." She briefly looked up to check that I understood. I nodded despite my confusion, and she returned her focus to the bird, gently twisting its legs out of joint and parting the feathers away from each side of the ster-num. With a knife's point placed exactly at the center of the bird, she sliced tenderly down along the right side of the breast bone to just under the tail. With the metal tip, she then loos-ened the skin in every direction, reversed the bird and repeated the process on the left side. "One must persuade the skin from the flesh. Do you see?" She delicately pushed until the legs could be cut away from the skin with the scissors. Her knife teased the skin away from the root of the tail, the wings, neck, ears and eyes until, finally, the skin was severed from the body. Miss Loddiges paused for a moment, pointing with a scalpel to emphasize her soft words. "Now I must cut the skull from the neck, pull out the tongue and excise the brains." As she spoke, the heat became increasingly oppressive, the light draining away into darkness. "And then I will remove the eyes, but great care must be taken not to burst them as the vitreous humor will stain the feathers."

I do not know how her instructions went from there for queasiness overcame me, and I rushed to a potted palm where I thoroughly disgraced myself. When at last I felt less wretched

and reasonably sure that I had tidied myself as best I could with
my handkerchief, I made my way back to my benefactress's
dissecting table, my face burning with embarrassment.

"I am so sorry. I do not know what came over me." I searched
for a convincing excuse, but Miss Loddiges shook her head,
dismissing my apology.

"It is I who must apologize. I forget that the minutiae of taxidermy unsettles many people. Jeremiah was fascinated by the
process of bringing the birds back to life, but my father will not
watch me at work, despite his extensive avian collection. Come,
sit and drink some water."

She led me to a chair next to a small table with a pitcher of
water upon it and poured some for me. As she handed me the
cup, the downy wisp of a feather adhered to her finger caught
my eye and bile rose up into my throat again. I pressed my hand
to my mouth and coughed, setting the cup back on the table.

"Thank you, I feel much recovered now."

"Very good," she said, her eyes full of concern. "Perhaps I
should simply tell you as much as I know about the murders?"

"Yes, although I confess I feel unconvinced that I shall be able
to assist you."

She ignored my deprecation. "Andrew Mathews was killed
on the twenty-fourth of November 1841 when on an expedition
in the Chachapoyan mountains of Peru," the lady announced.

I heard her words with some shock. "Chachapoyan mountains, you say?" I pictured the diorama with its mountainous
backdrop and the man with the sack of miniature birds interred
in a rough grave. And then there was the table with the implements, the female figure all dressed in black that was in my coat
pocket, and the dead raven parts. How could I have missed the
connection earlier? So shaken had I been by the reappearance
of my nemesis that my mind could focus on nothing else. "I
believe you are in terrible danger, Miss Loddiges," I blurted out.

"My father may think so too," she said calmly. "Or he does not trust me. Or he considers me an embarrassment. I really do not know. But as he refused to allow me to communicate with anyone outside of our home, I was forced to travel here without his knowledge and to alert you of my arrival so cryptically."

"But I did not receive a letter."

Miss Loddiges stared at me with round green eyes that might have belonged to some exotic species of owl. Her gaze was solemn and infinitely patient. After a long minute of silence, I understood at last.

"The diorama? It was from you?"

"Of course." She looked at me as if it were the most obvious thing in the world.

I could not think of anything to say for a time, such was my confusion. Certainly Miss Loddiges was eccentric, yet she had seemed logical in our previous dealings, a student of the scientific arts to her core. But her story of murder with no proof, the strange diorama with cryptic message and her unannounced arrival in Philadelphia strongly suggested that the lady had lost her wits.

"It was a most complicated message," I finally said, "which would have caused you great trouble to put together. Why not simply send a letter?"

"My father confiscated all the letters I tried to send. He refuses to believe the truth—that Andrew and Jeremiah Mathews were murdered."

I was not surprised at all by this. From what I had heard about George Loddiges, he was a man of science and logic who was unlikely to put much stock in his daughter's wild fantasies.

"When I told him that I would approach the authorities in London myself, he refused to let me leave the house. Of course I immediately wrote a letter to you about my fears, but he intercepted it. And the next one I wrote. He instructed all who work for him to confiscate any notes written by me and to turn them over to him. Truly, I was treated like a criminal," she said indignantly.

Or a woman who had lost all reason. "He was trying to protect you, I'm sure." And I truly meant my words, for Miss Loddiges's tale of murder in the wilds of Peru was unlikely to solicit a sympathetic response from the authorities if her own father did not believe her tale.

Miss Loddiges stared at me with her disconcerting eyes. "My father is hiding something, that is for certain. And I promise you that I am being objective when I say that. He is distracted and indecisive, which is most unlike him. Something preys upon his mind, and I believe it is the suspicious deaths of Andrew and Jeremiah Mathews. But he will not confide in me, and I will not bury my head in the sand. That is why I had to contact you in such a surreptitious manner. I remembered how you admired the bird dioramas I constructed and said you could read the stories within them—indeed you fully gathered my intentions for each of them. I knew you would grasp the dark tale behind this one."

I thought back to the afternoon when I met Miss Loddiges in her parlor full of birds and recalled how I had briefly improvised my interpretation of the bird displays she showed me, simply to make conversation. Her confidence in me to interpret the bizarre diorama of waxen figures had been utterly misplaced.

"But how did you manage to send the Wardian case and its contents if you were stopped from sending a letter?"

"I secreted them in two shipments of plants and seeds to Bartram's Gardens. They were wrapped in paper and addressed to you. I told the boy who helps our gardener pack the crates that they were birds I had worked on—a special order for a friend of Mrs. Carr."

"And you believed that Mrs. Carr would forward the packages to me?"

"Of course. She is very reliable. We often send my taxidermy for clients in Philadelphia or New York in crates to Bartram's, as they tend to be better accounted for than when shipped on their own. Mrs. Carr simply has them taken to the post office and they are forwarded on or collected."

"Which is what she did with the five packets addressed to me," I murmured. I wondered what Colonel and Mrs. Carr thought of Miss Loddiges's tales of murder, for she must have told them why she had come. "And have the Carrs sent your father notice as to where you are?"

Miss Loddiges scowled. "Of course, but it will take two weeks or more for her letter to reach him and longer still for someone to come and fetch me. I am certain we will capture the villain by then."

Miss Loddiges looked so earnest and determined that I did not bother to repudiate her assertion, despite my own lack of faith in the enterprise she had ensnared me in.

"Of course I would like to be of assistance," I said, "but truly I have little idea of how I might help you."

"You are too modest. I read about your successes with the villainous ourang-outang and the murder of that poor girl who sold cigars. You will find out the culprit."

I was taken aback by her words. Did she not understand the boundaries between fact and fiction? That the tales I wrote were not directly based on my own adventures?

"So let us begin our quest as soon as you are able." Miss Loddiges retrieved a leather-bound book from her pinafore pocket and placed it before me. "This is for you to study. It is Jeremiah's journal from the 1843 expedition. It notes their route, the birds he observed and those he collected."

I opened the book and found pages of Jeremiah Mathews's precise handwriting and admirable illustrations of plants, birds and other creatures.

"But please take great care of it. It was my gift to Jeremiah before he left for Peru and now it is all I have to remember him by."

"It will be my pleasure to read this, and I will take immense care of it."

She nodded, her pain at relinquishing the journal clear. "He sent it to me from Panama. I received it in late November and was glad of his imminent return. Just two weeks later we had news of his death."

"I am so sorry," I murmured.

"His letter is at the back," she added.

I turned to the back of the journal and found a folded piece of paper. Miss Loddiges gestured for me to open it.

Colón, Panama
4 October 1843

Dear Helena,

The expedition was a success. I have retraced my father's footsteps to the lost city and have gathered a quantity of specimens that is sure to please your father. The journey to Cuzco was, in many ways, more arduous than that into the Chachapoyas, and all that I have witnessed and experienced leads me to believe that our suppositions must be true. We set sail for Philadelphia tomorrow, so I am posting this treasured gift back to you for safekeeping. You will find its contents illuminating, and I trust you will ensure that my work is completed if the journey home is as treacherous as I fear.

I pray to see you before Christmas.

Your true friend,
Jeremiah

"He sounds satisfied with the expedition, and that he accomplished all he set out to achieve."

Miss Loddiges dismissed my comment with an impatient flick of her fingers. "Our suppositions were that his father had been murdered. And it is odd that Jeremiah posted the journal to me from Panama rather than simply bringing it home with him."

It did indeed seem rather strange, but I could not shake the notion that Miss Loddiges's imagination had gotten the better of her, and so I felt obliged to challenge her assertions

"There could be any number of reasons he posted the journal back to you from Panama," I said, though I was struggling to think of one. "Perhaps he thought you might like the list of the birds he collected in Peru before his arrival in London?"

"I don't think so," she persisted. "He speaks of the journey being treacherous, and I believe he is referring to a threat from a person rather than the sea. And look here at his entry on the third of October. Surely it is relevant."

I opened the journal and leafed through its pages until I found what was the last entry before Jeremiah Mathews's inventory of birds.

"'They seek the Jewel. All is within,'" I read out loud. "A rather cryptic message. Do you understand what he meant by it?"

"Not precisely, but it must be enormously important, for if you remember, he asked after a jewel on the night of his visitation. I believe that whoever was seeking this jewel murdered Jeremiah and perhaps his father too."

I nodded, even though I felt certain that Miss Loddiges's vision of the drowned Jeremiah Mathews was a nightmare provoked in part by the mysterious journal entry, which had succeeded in piquing my own curiosity.

" 'They seek the Jewel.' It sounds as if Jeremiah expected you or perhaps your father to know what he was referring to—that you had spoken of a jewel before his journey. Is that the case?"

Miss Loddiges thought for a moment, then said, "When Andrew Mathews was visiting with my father before his final expedition, I remember they spoke of old legends regarding a king's treasure trove hidden in the mountains of Peru, but neither seemed to believe it truly existed. I did not find any other reference to a jewel in his journal, but perhaps Jeremiah uncovered something and was murdered for it. My father complained that some items listed on the inventory were missing, but I cannot tell you which ones."

"A legendary Peruvian jewel," I murmured. "Well, I will read the journal with curiosity and hope to find something that may shed light on this mystery," I said truthfully.

"Thank you, Mr. Poe."

"It is an honor to assist you." We sat in awkward silence until I recalled Sissy's request. "My wife wonders if you would care to join us for an excursion tomorrow. There are many fine things to see in Philadelphia, and she feels it would divert your attention from your grief."

Miss Loddiges nodded gravely. "That is very kind. I would enjoy that."

"Very good. Virginia will be pleased. Shall we meet at our house at one o'clock?"

"I will be there." She paused a moment, then said tentatively: "There is one thing I would like to do while I am here in America."

"I will do my best to help you achieve it, of course."

"I would very much like to see a flocking of passenger pigeons."

For a moment I was startled by her request, then realized what a wondrous sight it would seem to an amateur ornithologist from London. I hadn't an inkling of how to find the birds, but if anyone knew, it would be Father Keane.

"I will visit a friend today who may be able to assist with that."

"How wonderful." She smiled. "I know you will succeed. In everything."

She was like the small child who believes her father has supernatural abilities, and I felt the weight of that faith.

"I will do my best. That is all I can promise."

And so I left that miniature tropical paradise and made my way to see Father Keane, hoping to persuade my friend to embark on a bizarre investigation with me instigated by Charles Dickens's deceased pet, that infernal devil Grip.

11

TUESDAY, 12 MARCH 1844

Miss Loddiges stood very still, staring up, completely oblivious to the pedestrians forced to skirt around her on the footpath; they, however, gawped unashamedly at her, betraying their polite Philadelphian upbringings. In truth, her costume was more than startling. The lady had protected herself against the chill with a vibrant azure woolen cloak composed of four voluminous layers, each finished with a furbelow of daffodil yellow. The fussiness of the garment was exacerbated by the silken bonnet she wore, also blue and decorated with a quantity of artificial posies which harbored several feasting hummingbirds. I had innocently asked if Miss Loddiges's garments were the current fashion in London, where I had noted a flair for the eccentric compared to our more conservative attire. Sissy tried to interject, fearing the lady would take offense, but Miss Loddiges was merely bemused.

"No, no, it is my creation. When I have no birds to work on, I often sew articles of clothing. I find that my taxidermy work inspires me, for what is more perfect than the artful plumage of a bird designed by Nature herself?"

"What a wonderful talent to have," my wife said somewhat disingenuously, given her own considerable skill as a seamstress.

"Too many simply buy what they are told is fashionable by ladies' journals."

"Perhaps," Miss Loddiges murmured, her eyes still directed upwards. "That is a wonderful eagle," she finally remarked. "Quite perfect in form and demeanor. Truly it should be inside the museum rather than outside."

I followed her gaze to the grand eagle carved from wood that was mounted above the doorway to the Pennsylvania Academy of Fine Arts. "Ah, indeed. It is by William Rush, who was an exceptional artist. I believe his master work is a life-sized statue of the Crucifixion at St. Augustine Church. Perhaps we will have time to see it, for we are meeting my friend Father Keane at the church tomorrow after he finishes teaching. He has an idea of where we might see a flocking of passenger pigeons."

Miss Loddiges whirled around, her face luminous with joy. "How marvelous! It has long been a dream of mine to see the pigeons."

"Please remember that our trip is but a hope and not a certainty," I cautioned. "One cannot truly predict the flight of the birds."

Miss Loddiges raised her brows as if she did not believe me. "Yes, of course, I understand. If I witness the pigeons darkening the sky, even at a distance, that will be something. Thank you, Mr. Poe. I am ever grateful that I made your acquaintance," she said solemnly. "Shall we go in?" And our guest was through the door before I could return the nicety.

We spent nearly two hours exploring the Academy, home to the best collection of art in the country, including works by European masters and contemporary American artists. There was an impressive exhibition of religious art on show, but this did not seem to move Miss Loddiges at all. She was equally unimpressed with some very fine works by Claude Lorrain and Benjamin West's *Death on the Pale Horse*, which was the pride of the Academy and had been purchased at great expense. Elegant portraits by West's protégé, Gilbert Stuart, did not capture her interest, nor did the works of Thomas Sully and Joshua Shaw, despite my efforts to explain why they were so highly regarded.

"I am sorry, Mr. Poe," she finally said. "I did have sketching and painting lessons as a young girl, and of course I realize that it requires great skill to paint a portrait that so captures the essence of a person or the atmosphere of a landscape, but I fear such works fail to move me. They are so *flat*, so lifeless. Perhaps that is my attraction to taxidermy—the bird is rendered immortal by capturing it in a life-like pose and the spectator can view it from different aspects and see something new each time. If a work is well done, it should evoke a sense of anticipation in the observer, a feeling that the bird might take flight at any moment."

I did not know how to respond to my guest's admission that she was unenthused by the art of painting—most would have pretended interest out of politeness. And I did not understand her passion for the birds she reconstructed, as to me the smell of death lingered on her creations. Thankfully my wife intervened.

"What of the illustrations by Mr. Audubon?" Sissy asked. "Do you think they capture the essence of his subjects?"

Miss Loddiges smiled. "Mr. Audubon is exceptional. I do enjoy how he depicts birds, often in motion or feeding. It gives them such life and spirit. I especially admire how he studies creatures in their habitat, for it is something I have had little opportunity to do."

"It sounds as if you know Audubon's work very well," I said as I paused to admire a Sully portrait. To my mind, Sully's art was more sublime than Audubon's, but Miss Loddiges seemed hardly to notice the painting in front of her.

"My father gave me Audubon's *Birds of America* and John Gould's *Birds of Europe* as he felt they would help me with my work. Both are treasures and I have studied them extensively. And while the artistry of Gould's books is exceptional, I find that Audubon's positioning of the birds and his backgrounds have been the most inspirational. I do my best to pose my birds in an equally life-like manner."

"And you succeed admirably," I said.

Miss Loddiges shrugged. "It is difficult to achieve much veracity when displaying a bird in a glass case. My humming-bird cabinet is quite a successful work, I think, but hardly natu-ralistic. My father wished to display a great quantity of his collection in one place—a symptom of his pride rather than any predilection for science—and so I complied. I tried to imagine a kingdom of hummingbirds and what its hierarchy might be. My arrangement reflects that vision."

"Eddy described the cabinet to me, and that night I dreamt of just such a kingdom of birds. You cannot imagine how much I have wished to look at the piece."

Miss Loddiges seemed thrilled with my wife's words. "Then you must come to Paradise Fields to see it. It would be such a pleasure to have you as our guests in London." She glanced at another masterpiece, then turned to face Sissy. "I think you would enjoy it. People come from all over to see our glass-houses and the array of plants we have. And I hope to make Jeremiah's dream a reality some day, to include living exotic birds in our glasshouse gardens. Wouldn't that be extraordi-nary? Jeremiah was both a man of science and a visionary—an artist, truly."

"What a wonderful notion. Jeremiah sounds an exceptional man." Sissy looked at Miss Loddiges with quiet compassion—she had a gift for putting people at ease. "And I would very much enjoy a trip to London and to see your home," she declared. "I have never left these shores, which is a particular grievance of mine."

Miss Loddiges became so absorbed with the notion of us traveling to London that she no longer bothered to give the paintings anything other than a cursory glance, almost chivvying us along whenever I paused to examine a work more closely. But then she stopped abruptly and stared, and when I joined her in front of the painting that had captured her attention, my breath caught in my throat, for it was a portrait my wife and I had viewed at an Artists' Fund Hall exhibition three years previously. The portrait was in a gilded, oval frame and done in a vignette manner; its background was shadowy, but the subject's eyes were luminous, almost alive. A small brass plaque was attached to the frame with the words:

Mrs. Reynolds, actress
(Robert Street, 1840)

The irrepressible Mr. Street had painted Mrs. Rowena Fontaine, an anonymous immigrant recently arrived from London in October 1840, and in three short years that work had been transformed as if by magic into the portrait of the very popular actress Mrs. Reynolds, and deemed worthy of display at the Academy of Fine Arts.

"I remember her," Miss Loddiges murmured after studying the painting for a time. "She came to see our glasshouses."

I was rather surprised by Miss Loddiges's pronouncement and noticed that she seemed troubled by the portrait. "Are you certain it was her? The lady emigrated to America more than three years ago and surely any number of people visit Paradise Fields."

"Yes, I am absolutely certain. In fact, she came to the glasshouses the day you called on me—the day you met Andrew and Jeremiah."

"Why did Mrs. Reynolds make such an impression?" my wife asked.

Miss Loddiges thought carefully for a moment, as if she were looking back in time and reliving the memory. "It was a peculiar day from the beginning, in truth. Mr. Poe's visit occurred on the date of a meeting my father had arranged to plan an expedition to Peru. My mother wanted me to find an orchid for the table and as I was searching for something suitable, a small group of visitors entered the glasshouse with my brother, who was conducting a tour. This lady"—she indicated the painting—"was amongst them. I noticed her because she seemed to have no interest in anything inside the glasshouse, and kept looking outside as if searching for someone or something. And then there was the screech of a bird in distress and a magpie swooped down from Lord knows where and struck at the lady's head—once and then again. She screamed in the most horrible manner until my brother chased the bird out of the door. And then the serving girl came to fetch me as you, Mr. Poe, had arrived and were waiting in my sitting room." Miss Loddiges shivered. "I had terrible dreams that night. I felt certain it was a warning—one for sorrow."

I nodded, my gaze caught in the violet eyes that were so perfectly rendered they seemed to be staring back at me. Miss Fontaine was at Paradise Fields on the one day I had travelled there? She had followed me, without doubt, and then she was attacked by a bird that was where it should not have been. I did not know what it meant, but I felt as unnerved as Miss Loddiges.

My wife put her hand in mine and squeezed it gently. "I would like some tea," she said. "I think I have had enough art for today and the recital at the Musical Fund Hall begins in one hour."

After Miss Loddiges's revelation, I knew there was little point in trying to sit through a musical evening when my mind would be fully elsewhere. I also knew that my wife was likely to enjoy the recital more if solely in the company of Miss Loddiges, for

I doubted the performance by the Hutchinson Family Singers would be entirely to my taste.

"I fear I have some work to be getting on with this evening, particularly as Miss Loddiges and I must set off by noon tomorrow to meet Father Keane, but you ladies should go to the Musical Fund Hall. It is a very American entertainment," I told Miss Loddiges. "I think you will enjoy it."

"Oh, you will!" Sissy's delight was clear. "It will be a wonderful evening."

"I will come back to meet you after the entertainment finishes."

"There is no need, my dear."

"If you are certain?"

"Of course. If Miss Loddiges is capable of finding her way from London to Philadelphia on her own, I believe I can find my own way home." The two women exchanged a smile.

We walked back through the door of the Academy and onto a bustling Chestnut Street. "I shall take my leave then," I said. "Thank you for a most pleasant afternoon."

Miss Loddiges gave a tentative smile. "And thank you for your extraordinary kindness, Mr. and Mrs. Poe. I believe you are the truest friends I have now that Jeremiah is gone, and it makes my heart glad."

Sissy caught her breath as she heard those words and she grasped Miss Loddiges's hands in her own. "And we are so very glad of that."

Any lingering annoyance I had harbored at the lady's lack of interest in the paintings had disappeared with her words, for I had known the cruelty of loneliness in the past.

"Very glad indeed," I said, meaning every word. If assisting her to find out more about Jeremiah Mathews's death helped in some small way to assuage her loneliness, then I would do all I could with an open heart.

After my ungentlemanly abandonment of my wife and Miss Loddiges, I made my way home, more than certain that the two would enjoy the recital much more now that they had the opportunity to talk about whatever it was ladies discuss when not in the company of the opposing sex. Once arrived, I immediately went to my study and wrote Dupin a letter.

234 North Seventh Street, Philadelphia

12 March 1844

My dear Dupin,

I have the most extraordinary news to relay about events that have occurred since my last letter—certain surprising facts have been revealed to me and my fears that George Williams was planning to murder you now appear groundless.

I had believed that Williams was tormenting me again by delivering macabre poppets that suggested murder—indeed, your murder. There was a reference to Peru in the threats I received and I recalled that you had journeyed there, which made me think you were

his intended victim. Recently I was sent another manikin, this time in the shape of a woman, and I had
presumed it to be Sissy, which terrified me. On that
very day, however, we had an unexpected visit from
Miss Helen Loddiges, the English ornithologist. You
will remember that I edited her book and met with her
one day during our time in London. The lady had
made the journey here on her own, against her father's
wishes, and it was she who had sent the strange dolls in
an attempt to inform me cryptically of a mystery she
wishes me to solve. Miss Loddiges ardently believes
that her father's bird collector and his son were
murdered, despite official verdicts of succumbing to
an accidental fall and drowning. She has asked me to
investigate their deaths, for she seems to credit me
with your skills of ratiocination. How I wish you were
here, my friend! I cannot see where to begin, for there
is no real evidence that either man was a victim of
malice. In my opinion, the lady is overcome with grief,
for she loved the young man, Jeremiah Mathews, who
died this past October in Philadelphia. She speaks of
seeing ghosts, of receiving messages from birds and of
a mysterious jewel from Peru. I would not get involved
in the matter at all, but my wife insists that I help the
lady.

As for George Williams and his paramour, Mrs.
Rowena Fontaine, they are indeed in Philadelphia, but
they now go by the name of Reynolds, perhaps to
escape some crime committed under their true appel-
lations. They are also married, or claim to be, and the
lady is a popular actress who performs in plays written
by her husband. My wife and I had an audience with
Mrs. Reynolds, who swears that she has persuaded her

husband to let go of the past and to absolve me of the crimes of my grandparents. I have not had that pledge from Williams himself, however, but I am gratified that he does not seem to be a threat to you as I had presumed. I would not forgive myself if our friendship brought you to harm.

I hope that your own quest has progressed. Please write soon and tell me any news of Valdemar. In your last letter you mentioned a sighting of him in the Bibliothèque de l'Arsenal. Have you discovered anything further?

With greatest respect,
Edgar A. Poe

I gave my letter to my mother-in-law to post the following day while we undertook our quest to find passenger pigeons, then sat down to do a final review of a tale entitled "The Spectacles" that I had written for *The Dollar* newspaper. I could not help but think of Mrs. Reynolds when working on it, for truly she too suffered from the vice of vanity, which was likely to be her undoing. Despite all the ways she had tormented me, I pitied her ill health and ravaged beauty.

Later, at eight o'clock, I was seated in the kitchen, Catterina warming my knees and rumbling with contentment while I was restless with worry. The recital was long over, and I had presumed Sissy would be home for supper, but she still had not returned. I had reassured Muddy that nothing was amiss and so she had retired, but I had little confidence in my own words. At last I heard the door open and the rustle of outer clothing being removed.

"Eddy! Dearest, I'm home."

Sissy walked into the kitchen, beaming, and I pretended that I had been engrossed in my book rather than anxiously waiting.

"How was your evening?" I asked.

"Oh, it was marvelous. The Hutchinson family truly are a wonder. Their four-part harmonizing is perfect and young Abby has such poise—as much or more than her brothers."

"Did Miss Loddiges enjoy the recital?"

"Very much, I am delighted to say. I wasn't certain at first as Helena sat so quietly and stared at the singers, head tilted to the side much like a bird, while those around us hummed along or tapped their feet and applauded most furiously."

"Did any of the songs offend her?"

"Not at all. She was surprised by the forthright lyrics and had never before heard songs about abolitionism and women's suffrage, but she did not disagree with the sentiments expressed, unlike some others in the audience."

"I hope there was no violence," I said with alarm.

"Just unpleasant hissing. A newspaper described the Hutchinson family as 'native talent', which led a few people to expect Nativist singers, and so they did not care much for 'The Lament of the Irish Emigrant'."

When in the vicinity of St. Augustine's, I had noticed a further worsening of tensions between the "Nativists" and the Irish Catholic immigrants there, but I did not wish to ruin my wife's evening with talk about conflict in a city built on the notion of brotherhood.

"It's a good thing the dissenters were in the minority, and I'm very pleased that you both enjoyed the performance."

"We did. In truth, I fear Helena goes to few entertainments at all, that she spends her life a virtual prisoner at Paradise Fields."

"A prisoner by choice, surely. I did not have the impression that her father kept her locked up in any way and certainly he encouraged her study and work. If he confiscated her letters to me, I think it was to save her reputation."

Sissy nodded, her face sympathetic. "I fear you are right that her home has become a prison by her own design. Helena is convinced that birds speak to her in the most uncanny ways and it frightens her when she is away from her little sanctuary. It was only her love for Jeremiah that enabled her to make this journey. We really must help her."

"I will do my best to find out the truth," I said carefully. "Miss Loddiges's story is most odd."

"Well, I believe her. And I am so glad I had the chance to get to know her today," Sissy declared. "If I had a sister, I would wish her to be exactly like Helena."

"Truly? Someone so . . . unusual?"

Sissy laughed. "I think you underestimate the dear lady. Her clothing may be exuberant, but it is merely the extension of an original mind. And she is very well read."

"And she believes in ghosts and messages sent from birds and hidden Peruvian treasure."

" 'There are more things in heaven and earth, Horatio, than are dreamt of in your philosophy,' " my wife quoted, smiling.

"Perhaps. But oft times those things we believe to be the product of some supernatural and ungodly force are truly the work of man." How well I knew this to be true!

"Then that is where you begin with Helena's mystery. Ascertain why someone might wish Jeremiah Mathews dead and then you will quickly work out the 'who'." My wife leaned closer as if to study every aspect of my face, then kissed me. "How lucky we are, dearest. How very lucky."

I was glad to hear her say the words that were always in my heart.

13

WEDNESDAY, 13 MARCH 1844

We made an unlikely trio in the open carriage borrowed from St. Augustine Academy as we travelled westward from the city along Ridge Road. Wedged in between Father Keane and I, Miss Loddiges resembled an exotic parrot accompanied by two ravens, her peculiar azure and yellow cloak flapping in the breeze like wings, her bonnet a convenient nest for her tiny avian acolytes.

Once the city was behind us, we drank in the beauty of the surrounding woodland, a mix of tulip trees, black birch, sassafras, beech, red maple and the nut-bearing hickories and grand oaks that attract passenger pigeons. Father Keane had received word that a flock of the birds had been roosting about twenty miles southwest of Philadelphia and were again migrating north. Such was the speed of the birds in flight—far faster than a horse and carriage—that he believed we had every chance of observing them in the Wissahickon area, where they might forage successfully for food. As we moved through seemingly endless forest, the air grew ever cleaner and colder. White-tailed deer froze where they stood as we drove past them, whereas squirrels continued their frantic scurrying up and down tree trunks, or leaping from bough to bough. The leaf buds were fat on the branches and clumps of violets and spring beauties were scattered through the forest floor. Father Keane pointed out each new bird he spied as we drove along, much to Miss Loddiges's delight.

"Nuthatch on the elm there," he said, pointing at a slate-gray bird with a white breast and stripe of black like a bandit mask over its eyes.

Our companion clapped her gloved hands together as the bird descended head first down the tree trunk like an acrobat.

"It's almost as if I'm in the Peruvian forests. Jeremiah grew up there and would watch the birds with his father. The stories he would tell me! He had a way of describing birds that made me feel I myself had seen them soaring through their habitat."

My fears that the journey would be cloaked in ponderous silence had thankfully come to naught. Miss Loddiges and Father Keane discussed their ornithological interests ardently, each impressed with the other's knowledge.

"You must show Father Keane Jeremiah's notebook," Miss Loddiges said. "He will surely appreciate it and will understand immediately the clues within it."

I had briefly shown my friend the notebook, suggesting exactly that, and was glad that I would not be obliged to hide Father Keane's involvement in what I hoped would be a short-lived investigation. He had been impressed with the illustrated journal and could scarcely hide his enthusiasm at my invitation to read it.

"I cannot promise that I will find any useful clues within the journal, for I have little expertise in the birds of Peru, but I am more than curious to examine Mr. Mathews's work," he had said to me. "And it must be a relief to learn that the diorama was not a threat from your enemy. I am certainly curious to meet this unusual lady—she would seem to be singularly determined with an original mind."

"And I am more than curious to see what you make of her," I had replied.

The two had an immediate affinity when I introduced them. Father Keane appeared genuinely to admire the gruesome embellishments she wore upon her hat and did not flinch when she described how she had fashioned them from hummingbird skins that had been too damaged to include in her father's collection.

There was a flash of red overhead and Miss Loddiges gasped. A cardinal landed in a tree, holding twigs for a nest its mate was building. My benefactress frowned slightly.

"An omen?" I asked.

She jumped at my words, as if jarred from a dream, and made as if to speak—but nothing came out.

"We are nearly there," Father Keane said, breaking the moment. "Do you hear it?"

Both Miss Loddiges and I tilted our heads and listened.

"Yes!" Miss Loddiges exclaimed just as I was about to reply in the negative. I listened again, more intently, and heard a strange, low noise like thunder in the distance.

"Let me tie up the horse. It will do us no good if she bolts and we are stranded here," Father Keane said.

Miss Loddiges and I stepped out of the carriage and waited. The noise gradually escalated—as though a herd of galloping horses was approaching—then the sky began to darken, gradually at first, until all above us was rendered black, and I could not help but cower as the passenger pigeons began to descend like a typhoon wave. Father Keane had taken the precaution of adjusting the horse's blinkers so that it might see little but the trees directly in front of it; even so it whinnied and pulled against its tether, frightened by the change in atmosphere as the shadow engulfed us. But Miss Loddiges did not scream with terror as many of the feminine persuasion might. She wandered through the trees as if in a trance, face lifted up toward that infernal cloud and the rattling of a million wings.

I gawped like a simpleton as the birds landed in the oaks. At first I could see only dark forms, but as they settled on the lower branches, the beauty of the birds was discernible: their slate-blue feathers, soft rose-tinted bellies and iridescent patches near the throat that shimmered purple, bronze, green. Nearer they came, seemingly without any fear, staring with bright red eyes, their feet and legs that same vivid hue. As the creatures continued to fill the branches, my heart trembled with awe at the sight. And yet more of the birds swooped down from the heavens, bills thrusting into the earth, searching for worms or insects, until the very ground seemed a living, moving thing. Overhead, many branches dipped and swayed under the weight of the pigeons and the creatures thrashed and chattered in the air as they sought a safe new roost. All was unearthly pandemonium, a wild scene from a fever-induced nightmare.

And suddenly we were not alone. Gunfire rang out and men appeared amongst the trees. In moments the thrumming of wings and cries of dying birds filled our ears as one shot extinguished several pigeons at once and they fell from the trees in dozens. But the dark swarm of live things overhead did not abate. More of the creatures swooped down to the branches, only to drop with a soft thud to the forest floor, their lives ended by men who merely aimed for the sky and brought down bird after bird. The smell of death polluted the air as if we were lost on some terrible battlefield. I turned to Father Keane and saw that he was trying to soothe the horse, a grim look upon his face as he watched boys stuff the dead and dying birds into huge sacks of burlap.

"Let us leave this infernal place," I called out to him.

He nodded, and we both looked to Miss Loddiges, who was perhaps fifty yards away, her bright azure cloak billowing around her as she turned in circles, watching the birds, her face tilted toward the heavens like a saint in ecstasy.

I began to make my way toward her, but was buffeted by hunters charging further into the trees, recklessly firing in all directions. The fusion of gunfire and screaming birds became ever more gruesome and yet the flock still descended into the trees or onto the ground, flapping wildly around those who were there to kill them. There was an almighty crack as a branch covered with pigeons broke from a tree, sending the birds clattering up into the air and feathers raining down. I felt enveloped in a whirlwind of beating wings and threw my arms over my head as birds fell ever closer to me. When I turned back to where Miss Loddiges had stood just moments before, there was nothing to see but dead or dying birds upon the ground.

14

Father Keane and I commenced a frantic search for Miss Loddiges, a potentially deadly endeavor with slingshots and shotguns discharging around us. I was initially dismayed when my friend retreated to the carriage, but he stood upon the seat, stretched his arms out wide and in a sonorous voice bellowed: "Gentleman! Gentleman! Desist!" Unbelievably, quiet descended onto the forest—the birds themselves stilled to listen to the priest.

"A lady has just vanished. We fear something terrible may have occurred and greatly need your assistance. She was wearing a bright blue cape and was just there, watching the birds." He pointed at the spot where she had last stood. "Now, has anyone seen her?"

I stared at my friend as he stood upon the carriage seat, the very picture of authority. The hunters muttered amongst themselves. A number had observed Miss Loddiges watching the birds, but no one could recall seeing her walk away from that spot.

Father Keane nodded gravely at each brief recollection, then said, "Gentlemen, we must search for the lady. She is a stranger in these parts and may have become lost, for certainly she would not venture off intentionally. Or perhaps she has been injured and is disoriented or—" He paused briefly, dramatically. "It could be that some ruffian has abducted the lady, forced her to go with him against her will. If that is the case, we must all fear for her safety." He glared out at the crowd, his gaze informing all the men that they were somehow responsible for the lady's disappearance. "Now let us work together and comb through the forest."

The men nodded to each other and muttered "Aye".

Father Keane instructed the hunters to gather together in a ring with their backs to each other, and all walked straight ahead, like an ever-expanding circle, checking every inch of ground, using sticks or even rifles to rustle the bushes like pheasant-beaters. We walked for at least half a mile, covering all points on a compass, the dead and dying birds momentarily forgotten as we searched for Miss Loddiges.

And then a boy yelled out, "Look, Father! A tiny bird!"

The boy and his father were about one hundred yards from where I was searching, and I rushed over to them.

"What strangeness is this?" the man muttered. "A hummingbird in March?" He cautiously picked up the carcass of the luminous creature that lay amongst the dead pigeons.

"It is from her hat—a decoration," I explained, hope stirring within me. I saw a faint pathway through the trees and dashed up it, hoping desperately that Miss Loddiges would be waiting patiently under a tree for help to come. Hunters clambered after me, feet rustling through dried leaves, snapping twigs and sticks. If Miss Loddiges were nearby, surely she would hear our approach and call out. I caught a glimpse of something yellow further along the path, as did the boy, who ran ahead to pick it up.

"A lady's glove!"

It was petite, butter-yellow and unmistakably Miss Loddiges's. The boy ran forward again and held up the glove's mate. It had been lying just on the edge of the forest, near the track that led to the west. Father Keane appeared at my side.

"I believe Miss Loddiges has been abducted," I told him. "She has left behind her gloves and the hummingbird to show us that she is not lost."

Father Keane looked from one item to the next and then examined the ground before us. "Fresh tracks in the mud. The carriage arrived from the east," he said, indicating its route, "then it waited in that quiet spot and travelled back in the same direction from whence it came."

"With Miss Loddiges held hostage within it," I murmured.

Father Keane nodded. "We will need to inform the officers of the police," he said slowly. "And after that we will discover for ourselves who has been stalking our dear lady and where he has taken her."

"Of course," I said, pretending confidence I did not feel.

* * *

It was after eight o'clock by the time I arrived home, and Sissy was waiting up for me, a blanket wrapped around her and Catterina on her lap. Her face softened with relief when she first saw me, but that shifted quickly to concern when she perceived my own expression.

"Miss Loddiges has vanished," I said, collapsing onto a chair next to her. "It is as if she flew away with the birds." I bowed my head in worry and shame, and my wife wrapped her arms around me. "We searched until it was dark, but found only these." I placed the corpse of the hummingbird and the two yellow gloves upon the table. I did not describe the gruesome scene to Sissy.

"Was she spirited away by someone who means her harm?"

"It certainly appears that way."

My wife bit her lip anxiously, then said: "Helena's tale of Jeremiah Mathews's murder truly does not seem a figment of an overly vivid imagination, for surely only someone who has been spying upon her would know she is here in Philadelphia—someone who perhaps followed her from London."

I flinched at my wife's words, for that was what had happened to me during my journey from Philadelphia to London and my fear for the lady's well-being increased.

"We cannot deny that Helena's intuitions were accurate and whoever harmed Jeremiah Mathews may have our dear friend held captive," she added.

Or worse, I thought, but did not say. And when my wife embraced me again, I knew she thought the same.

"You will find her, I know you will," she whispered.

"I will try, of course," I said softly in return, unable to turn my eyes from the forlorn hummingbird lying upon the table, its tiny feet splayed and broken, its dead eyes filled with pure darkness.

15

THURSDAY, 14 MARCH 1844

Muddy was startled when I appeared in the kitchen a full hour before I normally arose. She paused at sweeping up ashes from the hearth and said with ill-disguised exasperation, "The fire is not yet laid, Eddy."

"I am sorry, but I have an early appointment and could not fall back to sleep. There seemed little point in remaining in bed. Here, let me do it."

In fact, I had been unable to sleep the entire night, such was my worry for Miss Loddiges, for truly I was at fault for her disappearance, despite Sissy's reassurances to the contrary.

Muddy frowned and grumbled, displeased with the disruption of her daily routine, but she rose to her feet and bustled about until the kitchen was filled with the aroma of coffee and porridge. Once I had fortified myself against the cold and written down all that I could remember about the time just before and after Miss Loddiges's disappearance, I made my way to the quarters of the police, where I had agreed to meet Father Keane at eight o'clock. He was waiting at the door, shuffling his feet to keep warm.

"You went to the river after all." I nodded at the boots he wore for his bird observation walks.

"I could not sleep and thought a dawn walk might prove calming and perhaps provoke some thoughts about yesterday."

"And did it?"

He shrugged. "Not particularly on either count. I cannot lie—I fear greatly for Miss Loddiges."

"As do I. And I feel terribly responsible."

"Let us do what we must and pray for the best."

We entered the building and found the lieutenant of the police and the captain of the watch reading newspapers and drinking coffee.

"Good morning, sirs," I said. "We are here to report an abduction."

The lieutenant looked up from his newspaper, while the captain continued reading without a glance at us.

"And you are?" the lieutenant asked. He had the build and demeanor of a fighting dog and looked us over as a canine of that ilk might before lunging at one's throat.

"Edgar Poe of 234 North Seventh Street, above Spring Garden."

"Father Michael Keane of the St. Augustine Academy."

"And who have you lost? Some of your flock?" The lieutenant's eyes lingered on Father Keane. The captain of the watch, a red-faced man who smelled of last night's whiskey, gave a snort of laughter.

"Miss Helena Loddiges. A visitor from London," I told him. "We were at Wissahickon Creek observing the passenger pigeons and the lady was taken. We are fearful that her abduction might be connected to the death—perhaps murder—of Mr. Jeremiah Mathews last October when on board a vessel that had recently arrived in Philadelphia from Peru."

"Are you writing that down, Johnson?" the pugnacious lieutenant asked.

"Of course, sir."

I was surprised to see that Captain Johnson had a pen in hand and was diligently transcribing something onto a sheet of paper before him.

"Are you familiar with the murder of a Jeremiah Mathews, Johnson? Around the docks?"

"No, Lieutenant Webster. Notorious spot, Hell Town, for characters of ill repute. Murder is all too common."

"Jeremiah Mathews was not a criminal. He was a bird collector who worked for Miss Loddiges's father. He was waiting to board a ship back to England, but died before his departure."

"Ill-advised to go to Hell Town at night," Johnson said, as if it were Jeremiah Mathews's fault entirely that he had died.

"When did Miss Loddiges go missing?" Lieutenant Webster asked.

"Yesterday," I said.

"A day is twenty-four hours long. *Exactly* when?"

The red-faced watchman guffawed again.

"We arrived at Wissahickon Creek at three o'clock in the afternoon," Father Keane interjected. "We watched the pigeons for one hour until a large number of hunters arrived, and it became perilous as they were firing recklessly at the birds. Mr. Poe and I agreed that we should leave, but when we looked for Miss Loddiges she had disappeared."

"One moment she was there, gazing at the pigeons, and the next she had vanished," I added.

"Like a conjurer's trick," Webster smirked.

"No," Father Keane countered evenly. "Like an abduction. We and all the hunters combed every inch of the surrounding area and found an embellishment from her bonnet and two of her gloves, but the lady herself was nowhere to be seen."

I unfolded the brown paper in which I had wrapped Miss Loddiges's discarded possessions. Webster examined each glove, then poked at the hummingbird with a cautious fingertip.

"What is this?"

"A decoration from her bonnet. She knew that if we came across the hummingbird we would identify it as hers. Miss Loddiges is partial to the creatures," I explained. "And there are none this far north this time of year."

Webster stared at me as if I were mad. "Is that so?"

"Yes," Father Keane said. "She dropped the gloves on a pathway from the woods to the road that leads east toward Philadelphia. It was clear from tracks in the earth that a coach had been stationed on the side of the road and presumably she was forced into that coach."

Webster pursed his lips as he considered Father Keane's words and absently smoothed out the gloves until they were like two dismembered yellow hands resting upon the paper.

"Small woman," he observed.

"I would say she is about five foot tall with auburn hair and green eyes. She was wearing a bright blue cape trimmed in yellow the same shade as the gloves, and a bonnet decorated with several hummingbirds and artificial flowers," I said. "And she is English, visiting from London. Staying at the Bartram estate with Mrs. Carr."

"The lady is a friend of Colonel Carr and his wife?"

"Wealthy then," Johnson noted.

"And why didn't Colonel Carr report the abduction?" Webster asked suspiciously.

"We thought it best if we made the report first thing this morning as we were with the lady when she disappeared," I told him.

"To suggest your innocence," Webster said. Both officers stared at us in a manner that could only be described as challenging.

"Miss Loddiges is my benefactress," I protested.

"Benefactress? She gives you charity?"

"No! What I mean is that I edited a book for her several years ago, and she paid me for the work. She has just employed me to edit a second book for her."

Webster looked to Johnson, who raised his brows and scribbled faster.

"The lady writes books?"

"About birds. She is an ornithologist and taxidermist, hence her interest in the passenger pigeons," Father Keane said.

"I do know what an ornithologist is." Webster's eyes narrowed as he turned his gaze to Father Keane. "Philadelphians receive a free education. We have no need here for papist academies, do we, Johnson?"

"No, we don't, sir."

"There is no denying that Philadelphia offers an admirable public education system," I said. "Father Keane's occupation is surely not relevant to the fact that a young woman is missing and likely to be in terrible danger."

Webster turned his cynical gaze to me and seemed to absorb every detail of my countenance and frame. "Consider my point of view, Mr. Poe. Two men take a young, wealthy English woman, who is a visitor in Philadelphia, out to Wissahickon Creek to watch a flock of pigeons, and she mysteriously disappears. One man is a writer of little means and the other an Irish priest newly arrived on our shores to spread the Pope's word. Should I receive their story as innocently as Miss Helena Loddiges supposedly did? What do you think, Johnson?"

"You'd be a dunderhead if you did, sir."

"That's just what I think."

My face began to glow, but Father Keane spoke before my anger sparked into words. "We appreciate that you are leaving no stone unturned in considering what might have happened to Miss Loddiges. We will, of course, be ready to answer any of your questions and to assist in any manner. Now, would you like to keep Miss Loddiges's possessions for your inquiries?"

"Yes, we will keep them." Webster folded the paper up and handed the packet over to his colleague.

"Is there anything more you need from us at this time?" Father Keane asked.

"We know where to find you," Lieutenant Webster said, his words an unambiguous threat.

"And you will keep us informed about your investigation—if you unearth anything at all?" I suggested.

Webster frowned. "You'll hear from us if we need anything from you," he said flatly.

"Good day, sirs." Father Keane nodded amiably to each officer of the police, then left the station without a backward glance. I could do nothing but follow without looking entirely foolish.

Such was Father Keane's pace that it took me several minutes to draw aside him.

"I did not expect to be treated as a criminal," I said angrily. I presumed to see fury on the priest's face, but he was perfectly calm.

"I don't think anything will come of the insinuations. Truly their ire was directed at me."

"You were nothing if not cordial."

Father Keane sighed. "There is the Bible business, as you must know. Bishop Kenrick wrote to the Board of Controllers of Philadelphia's public schools to request permission for Catholic children to read the Douay version and for the children to be excused from any religious teachings while at school, which was agreed, but the Nativists complained that this was an attack against the Protestant Bible." He shook his head. "Of course it should not matter to anyone else which Bible we use at St. Augustine's. The truth is there are those born in this country who mistrust newcomers, believing they will bring unwelcome change by introducing new faiths and customs. Or that they will steal, as they put it, opportunities away from them. And then violence follows."

I nodded reluctantly, knowing the truth in his words. "I had not expected it from officers of the police."

Father Keane shrugged. "It is everywhere, even the academy."

"Your students have been attacked?"

"Not by adults, no, but children learn from their parents and have threatened our pupils. The worst violence has been inflicted by adults, particularly against newly arrived Catholics, and people have died, but the police have been oddly ineffectual at catching the perpetrators, despite the assistance of witnesses."

"I am surprised you wished to accompany me to the police office."

"It is, of course, my duty. We cannot hide away from those who persecute us or they have beaten us by default. And then the children will become precisely what the Nativists accuse their parents of being: criminals."

I could see Father Keane's point, but was still smarting from the way we had been treated.

"If Miss Loddiges is to be found," I said, "then it appears we will have to search for her ourselves."

"Yes, I believe you are correct and that it is our duty to find the lady, for she disappeared when in our company. Shall we go to the academy? I noticed a few anomalies in Jeremiah Mathews's journal that might prove of interest. We have nearly two hours before I must be with the students."

"Excellent."

And we both increased our pace until the vapor of our breaths streamed behind us in the cold air, like steam from a locomotive engine.

16

The yard of the St. Augustine Academy was lively with boys engaged in rambunctious play before their classes began, and when we entered the school itself, the cheerful din ebbed away, replaced by a thick stillness that threw the noise of our footsteps all around us. The atmosphere changed again as we entered Father Keane's study with its book-lined walls, proudly displayed bird egg collection and the assortment of scientific implements on his desk. The overall effect was of organized scholarship, but for the macabre diorama that disturbed the harmony of the room.

"Please." Father Keane indicated the chair situated in front of his desk. He took the seat behind it, unlocked a drawer and withdrew Jeremiah Mathews's journal, which he placed between us on the desk top. I had not looked at it carefully when Miss Loddiges had given it to me, such was my lack of enthusiasm for assisting her in what I had thought was a mere fantasy. The journal's binding was of cordovan brown leather, once handsome, but it had been attacked by mildew. Two initials were embossed in gold on its spine and the lower right of the front cover: *J.M.* The edges of the journal were gilded, but sadly that too had been spoiled by rough treatment and an unsympathetic climate. All in all, it was an impractical item to take into the wilds of Peru, which either made young Mathews foolish or overly romantic.

"I presume the journal was a gift, perhaps from his father, the bird collector?"

"It was a token from Miss Loddiges," I explained.

Two feathers were tucked into the journal's pages, taken, it appeared, from the jar of waterfowl plumes Father Keane kept on his desk to use as bookmarks. He opened the journal where one was situated and revealed a page filled with small, meticulous handwriting and neat ink drawings of exotic birds.

"This is an *Agyrtria franciae*—an Andean emerald hummingbird," he said, pointing to one of the images. "Indigenous to the mountains of Peru. The drawing captures its key aspects, and note how he describes the coloring and markings of each bird and that he has attached feather samples in some instances."

"Very neatly done."

"Yes." Father Keane nodded. "It is a clear and precise record of the birds Mathews observed and captured. Here at the back he has listed all the specimens collected on the expedition by date and location of capture, the bird's scientific classification, its condition and the number of the box it was stored in."

I scanned the entries and saw that several birds were noted as spoiled when shot, but most others had been skinned and were in good to excellent condition.

"I see. I presume this sort of log is common practice for bird collectors, so their employer has a record of their activities?"

"It would seem logical," Father Keane agreed. "There is one anomaly, however. Look here." He turned the page.

"'*Mathewsii nubes* of the *Trochilidae* family,'" I murmured. The word in the next column took me by surprise. "'Live'?"

"Yes, most unusual. Of course, exotic birds such as parrots, macaws and peafowl have been successfully transported live, but a hummingbird? It would seem quite a feat to transport one from Peru to Philadelphia given its fragile nature."

"It has been achieved," I said. "Andrew Mathews succeeded in bringing one to London. I saw it with my own eyes when I was there. He had dreams of establishing a colony of them in the Loddiges glasshouses."

"How interesting," Father Keane said. "I wonder how he transported it."

"That I cannot tell you, unfortunately. I was too struck with the wonder of it to question Mr. Mathews and our meeting was very brief."

"And what of this hummingbird?" Father Keane said, tapping the journal page. "Did it arrive in London with the rest of the cargo?"

"I don't know. Miss Loddiges did not mention it. She did say that items from the inventory were missing, but did not specify a hummingbird."

Father Keane nodded. "There is something else I noticed, which may be connected to the last journal entry: 'They seek the Jewel. All is within.'"

He turned to the very back of the journal and indicated where heavy marbled paper bound the cover to the pages. He gently peeled it back, revealing a paper sleeve where additional pages had been stored, which he removed and spread onto the desk. If Jeremiah Mathews's journal entries were neat and organized, these pages were far more lively. The handwriting was larger and highly expressive, the illustrations exuberantly rendered and colored with bright inks.

"Do you see the date?" Father Keane asked. "1841. This must be the work of Andrew Mathews, recording his own expedition to the Chachapoyan mountains."

I looked more closely at the loose pages. The descriptions of the birds were incorporated into the journal entries, creating a lively narrative, and it was clear from the pages in front of us that the author and artist had the deepest affinity for birds.

"These are glorious. What would possess young Mathews to ruin his father's expedition journal by removing these pages?" I murmured, impressed by the artistry of *père* Mathews.

"I believe it is because they contain errors. Peculiar errors."

"What sort of errors?"

"See here." Father Keane indicated a drawing of a seagull. The white bird had a silvery gray back and wings, yellow legs, and a black band encircled a lemon-colored bill. Its glaring yellow eye rimmed with red captured its thieving nature. "*Larus delawarensis,* more commonly know as the ring-billed gull. As you will have guessed from its name, it is a bird found in these parts, very common along the Delaware River. It migrates south, but only as far as Mexico."

"In other words, it is not a gull found in Peru."

Father Keane nodded.

"Might Andrew Mathews have made an error? Confused it with another type of gull endemic to Peru?"

"Such an experienced bird collector? Certainly not. It is so common a bird that any amateur ornithologist would readily identify it. And here on this page is another error."

The creature was standing on a pine bough and looked to me like a blackbird, but with a green and purple sheen to its feathers. Its eye was pale yellow and it wore a startled expression.

"*Euphagus carolinus,* the rusty blackbird. It lives in the coniferous forests of Canada and winters in this area, particularly near acorn-producing oaks."

"And a bird collector would be well aware that rusty blackbirds are not to be found in Peru."

"Correct. I believe Andrew Mathews made intentional errors in his journal, which his son detected but did not fully understand. Perhaps he felt the answers would be in the Chachapoyas."

Father Keane's supposition seemed plausible. "And perhaps the intentional errors are clues to something he came upon there, something that led to his murder," I suggested. "Is there any connection between the ring-billed gull and the rusty blackbird? What they eat? Some peculiar habit?"

"Beyond the fact that they can both be found here, they would seem to have little in common, the gull being of the *Charadriiformes* order and the blackbird of the *Passeriformes*."

"That both birds are found in Philadelphia seems beyond mere coincidence," I said.

"It does require further thought."

"And what of this drawing?" I said, picking up a sketch of a strange and wondrous tree growing inside a chamber, almost like a plant ready to emerge from a seed. Its roots twisted like an octopus's tentacles into the earth and large branches reached up to a hole in the chamber's domed roof. The leaves were long and narrow and grew from a stalk so that they resembled ferns hanging from the branches. Clusters of pink berries decorated the tree and vivid tropical birds roosted in its branches. "'Schinus molle,'" I read out. "What a peculiar drawing. It's quite fantastical."

"The branches and the roots make me think of *crann bethadh*—the tree of life in Irish lore. But the berries and the birds . . ." He shrugged.

"It reminds me of George Loddiges's famous hummingbird cabinet—an exquisitely constructed kingdom of the birds that Miss Loddiges created, derived from the imagination more than nature."

"These all look to be birds endemic to Peru, but certainly they would not roost together. And the drawing is unfinished." Father Keane indicated a hummingbird with long tail feathers near the top of the tree, outlined in ink but without the watercolor-tinted feathers that made its companions so vibrant.

"And these little drawings are most strange, almost primitive." I indicated a row of images to the left of the tree, line drawings of what I presumed to be indigenous Peruvian creatures sketched in ochre crayon: a lizard, a monkey, a spider, all in single file, following the lead of a bird in flight whose long bill pointed towards the *Schinus molle*. "Why would Andrew Mathews include such a peculiar drawing in his journal when his task was to record the birds and plants he saw on the expedition?"

"I suspect that Jeremiah Mathews wondered that same thing when he saw this," my friend replied. He moved the seven pages into a line and stared at them for a time, then shook his head. "Perhaps I am missing something. May I keep the journal a bit longer so I might scrutinize it in more detail? There are some books in our library that should prove useful."

"Yes, of course. I feel ill-equipped to locate any further errors in the journal. Indeed, I feel overwhelmed by this entire situation."

I could not help but glance at the diorama. Father Keane had positioned the peculiar figure of Helena Loddiges at her miniature dissecting table and the manikin appeared to be staring directly at me, its eyes accusing, one tiny hand gripping a black feather and the other clenched tight in fury.

17

FRIDAY, 15 MARCH 1844

Dawn had just retreated, its rosy glow cooled to blue. Catterina was stretched across my desk, gazing at me with one half-open eye, wondering why I was at work at such an early hour. I had not been able to sleep, such was my worry for Miss Loddiges, so I had retreated to my study to work on a tale of a man entombed alive. I felt the emotions of that situation acutely, for I was unable to assist my benefactress in any way. It did not seem likely that the officers of the police would act upon our report of her abduction, and it was difficult to see how Father Keane and I might discover who had spirited the lady away. Her notion that Jeremiah Mathews had been murdered seemed credible now, which made her situation all the more disturbing. Catterina stretched out one paw and tapped the edge of the page where my pen was hovering; when I looked up, both green eyes were fixed upon me, as if she were commiserating.

"We must do something," I muttered to her. "But I cannot fathom what."

A ferocious pounding on the front door interrupted my thought. Catterina dived under my desk and I leapt to my feet, certain that ominous news awaited me. Was it a miscreant demanding ransom, or, worse still, had time run out to rescue

Miss Loddiges? I hurried down the stairs and arrived at the door just as Sissy did.

"Let me, please," I said in a low voice. "It might not be safe."

Sissy backed away from the entrance, but remained in the hall, determined to see who had arrived so unexpectedly. I took a breath to calm myself and opened the door to find a boy of perhaps fourteen years of age.

"Mr. Poe?" His face was contorted with fear.

"Yes?"

"Father Nolan sent me—it's Father Keane. Something terrible has happened. Will you come with me to the school?"

I turned to Sissy, and she held my overcoat and hat toward me. "Go."

"We must hurry," the boy urged. "Father Nolan made me promise."

He and I ran and did not stop until we reached St. Augustine's. When we arrived at the academy's entrance, I was none the wiser as to what had happened, for the boy had been too terrified to tell me anything.

"Father Nolan is waiting in the library," the boy informed me.

"I know the way."

Relief was plain on his face, and the boy disappeared before I could thank him. I hurried down the empty corridor, disconcerted further by the heavy silence. Father Nolan was pacing anxiously at the library entrance and beckoned me inside, shutting the door behind me. He was the academy's librarian, a particularly esteemed position given the quality of the library and its prestige as a center of knowledge. It went without saying that he was an extremely learned man, and I had been privileged to engage in many fruitful conversations with him about a variety of topics. His habitual expression of gentle commiseration had deepened to utter sorrow.

"Is he badly hurt?" I asked, hoping not to hear what I felt to be inevitable.

"He has passed to God," Father Nolan said, his words thick with grief. We were both struck silent for a moment, then the priest said quietly: "When Father Keane returned from an errand last night, he seemed most shaken. I have known him for many years and he is not easily intimidated, but something unnerved him yesterday evening, so much so that he made me promise to send word to you immediately should anything happen to him. Truly his words made me terribly anxious, but never did I believe for a moment . . ." His voice trailed off, and I feared the priest would begin to weep.

"Where is he?" I asked gently.

"He is where I found him, his soul already gone. It is a terrible sight."

"Take me to him."

He nodded and led me further into the tomb-like library. The chamber was spacious with floor-to-ceiling shelves crammed full of books and rows of wooden tables for the students to work at. The calm beauty of that empty place countered the beating of my heart as I followed Father Nolan toward a wall with a large stained-glass window that featured St. Jerome. And there on the floor, beneath that saint of scholars, lay Father Keane, spears of colored light illuminating his stilled body, flurries of dust motes glimmering around his head like a halo. His sightless blue eyes stared up at Heaven and his arms were flung back above his head. Slowly the terrible sight before me softened to a haze, blurred by the tears that veiled my eyes.

"How?" I asked, when at last my voice returned.

Father Nolan raised his shoulders and turned his palms upward in a gesture of hopelessness. "That I cannot tell you for certain. But this was pinned to his cassock." He handed me a folded piece of paper. When I opened it, I saw that it was an incendiary broadsheet with an image of the so-called "Nativist" flag and some anti-Catholic doggerel beneath it.

"Pinned to his garment—like a warning?" I asked, handing the paper back to him.

"That is how we read it." Father Nolan shook his head, the worry plain on his face. "Father Moriarty instructed me to remove it," he said. "The children are fearful enough."

"You think Nativists might be responsible for Father Keane's death? Inside St. Augustine's library?" I asked in disbelief.

"They grow bolder," Father Nolan said. "They want us gone."

I thought back to our visit to the office of the police and how Father Keane had been treated there and could not offer any words of reassurance. The sight of my friend sprawled on the floor, dead, was a nightmare I hoped to awaken from.

"I am more sorry than I can express," I said.

Father Nolan nodded solemnly. "Words cannot convey the pain inside us when forced to part with a friend. Know that Father Keane deeply valued your friendship. Indeed, he asked me to give you this." He reached into his sleeve and began to pull out an envelope, but an imperious voice sounded and he immediately pushed it back in place.

"Father Nolan, why are you in here and who is this?" A dark-haired man who resembled a bull and looked to be roughly forty years of age strode up to us, his robes flapping like sails.

"It is Mr. Poe, Father Keane's friend," he stammered, then turning to me, "And this is the Very Reverend Doctor Moriarty, pastor of St. Augustine Church."

"It is hardly time for superfluous introductions," the priest snapped. "I asked for the library to remain locked. Why is this man here?" Father Moriarty glowered at both of us.

Father Nolan became very red in the face and could not hide his fear. Before he could stumble through a badly told lie, I said:

"Father Keane arranged to meet me here this morning and Father Nolan broke the terrible news to me. I will assist in any way I can to apprehend the perpetrator."

"Perpetrator? Do you intend to apprehend Death himself? I do not understand what you suggest, sir." Father Moriarty stared at me. "And now I bid you good day. We must tend to our brother." Father Moriarty waved in two priests who had appeared in the doorway. "Father Nolan, if you would see your guest out, please. The library will remain closed today."

Father Nolan nodded meekly and ushered me from the library. Once we were outside, I thought of the journal my friend had been studying for me. If I did not retrieve it now then I might never be able to do so. "I need to see Father Keane's study," I told Father Nolan in a low voice. "He had a book that belongs to a friend of mine."

Father Nolan looked bewildered and his nervousness increased. "We must be hasty as Father Moriarty is likely to send someone there."

"Yes, of course."

I followed Father Nolan, who scurried down the corridor as if being chased. When he opened the door to Father Keane's sanctuary, we were both thunderstruck, for the normally meticulous place had been ransacked.

"My word," Father Nolan murmured. "How dreadful."

"The rogues. All his precious things destroyed."

Papers and books littered the floor, his scientific treasures were strewn across his desk, and I felt as if my sternum had received an egregious blow when I saw that his bird egg collection was crushed. Then I noticed something most peculiar. The Wardian case was intact upon the table, empty but for its layer of dirt, which looked as if someone had raked through it. Gone were the figures of Jeremiah Mathews and Miss Loddiges, the taxidermist's table, the Chachapoyan backdrop. I made my way toward it, stepping over the scattered tomes and searched around the table. The hatbox with its cache of raven parts was gone as well. Surely this was not the work of Nativists who had taken against a Catholic priest. Everything connected to Miss Loddiges's mystery had vanished.

"We must be quick, Mr. Poe."

"Yes, I understand, but this is very important. There was a peculiar diorama of miniature figures—they are gone. And a box containing taxidermied birds. Father Keane was keeping them for me. Would you happen to know when they were taken away?"

"I remember seeing the diorama yesterday afternoon when Father Keane and I spoke. It was a very strange diorama."

"May I look in his desk?" I was not hopeful that the journal would be there, given the state of Father Keane's study, but not to search would be folly.

"Yes, but quickly, then we must go."

I went through the drawers while Father Nolan stood sentry at the door, peering down the hallway. There was nothing, as I had suspected.

"Someone is coming," he said in a low, urgent voice, and I immediately followed him from the room. Father Nolan scurried down the corridor and I dogged his heels until we reached a door that led to the church gardens.

It was a relief to escape the building into bright sunshine. The sound of clucking chickens and restless pigeons made cheerful music, and the air smelled of freshly tilled earth.

Father Nolan gestured that we should sit on a bench that faced out over the garden and produced the envelope he had tried to give me earlier. "Father Keane said it was important that you receive this and that I help you with it."

The envelope was sealed and addressed to me in Father Keane's large, flowing hand. I immediately opened it and found a brass key with an elaborate bow through which a long red cord was looped.

"Do you recognize it?" I asked.

Father Nolan frowned as he scrutinized the key. "I believe it is from a ring of keys I keep in my desk—it unlocks one of the bookcases that house our antique books." He seemed surprised by his own words, as if unconvinced that Father Keane would either take the key or allow an outsider access to the library's most priceless tomes.

"It would seem that he wished me to look at one of the books. Is there one about birds, perhaps? Birds of Peru?" I wondered if he had left me a message about the inaccuracies in the journal, some clues that would help me to find Miss Loddiges.

"I am not certain. There are many precious books in the cabinet, and we are not encouraged to remove them."

"Is there a time when I might come to the library and examine them?"

Father Nolan sighed and stared up at the sky as if waiting for a message from Father Keane in Heaven. "Outsiders have never been allowed access to the treasure books without Father Moriarty in attendance," he said. "And I doubt he will be accommodating."

"But I must try. I owe it to Father Keane."

Father Nolan pondered for a moment, then said, "The best time would be when Father Moriarty breaks his fast, between half past seven and eight o'clock. His meal is brought to him in his office as a matter of routine."

"Might I come tomorrow morning?" I asked. "The culprits will never be brought to justice if I fail to act quickly."

He nodded solemnly. "Yes, of course. I will make sure to be in the library at that time."

"Thank you, Father Nolan. And I will do anything I can to help bring our friend's murderer to justice."

"Thank you, sir. Here, it's best perhaps to leave this way to avoid crossing paths with Father Moriarty again." He led me to a bolted door in the garden wall large enough for wagons to pass through, which had a smaller wicket door cut within it for pedestrians. He unlocked it and let me out.

"Go with God, Mr. Poe."

As I stepped outside the peaceful confines of St. Augustine Church, a vision of Father Keane sprawled on the floor sprang into my mind, and I wondered what kind of devil could have murdered such an estimable man.

18

The parlor walls shimmered with light and shadow cast from the fire, which danced to the metronomic *tick-tick* of Muddy's knitting needles. Sissy was softly playing a mournful air on the piano that reflected the mood set by Father Keane's death. Muddy had appreciated his practical knowledge, the way he could fashion useful objects from the gifts of Nature and knew which wild plants were edible. He was perhaps my only friend that she enjoyed conversing with. I had not conveyed the details of his strange demise, but Sissy had sensed that something untoward had occurred and was both saddened and anxious, her mood matching my own. The book I held under the glow of the Argand lamp was no more than a prop, for the vision of Father Keane lying on the floor kept drawing me back, like a doleful ghost, to the library at St. Augustine's. As night thickened, so did our melancholy, until Muddy sighed and put her work to one side.

"Goodnight, my dears," she said, but our replies were cut short by a firm rapping at the door. Sissy's eyes immediately met mine and my own fear was reflected within them—we were expecting no one and it was not the hour for a spontaneous social call.

Muddy murmured, "How strange . . ." as she stepped toward the door.

"Please wait here," I said, leaping to my feet. After the morning's terrible events, I feared that danger might be waiting impatiently upon our doorstep.

Again, there was a rapping.

"Do not open it!" Sissy cried out.

"I will just peer from the window." I left the parlor and made my way to the front of the house before she could protest again and drew back the curtains slowly, so that I might capture a glimpse of the visitor but remain unseen. I could discern a man on the doorstep hunched up against the cold, with his back to the door.

"Who is there?" I said, doing my best to keep my voice steady. The figure shuffled but did not answer. I rapped upon the glass and fairly shouted, "Who is there? What is it you want at this hour?"

The person turned, stepped toward the window and gazed in. "T'is I, Dupin."

Dupin? It could only be an imposter using my friend's name to gain entrance for some iniquitous reason.

"It cannot be. Now go, you rogue." My demand sounded weak to my own ears, but I could not think of anything more persuasive, for surely we were prisoners within the house until morning and window glass was a fragile barrier against a determined villain.

"Poe, I received your letter and knew at once that you were in need of assistance—that you were in danger, not I—so I immediately set sail. The ship arrived in port several hours ago. Such was my rush to depart, I did not make any arrangements for accommodation, and hope you will assist me in finding somewhere suitable."

His words transformed my limbs to marble, my voice to empty air, until Dupin uttered my name again, releasing me like a magical spell undone. I undid the latch, threw open the door and embraced my friend. His body tensed, but he suffered my effusions until I pulled away and said, "Come in! Come in from the cold."

He picked up a small leather valise and stepped into the hallway, but abruptly halted. I followed his gaze and saw that Sissy and Muddy were peering from the parlor entrance.

"This is the Chevalier C. Auguste Dupin. You have, of course, heard me speak of him. Come, meet my wife and mother-in-law," I said, all fear transformed into relief at the surprise arrival of my friend.

My wife walked down the hallway toward us and her mother followed at her heels.

"Monsieur Dupin, I have heard so many good things about you and am delighted to meet you at last," she said.

Dupin bowed deeply but with the rigidity of a soldier. "Madame Poe, it is utterly my pleasure, and I hope you will find it in your heart to forgive my arrival at such an unseemly hour."

"There is nothing to forgive. You are a friend in a strange city, of course you must come to us."

"And this is my mother-in-law, Mrs. Clemm," I said, indicating Muddy, who was staring at Dupin with ill-concealed astonishment.

"My word, Eddy," she muttered, looking from me to Dupin and back again. "He might be your twin." Unease deepened the lines on her face and she shuffled back slightly as if Dupin were an unpredictable dog.

"Your son-in-law is like a brother to me, such is my high regard for him," Dupin said graciously. "And if that kinship has given us a similar countenance, then I am flattered."

Muddy nodded cautiously, and from her posture I could see that she was still wary.

"Shall we perhaps have tea?" I suggested. "It might prove a fine restorative for us all given the weather and circumstances."

Muddy immediately bustled into the kitchen, but not without gawping openly at Dupin as she passed him.

"Dearest, take Monsieur Dupin's coat, then let us settle by the fire," my wife instructed.

Dupin handed his overcoat and hat to me, then followed Sissy into the parlor as cautiously as an animal shy of a trap. I put his apparel on the coat stand and hurried after them.

"Please, make yourself comfortable." Sissy indicated my chair, which faced her own. "It's frightfully cold tonight."

Dupin did as he was bid and stretched his feet toward the crackling blaze. It was then, as the soft amber light glimmered over his features, that I understood why Muddy had reacted with such consternation, for my friend was seated directly beneath the portrait of me and one would be forgiven for thinking that it was his replica rather than mine. Indeed, every element of the portrait that I thought a poor depiction of me in flesh and spirit was a perfect reproduction of Dupin.

"Was the crossing rough?" Sissy asked, her voice bringing me from my reverie. "You look fearfully exhausted."

"There was a terrible storm two days before we reached the port of Boston. The waves that crashed over the steamship were so mighty I feared they would take us under, and of course I could not sleep."

"How awful," Sissy commiserated. "I enjoy short journeys by boat, but Eddy tells me that crossing the Atlantic can make one very ill in foul weather. I hope your trip from Boston to Philadelphia was less onerous."

Dupin nodded and scrutinized his hands as if they were some new addition to his arms, until the clatter of tea things sent his gaze to the doorway. Muddy set a tray down on the table and poured three cups of tea.

"Thank you kindly, madame." Dupin's words mixed with the chatter of the cup upon the saucer as he took the steaming beverage from her, the tremor of his hands audible if not visible.

Muddy nodded gravely. "I'll make up a bed in your study, Eddy," she said and left the room.

"Please do not go to any trouble," Dupin called after her.

"Dupin, you have traveled from France to Philadelphia with the sole aim of assisting me in a mystery I do not yet fully understand. It is most surely no trouble."

"And Eddy has told me of your hospitality in Paris. We are delighted to reciprocate," Sissy added.

The three of us then sat in awkward silence, sipping our tea.

"I sent a second letter," I finally began, "but it will still be making its way across the Atlantic. I do not know where to begin in describing all that has happened these past few weeks."

"And you will not tonight, Eddy," Sissy declared, rising to her feet, "for it is plain that Monsieur Dupin needs sleep. Shall I make you another cup of tea to take up with you?"

"Tea would be more than appreciated. I fear the night's chill has set into me," Dupin replied.

I stood up. "I'll make the tea, my dear."

My wife raised her brows but refrained from comment. "Goodnight then, Monsieur Dupin. I will retire now and leave you in my husband's care. Till morning."

"Thank you again for your hospitality. I am more than grateful."

I followed my wife to the parlor door and into the hallway.

"Do not stay up all night talking, dearest. He needs rest."

"I will see you shortly," I said and kissed her.

When I returned to the parlor, Dupin was perched warily upon his chair, looking wide awake despite his haggard countenance. I fetched a bottle from the cupboard near the fireplace.

"I cannot adequately describe how much your presence fills me with relief," I said as I tilted the bottle and a delicate stream of amber liquid flowed into two glasses waiting with open mouths. I offered a toast: "*Amicis semper fidelis*—you are as ever true to your words, Dupin, and I am forever in your debt."

"Please do not insult me with the presumption of any debt. If someone has threatened you or your family, it is my absolute pleasure to assist you."

Dupin and I both drank deeply from our glasses and sat in companionable silence for a moment, letting the whiskey and fire warm us through.

When the drink seemed to have banished the frost from my friend's blood and chased the pallor from his face, I said, "There is much I have to tell you—sad and fearful things—but my wife is right to insist that I let it wait until morning. However, let me repeat one question from my second letter—what of Valdemar? Have you unearthed anything further?"

Dupin gave a brusque shrug. "His name appears here and there in regard to some trivial social engagement or bequests he has made to advance his name."

"With your family's money."

"Of course. And each year he holds another *Bal des Victimes* in some obscure place, and sends an invitation to mock me," he added bitterly.

I knew from Dupin's expression that he was remembering events from a *Bal des Victimes* we had attended together at Madame Tussaud's macabre waxwork exhibition hall. He had come close to capturing the man who had stolen his family's property, leaving them penniless, but to his fury Valdemar had succeeded once again in getting the better of him.

"When you last wrote to me, you mentioned a sighting of him in the Bibliothèque de l'Arsenal. Was it rumor or did you see him yourself?"

"I saw him, I am certain, and immediately pursued him, but he vanished as if into the air itself. It was more than strange. There must be a pattern and I will find it—and *him*."

This had been the nature of Dupin's pursuit of his nemesis for years. It seemed hardly possible that Valdemar was human, so quickly did he disappear.

"I did manage to secure an item you will recognize, however." He tugged at something hidden beneath his neckcloth and brought forth a ring hanging on a golden chain. Dupin unclasped the necklace and passed it to me. The ring was also fashioned from gold and set with a charming painting of Cupid on enamel. It was a ring I knew very well.

"May I?"

Dupin nodded his assent and I opened the hinged front to reveal two beautifully rendered miniature portraits: Dupin's grandmother and grandfather. Both were executed during the Revolution, victims of M. Ernest Valdemar.

"I am relieved to see the portraits are still intact. How ever did you manage to re-secure the jewel?"

"I was wandering the rue d'Enfer and I came across a shop one might easily miss, it was so small and without character. There was a window filled with esoteric objects, things that would seem of little value to the untrained eye. It was there in the center of the display, and my gaze was immediately drawn to it. The interior of the shop was crammed with all manner of things and it took me quite some time to locate the old man who owns the place. When I asked about the ring, he presumed I was the person who had made an arrangement with the purported owner and simply gave it to me. Of course I did not reveal his error."

I handed back the necklace, which he slipped around his neck, and my fingers drifted to the locket hidden beneath my shirt that contained the miniature portrait of my own mother.

"Fate led you to the ring," I said. "Or perhaps it was the spirit of your grandparents." I smiled, anticipating Dupin's dismissal of such a fanciful notion, but he was silent, his attention focused on the floor. I followed his gaze and saw that Catterina had crept into the room and was crouched before him, staring as fixedly at Dupin as he was at her, their eyes uncannily the same shade of green, her tail swishing back and forth across the floor in agitation. Without warning, our gentle cat, who hid from most strangers, launched herself at Dupin and curled up in his lap like she belonged there. He looked horrified, as if she were a deadly creature he should not startle.

"What have you done to Catterina?" I asked, half in jest. "I have never seen her like this. Do you have catnip hidden upon your person?"

"Catnip? Certainly not. The animal is mad."

"You, sir, do not merit the affections of this most excellent feline. I cannot think why she is humiliating herself in such a manner."

"And I wish it would not," Dupin retorted.

"Catterina, come." I snapped my fingers at her, but she looked at me and did not move an inch. "Unfaithful beast," I said.

Dupin sat rigidly in my chair, utterly uncomfortable with the situation. "Go to your master," he said, waving his hands at Catterina. She merely looked up at him, then lowered her chin onto her paws. I tried to smother my enjoyment of his discomfort and was determined to make it last a bit longer, for Dupin had made me appear foolish innumerable times. There was no doubt that he was a true friend, the truest I had ever had, but when the chance came to deflate his pomposity, rarely could I resist it.

"Let me pour you another glass of whiskey to banish the chill completely, and I will tell you all that has happened since I sent you that first letter. Sissy will be asleep by now and will not know if we spend half the night talking."

Dupin's face tensed into a grimace as he looked down at Catterina; he seemed to believe he would invite dreadful consequences if he pushed her from his lap.

"I fear I am unable to keep my eyes open much longer, Poe, and will disgrace myself. Might we continue talking in the morning?"

"Of course." I stood and scooped up Catterina. He immediately rose to his feet, brushing at his clothing, removing invisible cat hair. "Come, I will show you where the study is and all you might need."

And as I climbed the stairs, Dupin padding quietly behind me, my heart felt infinitely lighter, for I was certain that through ratiocination, my friend would find Miss Loddiges and bring Father Keane's murderer to justice.

19

SATURDAY, 16 MARCH 1844

It was a glorious day, and I hoped to venture out for a brisk walk before Dupin arose, for surely he was exhausted after his arduous journey. I crept down the stairs, anxious not to awaken him, Catterina at my heels like a shadow. When I entered the kitchen, I was startled to see him seated at the table with a cup of coffee in hand while Muddy bustled around him nervously. Catterina stopped short and stared at our guest as if bewitched. He narrowed his eyes at her and immediately readjusted his position so that she could not claim his lap for a seat. Muddy handed me a cup of coffee and I drank deeply, enjoying the warmth coursing through me.

"Is it not your habit to walk along the river in the morning?" Dupin asked. "I thought we might go together and discuss the matters outlined in your letter."

Of course this was an excellent idea as I had no wish to frighten my mother-in-law with the pernicious events that had occurred since I had written to Dupin.

"It is indeed my morning ritual and if you are content to join me then let us go on our way and break our fast when we return."

Dupin stood up and bowed cordially to Muddy. "My deepest thanks, madame. The coffee was bracing."

She looked at Dupin, then me, then back at Dupin again, and shook her head in disbelief at the resemblance she perceived.

The morning sky was the color of a robin's egg and there was a faint scent of snow in the air mixed with sun-warmed earth and new grass. Dupin and I walked along the Schuylkill River footpath as the birds sang around us. It was a delightful morning, but the events of the previous day cast a pall upon it.

"Enjoy this splendid morning for a bit, Dupin, for I have nothing but dreadful news to relay to you."

"That is why I am here," he said. "To help ease your burden and to unravel whatever mystery plagues you."

"Your assistance is a godsend. I can make little sense of all that has occurred. My friend Father Keane of St. Augustine Church died yesterday. In truth, he was murdered."

Dupin was silent for a moment. "My deepest condolences. It is terrible when Death claims a friend and worse still when a fiend in human form is responsible."

"Thank you, Dupin. And that is not all. My benefactress, Miss Helena Loddiges, the English amateur ornithologist I have told you about, has been abducted, and I believe the two nefarious events to be connected."

"I see," said Dupin, his attention fully captured. "Please, tell me all from the beginning."

As we walked, I recounted everything that had happened, right back to the surprising arrival of Miss Loddiges on the tenth of March—how our lives had altered since then! I also outlined the mystery she had tasked me with and described the mysterious diorama she sent to me. Dupin was rather impressed.

"It is indeed an odd way to relay a message, but quite clever," he mused. "The tableau spelled out her imputations well enough and it is something one would take notice of, whereas you might have dismissed a letter detailing her accusations as the fears of an impressionable young woman. Instead, you and

Father Keane invested time in attempting to decipher the tableau she prepared and, thus, were more easily committed to helping the lady with her mystery."

"Perhaps," I said reluctantly. "It is difficult to imagine Miss Loddiges being quite so strategic."

"And perhaps you underestimate the lady? If I remember correctly, you admired her book on ornithology for being extremely thorough, and she is, it seems, a gifted taxidermist, which requires precision."

"If you had met Miss Loddiges, you might understand my hesitation better. She is certainly intelligent but highly eccentric in both her appearance and manner. For example, she seems to govern her life by ornithomancy."

Dupin shrugged. "It is not wise to repudiate such an ancient art. What we dismiss today as superstition, science may prove to be fully valid in future."

This I had not expected from Dupin.

"You are surprised by my lack of skepticism?" he said with a thin smile. "Remember our discussion of the cleverness of the raven when we met with Mr. Dickens's pet? It has long been known that birds sense things we do not—imminent earthquakes and other disasters of nature, for example. Consider their migratory pathways. Is there some invisible force they intuit that governs the direction of their flight? And what of the flocking of birds, the strangeness of a murmuration of starlings, which you must have witnessed in England as a child. Why does a group of birds cast such strange and marvelous shapes in the heavens, as if each avian being is but part of one larger creature? Civilizations more advanced than ours practiced ornithomancy. I would not dismiss Miss Loddiges's observations so readily."

Perhaps I should not have been surprised by Dupin's speech, as his relentless quest for knowledge made him expert in numerous esoteric studies, including, it seemed, ornithomancy. I continued on with my strange tale, telling Dupin all that I knew about Andrew and Jeremiah Mathews, their journeys to Peru, and the bird collecting journal that went missing the night Father Keane was murdered.

"Tell me more about his death. What precisely were the circumstances?"

"He was found dead on the library floor with an anti-Catholic broadsheet pinned to his cassock. His friend Father Nolan summoned me to the library as Father Keane had left me a message. According to Nolan, Keane had seemed fearful after he went on an errand yesterday evening. Nolan believes the nativists are behind his murder. The pastor of St. Augustine Church, Father Moriarty, is trying to suppress any such rumors."

Dupin raised his brows at this. "So, the same night your friend was murdered, the journal and the diorama disappeared. I agree that it is unlikely to be a coincidence."

He retreated into silent contemplation for a few moments, eyes restlessly examining the landscape, the end of his cobra-headed walking stick hitting the soft earth with regular beats as we made our way along the footpath.

"Tell me more about the journal," he finally said.

"In truth, I do not have much to tell, for I did not examine it carefully—I gave it to Father Keane as he knew far more about birds than I do."

"Tell me anything you can recall. The more facts and suppositions, the better," Dupin instructed.

"Miss Loddiges received a package that Jeremiah Mathews sent to her from Panama. In it was his journal, which she treasures as a memento, and a note. Not long after receiving the journal, Miss Loddiges had news of Jeremiah Mathews's death by drowning in Philadelphia. As you may have gathered, she loved him and he her."

Dupin nodded. "You say there was a note with the journal?"

"Yes, the letter from young Mr. Mathews asked her to take care of the journal for him. He said the expedition was a success, but the tenor of the message was guarded and suggested that he expected trouble on the journey back. His final journal entry on 3 October 1843 was oddly cryptic: 'They seek the Jewel. All is within.'"

"Cryptic indeed."

"I should add that when Miss Loddiges dreamt of seeing Jeremiah Mathews after his death, he asked her where the jewel was. She recalled her father and Andrew Mathews speaking of a lost treasure in Peru but did not think they truly believed in its existence. This journal entry added to her conviction that both father and son were murdered, perhaps by rogues in search of treasure."

Dupin contemplated this briefly. "Treasure hunters and looters," he said. "The bane of scholars of antiquity. A person of that ilk might resort to murder if he believed Mathews knew where to find treasure he was seeking. Perhaps the villain and his accomplices—for surely he has them—is convinced that the journal holds the key to the treasure's location."

"Yes," I agreed. "Miss Loddiges mentioned that her father complained that some of the inventory listed in the journal was missing when the shipment arrived in London, which could mean that a thief searched through the specimens Jeremiah Mathews collected. And Father Keane made a discovery that Miss Loddiges had overlooked: seven pages hidden at the back of the journal in a pocket with thick marbled paper pasted over it. The pages were apparently written by Andrew Mathews during his final expedition in 1841. Father Keane immediately noticed two errors in those pages."

Dupin slowed to a stop as a raft of mallard ducks launched from the shore and into the river with a noisy splashing of water. "Do you recall the errors?" he asked.

"Not precisely, but both were birds that Andrew Mathews claimed to have observed in the Chachapoyan mountains, whereas in actuality those birds are only native to this area, not Peru."

"Most interesting. Not mistakes an experienced bird collector would make. We must presume the errors were intentional."

"That is what Father Keane thought. He supposed they were clues of some sort."

"A very good deduction."

"Someone ransacked Father Keane's office and took the diorama. I believe they were looking for the journal, but don't think they found it. I suspect Father Keane has hidden it." I retrieved the key on the long red string, which I had secured to my waistcoat, and showed it to Dupin. "This is what he put in the envelope for me that he left with Father Nolan. Nolan believes it's a key to one of the cabinets in the library where the antique treasure books are kept."

"I shall look forward to investigating those," said my friend, who had made the libraries and book stores of Paris his second home.

"It will not be that simple," I cautioned. "Father Moriarty, who is in charge at the academy, has closed the library and was angry to find me there yesterday."

"We need to find a way. Certainly there must be a clue in the book cabinet as to the whereabouts of the journal. Perhaps your friend was alerting you to the presence of a book with vital information about the mysterious treasure the murderer seems to be seeking."

Dupin was right. We had to risk the fury of Father Moriarty, no matter what the consequences might be. "I did ask Father Nolan if I might come by early this morning, when Father Moriarty is breaking his fast."

"Excellent. Then let us go immediately. Time is of the essence. The sooner we find the journal, the sooner we will be able to locate Miss Loddiges. I fear her abductor may find her a burden before long if she cannot or will not provide him with the information he wants. And when he wearies of hiding Miss Loddiges, he is likely to dispose of her, as he cannot free her with impunity."

At that moment, the ducks that had been swimming languidly in the Schuylkill exploded into flight, setting my heart banging against my chest. I pivoted to look all around us, fearful that we had been tracked by Father Keane's murderer. Dupin was equally alert, eyes scanning the area for any movement.

"If a predator was stalking the ducks, it failed to capture its quarry," he observed. "And if it is a person stalking us, he is very well hidden."

I felt in my bones that someone was watching us and could tell from Dupin's increased vigilance that he felt the same.

"This way," I said, pointing to a path across a field that would lead us back into the city and on to St. Augustine Church. As we hurried away from the river, fear walked with me, larger and more brutish than it had been before.

20

We arrived at the academy library at a quarter to eight o'clock and, true to his word, Father Nolan was there alone, tidying up the bookshelves. He offered me a smile, which faded when he saw my companion.

"Father Nolan, may I present the Chevalier C. Auguste Dupin, who arrived last night and is here to help discover the identity of Father Keane's murderer. He is often called upon to assist the prefect of police when he is back home in Paris."

This clearly impressed Father Nolan, whose nervous expression transformed to one of hope. "It is my pleasure to meet you, Chevalier Dupin. I pray you will uncover something we have missed. Father Keane was well liked by the students and his brothers. It is impossible for us to believe that anyone from St. Augustine's might have harmed him."

Dupin nodded politely and refrained from expressing what I knew he was thinking: that "belief" often got in the way of perceiving the truth, and evil-doers used this to their advantage.

"May we examine the treasure books?" he asked. "It seems highly likely that Father Keane hid a message or clue there, given that he left the key for Mr. Poe."

"Yes, of course. I came in early this morning and checked the keys to the cabinets. The missing one opens this door." Father Nolan indicated a cabinet filled with magnificent treasure books, named as much for the artistry of their bindings as the value of their contents. Dupin's face was immediately suffused with a kind of lust, and I knew he wished he might spend a solid month examining every volume in that cabinet. I removed the key from my waistcoat pocket and inserted it in the cabinet door lock. It did indeed fit. As the door swung open to better reveal the books, their great beauty was more apparent— exquisite book bindings that encased important histories, memoirs, scientific studies and religious texts.

"Are they organized by title or author?" Dupin asked.

"Title," Father Nolan replied. "Many do not have an author attributed to them."

Dupin nodded as he scanned the double row of books. The more elaborate treasure books were bound in gold or silver, decorated with intricate designs and embellished with precious gems. I was amazed that Father Keane's murderer had not stolen any of the valuable books. Had he somehow managed to miss them in the dimly lit library or was there only one book that was of any value to him: Jeremiah Mathews's bird-collecting journal?

Dupin was moving down the row of books, scrutinizing each one without touching any of them. He paused for a time in front of one volume with a golden spine studded with rubies and amethysts in the shape of a cross, but moved along down the row and then made his way back again. He finally stopped in front of a green leather book, its title in silver.

"*Conference of the Birds*," Dupin murmured. "Intriguing." He turned to Father Nolan and me. "See here," he said, indicating the volume. "It is the only book not in line with all the others."

It was perhaps an inch, if that, in front of the other volumes, but as they were all so perfectly aligned, it did seem intentional.

"I believe the book may contain a message, particularly given its title. May I?" Dupin asked Father Nolan.

"Yes, of course."

Dupin removed the book from the shelf and its full beauty became apparent. The green leather was thick and soft, the front patterned with delicate silver leaves and decorated with emeralds and peridots. He opened the book and the frontis-piece was sublime—it depicted a conference of luminescent, exotic birds presented in a medieval style.

"How magnificent," I said.

"And in excellent condition. The text was written by Farid al-Din Attar in 1177. This is not quite that old, but is an ancient volume nonetheless." Dupin carefully turned the pages of the book, which were filled with extraordinary images. The callig-raphy alone was beautiful, made all the more exquisite by the illustrations of birds that spilled down the margins. I wished I had asked to look through these astonishing works previously, when I had the leisure, but we all knew there was little time to admire the artistry of the tome. If my murdered friend had left a clue, we had to find it before Father Moriarty finished his breakfast and began his rounds of St. Augustine's. Dupin contin-ued to turn the pages carefully, seemingly unconcerned. When he had leafed through more than half the volume, he paused. Pressed into the fold of the book was a strip of paper so small it would be missed if one were not searching for it. He opened it and in Father Keane's tiny handwriting were the words: *1 Kings 17:2–6*.

"Elijah and the ravens," Dupin and Father Nolan said in unison. Father Nolan's face lit up with joy.

"You are of the faith?" he asked Dupin.

"I was raised by a family who were ardent believers."

"Very good." Father Nolan beamed, presuming that Dupin too was a believer.

Dupin did not bother to correct him. Instead he asked, "Is there a depiction of Elijah and the ravens somewhere in St. Augustine's?"

Father Nolan thought carefully while Dupin stared at the two pages between which the note had been wedged, as if memorizing all that was there. Indeed, that was his wont, as his memory for detail was near infallible. I peered over his shoulder at the exquisite work, which featured a conference of birds beautifully arranged over two pages. Flowering vines crept around the margins, providing elegant perches for a nightingale, parrot, goldfinch and turtle dove on the left page. On the right, an owl gazed down on a partridge and a peacock in full display. There was a soaring falcon, a swimming duck, a heron balanced upon one leg. At the top, presiding over them all, was an elegant hoopoe, its crest fanned out, its striped wings flared.

When Dupin had absorbed every detail of the composition and content, he shifted his gaze to Father Nolan, who grew flustered under his scrutiny and stuttered: "I cannot think of any such depiction. We have St. Jerome." He indicated the stained-glass window that hummed with color in the morning light. "And St. Augustine, of course, and St. Antony." He furrowed his brow and closed his eyes as if imagining various parts of the church.

Dupin slipped the small note into his pocket and closed the treasure book. "Poe, perhaps you would look to see if there is any reference to Elijah or a raven within the library. We must make haste as Father Moriarty may have begun his rounds." He carried the treasure book to the cabinet, and I made my way to a stone relief on the wall opposite the entrance. It was a simple plaque of marble affixed to the wall on which two words were emblazoned in bas relief: *Tolle Lege*. I had of course observed it each time I entered the library and knew that the exhortation to "Take up and read" was both a command to the students and a reference to the legend of St. Augustine. Was there some other inscription or symbol upon those hallowed walls that might refer to Elijah or his ravens? I looked all around me, but there was none that I could immediately see. I tried to imagine where Father Keane might hide the journal, but my thoughts fluttered like a moth against the window glass, so worried was I that Father Moriarty would interrupt our search. My friend would have known that his office would be the first place his aggressors would search for the book and surely more than one villain attacked him, for Father Keane was a burly man who would not succumb easily, even if taken by surprise. Only frustration would lead the villains to disrupt his office so completely and to murder Father Keane. The journal was cleverly hidden so that only I might find it, either in the library or some other place at St. Augustine's that I could easily gain access to. My thoughts were interrupted by the imperious voice I dreaded hearing.

"Father Nolan, did I not request that the library remain closed this week in honor of Father Keane?" Father Moriarty presented a calm face, but the strength of his anger was apparent from the rigidity of his stance and the fierceness of his eyes.

Father Nolan did not have time to stumble over an excuse, for Dupin stepped forward. "I am afraid I must take full responsibility for convincing Father Nolan to let us into the library. He did his best to dissuade us, but I have travelled all the way from France and he took pity on me. My father, the Chevalier Dupin, had expressed a desire to visit St. Augustine Church in Philadelphia, but his wish was never achieved as he was lost on a pilgrimage to the Holy Land. I have taken it upon myself to visit in his stead."

"How admirable of you, sir," Father Moriarty said coolly. "T'is a pity you did not write to us, as we would have been delighted to organize a tour for you. As it happens, you have come at a most terrible time."

"So I understand. Please accept my condolences regarding Father Keane and my apologies for arriving unannounced, but Bishop Kenrick himself requested that I visit St. Augustine Church, and it would be awkward to refuse him, I am certain you will agree." Dupin stared at Father Moriarty, his threat disguised as an apology. I did not think that Dupin knew the Philadelphia bishop, but it was not impossible given his secretive nature.

Father Moriarty's heavy brows shifted downward, as if he too were evaluating Dupin's words.

"Some believe that Father Keane's death was unnatural. Is there any truth in that rumor?" Dupin asked, as if voicing a query from the bishop himself.

A look of surprise flickered across Father Moriarty's face. "We believe Father Keane succumbed to a weak heart."

"Frightened by his attackers, no doubt," Dupin said. "If nothing was stolen, then it would seem likely that an enemy of the Church committed the act—the Nativists, for example."

"That is not likely at all. The Nativists would not dare to enter our premises," Father Moriarty declared.

"And yet common thieves would not commit murder unless under duress," Dupin observed. "That does not seem to be the picture here."

"The Nativists grow bolder," Father Nolan said. "They have attacked our brothers on the street. The devils might have followed Father Keane into the library and taken him by surprise."

Father Moriarty's face turned to thunder. "Enough of this talk of the Nativists, Father Nolan. You stir unease amongst our brothers and the students. Let us stick to the facts. No intruders were seen in the building last night or this morning, until now," he said, glowering at Dupin and I. "And until we are certain what caused the death of Father Keane, there will be no more talk of Nativists committing murder in this library. Am I understood?"

Father Nolan nodded, his expression contrite.

"Now, you will excuse me, sirs, I have much to do. I trust you will gain comfort from your visit to St. Augustine's, Chevalier Dupin, and that Father Nolan proves a worthy guide. Go with God," he said, dismissing us.

"Thank you, Father Moriarty. I will remember you to Bishop Kenrick," Dupin said, before turning and leading Father Nolan and I from the library. The heavy doors immediately closed behind us and the lock clicked into place.

"Let us go to the church," Dupin said, "before Father Moriarty sends someone to follow us."

Our hurried footsteps echoed around us and the very air was charged with solemnity as we entered the church and made our way up the nave. Upon nearing the altar, the shadows were unexpectedly fractured by splinters of dazzling colored light. An assembly of saints hovered above us, as in a painting made of glass, and the light that spilled through brought the figures to life. We stood in awe for a moment, so wondrous was the sight, and as my gaze drifted downward, I perceived large golden letters above the altar that declared: *THE LORD SEETH*. A chill settled into me.

"There," said Dupin in a low voice. He nodded at the glowing windows and, looking more closely, I saw a raven, something grasped in its beak, hovering above a ragged man.

"St. Elijah," Father Nolan muttered. "Why did I not recollect he was there?"

"He may be above us, but surely the journal is not," I said.

Dupin walked in a careful circle, gazing up at the depiction of Elijah and the raven. He then turned to face the direction in which the raven was flying and raised one hand straight in front of him and pointed. We all looked at the spot he was now indicating and saw a quiet alcove, illuminated with the tiny flames of votive candles.

"St. Francis," Father Nolan murmured.

"Who preached to the birds," Dupin said in a low voice. "We must search there, but cautiously. There are many places in here where a person might observe us without our knowledge."

Father Nolan's apprehension was clear and he stayed close to us as we walked to the statue of St. Francis, which was glazed with shimmering light. At first glance, I could not see where the journal might be hidden, but then I spied a small door beneath the table where the votive candles were arranged.

"Perhaps you might tell me something about this shrine while Mr. Poe looks for the journal? If we stand here, we should obscure his activity from anyone who might be watching."

"Yes, of course," Father Nolan said cautiously. "What would you like to know?"

"Begin, perhaps, with the history of St. Augustine Church."

Father Nolan began a rambling account of all that led to the establishment of the church and I hoped I would soon find the journal, as Dupin's patience would quickly wear thin. At first I saw nothing in the small cabinet but a store of votive candles, but when I reached into the far corner, my hand touched soft leather and something cold—metal. I gingerly pulled out the items and, by the flickering light, could not help but gasp when I saw that I held Jeremiah Mathews's journal and a treasure book that was simpler in design than those we had looked at in the library, but quite obviously very ancient. I tucked both under my coat.

"Success?" Dupin asked.

"Indeed. Is there somewhere safe that we may look at the books?" I asked Father Nolan.

"Books?" Dupin asked.

"Yes. A treasure book was with the journal."

"Then there is nowhere safe here to study it," Dupin said. "We must take it to your home, Poe."

"A book from the library?" Father Nolan was clearly very distressed.

"We cannot know that right now, but rest assured, it will not be lost or damaged. Father Keane will have hidden it there for an important reason, so I beg you to have faith in him and us," Dupin said firmly.

Father Nolan nodded, his expression miserable. "Please God that it helps you to learn who murdered Father Keane," he said softly. "And that you bring him to justice."

21

The flames hissed and fluttered and filled the parlor with a welcome heat. We had ignored Muddy's entreaties to partake of a late breakfast, immediately setting to work. Sissy joined us, and I recounted what had transpired at St. Augustine's.

"Am I correct in understanding that Father Keane's death was not natural? That someone took his life?" Sissy asked.

"Yes," I confirmed softly.

Her face revealed a mix of sorrow and anger. "Such a good man," she murmured.

"Father Moriarty is hiding something," Dupin said.

"It would do the church little good if it were widely known that one of the priests was murdered," I agreed.

Sissy frowned. "Surely it is more than that."

"It is likely that your instincts are correct, Mrs. Poe. Father Moriarty did not quite dare order us to leave as he could not be sure of the veracity of my claim to know the bishop, but he certainly does not want any officers of the police at the church or academy."

"That is scarcely surprising, given how they treated Father Keane when we reported Miss Loddiges's abduction. Truly they acted as if he were a criminal."

"It is a pity your friend was treated without respect," Dupin said. "I would presume from your descriptions of him that Father Keane was an honest man. But someone at the church is not."

"And why do you presume this?" I asked.

Dupin retrieved his overcoat, which he had declined to hang up in the hallway, and from a capacious inside pocket he retrieved a book about the size of his hand, a thing of such beauty that both Sissy and I gasped at the sight of it. It was bound in silver inlaid with golden squares to make a checkerboard effect and each silver square was set with a precious gem. The spine was gold and adorned with amethysts and rubies that formed a cross.

"Is it from the cabinet in the church library?" I asked tentatively, remembering the spine and knowing that there was no other possibility, yet reluctant to believe that Dupin would take such a precious item without permission. My astonishment was acute, and Sissy's horrified expression made me feel mortified for my friend.

"That is where I found it, of course," Dupin said evenly. "Its true home is in quite another library, however."

Dupin undid the jeweled hinges that clasped the book shut and opened it to the frontispiece, which was magnificently illuminated and featured a variety of birds. The title was in French: *La Langue des Oiseaux.*

"It is a very rare volume, several centuries old. I was aware of the book's existence but had never seen it myself, for it was stolen before I was born. As I've told you previously, Poe, my grandfather kept very detailed descriptions of his most valued possessions and this book was indeed a treasure to him. When you and Father Nolan were searching for signs of Elijah and the raven in the library, I examined the frontispiece and my suspicions were confirmed." He pointed to an insignia beneath the title: against an azure field, a large golden foot crushed a serpent that had embedded its fangs in its heel. I immediately recognized it as the Dupin coat of arms.

"Valdemar stole it?" I asked.

"Of course. This esoteric volume is most rare and was very precious to my family, more valuable than mere gold and jewels."

"Who is Valdemar?" Sissy asked.

"A thief, a murderer and my sworn enemy," Dupin said.

"He was responsible for events that led to the execution of Chevalier Dupin's grandparents and the death of his mother," I quickly explained. "Valdemar plundered the Dupin family's possessions during the revolution in France."

"How terrible," Sissy murmured, her judgmental expression softening.

"Do you suspect that someone at the church is in league with Valdemar?" I asked.

Dupin contemplated my words briefly. "It is unwise to underestimate Valdemar's wickedness, but in this instance I believe he simply sold the volume for a great deal of money."

"And someone at St. Augustine's is purchasing stolen treasure books, hence your suspicions regarding Father Moriarty?" Sissy offered.

"Indeed."

I thought of the locket ring Dupin now wore on a chain with its hidden miniature portraits of his grandparents. He had tracked it to an auction in London, and I had impetuously bid on it until Valdemar had snatched it from our very fingertips.

"And that is why you removed the book without informing him that it was stolen from your family. You thought that you would never see it again," she added.

"Yes," Dupin said. "I simply recovered what by right belonged to me. I cannot see that as theft, but my sincere apologies if you view my actions otherwise. If you knew how my family has suffered at the hands of the immoral Ernest Valdemar, you might judge me less harshly."

"I do not judge you," my wife said. "You are Eddy's dearest friend and that makes you a friend to us both."

"That is a precious gift," Dupin said, his expression solemn.

The silence that followed soon became too airless, so I said: "Shall we examine the volumes Father Keane hid away?"

Dupin nodded with obvious relief. "Yes, of course." He prodded the journal and the treasure book that lay on the table around which we were gathered. "We know the journal contains intentional errors that are likely to provide a clue about a mysterious jewel and a legendary treasure in Peru. Father Keane thought this book—*Las Costumbres de la Gente de las Nubes*—pertinent to the investigation." He was silent for a moment, scrutinizing the exterior of the tome. The leather had once been supple and a rich scarlet, but was now scuffed and faded. The spine was of hammered gold, which also edged the binding, and the title was printed simply, again in gold, across the front. There was no other decoration, but for two small emeralds set in the golden clasps that held the volume closed.

Dupin opened the book to the frontispiece, which was a beautifully rendered landscape, an exotic setting of immense tree-covered mountain peaks that pierced the clouds, and above those clouds a majestic city carved into the rocks, smiled upon by a sun with a benevolent human face. At the edge of the city, perched on a cliff face, were a cluster of peculiar statues with solemn expressions that looked out from the mountains like gods. The author of the work was noted as Diego Fernández, the date 1560.

"Most interesting," Dupin said. "Fernández was a respected Spanish historian who lived in Peru for a time. I have read his book *Primera y Segunda Parte de la Historia del Peru* which is a definitive work on the subject."

"Why does St. Augustine's have such a singular tome in its library?" Sissy asked. "One would presume it would be held somewhere in Spain. Is it stolen also?"

"I don't think that is the case in this instance," I said. "The library holds many rare books as the Augustinian friars wished to establish an exceptional center of scholarship at the academy. Father Keane told me that the Augustinians have a connection with Peru—Spanish Augustinians traveled there in the mid-sixteenth century."

Dupin slowly leafed through the pages, many of which were beautifully illuminated with images of exotic flora and fauna, the calligraphy of the text graceful enough. And just as Dupin began to turn the page again, I spied another slip of paper nestled in the fold of the book.

"Wait." I pointed at the paper. "Another note."

Dupin extracted it and unfolded the paper. We leaned in to read its contents and saw another quotation from the Bible written in Father Keane's hand:

> *Ecclesiastes 10:20*
> *Detract not the king, no not in thy thought; and speak not*
> *evil of the rich man in thy private chamber: because even the*
> *birds of the air will carry thy voice, and he that huth wings*
> *will tell what thou hast said.*

"A warning," Sissy murmured.

"A warning about someone with power, someone not to be trusted," I said. "Could it be that he knew the person who murdered him? He feared no one previously, of that I am certain."

"It is possible, of course. If so, it would seem that Father Keane came upon something of consequence, something that would damage that person's reputation enough for him to commit murder," Dupin observed. "'Detract not the king'— that insinuates someone high up at St. Augustine's. Someone who may have any number of people spying for him—'he that hath wings will tell what thou hast said.'"

"Father Moriarty immediately springs to mind," I said.

"Indeed. But might he be protecting someone else? Certainly it would be unwise to trust him. And we must also consider why Father Keane left his warning within this book at this particular page, for it must be relevant," Dupin said.

I wondered again why Father Keane had not made the journey to our home, where he would have been safe if he believed that someone at St. Augustine's was such a threat to his very existence. Father Nolan said that our friend had been highly disconcerted when he returned to the academy after an errand. What was that errand and what happened to him on his journey back? Had someone threatened him? Had he seen something that shocked him? Perhaps someone he trusted or deemed above corruption had proved otherwise? And why hadn't he left a note for me that plainly said what had transpired?

"It seems likely that your friend feared for his life and left clues for you regarding the identities of his murderer and Miss Loddiges's abductor, who may or may not be one and the same person. He may have intended to tell you in person what he discovered, but his fears were realized. I am sorry, Poe."

"As am I. Father Keane was an exceptional man."

"We will avenge him. But first we must read the journal and the work by Diego Fernández. Shall I begin with the journal, as I have some knowledge of Peruvian ornithology, while you study *Las Costumbres de la Gente de las Nubes,* beginning with this chapter?" Dupin placed the slip of paper back where it had been hidden and handed the tome to me. He then picked up the treasure book he had reclaimed and held it toward my wife.

"Would you care to read it?" he asked. "It is a rather obscure text about the secret language practiced by my ancestors several hundred years ago, but quite fascinating."

I was astounded at Dupin's offer, as was Sissy, who did not seem certain whether to accept or demur.

"I do not wish to immerse myself in the work until I have time to study it seriously," he added. "It is a most beautiful illuminated volume. You may enjoy its artistry."

Sissy took the exquisite treasure book with wide eyes and a slightly trembling hand. "I know I will enjoy it and promise to treat it with great care."

"I had no doubt," Dupin said lightly. "Shall we reconvene later this evening to discuss what we find?"

I looked at the thick volume I was tasked with reading. "I will do my best, but may not fathom enough so quickly. And you will find, I think, there is much to unravel in the journal. Father Keane was quite an expert ornithologist and found only two intentional errors, although he was certain there were more. Deciphering what Jeremiah Mathews was endeavoring to communicate surreptitiously might take longer than you imagine."

Dupin raised his brows, but did not contradict me.

"Certainly we might share anything that seems relevant before the day finishes," my wife said, "and reconvene tomorrow morning to fully discuss both volumes and formulate a plan to rescue Helena."

Again Dupin raised his brows, this time at Sissy's presumption of her inclusion. "That seems a good idea," he said politely. "But let us not forget that Miss Loddiges's abductor is without scruples. We know that he wants the journal in our possession, as it is a key to gaining something he desperately desires. It is not yet clear why he has taken Miss Loddiges. Perhaps he thinks she knows where the journal is or that she has some other knowledge he seeks. Or perhaps he has demanded ransom from her father and is waiting for his demands to be met. But one thing seems certain. If Father Keane's demise is connected to her abduction, as the evidence suggests, the devil will simply murder the lady if he does not get what he wants. Time is of the essence if we are to save your benefactress."

"And friend," Sissy added. "Certainly I will find it impossible to sleep until we make Helena safe." She carefully placed the treasure book on the table next to her chair and stood up. "I will organize coffee and, Eddy, if you would ensure there is enough wood for the fire so that we might continue to work unabated."

I could see that Dupin was not completely comfortable with Sissy's involvement in our quest, but he did not object. It would be up to me to ensure that my wife was kept out of harm's way.

22

It was unbearably hot and moisture thickened the air. The tails of our mules twitched and flicked as the flies jumped from one flank to the other or buzzed in circles around us, but the patient creatures continued onward led by the native Peruvian porters who had packed our supplies. We were in excellent botanizing territory, but the trail was rough and narrow, frequently disappearing into primeval forest, which seemed a cognizant entity—quarrelsome, powerful and constantly at war with our little troupe, rebuffing our efforts to collect specimens of its grasses, herbs, shrubs.

We followed a fast-moving stream that cut through the greenery, and it too was remarkable, as emeralds and lumps of gold were mixed through the gravel of its bed. There was no time to collect these riches, however, as it was imperative that we reach our destination by dusk, which was almost upon us.

Night enveloped the cloud forest with speed, and with the darkness came a myriad of dangers: venomous insects that might paralyze or kill us, deadly serpents and fierce jaguars on the prowl, or so we were warned by our expedition leader, known to us only as "the captain". He was a man of medium height with the noble features and blue-black hair of the people indigenous to that area, but with surprisingly fair skin and eyes of turquoise. The porters whispered that our captain was descended from the Cloud People, fierce warriors that had staved off the marauding Incas and conquistadors, protecting their celestial cities that held secret troves of gold, silver and emeralds. The captain knew where these mysterious cities and their riches were located and believed it was his destiny to return there as rightful king, when his gods decreed it was time for his people to rise again.

Three Peruvian guides slashed through the verdant foliage with machetes, and birds chattered above us, following our course with interest, as did other creatures we heard but did not see in the undergrowth. A quick-flying arrow sent a python slithering into the depths of the forest and a throng of parrots exploded from the tree canopy; airborne jewels that chattered noisily until retreating back into the leaves.

The sky was a mix of bright pinks and yellows as the sun slipped down to the mountain tops and there was a rumbling sound as if the forest were ravenous, and the sound increased as we progressed until it was an angry roaring. Our guides signaled caution and hacked at low-hanging branches draped in vines and exotic flowers. The window in the green revealed the source of the noise—a monstrous waterfall. A few more oblivious steps had it been dark and we would have plunged into that watery maw.

Onward we climbed, stumbling, sometimes crawling, through loose scree, as the captain urged us on to the place where we would make camp for the night. Fear made us scramble faster as the sun had dropped below the horizon and all the color leaked from the sky. We had to make our way by torchlight for a time until the landscape was immersed in silver spilled from an immense full moon.

Moments later, we came to a plateau at the foot of a mountain, the place the captain had designated as our campsite. As we each looked up, our group fell into utter, breathless silence, for illuminated in the silvery light was an assembly of giants—white figures with large heads and enormous, dark eyes—and this host was suspended in the air like the strange ghosts of some alien race. I half-expected to be mown down by those frightful, silent creatures and retreated several steps, as did my companions.

"Fear not," the captain said. "They wait for their time."

I wished to believe there was nothing to fear from those Chachapoyan giants, but an unearthly screech pierced the quiet—a bird crying out as if in warning. And again it came, louder still . . .

But I found myself awake in my bed, disoriented, the darkness of the mountains replaced with the shadows of our house immersed in deepest night. The peculiar bird-call sounded again, pulling me more firmly into the corporeal world. Had another crow inched its way down the chimney and into the kitchen? I slipped out of bed and crept to the stairs, hoping not to wake anyone, but was startled by the unmistakable sound of pottery shattering on stone. I did not think, merely ran down the stairs, determined to rescue Sissy's crockery before the winged creature could do more harm. My heart near stopped its beating as a shadow loomed before me in the hallway.

"Take heed," whispered Dupin. "I fear it is an intruder."

He ran for the parlor, and, still groggy with sleep, I turned into the kitchen, determined to arm myself. The fire had long been extinguished and the room was empty of light. I located the fire iron by memory and stood with my back to the wall, allowing my eyes to further adjust to the darkness. Moments later, a flickering glow crept along the hallway and I gripped my weapon more tightly. Dupin appeared in the doorway, his cobra walking stick in his left hand, a lit oil lamp in his right. Before I could speak, he took three quick strides into the kitchen and lunged forward, swinging his stick viciously. I threw myself to the wall and heard a yelp of pain as a person fell to the floor near my feet. Dupin pinned him with his walking stick.

"Do not move," he growled.

"I won't, sir," a voice sniveled. "I'm not moving, sir." He squealed again with pain as Dupin prodded him. I placed the fire iron against the wall and quickly lit two tapers and the mantelpiece lamp. The soft glow revealed that our adversary was but a boy of twelve or thirteen, tall for his age, but severely underfed with a pale freckled face and mop of ginger curls.

"Rope?" Dupin asked.

I spied a bundle of rosemary that Muddy had suspended from the ceiling rafter and fetched it down—the twine would have to suffice. I tied the boy's hands behind his back, and Dupin searched him. He found no weapon, but located the tools of a housebreaker's trade: a jemmy, several picklocks and a knife, along with a folded note. He opened the paper and showed it to me; the letters "J M" were scrawled upon it. We hoisted the boy into a chair and the roving shadows created by the candlelight enhanced the look of fear on the boy's face.

"Who sent you?" Dupin demanded.

"No one! It's my family, sir. We haven't enough for food. There is a man who will buy valuable things—paintings and books and the like," he said, his high-pitched voice cracking either with fear, his youth or both.

A bitter laugh escaped me at the thought of our meager possessions being purchased by the criminal fraternity. "If you persist with your lies, we will fetch the night watchman, who will take you directly to prison, and I will personally ensure that you are not released for many years," I improvised.

Perhaps my imagination got the better of me, but it seemed that the boy met the notion of life in prison with resignation rather than outright fear, and it occurred to me that he might already be in prison, or the nearest thing to it—Old Blockley, the city's almshouse. It was a brooding complex, with its poorhouse, orphanage, infirmary and insane asylum, crouched like a hungry beast on the west side of the Schuylkill, south of the city's thriving center. When I took walks in that direction, its ominous presence left me feeling morose, for I knew that it was not difficult to end up in such a place. If one were unable to find enough work and debts accumulated, Old Blockley laid claim to even the most industrious.

"Tell us who paid you and what you were looking for," Dupin continued.

The boy tried to appear brave, but as his eyes flicked from Dupin to me and back again, his face sagged in fear and his lower lip trembled. I began to feel sorry for him but tried to banish the emotion—it would do Miss Loddiges no good to feel sympathy for a thief, even if driven to his trade through his family's impoverishment or through having no family at all.

"We will let you go without charge if you give us the information we need," I said. "And you will be able to keep the money from the villain who put you up to this."

"I wasn't given any money," the boy protested.

"Your employer will not know that you've told us," came Sissy's voice from behind us. "What is your name, dear?"

We turned as one to the kitchen doorway, where Sissy and Muddy stood huddled together, wrapped up in their woolen dressing gowns and nightcaps, each clutching a taper. Muddy was armed with her own walking stick and a very fierce expression.

"Billy Sweeney, ma'am. My name is Billy."

"And who forced you to break the law, Billy?" she asked gently, and her kind words seemed to crumble the boy's determination to protect the rogue who had put him up to his devilry.

"It was a man who drinks at the Mermaid in Hell Town. I was to fetch a journal for him. He said I would know it from its leather cover, the letters on its edge and the drawings of birds inside."

Dupin held up the note. "These letters?"

The boy nodded.

"What else did your employer tell you?" Dupin asked.

"If I found the journal, I would be paid double what he promised me to get inside. If I told anyone, he would murder me." He grimaced with the last words, as if a dagger had already pierced his heart.

"You will assist us if you wish to gain your freedom," Dupin advised. "Then you will simply tell your employer that you could not find any journal."

The boy remained silent, a stubborn expression fixed upon his face, his eyes avoiding Dupin's.

"Truly you have nothing to gain by continuing to help a criminal," Sissy reasoned. "There is nothing to say he would have paid you at all, for there is no honor amongst thieves."

"But he is not a thief!" the boy blurted out. "He told me that the man who lives here is a thief. That he stole the book from a lady friend of his."

Dupin and I looked at each other. Miss Loddiges's abductor was undoubtedly behind this housebreaking.

"Have you met the lady?" I asked.

The boy shook his head, and Dupin shifted restlessly, his patience at an end. "It is clear we will get nothing more of interest from this miscreant, nothing that we cannot fathom ourselves. I believe there is only one course of action to be taken at this time." He strode to the hall and returned with his overcoat, hat, and muffler. "You will take me to the tavern where you met with your employer."

"But it is the middle of the night," Sissy objected.

"In my experience, the haunts of thieves and liars rarely close," Dupin said, a remark which only served to deepen the expressions of consternation on the faces of my wife and her mother.

"It will take me but a moment to dress," I told Dupin.

"Shouldn't you bring someone from the night watch with you, Eddy?" my mother-in-law said with alarm.

"That would defeat what we hope to achieve," Dupin said. "We will be quite safe, I assure you, madame." Dupin deftly tossed his walking stick from one hand to the other and back again. Muddy frowned slightly, but handed her own walking stick to me. It was a rustic thing that she used on woodland rambles, and utterly unlike Dupin's ebony cane topped by its golden cobra head with ruby eyes—an elegant accoutrement with a secret bite. But when I felt the weight of the wood and the solidity of its knotted handle, I realized that it might indeed serve me well should we find trouble at the Mermaid tavern and looked at my mother-in-law with additional respect.

23

We made our way down Seventh Street with linked arms, Billy the picklock between Dupin and I, his hands still bound behind him, our staggering walk lending us the air of a trio who had spent many hours in a tippling den. The young ruffian did his best to persuade us that we would gain nothing by accompanying him to the tavern, that his employer was not likely to be there waiting for him. Dupin countered this with the suggestion that if the boy preferred to spend the night in jail, we would take him there instead. We turned left on Sassafras Street and headed toward the harbor.

The night itself seemed to grow darker once we stepped into the area known as Hell Town, and yet the place was perhaps the liveliest part of the city at that hour. There seemed to be a tavern or beerhouse on every corner, with their clientele spilling out into the streets, immune to the cold due to the quantities of rum or grog they had imbibed. Plumes of smoke mixed with laughter as mariners swapped tales of the sea or ladies intent on securing a man's attentions pretended mirth at muttered inanities.

A sign suspended above the tavern door featured a golden-haired siren perched on a rock, waves crashing around her as she strummed upon a small harp. We had at last reached our destination.

"Go directly to the person who employed you, but do not attempt to alert him to our presence or you will regret it." And with those words, Dupin surreptitiously revealed the rapier hidden within his walking stick, and young Billy's eyes opened wide with fear. Dupin cut the boy's bonds, then concealed the weapon again. "Tell your employer that you searched everywhere, but the journal was not at the house. Ask if they wish you to look elsewhere for it. You will inform us if he devises another plan."

"Remember, we know where to find you at Old Blockley," I tested and the boy's face revealed that my guess was accurate. "If you betray us we will have both you and your mother taken to prison."

Again my guess about his family circumstances proved correct as Billy nodded, his expression doubly fearful.

We followed him inside as surreptitiously as we could, hats tipped low and mufflers pulled up to hide our faces, and sat at a grimy table in the shadows while Billy made his way across the room. Dupin handed me the green-tinted spectacles he often wore when applying his skills of ratiocination at the location of a crime.

"In case his companions recognize your face," he said. "They are less likely to know mine."

I quickly put on the glasses and had the sense of being submerged beneath murky seawater. I knew from previous experience in Dupin's company that the darkened lenses obscured the wearer's eyes and functioned as a useful disguise.

Billy had joined two men at a table in the corner, one a hulking beast of a fellow, red-faced and round-bellied, the other as small and furtive as a rat, wearing a voluminous black coat and a wide-brimmed hat that successfully hid a good deal of his face. It was impossible to hear what was being said, such was the din from drunken revelers, ill-advised songsters, a chattering parrot at the bar and an old dog near the fire that howled at regular intervals. I hoped the two rogues would soon go so we might follow them to the place where Miss Loddiges was being held captive. Unfortunately, they decided to deplete their bottle of rum before leaving the establishment, so I bought us two tankards of beer and we waited.

The tavern was a peculiar theater, full of drama, its cast drawn from around the world due to its proximity to the docks. There were characters that Mr. Dickens himself might people his novels with—thieves, vagabonds, ladies of dubious repute, eccentrics in dandified attire and servants who had sneaked out to enjoy the entertainments Hell Town had to offer. A card sharper lured a group of innocents into playing cards for money, while a group of seasoned gamblers threw dice at another table. An elderly woman in greasy clothes with an aged hyacinth macaw perched upon her shoulder was ensconced at a table near the fireplace, sipping at a tankard of ale and playing the part of local apothecary. A constant stream of customers paid their respects to "Mrs. Mermaid" and, after slipping her a few coins, left her company with some useful potion—a tonic for seasickness, salve for bug bites, tincture of opium, Jesuit's Bark for swamp fever, or Spanish flies for a sailor's carnal woes, according to her loud commentary. If the buyer did not have the requisite coins to pay Mrs. Mermaid, I noticed she was willing to accept odd bits of jewelry or other items of value that looked unlikely to belong to her customer.

There was a yard out behind the tavern, and I watched as disagreeable-looking fellows collected bets on that night's cockfight, then lugged cages of unlucky birds through the back door, where they would battle to the death. Thankfully, we were spared the roars of that despicable contest, for the two ruffians seated with the young housebreaker stood up to leave. I gulped back the contents of my tankard, and Dupin and I slipped out of the door. Water Street was still crowded with people, many of whom staggered one way, then the other, interfering with our view, but we managed to stay with them as they proceeded west on Sassafras Street and watched as the trio split at Second Street, Billy heading south and his employers walking north. We continued to follow the ruffians, who seemed unaware of our presence as they turned onto Vine Street, moving west. So intent was I upon concealment that I did not consider our surroundings until our quarry's destination was clear.

"You are surprised?" Dupin whispered.

"Most completely, but you are not?"

"Why would I be, given the book I found in the library and the fate of your friend there? Now we know for certain that someone at St. Augustine's is in allegiance with the person who kidnapped your benefactress or possibly did the deed themselves."

"Father Moriarty," I muttered.

"Perhaps, although we must not presume so merely because he strives to hide the fact that Father Keane was murdered. But we do know that the person responsible has two accomplices and now it seems very likely they are priests. And then there is the third person," he murmured.

"Young Sweeney?"

"No, the person who made the bird call outside your house—something like the sound of a crow. Did you hear it?"

"Yes, it woke me up. I purely forgot about it with all that has happened."

"Most strange," Dupin murmured. "If Sweeney had an accomplice, his bird calls made me aware something was amiss, which was clumsy, yet he was skillful enough to remain invisible if he followed us to the tavern. And if he is trailing us still, he is like a ghost."

I peered into the darkness that surrounded us, but could only see the two men who had hired the young lockpick to break into my home. They stepped through the door in the stone wall that surrounded the hulking shadow that was St. Augustine Church.

24

SUNDAY, 17 MARCH 1844

"There were nine in the band and each was almost ten feet tall; they crouched on the very edge of the cliff face, morose giants transformed into stone, who might awaken should their eyrie kingdom be threatened. The altitude and precarious location gave them supreme protection from marauders and the ideal vantage point from which to watch over their city and its people." I did my best to convey Diego Fernández's wonder and excitement at first setting eyes upon that remote Chachapoyan city, as described in his book *Las Costumbres de la Gente de las Nubes*, but it was difficult to adequately describe such a wild and strange place when in the hallowed confines of the Academy of Natural Sciences. Dupin, Sissy and I had traveled there at Dupin's suggestion, due to its reputation for having the largest and taxonomically most complete ornithological collection in the world. We moved from display to display as I continued to recount what I had read in that ancient tome.

"The giant figures captured the imagination of Diego Fernández and he was determined to examine them more closely. He and several intrepid men climbed up to the precipice and saw that one figure had been considerably damaged,

enough to reveal that it was a sarcophagus. Inside was a mummified person wrapped in layers of wool and cotton, then covered
in clay. A wooden frame, almost like a bird cage, had been
constructed around the mummy, covered with layers of mud
and straw to form the giant figure, then painted with sepia and
ochre patterns in imitation of elaborate ceremonial robes.
Fernández hypothesized that each of the giants contained a
mummy and that the imposing sarcophagi had been built in
situ."

"The figures he describes sound identical to those Jeremiah
Mathews writes about in his journal," Dupin said. "It seems
likely that Andrew Mathews, or someone who organized the
1841 expedition, read Fernández's book, *Las Costumbres de la
Gente de las Nubes*, and used it as a guide to find the site—or
that is certainly what your friend Father Keane thought if he
hid the book for you. Jeremiah Mathews retraced his father's
footsteps, either following a map or perhaps with the
same expedition crew that traveled to the lost city with his
father." Dupin paused to scrutinize a cabinet full of parrot
skins that had been gathered in South America. A carefully
written notice informed us that this was the most complete
selection of birds from the Andes in any ornithological
collection.

"That sounds plausible, Dupin. Fernández notes that the
local native population was aware of the ruined city and its
tombs, but feared that the giant statues were the Chachapoyans'
gods waiting to take revenge for the city's destruction. They
also believed that dangerous, unearthly creatures inhabited the
area. There was said to be a fair-haired mermaid living in the
pool beneath an immense waterfall who would bring a curse
upon any person unwise enough to swim there."

"Perhaps, in truth, the curse was to come upon the waterfall
unawares and plunge down it," Sissy observed.

"You have read my thoughts again, my dear," I said, smiling. "Last night, after reading the book, I dreamt that I near plunged into that waterfall."

"That is often how these superstitions begin. The frightening tale works as an effective warning," Dupin observed as he led us to yet another cabinet of taxidermied birds, this time from Asia. He paused in his restless wandering before an elegant figure of a white crane standing upon one leg, and peered more closely to read the identification tag affixed to it. "'Leucogeranus leucogeranus,'" he read out, "'Habitat, Siberia, wintering in China.'" He turned to face us. "It is impossible that Andrew Mathews saw this bird in Peru."

"This was a bird noted in the pages from Andrew Mathews's journal?"

"Indeed. Your friend the priest was correct. There are several birds described in the journal that he could not have observed in the Chachapoyas region."

"Dupin has an unparalleled memory," I told Sissy. "He observes something once—a person, a location or a page in a book—and can describe it as if it were still there in front of him."

"What a remarkable gift," my wife said.

"A useful one when faced with a mystery, but of little consequence without the skill of deduction," Dupin said. "Please continue, Poe. What did the Spaniards discover?"

"Fernández writes that the figures obscured a hole in the cliff face. When they ventured inside, he and his men found a cave decorated with strange paintings that were similar in style to those on the sarcophagi. Some were geometric designs and others were primitive depictions of animals: jaguars, snakes, hummingbirds, eagles, condors."

"Figures like those depicted in Andrew Mathews's strange drawing of the tree full of birds?" Dupin wondered.

"The description would seem to fit them," I said.

"Most interesting," Dupin mused. "We must then presume that the drawing is not merely an artistic fantasy, but provides a clue to something Mr. Mathews discovered on the expedition, particularly if his son chose to bring the picture with him to Peru."

"Father Keane and I discussed that very thought. He believed that all the birds depicted are found in Peru, as is the tree."

"*Schinus molle*," Dupin said. "The Peruvian pepper tree. Andrew Mathews would be well acquainted with it. The Spaniards brought it to Europe as an ornamental tree because of the berries, which are used as a spice. The Peruvians make an alcoholic beverage from the berries, and indeed I sampled some when I was there."

"Would you recommend it?" I smiled.

"Not that vintage," Dupin replied. "Particularly as scholars write that the Incas used the berries in the mummification of their dead."

"Mummification of the dead? That is more than relevant given Fernández's description of the chamber. He said it had numerous alcoves, all of which were filled with mummies."

"Fascinating," Dupin murmured.

"So Fernández thought. He writes that at first the bodies appeared to be children until they unwrapped one and saw it was bound with its knees bent to its chest, arms twisted around its knees. Its mouth was gaping open as if screaming and its mummified skin was stretched as taut as a drum. The illustrations in the book were quite gruesome, like shrieking demons in a medieval codex."

"How awful." My wife shuddered.

"Was anything placed with the mummies?" Dupin asked. "Any possessions or religious artifacts?"

"In the first burial alcoves they found earthenware pots, trinkets made from feathers and a woven article he called a quipu."

"But surely there was more than that. If the site described in Jeremiah Mathews's journal is the same as that explored by Fernández and his men, whoever so desperately wants the journal is searching for something other than a few sarcophagi," Sissy argued. Dupin's face was the picture of discomposure, for Sissy laughed. "Truly you cannot believe that the murder of three men, a housebreaking and Helena's abduction were all for the sake of a few mummies and ancient artifacts?"

"It has happened," Dupin muttered, but did not elaborate.

"Do correct me if I am wrong, but most looters are desirous of what might commonly be called treasure: gold, silver, jewels. The Spaniards were renowned, or perhaps notorious, for the riches they plundered," she continued. "What of the mysterious jewel mentioned in Jeremiah's letter? And the lost Peruvian treasure Helena's father talked about?"

Dupin nodded almost imperceptibly, unable to relinquish the notion that Chachapoyan artifacts were as coveted as jewels or precious metals. He continued his meandering journey around the display cabinets, scrutinizing the birds inside them, while we followed in his wake like anxious ducklings.

"In truth, Fernández's book suggests that Sissy is correct," I said, feeling no small amount of triumph at my wife's cleverness and Dupin's discomfiture. "As they moved further into the burial chamber, he claims to have found gold and silver goblets, jewelry and other decorative items left with the mummies. And still deeper inside, where they had to rely upon torches to banish the darkness, they found the most exquisite jewels: emeralds cut into the shape of flowers, fish and birds. There appeared to be a hierarchy to the placement of the mummies, which led Fernández to believe that the greatest riches would be found at the far end of the chamber, where the most venerable were laid to rest. They pocketed a quantity of the precious gems as they made their way to the back of the cave—or what they had presumed was the back. Torchlight revealed a mud brick wall, which they immediately set to knocking down, hoping that it concealed the legendary king's tomb with all of its treasure. But once through the wall, they were surprised to discover daylight spilling into the gloom, illuminating more of the strange wall paintings, and a cascade of flowering vines that perfumed the air. The light fell through a hole pierced through the roof of the cave, and the vines had crept after it, making their way down to what appeared to be a simple altar constructed of earth and fronted with a large stone. And there, sitting upon that earthen altar, glittering in a splash of sunlight, was a green rock, larger than an ostrich egg—the most rare and precious jewel of all."

"An emerald?" Sissy asked.

"That is what Fernández believed. But as he entered the inner chamber, there was a fluttering in the air and suddenly he and his companions were attacked by a swarm of bees—or so they thought, until they realized it was gravel showering down upon them. There was a terrible rumbling and it seemed that the roof might collapse, so they ran from the tomb, leaving the cache of treasure behind, but for the carved emeralds they had collected. As the men readied the ropes they had brought to help them descend, the earth shook more violently. The huge, damaged sarcophagus teetered on the cliff's edge until the mummy fell at their feet as if alive, and the sarcophagus tumbled from the precipice. The local men howled at the sight of the mummy and almost threw themselves from the cliff, but Fernández managed to get them all down safely."

"But without the enormous emerald," Sissy added.

"Indeed. When Fernández spoke of what he had seen, there was a muttering amongst the local men, who claimed that the emerald had caused the small earthquake they had endured."

"Most fanciful," Dupin said.

"Perhaps. But according to the local native people, the emerald was cursed and whoever touched it would, in turn, be touched by madness."

"A common enough tale designed to deter thieves." Dupin stared at another collection of exotic birds. "'They seek the Jewel. All is within.' If a person on the expedition with Jeremiah Mathews was seeking the emerald that Diego Fernández described, he must believe that Jeremiah Mathews or his father knew where it was hidden."

"And the clue to the jewel's location is in the journal, or so his murderer believes," I added.

"The journal most certainly contains a message hidden in the pages excised from Andrew Mathews's journal," Dupin said. "This bird, for example." He pointed at a display case, where a luminous green parrot with scarlet brows and stripes above its wings was perched. "*Rhynchopsitta pachyrhyncha.* Found only in Mexico. And this bird here." Dupin indicated another bird in the same display case. "*Euptilotis neoxenus*— commonly known as the eared quetzal. It is indigenous to the pine-oak forests of the Sierra Madre mountain range of Mexico. Occasionally it is found as far north as the southwest United States, but not to the south in Peru."

Sissy and I peered down at a striking, dark-green bird with a red breast and white outer tail feathers and iridescent blue feathers at the center. It had delicate hairs about its ears, a small head in comparison with its rather plump body, and was approximately a foot long.

"Two birds that are found in this area; two from Mexico and a crane that lives in Siberia and China," my wife said softly.

"And this bird," Dupin said, leading us to another display cabinet. "*Numida meleagris,* the helmeted guinea fowl. A type of partridge indigenous to Senegal."

"Certainly not to be found in the Chachapoyas region of Peru," I said.

"No."

We three stared at the peculiar-looking bird that stood about two feet high and had a body with silvery-black spangled plumage and short wings. Its featherless head had an odd crest of flesh upon it and there were red and blue patches upon its cheeks.

"And here is the saddle-billed stork—*Ephippiorhynchus senegalensis*—also from Senegal as the name suggests."

It was an enormous and handsome bird, nearly five feet tall, with very long legs and a startling beak of red with a black band and yellow wattle above it that contrasted wonderfully with its black head and yellow eye. The body was white, but with iridescent black wings, back and tail.

"How beautiful," Sissy murmured. "Are there other anomalies in his bird drawings?"

"I do not think so. Andrew Mathews put his intentional errors on pages with the more recognizable Peruvian birds, certainly ones familiar to me from my time in Peru." Dupin retrieved the journal from his pocket and showed us the loose pages. "For example, here we have a mountain toucan, amazilia and Peruvian sheartail hummingbirds, three different tanagers and a versicolored barbet." The barbet in particular was beautifully painted in an array of colors. "There may be additional anomalies in Jeremiah Mathews's journal that I have yet to uncover, but I believe I have located all the avian clues his father recorded."

"I am certain you have, Dupin."

"It is frustrating not to have Andrew Mathews's complete journal," he complained. "A full record of precisely who he was with and where he went and all that he saw and collected would make unraveling what truly happened to him much simpler."

He quickly cast his eyes over each sheet. "If we look at the dates, these are all entries from the twentieth to the twenty-third of November 1841. Mathews's descriptions of the flora and fauna seem genuine, bar the rogue illustrations, but we have only fragments of what he experienced each day. He expresses admiration for their local guide and remarks on the strength of the porters carrying supplies, but no one on the expedition is mentioned by name in these pages," Dupin said. "Did Miss Loddiges tell you of anyone who assisted Andrew Mathews when he was in the Chachapoyas?"

"I have no recollection of her doing so."

Dupin shook his head with frustration. "I cannot, at this point, offer any theory as to what these clues might mean. We need to visit St. Augustine's again. I am certain there are secrets at the church and the academy connected to the journal, and we must ascertain what those secrets are."

"Indeed, but it will be difficult to gain access to the library, I fear, as Father Moriarty made it abundantly clear that we were not welcome there."

"We must hope that Father Nolan's desire to regain *Las Costumbres de la Gente de las Nubes* without Father Moriarty learning that it is missing will allow us to spend some time in the library," Dupin said. "We should also speak with the young lockpick again and discover what transpired during his meeting at the tavern. You seemed to know where he might be found, Poe?"

"The city's almshouse. In his fear, the boy confirmed that he lives there with his mother."

"Then I would advise visiting him this afternoon. The boy was too frightened to disobey our orders last night, and his employers did not appear to be aware of our presence, but we cannot be certain that he will not confess all to them, for certainly he feared those two men we followed to St. Augustine's."

"He was employed by priests?" my wife said with surprise.

"Maybe. Or they themselves were hired by a priest who resides there. We must learn the truth from our lockpick."

"Do you think Billy is in danger?" my wife asked.

"It is possible," Dupin said. "If we consider the fate of Father Keane."

She nodded, twisting her hands anxiously, then she drew herself up into a determined stance that I knew too well. "We must go there now," she announced. "I would not forgive myself if harm came to Billy Sweeney as well."

I glanced at my pocket watch. "We will take you back home, and Dupin and I will make our way there immediately. Young Billy is likely to be at some task assigned by the almshouse until supper time, after which it may be more difficult to locate him."

"I am coming with you," my wife said.

Dupin pretended to be engrossed in an array of colorful finches pinned to a board, paper tags with their names dangling like ornaments from their stiffened legs, but I knew that he was listening acutely.

"It is a terrible place," I began. "I would rather that you were safe at home."

"I hardly think the almshouse is dangerous. Its inhabitants are impoverished, not murderous criminals."

"Most," I agreed, hoping to plant seeds of doubt.

"And I believe my presence will make it easier for us to speak with Billy. Perhaps we might pose as distant relatives visiting Philadelphia who wish to see the boy with a view to taking him in."

My face must have betrayed some of the alarm I felt, because Dupin cleared his throat to disguise a low chuckle.

"Dearest, we cannot be so persuasive that anyone presumes we might cover his family's debts or, indeed, that we might take the boy in, for we cannot do either," I said firmly.

"We will have to pay him something to act on our behalf," Dupin said. "But I will meet his price. As time is of the essence, shall we?" he added, indicating the door.

My wife preceded us through the doors of the Academy of Natural Sciences, and we followed her down Broad Street, searching for a carriage that would take us to Old Blockley.

25

The Schuylkill was crowded with boats of all shapes and sizes, moving across the water in a complex dance, the sight of which was uplifting to the spirits. The cheerful tableau made Sissy long for warmer weather and the chance to perhaps go for a sail along the river. Her enthusiasm for such an interlude was not diminished when I pointed out that a number of those inno-cent-looking vessels were manned by the Schuylkill rangers: river pirates who demanded taxes from barges on the way to the city or robbed them of their cargo; she declared it unlikely that a pirate would waste his time on a small pleasure craft. We had lived in Philadelphia for seven years, and I had done my best to shield my wife from the less salubrious aspects of the city, but now I felt it necessary to reveal some of its darkness so that she was more fully aware of the dangers we all faced if we were to save Miss Loddiges.

When our destination came into view, it dampened all our moods. An air of menace emanated from Old Blockley, a disturbing mix of power and the threat of pestilence. Its four stark, mushroom-pale buildings squatted behind a high board fence, the busy river separating the compound from the city of Philadelphia.

"How will we find the boy?" Dupin wondered. "I had not thought the place would be so vast."

"The four buildings have separate uses. One is an asylum for the insane, one an infirmary, the third an almshouse and the last an orphanage and ward for children. From Billy Sweeney's reactions to my questions, I believe he was admitted with his mother, but I think the practice is to separate debtors from their children until the debts are repaid."

Sissy was horrified. "They are punished for their poverty by taking away their children? How terrible. He is still a boy."

"This practice is meant to encourage industry and sedulity in debtors, and their children are indentured so they may learn a trade."

Sissy pressed her lips tight and lapsed into silence.

"I presume the intention is to provide the children with a skill to make them less of a burden on society," Dupin offered. "Is it an effective course of action?"

"That I cannot tell you."

We were admitted to Old Blockley without much interrogation, after Dupin explained that he was writing a scholarly paper on the Philadelphia system for dealing with the impoverished, which was much admired in France. We were directed to a somber-looking fellow, Mr. Cowperthwaite, who did not question our arrival without prior arrangement once he was told Dupin's fabrication.

"Father Keane at St. Augustine Church recommended that I interview a boy called Billy Sweeney," Dupin said. "He believed that Billy's story would be of interest for my paper."

Mr. Cowperthwaite shrugged and shook his head. "A common enough story, in truth. But Billy is a hard worker and a good boy at heart," he added, turning to address Sissy and me, no doubt hopeful that we might offer the boy an indentureship. "Indeed, he is busy in one of the workshops as we speak."

Mr. Cowperthwaite led us on an impromptu tour of the orphanage as he took us to Billy, and it proved to be an austere place, the dormitories crammed full of narrow beds, the few windows without curtains. An unpleasant and indefinable odor pervaded the air.

"Are all the children who reside here orphans?" Sissy asked. It was clear she did not wish to believe my explanation of how Old Blockley operated.

"All are orphans in a sense," Mr. Cowperthwaite said. "They are children left alone when their parents have either died or become unable to care for them adequately. Indeed, those with cruel fathers or mothers have a better chance of survival under our tutelage," he added.

This unsettled Sissy further, particularly as it was obvious Mr. Cowperthwaite believed the orphanage provided refuge for its charges, and that they would perish if not taken in there.

"And they remain with you until adulthood?" Sissy asked hopefully.

"We do our best to furnish all children with an indenture-ship," he said, leading us down a corridor. "Normally between six and ten years old. In return for their labor, the children are given room, board, clothing and some education by those they are indentured to, which is much more than their parents can provide. When they reach the age of eighteen, the indenture-ship ends and they receive freedom dues, about twenty dollars. Then they are free to look for a paid position," Mr. Cowperthwaite explained, his face full of pride.

"What an interesting system," Dupin said carefully. "Has it proved effective? Do those who pass through it become useful citizens?"

A shadow darkened our guide's face. "There are times when a child is ill-suited for life with a particular family and is returned to us or, on occasion, they abscond. We try to find a new indentureship for children returned here. There is little we can do for those who abscond, I fear."

I wondered how many times Billy Sweeney had been returned to Old Blockley. Mr. Cowperthwaite led us into a workshop where the young people were seated quietly and working with great industry at repairing shoes. They were dressed in neat but ill-fitting uniforms which added to their maudlin air.

"Are these children you were unable to find an indentureship for?" Sissy asked in a low voice. "Or children sent back by those you placed them with?" she added.

"Both, I'm afraid. Despite our best efforts, we cannot find enough good Philadelphians willing to offer these poor wretches such a position. Is this something you might consider doing?" Mr. Cowperthwaite asked hopefully.

"Quite possibly," my wife said before I could answer. "That is why my husband and I were so pleased to be able to accompany Monsieur Dupin. Our visit has been most illuminating so far."

"Very good," beamed Mr. Cowperthwaite. "And you, sir?"

Dupin looked alarmed at Mr. Cowperthwaite's query. "I live in Paris," he said quickly. "I am here purely for research purposes."

Mr. Cowperthwaite nodded sadly, then made his way further into the room and faced the industrious young people. "We have visitors," he announced, and the children immediately abandoned their tasks and stood up. He raised his hand as if he were a conductor holding a baton.

"Good afternoon," they said in unison.

I spotted Billy Sweeney at the back of the group, as did Dupin and Sissy. Fear made his face all the more pale and he looked as if he might try to run, but any such plan was scuppered when Mr. Cowperthwaite drew a circle in the air. The children assembled in a line and marched around the room in military precision; Billy Sweeney was by far the tallest and his ginger-colored curls marked him out further. After one circle had been completed, they returned to their desks and stood to attention, facing straight ahead. Mr. Cowperthwaite traced a vertical line in the air and the children sat down in unison.

"Billy Sweeney," he said. "Our guests would like to speak with you." I thought that I perceived a flicker of envy on the faces of the youngest children, but Billy's dread seemed to increase. "You may speak in the yard." Mr. Cowperthwaite gestured toward the door and Billy headed in that direction. We three hurried after, fearing the boy might bolt and our mission would be in vain. Billy stopped a good distance into the dusty yard, far enough from the workshop to avoid being overheard.

"You have nothing to fear, Billy," my wife immediately said. "We just have some questions for you."

Billy nodded cautiously, mistrust stamped upon his face.

"Have you seen your mother recently?" Sissy asked. "She is here too, isn't she?"

Billy's only response was to shrug, which Sissy took for sorrow.

"Would you like us to take a message to her? I'm sure Mr. Cowperthwaite will allow us to deliver a note."

Billy shook his head. "She cannot read, miss."

"Well, I could read the note to her, and certainly she would treasure something written in your hand even if she cannot read the sentiments within."

"What are the names of the men you met with at the Mermaid tavern?" Dupin interjected, before Sissy could ask another question. He was as abrupt as she had been gentle and Sissy's face tightened with annoyance. The boy's mouth dropped open, giving him the unfortunate look of an expiring fish.

"We followed them to St. Augustine's," I said, "so please do not lie."

The boy considered this for a moment, then said: "Father Healey and Father Carroll."

"Why must you do what they bid?" Dupin asked.

The question surprised me as I had presumed the fee for his nefarious work was persuasive enough.

The boy was stricken with shame and mumbled: "When my pa left, my ma had trouble getting work, so it was up to me. Father O'Byrne in the kitchen at St. Augustine's would give me food if I worked in the garden for him. But it wasn't enough. So I did jobs for Old Skipper too. He taught me and some others to pick locks and would send us to fetch things that he would sell at the Mermaid. Father Healey and Father Carroll drink there and never bothered Old Skipper about his business, but when they saw him give me money at the Mermaid one night, they said they ought to turn me in for stealing and both me and my ma would die in prison."

"And so you are indentured, in a sense, to Fathers Carroll and Healey," I said.

The boy nodded grimly. "That's what they told me. And it didn't stop when we were sent here two years ago. Or even when Mr. Cowperthwaite got me a proper indentureship. They would find me and give me jobs and then I would be sent back here for sneaking out at night," he said bitterly. "My ma told me we left Ireland for food and freedom and we couldn't find neither here and that's the truth of it."

"Surely the priests can't make you steal. Why not just refuse them?" Sissy asked.

"I can't abscond from them. God will help them find me and will send me and my mother to hell."

Dupin snorted at that.

"What else have they made you do?" Sissy asked.

"Deliver messages. Show people where to bring supplies for St. Augustine's. Open some locks."

"And you just come and go as you please?" I asked.

"As the fathers please," he said. "They send me a message and I show it to whoever is on the gate and I'm let out."

"Who do Fathers Carroll and Healey work for?" Dupin asked. "Who wanted the journal they sent you to steal? Surely it was not for them."

Billy shrugged. "They said it was for their lady friend, as I told you."

"Do you not see how untrue that is likely to be?" Sissy asked.

"I thought it was a lady from the church," Billy said, his hesitancy indicating that he'd given it no thought at all.

"Are they good friends with the pastor of St. Augustine's, Father Moriarty?" I asked him. "Have you observed them talking together much?"

The boy looked mightily confused by this. "Father Moriarty doesn't seem to have friends, sir. At least not true ones. The priests listen to him because they have to. And I don't think he would try to get a lady's journal back for her."

"The best dissimulators are the most difficult to recognize," Dupin observed. "We therefore have some work we would like you to do for us in recompense."

Billy nodded warily.

"You said that Father O'Byrne gave you work in the church gardens. Is that still the case?"

"When I go to Mass he does—Mr. Cowperthwaite lets us go, but he doesn't truly like it."

"I want you to watch what Fathers Carroll and Healey do and to whom they speak when you are next at St. Augustine's or called upon to work for them. Then report back to us. Take this for your efforts." Dupin took out a small purse and retrieved some coins that he spilled into Billy's palms. The boy looked stunned by the amount and quickly secreted the coins in his pockets.

"Yes, sir. I will do it, sir. You have my word."

"You know where to find us should you learn anything at all," Dupin added.

The boy nodded guiltily.

Silence settled down on us, and naturally we turned to make our way back into the workshop.

"One other thing," I said, as a thought occurred to me. "How do Fathers Carroll and Healey summon you when they wish for a job to be done? You mentioned receiving notes from them. Does Mr. Cowperthwaite deliver them? Is he friendly with the priests?"

"No, sir, not at all," Billy said, his eyes widening at the thought. "He is a Quaker, not of the faith. He would not support the fathers' activities."

"Then how?" I persisted.

"The birds," Billy answered. "They send a bird and Mr. Cavelli gives me the message."

Sissy and I exchanged a confused look but Dupin instantly understood. "Pigeons? There are pigeons here?"

Billy nodded. "I help Mr. Cavelli with them and sometimes Father Healey makes me wash out the pigeon house at St. Augustine's." He grimaced. "He tends the birds there."

"Where are these pigeons? Show us," Dupin instructed.

"Just over here." Billy took us across the yard to a set of stairs that led to a flat roof, upon which a pigeon loft was situated. "Mr. Cavelli!" he called out.

Moments later, a wizened, elderly man peered down at us. He exhibited a toothless grin when he saw Billy. "Good afternoon," he said, his accent still flavored with the sound of his homeland.

"We are very interested in your pigeons," Dupin said. "Where do you fly them to?"

"Many places," Mr. Cavelli said. "We are quite far from the city and it is safer and faster than sending messages by boat."

"Do you exchange messages with St. Augustine's?" I asked.

"Yes, certainly. Would you like to see one fly?"

"Please," Sissy answered.

The man disappeared and returned later with a bird in his hands. "The message is put here," he explained, indicating the bird's leg. "She takes it with her when she flies back to her home." He threw a bird up in the air and it flapped noisily skywards, circled over us once, then disappeared into the blue. The old man and Billy gazed wistfully after it.

"'Even the birds of the air will carry thy voice, and he that hath wings will tell what thou hast said,'" Dupin murmured.

"Father Keane's warning," my wife said.

"I believe so," Dupin agreed.

26

Lamplight shimmered over feathers of red, purple and green, beaks of orange and yellow, and staring eyes, heads cocked with curiosity. So life-like were Andrew Mathews's drawings that it seemed the birds on those pages might suddenly take to the air and swoop around us.

"I can almost feel the breeze in their wings," my wife said, voicing my thoughts.

Dupin, Sissy and I were grouped around the table in the parlor, examining the pages torn from the bird collector's journal. Dupin's hands sifted through each of the sheets yet again, his brisk movements revealing a certain frustration, then he returned his attention to the paper on which he had written out the names of the birds alien to the Chachapoyan mountain region.

"*Ephippiorhynchus senegalensis, Euphagus carolinus, Euptilotis neoxenus, Larus delawarensis, Leucogeranus leucogeranus, Numida meleagris, Rhynchopsitta pachyrhyncha,*" Dupin murmured. "The eared quetzal, helmeted guineafowl, ring-billed gull, rusty blackbird, saddle-billed stork, Siberian crane, thick-billed parrot."

"We have established that two of the birds are found here in Philadelphia. Another two are from West Africa, a further two are from Mexico and the final bird lives in Siberia and winters in China," I said. "Is there some pattern to be found in the different habitats? Or was Andrew Mathews merely attempting to make it obvious that the birds noted could not be found in the mountains of Peru?"

Dupin grimaced. "There may be a pattern, but I cannot see it. Certainly it would seem relevant that two birds are found in this area, particularly as Jeremiah Mathews died here. Why did he travel back via Philadelphia? He was bird collecting for George Loddiges, as was his father. Might it have been a jointly funded expedition with someone here? You mentioned the Bartram estate. Were they somehow involved?"

"In truth, the thought had not occurred to me. Miss Loddiges was staying with Mrs. and Colonel Carr before she was abducted and certainly the Loddiges and Bartram nurseries conduct business together, but Miss Loddiges made no mention of their involvement in the expedition."

"I believe Helena would have told us if that were the case," Sissy added with a touch of over-formality, which meant she was still annoyed with Dupin for talking over her when at Old Blockley. Dupin was not a man who took much note of the fairer sex's subtle emotions, but surprisingly he noticed her frosty tone.

"Mrs. Poe, I beg you to forgive me for my rudeness this afternoon and for my unpardonable lateness in offering my apology. I am so quickly immersed in the process of ratiocination that I lose sight of decorum. While there is no excuse for rudeness to a lady, may I at least offer an explanation?"

Sissy nodded with a touch of reluctance.

"You were making an admirable effort to assist the boy in communicating with his mother, but in the course of your conversation and in watching the boy, I came to realize that his mother is not in the almshouse, but rather the asylum for the insane. In attempting to spare the boy embarrassment, I fear I offended you."

Sissy caught her breath with a soft gasp. "Oh, my word. I did not see it. How awful of me."

"Not at all," Dupin said. "I am certain he understood your good intentions."

"Of course he did," I added, feeling my face redden, for I too had failed to perceive what Dupin had fathomed and now it seemed absurdly obvious. "But let us not dwell on our errors; let us instead solve this puzzle. Doing so will not only allow us to rescue Miss Loddiges, but might also assist Billy in escaping those rascals."

"Yes," Sissy agreed firmly.

"What about the bird names themselves. Might they be a cryptograph of some sort?" I wondered.

Dupin nodded. "I thought something simple like an anagram using the first letter of each bird name." He pushed a sheet of paper toward us. "E-E-E-L-L-N-R. I cannot see any meaning in this. If we add the first letters from the full scientific names, we have: C-D-E-E-E-L-L-L-M-N-N-P-R-S." He tapped the letters he had written neatly upon the page.

"Perhaps this will assist us." Sissy reached into her sewing box and took out a pair of scissors. "Shall I?"

Dupin handed her the paper and my wife quickly cut the letters into individual squares, then grouped them on the table, the consonants in one pile, the vowels in another. We scrutinized the letters for a time, as if willing them to arrange themselves into a message, and when that failed we took turns pushing the letters this way and that to form words: *men, creep, speed, spree, scree.*

"Should we use all the letters in the bird names?" Sissy wondered.

Dupin shook his head. "That would be rather complex and Andrew Mathews was a bird collector not a cryptographer. But of course it might not be the first letter, but rather the last, for example."

"Given that 'Larus' is the shortest word with only five letters, perhaps we should try the fifth letter of each?" I suggested.

Dupin shrugged. "Overly complicated, I fear, but let us try."

He quickly wrote down the fifth letter of each word and Sissy cut them into squares. We examined the jumble of letters before us: A-A-C-D-E-G-I-L-O-O-P-S-W-Y. The word *legacy* seemed promising, given the journal and its contents. The remaining letters formed *aid* and *swoop* or *paid* and *woos*, but we could not discern a message within those words. *Go copse waylaid* also seemed to have potential, but if this were a summary of something that had happened to Andrew Mathews, it did not reveal the identity of the perpetrator or anything else particularly useful.

"I believe this is a cipher and we are missing the key," Dupin said in frustration. "It is either hidden in these pages or it is in some other part of the journal that Jeremiah Mathews left behind in England."

"Let us hope that is not the case. I would like to study the journal pages tonight. May I suggest that you read the passages I marked in *Las Costumbres de la Gente de las Nubes* that relate to the Chachapoyan mountains," I said to Dupin, handing him the tome.

"Yes, of course."

Sissy gathered up the letters scattered on the table and a page upon which she had copied down the names of the rogue birds in both Latin and common English.

"And I will experiment with these a bit longer. I feel we have missed something." Sissy ran her fingers lightly across Andrew Mathews's bird drawings and her hand paused at the sketch of the Peruvian pepper tree and its flock of disparate birds. She stared at the page for a moment, then said, "This drawing caught the attention of Jeremiah Mathews, but not because of any non-native birds hidden in plain sight on the page. I wonder if it was because these Peruvian birds would never roost together in the same tree, particularly a tree that is growing inside what appears to be a cave. The drawing looks fantastical and might be easily dismissed as such, but what if it too has something of importance hidden in plain sight? Some valuable clue? Might it represent an actual location of significance that is disguised by these elements of fantasy?" she said, indicating the birds. "The king's tomb, perhaps?"

I half-expected Dupin to dismiss Sissy's comment, but he went very quiet and stared into the flames, politely ignoring her hypothesis, or so we thought. Sissy's face dropped and I said, "You're correct that those birds would never roost together, and surely no tree could grow inside a cave, for that is what the structure appears to be. It seems to be an artist's idle daydream, unless it is a metaphor of some sort."

"If there were a hole in the cave roof that let in light and water, as depicted in the drawing," Dupin said slowly, "it would not be impossible to find a *Schinus molle* in such a location. The Peruvian pepper tree often lives several hundred years and, as we know, they were used to mummify the dead. The trees may have been important to the Cloud People in their burial rituals."

Sissy nodded slightly and picked up the drawing of the *Schinus molle*. She examined it for a time then placed it back on the table. "Diego Fernández's description of the hidden chamber behind the mud brick wall they knocked down—he mentions primitive wall paintings," she said, indicating those depicted in the drawing. "And a gap in the chamber's roof through which a shaft of light fell, illuminating a large emerald on an earthen altar." She pointed at the branches of the pepper tree reaching up toward the hole in the roof of the cave in Andrew Mathews's drawing. "What if this is a drawing of the hidden chamber that the Spaniards explored and Fernández described in his book? If a *Schinus molle* seed sprouted in the earth after their discovery, might there now be a tree something like this?" She gently traced the roots of the tree snaking into the earth. "And if so, might its roots have grown around the emerald Fernández saw on the altar?"

Dupin gave my wife a curious glance and leaned in to study the drawing. "It is not an impossible theory," he finally said.

My wife smiled and added, "If this tree exists, Jeremiah Mathews may indeed have found the legendary jewel and perhaps even the entrance to the king's tomb. What if the stone at the front of the altar that Fernández mentioned hid yet another chamber, and the emerald was situated there to mark its location?" Her eyes were gleaming with excitement.

I stared at the drawing, my own imagination ignited. Sissy's theory did not seem to me any more fanciful than Fernández's descriptions of what he had seen in the burial chamber of the Cloud People so many years previously. Had Jeremiah Mathews been led to the jewel of Peru by his father's peculiar drawing? Dupin's distracted expression suggested that he was pondering those same thoughts. Sissy ran her finger lightly over the edge of the drawing then stood up.

"Unfortunately we will not, tonight, solve the mystery of whether Andrew Mathews truly did discover the king's tomb or if he or his son found the notorious jewel," she said with a smile. "Perhaps we should visit Bartram's estate in the morning and speak with the Carrs. Helena told me that they knew Andrew Mathews very well and met Jeremiah—perhaps they will see something in the journal pages that we missed, or have a thought that might help us find Helena. Mrs. Carr must be deeply worried about her and will be eager to assist us. Goodnight, gentlemen." And my wife was gone before we could wish her the same.

27

MONDAY, 18 MARCH 1844

We did not make the journey to Bartram's estate the next morning, for a smartly dressed boy arrived at the door with a letter.

"From the United States Hotel, sir." He handed it over and was off down the road before I could muster my thoughts to question him. I brought the letter to the kitchen table, where Dupin sat with Muddy, the oppressive silence alleviated only by the chatter of teacups on saucers.

"From the United States Hotel," I repeated and tore open the envelope.

"An unexpected missive, I take it?" Dupin said.

"More than unexpected," I muttered when I saw the contents.

"How so?" Dupin put down his coffee and turned his full attention to me. I allowed the letter to flutter down in front of him, and he quickly scanned it, his frown deepening as he read each word. "Do you believe it genuine?" he finally asked.

"It is most definitely her handwriting." I indicated the elegant and precise copperplate script. "Few have the skill to mimic such elaborate penmanship."

"Whose handwriting?" Sissy entered the kitchen, her face still soft with sleep.

"It is a letter, from Helena Loddiges." I handed her the page and my wife read it aloud.

The United States Hotel, Philadelphia
Monday, 18 March 1844

Dear Mr. Poe,

I must apologize most profusely for the inconvenience I have caused you with my abrupt departure. My father arrived in Philadelphia earlier than I expected, determined to bring me home to Paradise Fields.

I am sorry that I did not tell you, but I so wished to see the passenger pigeons. Mrs. Carr worked out where I might be and my father collected me at Wissahickon wood. He had business in New York, so we left directly from the forest, and, in truth, he was so angry I thought it best not to make introductions at that time.

We set sail this evening, and I am desperate to have the journal with me as it is my last keepsake of Jeremiah's. Father will not let me out of his sight, so I hope you will bring the journal to me at the United States Hotel today at noon. I apologize once more for the immense inconvenience I have caused you. Jeremiah's untimely demise filled me with so much grief I failed to see what a misguided and dangerous adventure I had undertaken and profoundly regret that I involved you in it. I look forward to wishing you bon voyage.

Your most sincere friend,
Miss Helena Loddiges

"The girl is safe?" Muddy asked. "That is a relief."

Sissy shook her head, frowning. "Helena did fear that her father would send someone to fetch her home, but I am not convinced. She may seem eccentric and unworldly but she is most certainly not so thoughtless as to wait this many days before telling us where she is. Helena knows we would be frantic with worry given all that she told us."

"Very true," I said. "Furthermore, I cannot believe her father managed to locate her so easily at the woods and persuaded her to leave us without a word. And we did, after all, find her gloves and the hummingbird from her hat on the forest floor."

"She will be pleased that you have found them," Muddy said.

"We think she dropped them intentionally, Mother," my wife told her.

Muddy shook her head in bafflement and began to clear the table. "It seems to me that you are making a mystery out of nothing. The girl is safe, that is the most important thing."

"We do not know that she is safe, unfortunately. Her abductor probably forced her to write the letter so we deliver the journal to him," I said.

"I do not know the lady," Dupin said. "But from what you have told me, it seems unlikely that such a determined person would abandon her quest to learn the true circumstances of Jeremiah Mathews's death without a more detailed explanation in person, or in a private note." He tapped at the letter on the table.

"The Carrs will know if Helena's father has truly arrived in Philadelphia," Sissy observed.

"Of course, but we will find out soon enough if Miss Loddiges is waiting for me at the United States Hotel, or if it is the man who killed Father Keane and, we must presume, Jeremiah Mathews," I said.

"Which would mean that Helena is still being held hostage," Sissy explained to Muddy.

"Dear Lord," my mother-in-law muttered.

"Such a trick is most revealing," Dupin observed. "Only a man who believes he has a far superior intellect would underestimate an adversary's ability to see through such a ruse." The way in which Dupin said each word made it perfectly clear what he thought of that notion.

"May I suggest that you take a false journal with you?" my wife said. "If Helena is acting under duress, her abductor may force her to collect the journal from you and they may still harm her to ensure her silence."

"A valid point," Dupin agreed.

"I have a small notebook for sketching that will suffice. If I quickly copy some of the birds and text from Jeremiah's journal, and put his name to it, that should persuade them. I do not think there is any need to color the drawings," she added.

"Will you have enough time?" I asked.

"I think so. Helena's abductor has not seen the journal and therefore cannot know how adept an artist he is. They certainly don't know of Andrew Mathews's drawings as Helena herself seems unaware of them."

Dupin nodded. "Excellent idea. We will take whatever you manage to put together and use it to lure the villain at the hotel, then we will seize him and free Miss Loddiges," he said as he retrieved his green spectacles from his waistcoat pocket and put them on. "If I proceed to the hotel before you, and station myself somewhere unobtrusive in the foyer, I will be able to observe and, I hope, take our adversary by surprise." He looked at his pocket watch. "We have three hours. Where is the hotel?"

"Not far. It is located on Chestnut Street between Fourth and Fifth Streets, opposite the United States Bank."

"What an appropriate location for a treasure seeker," Dupin said wryly.

28

It was a grand building, five stories high, rectangular and pale, with the American flag waving in the breeze from the top floor. As I entered the foyer, I remembered the feeling of expectation tempered with nervousness that enveloped me when I had first visited the United States Hotel two years previously for an assignation with Charles Dickens. Our attempts to meet in London had come to naught, and I had hoped that Dickens—an author I admired enormously—would prove a kindred spirit, but alas that hope had not been fulfilled. Suffice to say that one might greatly enjoy the fruit of another's imagination, but find little common ground in every day discourse.

I had no hopeful expectations for this meeting, however, and my senses were acute with watchful unease, for our adversary had murdered two innocent men and might intend the same fate for me and Miss Loddiges. I paused for a moment in the foyer to gather myself, dipping my hand into my coat pocket to touch the false journal like the lucky talisman I hoped it would be. Sissy had done a wonderful job of reproducing enough of the birds and innocuous observations in Jeremiah Mathews's journal to construct what we hoped was a convincing decoy with the initials J.M. painted on the spine. To my left, in a dimly

lit corner, was Dupin pretending to be engrossed in a newspaper, so I took a calming breath and approached the desk clerk, a
man who seemed designed to become invisible in any environment, a useful trait for his occupation.

"I am Edgar Poe here to see Miss Helena Loddiges. She is
expecting me."

The desk clerk's expression suggested that he was anticipating my arrival. "I am sorry, Mr. Poe. Miss Loddiges was unable
to keep her engagement. This was left for you." He handed me
another letter, which I immediately opened.

> The United States Hotel, Philadelphia
> Monday, 18 March 1844
>
> Dear Mr. Poe,
>   I am terribly sorry to inconvenience you, but I had
> no choice but to go with my father to a warehouse
> near the harbor in hopes of re-securing the remainder
> of the shipment Jeremiah Mathews collected. Again, I
> apologize, but would you please bring the journal to
> the Jolly Traveler tavern in Black Horse Alley near
> Front Street at half past twelve o'clock? I would deeply
> appreciate it as you are aware how dear the journal is
> to me, but of course will understand if you cannot
> make your way there. I hope to see you, but if not, I
> bid you farewell and will write upon my return to
> London.
>   Yours respectfully,
>   Miss Helena Loddiges

I stared at the letter written in Miss Loddiges's unmistakable
hand, feeling both disappointed and irked. If she had been
forced to write the missive, why would her abductor have her

send me to another location rather than simply ask that I leave the journal at the hotel? I recollected the lady's talk of murder, ghosts, doppelgängers—was she indeed unbalanced and weaving an elaborate fantasy? But my doubts quickly vanished. Surely it was a trick to give credibility to the letter. The United States Hotel was too public a place for Miss Loddiges to take the journal without putting her abductor in jeopardy. And it was obvious that I would not leave the journal at the hotel without seeing Miss Loddiges. I looked around me at the other men in the hotel foyer. It was likely that one of them had been tasked by Miss Loddiges's abductor with ascertaining whether I had an accomplice with me. And so I could not show the second letter to Dupin without making his presence known. There was no option but to make my way to the Jolly Traveler tavern in hopes of exchanging the false journal for Miss Loddiges. It was in all probability a trap, but I felt sure enough that Dupin and I would hold our own against any ruffian. We would have to try.

I left the United States Hotel, knowing that Dupin would follow me like a ghost until he was needed, and made my way down Chestnut Street, heading east toward the Delaware River and the docks. It was a long, straight road and therefore untroublesome to catch sight of Dupin trailing a distance behind me. It would, of course, be equally simple for a foe to keep me in sight. The pleasantness of the walk somewhat countered my apprehension, for it was a bright day imbued with the smell of spring. Industrious women scrubbed already-clean marble steps outside prosperous-looking homes and cheerful folk out for a stroll bid me good day. A cardinal followed my path, flitting from tree to tree, singing loudly each time he landed on a branch, his crimson feathers contrasting with the dark skeletal fingers of the trees. It did not take me long to reach Front Street. I turned left into it and proceeded north toward my destination.

When at last I turned into Black Horse Alley, I saw a crowd further ahead and was surprised by how very busy the tavern was in the middle of the day. The throng seemed to part then merge around me again as I made my way down the alley. I had the sense of being shadowed, but when I looked behind me, I could not locate Dupin. As I was pushed along by the mob, I soon perceived that they were not afternoon drinkers, but spectators of a boxing match, and the pugilists were not the usual bare-knuckle boxers one sees outside the less salubrious taverns of the area, but two ladies. Perhaps "lady" is not the correct description when considering their activity, but the pair were most certainly female, for each was stripped down to her under-garments: a chemise, short petticoats, Holland drawers and white stockings. One was an Irish woman of Amazonian proportions with pale skin and curls as black as a crow's wing, and the other a fair-haired, pink-faced female who looked as if she had stepped out from a Titian painting and was in a fear-some mood.

"Place your bets here! Taking final bets!" shouted a corpu-lent man wearing a yellow and brown checked coat and sport-ing a prodigious mustache. In exchange for coins offered he handed over a marked slip of paper. "The Dublin Duchess or Philadelphia's finest, Hell Town Helga. Care to place a bet, sir?" I was startled to find his pale blue eyes fixed upon me. I shook my head, but he continued to stare, which made me pull my coat a little closer, conscious that such a crowd was the delight of pickpockets. "Final bets now, final bets!" he roared.

As the spectators around me pushed forward to place their bets, I was herded closer to the alley's end, which functioned as a makeshift sparring ring. The two combatants circled each other there, waving their clenched fists, doing their best to ignite each other and the crowd.

"I'll give you a good anointing and send you to Hell—if the Devil will have your ugly arse," the Irish Amazon sneered. Cheers met her pronouncement, followed by the chant: "*Send her to the Devil! Send her to the Devil!*"

"I'm gonna blinker you, Cat-lick, and send you back to the bog with a push from this." Hell Town Helga shook her sizable fist at her opponent.

Her supporters shouted, "Cat-lick, Cat-lick, kill the Cat-lick!"

The Dublin Duchess flushed crimson and danced closer to her adversary, fists feigning left then right. "Shut your bone-box before I do it for you."

The subsequent cheers were pierced by a whistle and the corpulent fight-fixer shoved his way to the ladies. Despite my best efforts to exit the makeshift arena, I was held captive at the front of the crowd by boxing enthusiasts. The man who was both compere and fight-fixer threw his arms over the shoulders of each lady and leaned in to give them quiet words of instruction, gesticulating at the crowd, after which each nodded.

"The first down is out," he announced loudly. "Winner takes half the purse, the rest is split with those holding the right ticket. Everybody else gets nothing but a good show." The mob roared its appreciation at his promise and both women held up their arms as if already declared the winner. "Are we ready now, ladies?" the compere asked.

"Ready to give her a bunch of fives," snarled the Dublin Duchess.

"She'll be off her drumsticks before she tries it," snapped Hell Town Helga.

The compere clapped his hands to one and then the other while the crowd joined in, stomping their feet and cat-calling. He then separated the two pugilists until they were a good six feet apart. "Wait for my signal," he commanded, then scuttled back out of reach before putting his fingers to his mouth and whistling. The ladies immediately advanced upon each other, fists held high. The crowd jostled and shouted and each time I tried to back away from the action, I was shoved forward again.

"Go, Peg! Shut her saucebox!"

"Hit her, Helga! Smack her one!"

The Dublin Duchess landed the first blow and the sound of bare knuckles on shoulder-blade made me gasp. But rumbumptious Hell Town Helga came back at her with two punches that spun the Duchess in a circle. And on it went, the growling women throwing their fists just as a man would, until blood sprayed from noses and trickled from mouths, staining the white of their costumes in a ghastly manner. The crowd cheered each punch and booed when the pugilists collapsed into each other or lurched about in a punch-drunk waltz. Throughout this macabre dance I did my best to push my way out of the throng but I was netted in like a fish.

"Go, Helga! Knock back that potato-eater!"

And she did with a slash of the fingernails to the eye, which half-blinded the Dublin Duchess as blood flowed like tears. She looked as if she might collapse, but the native Philadelphian's supporters were disappointed when the Irish woman re-gathered her strength and charged Hell Town Helga like a bull, ramming her head into her adversary's belly and knocking the wind right out of her. She followed this with a flurry of blows that sent Hell Town Helga to the ground, insensible.

The mob erupted, some cheering, some booing, all jostling. The Dublin Duchess threw her fists into the air and shook them, roaring as a lion might. Her supporters echoed her victory bellow then danced in circles, chanting, "Du-blin Du-chess! Du-blin Du-chess!"

Chaos reigned until the voice of the compere rose above the noise of the crowd. "Winners collect inside the Jolly Traveler!"

he shouted. "Winners into the Jolly Traveler for your cut of the purse!"

I briefly caught sight of the compere in his plaid coat before he ducked into the tavern and the mob surged after him, each winner desperate to get their money first. I made my way in the opposite direction and was elbowed and kicked and shoved until I feared I might be crushed. And just as the sea of humanity parted and I dashed forward to freedom, I came face to face with the Dublin Duchess and her fist flew at me like a vicious bird.

29

It was as if a shell were pressed to my ear and all I could hear was the roaring of an artificial sea. Sunlight trickled under my eyelids, but they were so heavy I could not lift them. The gentle roaring continued for a time—I know not how long—until it transformed into words: "Poe, Poe, can you hear me, Poe?" My mind reassembled itself, and I eased my eyes open to see Dupin leaning over me.

"Gone, is the journal gone?"

"Yes," he said.

"And Miss Loddiges is not at the tavern?"

"I do not know. When I managed to push my way through the crowd I found you lying here. I have not looked inside."

I tried to sit up and felt as if I'd just awakened from a long night of heavy tippling.

"Take your time, Poe. Who pummeled you?"

"The Dublin Duchess. I now understand why she was the victor," I said, attempting some levity.

"It is likely she is in league with the two priests and their employer."

I remembered the piercing look the compere had given me. "Did you notice the compere—a stout fellow wearing a plaid coat? Dark hair, very large mustache. I believe he was involved. He whispered something to the pugilists and gave me a most knowing look."

"If the two priests who frequent the taverns here are aware of his business, then it is very likely he is in league with them. Careful now," he added as he gripped my elbow, helping me rise unsteadily to my feet. "We had best get a coach."

* * *

The jostling ride had conjured up a headache in me, and Dupin was forced to assist me to the house. Before I managed to unlock the door, it flew open. Muddy stood before us gripping a broom, her face full of agitation, which deepened when she saw that Dupin was supporting me.

"What have you done to our dear boy?"

"We were not in a tippling den," I began, only to be interrupted by a peculiar sound and my wife crying out.

"A bird is in the house, and I cannot catch the blessed thing," Muddy snapped. "Virginia is beside herself. Speaking of how it signifies death. She fears for you, Eddy."

"What sort of bird?" Dupin asked, before I could respond.

"A pigeon that will make a fine supper if I get my hands around its neck." She moved toward the kitchen, broom held aloft like a weapon. Dupin and I hurried after her.

"Quite the coincidence," he said, voicing my own thoughts.

A thrumming sound filled the air, and Virginia scurried through the door, arms held over her head. "The beastly thing! It came in through the window and will not leave the same way." She threw her arms around me, which caused me to huff in pain, and her face filled with concern. "What happened? It was all a ruse, wasn't it? Are you terribly hurt?" She gently touched where the Duchess's fist had connected with the side of my head.

"I am perfectly fine, dearest. Let us capture the bird first, then I will explain everything." I extracted myself from her arms and followed Dupin into the kitchen. He stood at its center, watching a fine-looking pigeon saunter along a shelf, pink feet high-stepping and head bobbing, its feathers a decorous gray but for the black stripes across its wings and gleams of amethyst and emerald at its throat like a fanciful neckcloth.

"It is well cared for," Dupin observed. "And, as we presumed, it did not enter your house by chance."

"Quite impossible," I agreed. "A homing pigeon only flies to its *home*. Someone must have purposefully released it here."

"With a message. Notice its leg." Dupin pointed at the bird, and I focused my gaze on the restless pigeon's feet. There was indeed something attached to its leg, but the bird flew up into the air before I could get a proper look at it. The creature circled the room once, tried to perch upon the door lintel, then returned to the shelf.

"Another threat? But surely our adversaries believe they have stolen what they were after."

"True," Dupin agreed, his eyes staring into those of the pigeon's like a mesmerist. He suddenly reached up and grasped the pigeon around its middle, pinning its wings to its body. The bird gave no resistance. "The message will tell us if the bird came from foe or friend." He held the bird toward me, and I removed the small slip of folded paper that was attached to its leg with a piece of string as Sissy crept back into the room carrying a large hatbox, its lid punched with holes.

"For the bird." She placed the box on the table and removed the lid. Dupin placed the now docile creature inside the box and replaced the lid. My wife nodded at the folded slip of paper in my hands. "What does it say?"

I quickly opened the note and read it out: "'Noon, tomorrow. The Philosophical Hall. Two sold. Bring two more.'" Silent contemplation stilled the air.

"It is, of course, obvious that the message was not meant for us," Dupin said. "The note suggests that the sender and the intended recipient have a usual meeting place at the Philosophical Hall, and that they are in league selling some commodity for mutual benefit. Given that Billy Sweeney's employers at St. Augustine's—the two criminal priests—relay messages to Old Blockley with pigeons, and considering the notes Father Keane hid within the treasure books in the library, I would venture to guess that it is treasure books that are being stolen and sold. They would, after all, be among the most valuable commodities at St. Augustine, yet they are relatively easily stolen and spirited away without raising suspicion—as I myself have demonstrated." Dupin paused to allow us to consider his words. "I also believe that the bird was sent from the would-be journal thief or his accomplice to someone at St. Augustine's."

"It is conceivable," I agreed. "If we station ourselves near the entrance of the Philosophical Hall prior to noon, perhaps we will discover who is after the journal and who murdered Jeremiah Mathews."

"But it does not tell us why this bird and its message ended up in our kitchen," Sissy observed.

"Indeed," Dupin nodded. "It is obvious that someone captured the bird and delivered it through your window. We seem to have an ally."

Sissy looked as surprised as I felt. She pondered Dupin's declaration for a moment then said, "Do you think it is Billy? That he intercepted a carrier pigeon somehow to help us?"

"No," Dupin said. "Your faith in the boy is admirable, but it is most certainly not his doing. Let us recall for a moment the ghost that haunted Miss Loddiges before her journey."

"The ghost of Jeremiah Mathews."

"Indeed. We have presumed that Miss Loddiges is overly imaginative," Dupin said generously. "That in her grief she saw things that were not there. But what if she were not dreaming when she saw her beloved?" He paused for a moment to allow that thought to consume our consciousness.

"What if the ghost is not a ghost at all?" Sissy ventured.

Dupin nodded. "What proof do we have that Jeremiah Mathews has been murdered, other than accounts of his death delivered to George Loddiges?"

"Surely the young man was sent home for burial. It was the duty of Helena's father to see to that if young Mr. Mathews died in his employ," my mother-in-law declared.

She was not wrong, and yet I could not recall that Miss Loddiges had made any mention of grieving over Jeremiah Mathew's lifeless form or of attending his burial.

"Miss Loddiges received a package sent by Jeremiah Mathews from Panama. It contained his journal and a letter asking her to take care of it for him. He hoped to see her by Christmas. Shortly after, George Loddiges received a letter informing him of Jeremiah Mathew's death by drowning in Philadelphia, which arrived with the bird and plant specimens the young man had collected for him in Peru," I summarized. "Miss Loddiges did not directly state that his body was returned to England, however. I had merely presumed that was the case."

"So it is possible that his death is a hoax," Sissy said. "But if Jeremiah Mathews is truly alive and Miss Loddiges caught sight of him in London, why did he not explain everything to her?"

"One step at a time," Dupin advised, "or we will miss something. Let us first ascertain if the young man is truly dead or if he might be alive and in hiding. There must be an office that keeps an official record of the deaths in this city."

"We might try the Lazaretto," I said. "All ships bound for Philadelphia must dock there first and go through a strict quarantine inspection of both crew and cargo to prevent them bringing contagion into the city. We know the rough date of Jeremiah Mathews's arrival in Philadelphia and where his ship came from. The quarantine inspection logs should record the date of arrival of all vessels, information regarding the crew and cargo, and the date each vessel was permitted to leave the quarantine station."

"Very good," Dupin said.

"As for that in the box," Muddy interjected, "will you be releasing it or will I be cooking it for supper?"

The thought of roasted pigeon made my mouth water and I could see that Sissy and Dupin entertained similar thoughts.

"We had best release it," my wife said, "with the message attached to its leg, or the intended recipient will not know about the meeting tomorrow."

"True," I agreed. "Dupin, would you do the honors, given your apparent ability to charm the creature?"

He refolded the paper, took the lid from the hatbox, and without any difficulty at all reaffixed the note to the pigeon, then put the lid back onto the box. "I have an idea," he said.

Dupin picked up the hatbox and exited the house with it. Sissy and I rushed after, but when we reached the front porch, he had disappeared.

"Dupin?"

"Here, near the kitchen window."

When we walked around the corner of the house, there he was, crouched on the ground, examining the dirt. "Did you find something?" I asked.

"Do not move," he instructed, raising a hand to halt my progress. He was staring intently at the ground, but I could see nothing. "Most of the footprints have erased each other, but here is a very good one," he added. "As it faces the window, I believe we might presume that it belongs to the person who released the pigeon into your home."

I crouched down and saw quite a clear footprint in the mud.

"From the size and depth of the print, I would suggest that the man who released the bird into the kitchen is smaller than both of us, but stocky—of a greater weight. And that he was wearing sturdy boots."

"You are able to ascertain that from the footprint?" Sissy shook her head. "If Eddy had not told me so many tales of your skill in ratiocination, I would think you a sorcerer, Monsieur Dupin."

"It is but an educated guess. I am as curious as you to see if it proves accurate." Dupin smiled slightly, then said in a low voice, "The trick, of course, is to obscure one's steps when explaining what one has divined through ratiocination. This gives the illusion of mystical powers, which can be advantageous if the adversary is wrong-footed by fear."

"But I suppose one's adversary might be adroit at the same game," my wife said. "Which makes a mystery all the more difficult to solve."

How right she was! Dupin and I had both lost at the game for a time in London.

"Correct again, Mrs. Poe. I hope we will always remain on the same side."

"Surely there is no fear of that?" she said, smiling. "Now go set the bird free to deliver its mysterious message."

30

A quarter of an hour later, I was striding along Vine Street with Dupin, who carried Sissy's makeshift pigeon carrier in his hands, while I had *Las Costumbres de la Gente de las Nubes* in my coat pocket. Dupin had pointed out that it made no sense to release the bird from our home as we would not be able to track it for long, but if we released the creature near St. Augustine's, we would soon know if someone at the church sent the message or was its intended recipient.

"What precisely is our plan now?" I asked as we neared our destination.

"The door in the stone wall that the priests entered by the night we followed them to St. Augustine's—it leads into the gardens, correct?"

"Correct. Father Keane and I sat in the gardens on occasion, but I cannot recall if there are pigeon lofts there."

As the stone wall that enclosed St. Augustine's came into view, we observed a man leading a horse and cart through the large double door in it. The wagon's contents were covered with a tarpaulin and the doors closed behind them.

"Interesting." Dupin strode up to the doors and tried the latch to the smaller wicket cut into one of them. It swung several inches and he peered through, then said, "I will release the pigeon, then let us enter and observe what happens."

"And if someone challenges us?"

"We are merely returning a book to Father Nolan in the library. Certainly he will gloss over our actions for fear of admonishment, or worse, from his superior."

I thought of the formidable and seemingly heartless Father Moriarty and knew that Dupin was right. "Let us begin then."

We stood on either side of the doors, obscured from anyone who might be in the garden, and Dupin lifted the lid from the hatbox. Nothing happened and I momentarily feared that the bird had met its end during our journey, but as soon as Dupin swept the hatbox up and back down again, the creature burst into flight and circled once high above us. We watched as it began to circle again, as if getting its bearings, then descended toward the garden. We immediately slipped inside the grounds of St. Augustine's.

"There," Dupin muttered, nodding his head at a turret built into the garden wall, and when our pigeon flew into a hole at the top of it, I realized it was an artfully constructed dovecot. A door at the base of the wall opened into the structure and another door on the side of the dovecot led to a walkway on top of the garden wall. We stood quietly in the garden, waiting for any indication that someone had received the pigeon's message, but time stretched on and just as I was about to suggest that our presence there was going to raise suspicion, a small, wiry priest exited onto the walkway, a pigeon cupped in his hands. His size and something in his movements made me wonder if he were one of the priests we had followed from the Mermaid. He threw his hands toward the heavens and the pigeon erupted from them, no doubt with another slip of paper tethered to its leg.

"Keep sight of the bird," Dupin muttered. "Try to gauge the direction in which it flies, for that is where the guilty priest's accomplice resides."

We stood and watched as the bird soared up, flying northwest until it disappeared into the blue.

"Not in the direction of Old Blockley," I observed.

"Indeed. And I wonder if that is Father Carroll or Father Healey," he murmured. "Presumably Healey, since he is the one who takes care of the birds here, according to our young lockpick."

I watched the priest, who seemed intent on observing the flight of the pigeon he had released.

"Let us make our way to the library on the pretext of returning the book to Father Nolan as promised. I'd like to find out who has access to the treasure books and where the list of those held by the library is kept," Dupin said.

I led the way inside and we found Father Nolan seated at a table in the library, engrossed in an ancient tome, oblivious to all around him.

"Good afternoon, sir," I said. "That appears compelling."

The priest shied like a startled horse at my voice and his face was the picture of surprise when he looked up at us.

"Mr. Poe and Chevalier Dupin. What an unexpected surprise. I was attempting to steal some reading time before attending to my students."

"It is difficult to find enough hours in the day to read," Dupin agreed. "So we will not keep you for long."

"I am more than happy to assist," Father Nolan demurred.

"We have brought back the treasure book." I retrieved it from my coat pocket and held it toward him.

"Thank you, sirs. That is a relief." Father Nolan's face was filled with that emotion as he took the volume from me. "I began to fear that Father Keane would be accused of theft, as the book's absence has been noted." He made his way to the treasure book cabinet and fished his set of cabinet keys from his pocket. Dupin joined him there as he opened the glass door, and I followed. We watched as he gazed at the books on the left of the shelf, then made space for *Las Costumbres de la Gente de las Nubes*.

Dupin stared intently at the books in the open cabinet, then began to scrutinize the display of books in the other locked cabinets. "I presume Father Moriarty takes an inventory of the treasure books on a regular basis?" Dupin asked as he looked at book after book.

"Indeed," Father Nolan nodded. "I dissuaded him from doing so yesterday, but he will not be deterred again, of that I am certain."

I wondered if Father Nolan did his own inventory and whether he was aware that the exquisite tome *La Langue des Oiseaux* was no longer in the treasure book cabinet.

"I noted during our last visit that the treasure books are arranged alphabetically by title. Is there an alphabetical listing of the books held here in the library?" Dupin asked.

"Yes, of course."

"May I see it?" Dupin asked.

"Sir?" The priest's shock at the request was more than clear.

"I believe that an illicit trade in treasure books is being conducted and would like to test my theory."

Father Nolan remained in stunned silence for a moment. "You cannot believe that Father Keane removed additional books," he said, indicating the tome we had returned.

"Of course not," I said quickly. "Father Keane may have come upon a person or persons in the act of stealing books and been murdered for it. And the perpetrator is likely to be someone who resides at St. Augustine's rather than a stranger."

Father Nolan blanched and staggered slightly as if he had just received a physical blow. He shook his head and struggled to speak, but could not.

"The list of treasure books," Dupin repeated. "May I see it?"

Father Nolan shut the cabinet and locked it. "Not today, I'm afraid. I would have to receive permission from Father Moriarty, who keeps the ledger in his office. As I mentioned, he does the inventory and is the only person who has access to the official list." A frown creased Father Nolan's forehead, as if the thought caused him concern.

"And therefore he is the only person who would know if any books went missing," Dupin said.

"In all likelihood," Father Nolan agreed.

"Thank you, sir," Dupin said, scanning the treasure book cabinets as he walked back toward us. "You have been most helpful."

"I am glad if I have been of some small assistance." Father Nolan looked to me, then Dupin, and back again, his demeanor and garb giving him the look of a nervous magpie.

"We will find Father Keane's murderer, have no doubt," I said. "And justice will be served."

"That is some comfort," Father Nolan said. "God rest his soul." He solemnly made the sign of the cross and dismissed us with a gentle nod.

31

TUESDAY, 19 MARCH 1844

"It was an oasis contained by glass, filled with palm trees and orchids made strange by moonlight, and creeping vines with trumpet-shaped flowers, around which a tiny bird of emerald hovered and darted. I made my way like a thief from that exotic space through a dark passageway and entered a candlelit chamber I recognized: Miss Loddiges's sitting room. It was crammed with Wardian cases filled with ferns and a flock of innumerable and diverse birds, frozen and silent, as if asleep. Then a glint, the flicker of something observing me from the darkness.

"'Hello, old girl,' a croaking voice said. 'What the devil is going on here?' With a flutter of wings, Grip the raven swooped down from a bookshelf and landed on a chair next to me. The bird observed me with its gimlet eye. 'I told her,' it said. 'I told her and warned her.'

This was not the bird's usual repertoire of nonsense.

"'Where is she? Where is Miss Loddiges?' I asked.

"'Miss Loddiges,' the creature chattered. 'Hello, old girl.' As he flew up to the bookcase, the sitting room door opened and in walked the lady herself, along with Andrew Mathews and his son Jeremiah. What an odd trio they were, Miss Loddiges in her peculiar clothing and hummingbird embellishments, the

solemn Jeremiah Mathews in a plain dark suit and Andrew
Mathews wearing a forest-green jacket with the diaphanous
bubble attached to its front.

"Miss Loddiges did not appear to hear or see me. Nor did her
guests. She gestured for the two gentlemen to sit. After a
moment's hesitation, I took the empty chair across from them
and immediately realized we were seated exactly as we had
been on that afternoon when we had all had tea in her sitting
room. Then a shadow swooped and feathers rustled as Grip
circled us. Miss Loddiges raised her arm as if to fend off the bird
before cowering back in her chair, visibly shaken. Grip swooped
again and said loudly, 'The Lord seeth. The Lord seeth all.'

"As the two men stared at Helena Loddiges with concern, a
subtle noise began, then grew louder—it was the rustling of
feathers and the shuffling of small feet. I watched in fascinated
horror as the lifeless birds in the room began to shift and stretch
their wings as if waking from a stupor. Soon they were scuttling
along the mantelpiece and tabletops or tapping their beaks
against the glass bell jars or cases that imprisoned them, and
cabinets full of hummingbirds came to life in a chaotic whir of
color.

"Andrew and Jeremiah Mathews seemed utterly unaware of
the growing chaos presided over by that demon Grip. They saw
only that Helena Loddiges had her hands pressed to her ears,
trying to shut out the frightful noise of the dead birds come to
life. Grip gave me a knowing look as he repeated, 'The Lord
seeth all,' then flew into the air, transforming it to the color of
his inky feathers."

"A strange dream, indeed, but interesting," Dupin said as I
concluded my tale. He and I were situated in the foyer of the
Philosophical Hall in a position that we had determined
would give one or both of us a clear view of anyone who
entered the building. The table between us was scattered

with papers to give the impression that we were two scholars discussing some philosophical treatise. "Does the dream reflect a good deal of the circumstances surrounding your meeting with Miss Loddiges and Andrew and Jeremiah Mathews?" he continued.

"The circumstances were somewhat similar. When we had tea we were seated in the same manner. Miss Loddiges did have some sort of premonition as we were touring the glasshouses—it was Jeremiah Mathews who noticed—but I don't recall her behaving as she did in my dream."

"And Dickens's pet raven was not there," Dupin added with a trace of a smile.

"No, but Miss Loddiges did inform me that it was Grip who told her I would help her find out the truth about the deaths of Andrew Mathews and his son. Our friend Grip haunts Dickens's study in quite a different way now, for he died and Dickens engaged Miss Loddiges to stuff the creature."

"I see. Well, it seems your slumbering mind made a connection between Grip, who was a highly intelligent if vexatious creature, and the ravens in the stained-glass window at St. Augustine Church, where the words 'The Lord Seeth' are emblazoned in gold above the altar."

"True, but to what purpose? I spent the remainder of the night trying to unravel my dream to no avail."

"Our minds continue to work as we sleep but in quite a different manner, I believe. At times our dreams explore things we sensed when awake but dismissed as we did not understand them or did not wish to believe them. Your dream also includes your own interpretations of Miss Loddiges's account of someone breaking into the glasshouse and freeing the hummingbird from its enclosure."

"And of the taxidermied birds in her sitting room being rearranged at night," I said. "It's true that when she related her story to me I could not help but imagine the birds coming alive at night, so life-like were the creatures."

"In your dream the birds appeared to be dead but were actually alive, just as there is the possibility that Jeremiah Mathews is not truly dead, but is in hiding from those who believe he has the jewel and would murder him to get it."

I considered this for a moment. "Miss Loddiges thought her father was concealing something and claimed he was holding her prisoner at home. Perhaps her abductor had threatened George Loddiges. I would presume that he does not know where the jewel is, as certainly he would give it up to ensure the safety of his daughter."

Dupin nodded. "It appears ever more likely that whoever is selling the treasure books is seeking the jewel and is holding your benefactress captive."

"Then let us do our utmost to end Miss Loddiges's ordeal quickly."

"Indeed." Dupin examined his pocket watch. "Five minutes until noon." He put on his green-tinted spectacles to obscure the direction of his gaze and I quickly adjusted my hat to better obscure my face from anyone entering the building.

We lapsed into silence as we watched for our quarry, but this lull was disturbed by two gentlemen engaged in voluble discussion as they descended the staircase. One was a portly, gray-haired fellow I recognized as Mr. Blackwell, who often introduced speakers giving presentations at the Philosophical Hall. The second man was close to six foot tall, tawny-haired and dressed expensively, but with a surfeit of pomp. His silk waistcoat was striped with vermilion and gold, and a large jewel sparkled on his pale yellow cravat. He appeared to be listening intently to his companion but his arched brows gave the sense that all he heard was met with disdain. I was certain I had met the man before, but could not quite place him.

"Thank you, Mr. Blackwell," he said in a booming voice that made all in the foyer glance in his direction. "The room is quite suitable and if my displays could be organized in the manner I suggested, I would be grateful."

The voice revived my memory—he was Mrs. Reynolds's admirer, the man that had delivered the basket of roses to her at the theater, and she had snubbed him.

"The audience must be seated by quarter to seven, as I will begin promptly on the hour," the man continued. "I will also need an assistant to take orders for the magic lantern slides and donations for the next expedition."

"Yes, of course. I will assist with that myself. If there is anything else you think of, do not hesitate to ask on the evening," Mr. Blackwell said.

"Thank you."

The two shook hands and Mr. Blackwell appeared somewhat wrong-footed when the man did not leave, but rather settled himself into a chair close to the door and opened a newspaper. Dupin immediately retrieved his meerschaum and began to fill it with tobacco, while I shuffled at the pages on the table.

"Keep your head down," Dupin murmured. "He is gazing this way."

I did as Dupin advised and rubbed at my brow as if in concentration, using my hand to obscure my face further while peering sideways at the fellow who might very well be our quarry. It was then that the door to the Philosophical Hall opened and someone stepped inside. Dupin exhaled a plume of smoke and joined me in leaning over the papers on the table.

"Do not look up," he commanded softly. He picked up one of the sheets and held it in such a direction that to view it I had to turn my head away from the door. "I have made a most fundamental error," he muttered, tapping at the paper as if debating some point with me. "And missed the truth hidden in plain sight."

I could barely contain my frustration. "Who is it, Dupin? I presume it is someone I know."

"Indeed. And a very fine actor Father Nolan is, or I have lost my wits entirely."

"Father Nolan?" I began to turn, such was my disbelief, but Dupin grasped my arm.

"Wait," he whispered. "Father Nolan has placed a satchel on the table." I could not see Dupin's eyes through the green glasses, but knew he was utterly focused on the priest. "He has taken two volumes from the satchel, both are bound in gold and I can perceive jeweled embellishments—undoubtedly treasure books from the library."

How I wished to leap from my chair and confront the wretched thief who had deceived us so completely!

"The scholar appears more than satisfied and has taken the satchel. And now they are readying to leave. I will follow the man who received the treasure books—you must learn his identity from Mr. Blackwell, then let us meet at your home." Dupin dashed for the door and was gone. Every fiber of my being wished to run after Father Nolan, but if he saw me pursuing him, he would quickly fathom that his duplicity had been uncovered. Dupin was right—it was best if I found out the identity of Father Nolan's co-conspirator, the man who perhaps had abducted Miss Loddiges.

I made my way upstairs in search of Mr. Blackwell. If he had invited the peacock of a man we had seen in the foyer to give a presentation, our quarry was more than a mere treasure hunter—an antiquarian, perhaps, or a botanist or an explorer. The topic of his presentation would reveal much. It did not take long for me to find the small room that served as Mr. Blackwell's office. The door was open, and he was at his desk reading. I rapped politely on the open door and he jumped.

"My apologies for disturbing you, sir. I could not help but overhear that a lecture will be presented here soon and I am curious to know the subject as I might like to attend."

"No trouble at all, sir. Do come in," he said, rising to his feet. "You are quite correct, there is a presentation tomorrow night by Professor Renelle." Mr. Blackwell shuffled through some papers on his desk and retrieved a broadsheet, which he handed to me. It was an advertisement for a lecture about a "Daring Expedition to the remains of an Ancient Civilization in the remote mountains of Peru", as undertaken by Professor Frederic Renelle, "Antiquarian, Scholar and Adventurer". An "Unforgettable Magic Lantern Show" would accompany the professor's talk.

"Peru! How fascinating," I said, meaning every word. It could only be the expedition that ended with Jeremiah Mathews's death. "And a magic lantern show? I will certainly attend," I said as calmly as I could.

"Very good. The more the merrier." Mr. Blackwell smiled jovially. "The Philosophical Society raised a subscription to help finance the last expedition, and Professor Renelle hopes to gain support for another, so do bring companions. If you would arrive at six forty-five for seven o'clock."

"Certainly. I look forward to it. Thank you for your assistance. You've been most helpful."

"My pleasure, sir."

I made my escape, clutching the broadsheet. When I stepped out of the Philosophical Hall, my mind was in a flux with all that had been revealed to us—indeed, it was filled with more questions than when I had entered the place. The day was bright, the air sweet with spring, and the proud red-brick buildings steeped in righteous rebellion that graced Chestnut

Street—City Hall and Independence Hall—had the effect of increasing my fury at Father Nolan's Machiavellian nature. The priest had an alliance with the man who had murdered Father Keane or, worse still, had done the deed himself, and we had naively confided in him, allowing him to reveal those confidences to his accomplice, Professor Renelle.

These thoughts filled me with self-recrimination—if only I had seen through the priest's façade, my friend might still be alive. I stepped into the first tavern I saw, but the smell of old ale and the noise of fortified revelry made me walk back outside. Instead I made my way to the river and strode along its banks, hoping to calm myself. If Father Keane's spirit remained anywhere in Philadelphia it would be there, wandering through the beauty of nature and conversing with the birds he loved so much. I did not catch a glimpse of him, but my memories of our morning walks along the Schuylkill were so strong I felt him there at my side, as surely did the stately, great blue heron that paused in his search for dinner to gaze my way. And when the bird tipped back its head and delivered a tuneless, trumpeting song, I could not help but laugh, for it was as if Father Keane had encouraged the creature to lift my spirits with its graceless holler. It gave me hope that my friend might forgive me for leading him into Death's arms, even if I could not forgive myself.

I saluted the heron and headed toward home to discover whether Dupin had managed to track Professor Frederic Renelle—antiquarian, scholar, adventurer and ruthless treasure-seeker. The sooner we knew where he resided, the more likely it was that we would find Miss Loddiges.

32

A luxuriant fragrance greeted me when I opened the door to our home—the earthy smell of roasting potatoes mixed with the sweetness of pork and baking apples lured me into the kitchen. Muddy looked up from the stove, her face radiant.

"Dinner will be ready shortly. Sissy and Mr. Dupin are in the parlor."

"Have I missed something?"

"He brought it all back from the market," she said, waving her hands at the cooking dinner. "I would not have thought a man capable, but he did very well." This was the highest of compliments from Muddy, and I knew that Dupin had won her respect, which was not easily bestowed.

When I neared the parlor I heard Sissy laughing and hovered just outside the door with surprise as I had half-expected to enter a room filled with awkward silence. I could hear the murmur of Dupin's voice, but not what he was saying. Evidently it was amusing, as my wife laughed again. Feeling somewhat disgruntled at such levity when we had only just learned of Father Nolan's terrible treachery, I made my way into the room.

"Dearest! I did not hear you come in," Sissy said. "Monsieur Dupin was telling me of the difficulties he had in communicating with one of the market ladies."

This was the happiest I'd seen my wife in several days, so I let my initial irritation pass.

"I do hope you remembered to speak in English, Dupin," I said.

"I am quite certain I did, but the accent defeated her and her confusion defeated me."

I settled into a chair. "It was most kind of you to go to the market. My mother-in-law is delighted."

"It was my pleasure and a fascinating experience."

"And what of your pursuit? Did you manage to track our quarry?"

"Father Nolan and the man who received the treasure books parted ways outside the Philosophical Hall. I followed the latter until I lost sight of him in the market. Perhaps he sensed he was being shadowed and intentionally took a diversion through the crowd there. Did you learn his identity?"

"I did. Mr. Blackwell informed me that Professor Frederic Renelle is giving a presentation at the American Philosophical Society tomorrow evening at seven o'clock."

"Renelle?" Sissy reached for the dish that held the squares of paper marked with letters that she had fashioned previously. She tipped them onto the table and quickly arranged them while Dupin closed his eyes and muttered the names of the birds we had discussed. Both arrived at the same conclusion simultaneously. "It fits," she said.

"A simple anagram. I should have seen it." Annoyance sharpened Dupin's voice.

"I am certain we wrote it down as a possibility," my wife said, "but the name could mean nothing to us without any knowledge of the person."

Dupin raised his brows, dismissing her excuse, but he was polite enough to refrain from voicing his opinion. "What is the subject of Renelle's presentation?" he asked instead.

I placed the broadsheet advertising the lecture on the table. "An expedition he made to a remote region of Peru last year. The Philosophical Society raised a subscription to contribute to the expedition's costs."

"Truly? Then there is no doubt that he is the culprit." Sissy's face was the picture of indignation.

"Little doubt," Dupin corrected her. "Did you find out where Professor Renelle resides?"

"I'm afraid not. I could not find a seemly way of inquiring."

Dupin nodded. "Caution is the best strategy. If the Philosophical Society has an interest in Renelle's expeditions, we cannot presume Mr. Blackwell to be innocent."

"That thought crossed my mind also, Dupin, but in truth I believe he has nothing to do with Professor Renelle's schemes beyond being used to raise money for his expeditions."

"Perhaps," he said, his caution no doubt springing from his anger at being successfully duped by Father Nolan.

Muddy appeared at the door. "Dinner," she announced.

We adjourned to the kitchen, where the rich smell of the food set my stomach gurgling with anticipation. Muddy had heaped our plates with roast pork topped with gravy, potatoes and baked apple. Once we were seated, Dupin cleared his throat and held up his glass of ale.

"To cherished friends. Thank you for your kind hospitality. I am forever indebted."

"It is I who is indebted to you for making the journey here," I said in return.

"Perhaps we might all agree that there is no debt between friends." My wife smiled.

"Well spoken indeed—" Dupin began.

"Enough!" Muddy looked at us with exasperation. "Please eat before it is cold."

We descended on the food with unseemly haste and conversation was replaced with the sound of cutlery on plates.

"This is delicious, madame," Dupin said to Muddy. "I do not think I have ever had a dinner of roast pork this fine in Paris."

"I'm pleased you're enjoying it," she responded with pride.

I watched Dupin for a time as we ate, looking for signs that his flattery sprang from mere etiquette rather than true feeling, but the sense of guardedness that was his normal demeanor had softened.

We continued eating in genial silence until Sissy paused and said, "It is a strange alliance between Father Nolan and Professor Renclle. Am I correct in assuming that both are benefiting from Father Nolan's theft of treasure books from the library at St. Augustine's?"

"I believe so. Father Nolan steals the books and presumably Renelle sells them, then they divide the takings—unless Father Nolan is contributing to Renelle's next expedition in the hopes that he finds the Peruvian treasure," Dupin said. "The other question we must consider," he added, looking at me, "is why Father Nolan summoned you to St. Augustine's the morning after Father Keane's murder and gave you the envelope with the library cabinet key. He could have concealed it and left you to discover that your friend was dead when you next visited."

"He must have worked out that Father Keane hid the journal, for surely it was Father Nolan who ransacked his office looking for it. He was devious enough to let us find it, and the treasure book, for him. Of course he did not have a subtle way of stopping us from taking either away from St. Augustine's without appearing guilty."

"Very true. I also suspect his claim that Father Moriarty conducts inventory of the treasure books is false—as librarian it would surely be his duty, giving him ample opportunity to conduct his illicit trade," Dupin said. "Certainly Nolan has proved himself to be utterly ruthless and manipulative when we consider Father Keane's fate. Your friend must have uncovered something that endangered Nolan's plans—perhaps his theft of the books or his association with Renelle."

The image of Father Keane sprawled on the floor, framed in splashes of colored light, returned to me like a bad dream. Dupin's supposition did seem the most likely scenario. And then I thought back to how I had been summoned to the library, how calmly Father Nolan had shown me my friend's body, which had been left on the floor since his life was stolen from him. Only a ruthless man could behave in such a way.

"Do you think Father Nolan's actions are driven purely by greed?" I asked. "I wonder if he seeks power. It is plain that he and Father Moriarty have little or no affection for each other."

Dupin considered this and nodded. "Father Nolan is an accomplished dissembler who plays the lamb to gain one's confidence and ferret out information. The lust for power often motivates such people. He pretends to be cowed by Father Moriarty, but it would not surprise me if Father Nolan covets his superior's role at St. Augustine's."

Sissy's face filled with worry. "Did he notice you at the Philosophical Hall?"

"I don't think Nolan observed either of us there," Dupin said. "I blocked your husband from his view and did my best to obscure my identity."

"Tinted spectacles and copious amounts of smoke from his meerschaum," I explained. "I myself could barely discern his features."

My wife smiled, somewhat reassured.

"The most pressing question at this time," Dupin continued, "is how to persuade Professor Renelle to invite you to his home.

We must find out if Miss Loddiges is being held there and if so how we might rescue her."

"That sounds a dangerous proposition," Sissy murmured.

"It is not without risk, but I believe we will prevail if Renelle and Nolan remain ignorant of what we have learned so far. While they both know that you have Jeremiah Mathews's journal, Poe, and that you realize someone desperately wants it, they don't know what we have gleaned from piecing together the evidence—quite literally with respect to Renelle's name. For example, they are unaware we have determined that Professor Renelle travelled to Peru with both Andrew and Jeremiah Mathews and is responsible directly or indirectly for their deaths. Or that we presume he abducted Miss Loddiges, given his desire to obtain Jeremiah Mathews's journal."

I could not fault Dupin's presumptions. Nolan knew of our determination to bring Father Keane's murderer to justice, but we had never spoken to him of our investigation into the deaths of Andrew or Jeremiah Mathews or the abduction of Miss Loddiges.

"Father Nolan may have told Renelle that we suspect treasure books have been stolen from St. Augustine's library, but will think he has duped us into believing his innocence," I said.

"But Professor Renelle certainly knows who you are, Eddy, from Helena, by name if not by sight. And Father Nolan has met both of you, so may have provided his accomplice with your descriptions," Sissy pointed out.

"We must indeed presume this is the case, hence why I stress the importance of feigning to know nothing of what Renelle is up to," Dupin said.

"Perhaps there is something to be gained by pretending to be a treasure hunter, too. If I approach Professor Renelle as an investor in his next expedition, asking for a percentage of whatever is found, he may then conclude that my interest in the journal springs from my own dreams of finding the emerald, and the king's treasure," I suggested.

"Which explains why you and your wife are at Renelle's lecture. Excellent idea. And I believe your attendance is crucial, Mrs. Poe," Dupin added, when he took note of her surprise to be included.

Muddy, who had been taking little notice of the conversation, looked as alarmed as I felt.

"How do you mean?" my wife said cautiously.

"From my assessment of the professor's attire and demeanor, he is a man full of arrogance and self-regard, the sort of man whose pride and vanity leads him into error. If you both approach him after the lecture and Poe professes a keen interest in antiquities, suggesting he wishes to invest in Renelle's next expedition, perhaps you might charm him into inviting you both to his home to discuss the proposal in more detail."

Sissy considered this and nodded. "And should we receive an invitation to Professor Renelle's, we will be able to keep him occupied while you investigate the premises and fathom the best way to rescue Miss Loddiges."

"Exactly," Dupin said. "If you have no objections. We must be bold if we are to rescue your friend."

"I have no objections. Indeed, I am determined to help."

"Poe?"

I did not like the sound of Dupin's suggestion at all, especially as it was presented in such a way as to make it difficult for Sissy to refuse.

"Let us take the measure of Renelle tomorrow evening," I said. "I will not promise anything that might put my wife in danger."

Muddy's expression was one of relief, which contrasted sharply with Sissy's look of determination.

33

WEDNESDAY, 20 MARCH 1844

The wind tasted of ice and the water was slate gray and choppy as we sailed on the steamer that would take us to the Lazaretto. We had made an early start and the morning sky still held a rosy glow that contrasted with the murky waves beneath us as we left the city, heading south along the Delaware River. Dupin was absorbed by the journey—the grand houses that lined the river, the simple design of Old Swedes Church, the factories further south. When we neared the Neck, the spot where the Delaware and Schuylkill rivers met, the smell of death permeated the air, from the industries of bone-boiling and manufacture of fertilizer. The gulls that reeled and screeched overhead were joined by more stately herons and egrets standing in the marshlands that softened the Pennsylvanian shoreline. This part of the river was renowned for its shad fishing and the animosity between the fishermen of Pennsylvania and New Jersey regarding where they might seek their prey. When Little Tinicum Island came into sight, I knew we were nearing our destination, and moments later I caught a glimpse of a yellow flag fluttering on the breeze.

"There," I said. "The Lazaretto. I am certain this place holds the truth of Jeremiah Mathews's last days. Any ship transporting collections of bird skins and plants from exotic places would be obliged to stop for what might be quite a lengthy quarantine inspection."

"I hope we will have the opportunity to see firsthand how the quarantine procedure operates," Dupin said, nodding at a ship that was moored. "It will assist us in unraveling the circumstances of Jeremiah's death—if he is indeed deceased."

"I suggest we interview both the quarantine master and the physician. There should be records of the ship's landing and all who travelled on board."

An imposing red-brick building came into view that seemed designed to give a cordial yet austere welcome to those approaching. Its central section was three stories high, with a cupola and weathervane at its top, with two wings on either side that were a story lower and gave it a pleasing symmetry. Once the steamship was docked, the captain gave a friendly nod as we disembarked. He had agreed to ferry us to and from the Lazaretto as he delivered supplies, satisfied with the handsome "gratuity" that supplemented my tale of misplaced permits to enter the station to conduct urgent business. The captain had informed us that the Quarantine Master's House was about forty yards to the southeast of the main building and the Physician's House mirrored it on the southwest side.

I began to make my way toward the quarantine master's accommodation, but Dupin paused to gaze at the moored ship, which was called the *Hopewell*. There were people on the deck, including some women with children huddled together against the cold.

"I wonder how long they have been moored here," I said. "It must be terrible to be so close to one's destination and yet forced to wait."

"Steerage passengers, I believe. The cold air must be preferable to that inside the ship."

"In my experience, that is the case even when one has a cabin," I muttered, remembering without any trace of fondness my own journeys across the Atlantic to London and back again.

"Let us go find out more," Dupin said.

When we reached the home of Mr. Pollard, the quarantine master, a servant let us in the door. We waited almost a quarter of an hour for him to appear and lead us into his study. Mr. Pollard was a lively man of about forty-five years, in well-made if ill-fitting somber clothing. From the traces of toasted bread and egg yolk in his gray mustache and beard, it seemed we had interrupted his breakfast.

"How might I help you, gentleman?" he asked after all the introductions were out of the way. "You have questions about bringing goods into the city of Philadelphia from foreign climes?" He looked from Dupin to me and back again with inquisitive dark eyes and the skittish manner of a squirrel.

"Correct, sir. We import plants and ornithological specimens of interest to the Bartram's Botanical Gardens here in Philadelphia and the Loddiges's nursery in London. We had a minor interest in a cargo that arrived from Peru in October of last year and wish to understand how better to organize our next expedition and subsequent cargo," Dupin announced before I could say a word. I hoped my face did not reveal my astonishment at his words.

"Very good," Mr. Pollard said with great approval. "If more were aware of the necessary procedures there would be far less trouble all round. My duty is to protect the city of Philadelphia from pestilence—it is of no consequence to me whether a ship is moored here for a day or a month and a day if that proves to be necessary."

"Quite right, sir. My own grandmother died of the yellow fever. No one should wish to revisit the horror of the 1793 epidemic," I said.

"Indeed," Mr. Pollard said with a shudder. "My parents survived it or I would not be here today."

"How lucky for you," Dupin said, with an utterly serious face. "If you please, tell us the procedure you go through when a ship arrives at the Lazaretto," he added.

"Well, as you will perhaps have noticed, the Lazaretto operates rather like an island, cut off from the mainland for its main purpose. Accommodation is provided for those employed here." He waved his hands at the four walls around us. "We also have extensive gardens for food, and necessary supplies are brought in by steamboat. Some of those employed here rarely leave the Lazaretto—"

"Interesting," Dupin interjected, with little attempt to conceal his impatience. "And what is the procedure when a ship arrives?"

"When inbound vessels are sighted, the lookout rings the Watch House bell to alert Dr. Henderson and myself. The ship is moored and no one is permitted to disembark. We travel out to the ship and examine both the cargo and the passengers. If the doctor finds that anyone is ill enough to require treatment in our hospital, they are then taken there and, of course, all is recorded."

"So all within the ship is examined when moored. No one disembarks and nothing is taken off the ship except under your direct instruction."

"That is correct."

"And how long does the quarantine process take?" I asked.

"Normally a day, if all are in good health and nothing on board needs fumigation. I present the ship's captain with a certificate of health and he may then sail up the river to Philadelphia."

"And what if someone is ill?" Dupin asked.

"If there is any sickness on board, or the ship has been to a port where there is known to be a contagious disease outbreak, the ship is detained here. Those afflicted are removed and taken to the hospital."

"And what of the others?" I asked.

"They must wait on board to ensure they are not harboring any disease. The ship is thoroughly scoured and its cargo fumigated with burning sulfur and alcohol."

"What is the procedure regarding ships with cargo from exotic climes, such as ornithological specimens from Peru?" Dupin queried.

"Fumigation, most certainly," Mr. Pollard said.

"Do you recall such a ship arriving from Peru last October?" Dupin continued. "It contained a cargo of ornithological specimens, plants, seeds and primitive antiquities?"

"Ornithological specimens, Peru . . ." Mr. Pollard squinted as if trying to look back in time and the frown deepened on his face. "I do have a recollection of such a cargo. There was a most troublesome investor. Came here several times and demanded to board the ship, which was, of course, not permitted."

A shiver crept up my back, like a spider. Dupin's eyes met mine and I knew he was wondering the same thing.

"Do you mean Professor Renelle?" I asked.

Mr. Pollard squinted again. "He was quite a tall fellow, or perhaps his bearing made him seem so. Hair like a lion's mane. Loud voice. Unpardonably unpleasant."

His description was very like the man we had observed with Father Nolan at the Philosophical Society.

"You say he came to the Lazaretto several times—you are certain he was not a part of the expedition?" Dupin asked.

"Sir, if he were a member of the expedition, he would be on board the ship, would he not?"

Dupin laughed. "Indeed, that is what we believed. I am afraid the fellow misled us not only about discoveries made on that journey to the mountains of Peru, but also about the fate of a young man who most certainly was on that expedition and the ship of which you speak—a young man called Jeremiah Mathews. His friends were informed that he drowned in Philadelphia, but they have no proof of his demise. We now must wonder if the young man died at all."

"The family should have received an official notification of his death," Mr. Pollard said.

"No official document was sent that we are aware of," I told him. Another shiver crept up my back. Given what we had just learned, Miss Loddiges's ghost might very well be flesh and blood as Dupin had suggested.

"I should be able to answer that for you," Mr. Pollard said. "For all is noted in the day books. October 1843, you say?"

"Indeed, sir," I confirmed.

Mr. Pollard made his way to the bookshelves and examined a row of volumes all bound in the same plain brown leather, but stamped with dates. He selected one and returned to us. "Now let me see." He opened the volume and carefully leafed through the pages, which were neatly annotated. "It is all by date. I keep a record of the ship's name, the captain, all the passengers, the ship's cargo and any notes that I deem relevant." Mr. Pollard's fingers flew through the pages until he finally said: "Twenty-fourth of October, 1843, the *Bounteous* arrived. The cargo and most of the crew originated in Peru. The expedition members sailed from Peru to Panama on the *Santa Theresa,* transported their cargo overland and then sailed north from Colón on the *Bounteous,* arriving here, as I said, on the twenty-fourth of October." Mr. Pollard looked up at us. "The ship was held in quarantine for five days. One crew member seemed to be suffering from dysentery but recovered in the hospital and no one else on board took ill."

"And was that crew member Mr. Mathews?" I asked.

Mr. Pollard glanced back down at the logbook. "It was a Peter Shaw, nineteen years of age, sailor."

"Interesting," Dupin said. "But no mention of Jeremiah Mathews?"

Mr. Pollard turned back to the log and ran his finger down the crew list. "Yes, yes. There is a Jeremiah Mathews, occupation noted as bird collector. He was quarantined on the ship with the rest of them."

"And he left the Lazaretto in good health," I said.

Mr. Pollard turned the page. "Ah, I am afraid not," he said. "The young man drowned two days after arriving. Terribly careless of him. Fell overboard."

"There were witnesses?" I asked, imagining young Mathews being pushed by some shadowy figure.

" 'The young man indulged in too much grog and was foolhardy on deck,' " Mr. Pollard read out. "That was the testimony of the captain."

"And you saw his body?" Dupin asked.

"I don't seem to recall. Many ships arrive here, you see. And it really is not my domain. Dr. Henderson will have been called to tend to the body."

"Of course," Dupin said. "You have been marvelously informative, Mr. Pollard. May I impose upon you for one more thing?"

"Yes?" Mr. Pollard said with a certain amount of caution.

"May I write down the names of the passengers who traveled with Mr. Mathews to Philadelphia?"

Mr. Pollard considered Dupin's request. "I cannot see why not," he finally said. He retrieved a sheet of paper, ink and a pen, then turned the day book to face Dupin, who quickly began to list the names of those who had arrived on the *Bounteous* with Jeremiah Mathews.

A thought occurred to me. "You say that the *Bounteous* was quarantined here at the Lazaretto for five days and then was permitted to sail on to Philadelphia. The final destination of much of the cargo from Peru was London. Did the *Bounteous* sail on to London from Philadelphia?"

"No, Philadelphia was recorded as the final destination of the *Bounteous* with that crew and cargo. If, as you say, the articles from Peru were to be sent on to London, it would be with another ship."

"And would you have inspected that ship on its way to London? We know the cargo arrived in London in early December."

"No, no," Mr. Pollard said. "A ship's cargo is inspected before it enters Philadelphia. There is no need for us to conduct a quarantine inspection when a ship leaves the city. There are warehouses up in what is known as Hell Town where cargo is stored, and ships transporting goods across the Atlantic often load up at the docks there."

Dupin and I exchanged a glance. "Warehouses near the Mermaid tavern?" I asked.

"I wouldn't know, sir, for I do not frequent Hell Town. If I wish to see drunken sailors I can watch them on the ships moored here," Mr. Pollard said smugly.

Dupin finished his handiwork with a flourish. Mr. Pollard picked up a whimsical pounce pot in the shape of a laughing goose and sprinkled the page with fine sand, then expertly tipped the pounce back into the silver goose's open bill. Satisfied that the ink was dry, Dupin folded the page and secreted it in his pocket.

"We cannot thank you enough for your assistance, Mr. Pollard," he said, rising to his feet.

"If only all were as courteous and helpful as you have proven to be. Thank you, sir," I added, as I too stood up. Mr. Pollard rose from his chair, a rather disappointed look on his face.

"It was my pleasure. It is not often that I have the opportunity to speak of my work with learned fellows such as yourselves."

"Perhaps you should make a presentation at the Philosophical

Society?" I suggested. "I believe you would find an attentive audience there."

Mr. Pollard brightened at the thought. "I will certainly consider that."

We left the gentleman dwelling on that idea and made our way to Dr. Henderson's accommodation. A housekeeper opened the door and informed us that Dr. Henderson had gone to the quarantined ship to do his rounds, so we walked over to the wharf and waited for his boat to return.

"This has been a most productive journey," Dupin said. "Miss Loddiges's fears regarding Andrew Mathews and his son seem to have basis in fact after all."

"Yes, I fear I was in error to dismiss the lady's story as nonsense."

"It is not unusual to disbelieve tales of ghosts and warnings from birds when we hear them and, indeed, skepticism is typically a logical approach to such matters," Dupin said. "I hope that we will be clearer still about Jeremiah Mathews's fate once we hear what the doctor has to tell us." He nodded at two men climbing from the ship into the barge that was moored to it. It wasn't long before the bargeman delivered the doctor to the shore and we introduced ourselves. Dr. Henderson was as reserved as Mr. Pollard was loquacious and his frame was so spare that it looked as if he felt the act of consuming food was a mortal sin.

"I do not recall the ship you mention," he said after hearing details of the arrival of the *Bounteous* and Jeremiah Mathews's apparent death by drowning. "As you might imagine, numerous vessels arrive at the Lazaretto and one would need a prodigious memory to recall even a quarter of them."

"Of course. But you must keep a log, as Mr. Pollard does," Dupin observed. "It would be most helpful if you would check your notes for us, please."

"I am extremely busy, gentlemen."

"And your time is valuable, sir. But it is imperative that I avail myself of your knowledge, for I will be returning to Paris in the next few days and there are certain facts I must present to the prefect of police there, for whom I have undertaken an urgent task. Here, let me present my card." Dupin removed a card case from his coat pocket and with some sleight of hand passed several gold coins along with his personal card. Dr. Henderson immediately became more accommodating.

"Remind me of the date the ship arrived at the Lazaretto?"

"Twenty-fourth of October, 1843."

"A ship from Panama with passengers and cargo from Peru?"

"Yes," I said. "And a young man, Jeremiah Mathews, who drowned according to Mr. Pollard. We wish to know more details of his fate."

"Come with me." Dr. Henderson led us back to his accommodation and into an office with a desk and a quantity of books. He had his own shelf of leather-bound logbooks and quickly selected the relevant tome, then leafed through it with his overly large yet dextrous hands.

"Here we are. Jeremiah Mathews. Born fifteenth of July, 1821, deceased twenty-sixth of October, 1843. His body was seen by the watchman that morning, but he was too long drowned to be revived. He was identified by the ship's captain, who received a certificate of his death."

"But not the body?" Dupin said.

"No, he is buried here," Dr. Henderson said. "That is normal procedure. We cannot release the deceased for fear of the spread of infection."

"Even if the deceased is drowned?"

Dr. Henderson shrugged. "It is procedure. In any case, sailors are a superstitious lot and reluctant to transport a corpse for fear of pestilence and ill luck from spirits."

"Would you mind showing us where he is buried? I should

like to be able to convey the details of his resting spot to a dear friend of his."

Dr. Henderson nodded. "I believe I will be able to locate it." He marched from the room, and we hurried after.

We walked through the pleasant grounds of the Lazaretto, which bustled with the activities of those employed there: farmhands, general laborers, nurses, washerwomen, cooks and cleaners. The outbuildings were attractive and the area pleasingly landscaped. The vegetable gardens were large and there was an array of farm animals—chickens, pigs, cows, goats—to provide food for those who lived and labored there. It wasn't long before we arrived at a burial ground that had none of the hopeful pomp of many cemeteries I had visited. Here each grave was marked with a simple wooden cross with a name and date of birth and death inscribed upon it in black paint. The oldest graves were the furthest away and the dead were buried according to date of demise. Dr. Henderson made his way to a small wooden cross upon which was written: *Jeremiah Mathews 1821–1843*. It was a forlorn sight, one that I felt would only add to Miss Loddiges's sorrow. It made me even more determined to bring the young man's killer to justice, for surely he had been murdered and thrown into the river.

Dupin broke the silence. "Thank you, Dr. Henderson. Your assistance is deeply appreciated."

"It was my pleasure."

"One more question, sir," I said, as we walked away from the burial ground. "You mentioned that the watchman spied Mr. Mathews's body in the water and you found that it was too late to revive him. Is there any way of knowing whether Mr. Mathews died from drowning or if he was dead before he landed in the water?"

Dr. Henderson thought about this as we made our way to the wharf closest to where the *Hopewell* was anchored. "Not decisively. If Mr. Mathews had a visible wound, it would have been considered as a possible cause of death. Obviously that was not the case and witnesses stated that the victim had imbibed a surfeit of alcohol," the doctor said stiffly.

"Of course you would have investigated any wounds upon Jeremiah Mathews's person," I continued. "But if he were poisoned or perhaps struck unconscious and thrown into the water, it would not be immediately apparent."

"No," Dr. Henderson conceded.

"I see."

Dupin laughed as if I had been jesting. "My friend has quite an imagination. If young Mr. Mathews survived the journey all the way from Peru to the Philadelphia Lazaretto with all who were on board the *Bounteous*, it makes little sense that he would be murdered here." Dupin raised his brows at me and I realized from that subtle gesture that he did not entirely trust the good doctor. An infant's wail sailed on the breeze to us and drew our gaze to the vessel moored in the waters before us. More passengers had gathered on the *Hopewell*'s decks since we had arrived at the Lazaretto, and the infant's cries seem to sum up the general mood of the ship's passengers.

"Before we part ways, good sir, tell us about the *Hopewell*. Where did she sail from? What is her cargo?" I asked.

"She is from Liverpool and her cargo is those you see on her decks."

"How long has the *Hopewell* been moored here?" Dupin's tone was casual.

"Five days. There were several cases of black tongue on board. Two have died. So we must wait and see if more fall ill or if we are to send forth more papists to fill the slums of Southwark and Kensington," he said without any effort to hide his contempt for the *Hopewell*'s passengers.

Dupin's expression suggested that something had been confirmed to him.

"Thank you again, Dr. Henderson," I said.

"My pleasure." The doctor turned to leave.

"*Phileo adelphos,*" Dupin said, voice slightly raised. The doctor turned his head to look back at him, brow furrowed. "The love of one's brother," Dupin continued, his tone acerbic. "The Quaker William Penn named your city with great optimism. Good day to you, sir." He bowed with mock gravity and walked toward the wharf without a backward glance.

34

We arrived at the Front Street wharf at half past two and made our way to the Mermaid tavern with the aim of uncovering information regarding the crew of the *Bounteous,* but my rumbling belly demanded sustenance, and I hoped we might also find something edible to ease the pangs of hunger. As we stepped from the afternoon light into the deep shadow of the tavern, the noise of tipplers who had imbibed too much and the smell of greasy food assaulted us. We made our way to a space at the counter and Dupin ordered two tankards of ale from the tavern keeper, a tall, brown-skinned man so full of muscle that few would dare to antagonize him.

"Might we also have something to eat? A plate of cheese and bread, perhaps," I suggested, as the tavern keeper passed us our tankards. I didn't think it wise to have any meat or even fish, despite our proximity to the river. Dupin surveyed the drinkers ensconced at the dingy tables, several of whom were wolfing down their dinners.

"What is the soup?" he asked.

"Oyster," the tavern keeper replied.

Dupin examined the food that was visible on the shelves behind the bar. "Two cups of the soup, bread, cheese, the smoked sausage and the pâté there."

"Liverwurst," the tavern keeper corrected him.

"And what is that?" He indicated a large jar of spherical objects in wine-colored liquid.

"Pickled eggs in beet juice."

"Two of those."

The tavern keeper began to fill two plates with food.

"Would you know if any of your customers might have sailed back from Peru last autumn?" Dupin asked.

The tavern keeper scrutinized him for a moment, then said: "There was some talk of Peru, but I can't recall more than that. She'll know." He nodded at Mrs. Mermaid, who was stationed in exactly the same place as before, her potions in baskets around her feet and her hyacinth macaw perched on her shoulder, snacking on tasty morsels he found lurking in her tufts of gray hair.

Dupin looked dubious. "There is no one with perhaps a better memory?"

The tavern keeper shook his head.

"Make up a plate of whatever she likes best," Dupin instructed. "And a drink." He placed a silver dollar on the counter. The tavern keeper slid some coins back his way, but Dupin held up his hand in dismissal and the tavern keeper pocketed them, his mouth edging toward a smile. The taciturn fellow heaped the third plate high with food and filled a cup with a noxious-looking drink from an unlabeled bottle. He nodded at Mrs. Mermaid.

"I'll bring it over."

We picked up our tankards and plates, then made our way to an empty table directly in front of the lady. Just as we sat down, the tavern keeper brought Mrs. Mermaid her dinner and whispered something into her ear. She nodded and fixed a rheumy eye of turquoise on each of us, which was a disconcerting feat in itself.

"Kind of you, gentlemen. I was getting quite peckish." She spit her chewing tobacco onto the floor and I fear I winced, for she laughed and raised her cup to me. "Here's to your good fortune." She took a deep drink of the stuff, then attacked the food in front of her with such ferocity I hoped I would never meet her in a lonesome spot at night. "So, my dears, you're wanting information about sailors gone to Peru."

"Indeed, madame. On a ship called the *Bounteous*, arrived at the Lazaretto on the twenty-fourth of October, then at the docks here a week later."

The old woman contemplated this as she gnawed on a link of smoked sausage, her teeth surprisingly large and sturdy-looking for one of her apparent age. I had expected the stench of her to be overpowering, but her ancient clothes were surprisingly clean, yellowed with age rather than dirt. She smelled of camphor and vinegar and had sprigs of dried rosemary pinned to her bonnet and breast as if they were brooches.

"I know more of the ships that depart from the port here, as the sailors come to me for various essentials."

"Some of the crew from the *Bounteous* sailed on to London with cargo from Peru—bird skins, plants, some artifacts from the natives there," Dupin said. "Would you know of any sailors who were on that ship?"

The old lady did not immediately answer, directing her attention to the remainder of her dinner. Dupin and I slowly spooned soup into our mouths and watched her.

"And your connection to the ship?" she asked.

I was not certain we should reveal anything of consequence to her, given that the insalubrious place we were in was frequented by priests who had sent a lockpick to my house and had, perhaps, murdered my friend.

"A young man, Jeremiah Mathews, died on the *Bounteous* at

the Lazaretto. Or, more precisely, he drowned. We believe he was murdered," Dupin said.

"Do you now." She drank back the remains of the liquid in her cup. "I'd enjoy another of those," she said, jiggling the empty vessel.

Dupin turned to the tavern keeper, who simply nodded and poured another dose of the stuff and brought it over.

"Fetch Davey down," she said to the tavern keeper. He nodded again and disappeared through a door that seemed to lead upstairs. Both Dupin and I tensed at this and she cackled. "Fear not, my friends, fear not." She reached into her bosom and removed a small cloth bundle. She gently unrolled it on the tabletop and I was horrified to see what appeared to be a human finger bone lying on the cloth. "Davey brought it back from that ancient city for me. It's the finger of an Indian emperor—very powerful magic. And very costly," she added, eyeing us with the gleam of avarice in her eyes.

Dupin looked at the bone, then said politely, "I'm sure you will get a very good price for it, madame."

She directed her gaze to me, but I quickly shook my head and with a sigh she wrapped the thing up and tucked it into her bosom again.

"You wanted me?"

Dupin and I turned to see a boy of about eleven years. My friend's face tensed with annoyance, certain that we had been duped.

"You sailed on the *Bounteous* with Jeremiah Mathews?" I said, skepticism sharpening my voice.

He nodded. "I did. My father was a sailor and my mother's dead," he added, as if that explained anything. "Mostly I'm on the ships—they send me up the crow's nest and I do whatever chores they give me. And if not on the ships I'm here at my uncle's tavern."

Dupin's face relaxed and he said, "Tell us what you know of Mr. Mathews."

"He drew lovely pictures—birds and plants mostly, but also the mules and sometimes the fellows to make them laugh." The boy was grinning with the memory, then his face dropped. "I was very sorry when he died."

"Had he too much to drink the night he drowned?" Dupin asked.

"That's what they told the men at the Lazaretto," Davey said cautiously.

"But you don't believe that was the truth of it?" Dupin pressed.

"Tell all, lad. You have nowt to fear," Mrs. Mermaid said.

"Jeremiah was a teetotaler."

"So you do not believe he was inebriated and fell in the water?"

The boy shrugged and shook his head. "I tried to tell the doctor at the Lazaretto but he wouldn't listen."

"I presume you were not on the expedition to the lost city and you took the bone from the cargo they brought back," Dupin said, and the boy nodded sheepishly. "Did you hear anyone mention a jewel? Or any kind of treasure?"

Davey's eyes went wide, as if Dupin had supernatural powers and had somehow read his mind. "There was talk that Jeremiah had found treasure in the ancient city, but no one saw anything but dead birds and plants and bits of pottery and cloth. Some of the crew said that Jeremiah kept the treasure in his cabin as the door was always shut and no one was allowed inside but him."

"What happened to all that was in Mr. Mathews's cabin after he died?"

"First the professor came and said he needed to get on the ship, but the quarantine master forbade it."

"Professor Renelle?" I interjected.

"Yes," Davey replied. "The quarantine master didn't like him much and said nothing could leave the ship until it was disinfected." The boy smirked. "He was terrible angry and said it was his expedition and everything on the ship was his, but nothing he did changed the quarantine master's mind."

"What truly happened to Jeremiah?" I asked.

Davey's face crumpled and for a moment he struggled to find his words. "The Schuylkill rangers came very late one night and took things from Jeremiah's cabin—I heard them board, but stayed in my bunk because you don't get in their way, you let them take what they want. Everyone knows that." He shook his head. "So I didn't see exactly what happened. But next morning Jeremiah was found floating in the water, drowned. And the captain told the story of him being on the grog and falling overboard."

"I'm sorry. That must have been terrible for you, Davey," I said. The boy nodded, like the young man's death was his fault.

"The items from Jeremiah Mathews's cabin—were they smuggled away from the Lazaretto?" Dupin asked.

"That's what I heard from those who saw the rangers. That's what always happens." He shrugged. Then a thought came to the boy and he looked at us with a glimmer of pride in his eyes. "But not his book with the bird drawings. They didn't get that. He had me send it to his lady friend in England when we were in Panama. He didn't trust the two priests that came along on the expedition with the professor. They were always watching him."

Dupin looked to me and I knew he was wondering the same thing that I was—were they the men we had seen at the Mermaid on Saturday night with Billy Sweeney?

"Do these two priests ever frequent the Mermaid?" I asked.

Davey nodded. "They like their drink all right."

"And pay for it with coin that falls into their laps direct from Heaven," Mrs. Mermaid guffawed.

"How convenient," Dupin said with a cynical smile.

"And were these priests friends of Professor Renelle?" I asked Davey.

The boy frowned. "I wouldn't call them friends. In fact I don't think they liked each other at all. The priests continued on the expedition when Professor Renelle stopped in Cuzco."

Dupin became focused, like a dog that catches its quarry's scent. "The professor stayed in Cuzco? Why?"

"He got very sick on the journey from Lima to Cuzco. He said someone poisoned his water."

"Why didn't they call off the expedition if Professor Renelle was ill?" Dupin asked.

"He wanted to call it off, but Jeremiah and the two priests refused. Jeremiah said that his job was to collect birds and plants for his employer in England who had paid for most of the expedition, and the priests said that the Church had made a big contribution too, and they would go with Jeremiah to the lost city. They took the professor to stay with priests they knew who were living in Cuzco."

"Augustinians?" Dupin asked.

Davey considered the word for a moment, then nodded. "That's it. They were in Cuzco to turn people Catholic."

"And what about you, Davey? We established that you didn't truly go to the lost city, but I presume you went to Cuzco from what you observed. Did you stay with Professor Renelle and the Augustinians?" I asked.

Davey shook his head. "I stayed with Jeremiah's aunt. I wanted to go to the lost city, but Jeremiah said it was too dangerous. And he wanted me to keep an eye on Professor Renelle, so I did." The boy smiled, proud that he'd done his friend's bidding.

"What did the professor do in Cuzco?" I asked.

"At first, nothing, because he was sick. A Peruvian lady Jeremiah's aunt knows brought him special tea and after a week he was better. The professor wanted to go after them to the lost city, but he couldn't get anyone to take him there, and not even he dared go into the mountains on his own. No one knew when Jeremiah and the others would come back, so after a few days waiting and causing a fuss everywhere, the professor decided to return to Philadelphia."

"Presumably it was not a decision he was pleased to make," I said.

"He was very angry. He said he hoped they would all die in the mountains." A smile twitched at the boy's lips. "The priests from the mission all went straight to the grog house after the professor left and raised a few to thank the Lord for persuading him to go back to whatever Hell he came from."

Dupin huffed at that. "And how did Professor Renelle get back to Philadelphia? The ship on which you sailed to Lima?"

"No, sir, not on the *Santa Theresa*. The ship waited for the expedition party. Professor Renelle made his own way back, but on what ship I do not know."

"If Renelle had sailed away on the *Santa Theresa* he would not have been able to claim he was with the expedition party and might have forfeited any share he negotiated in specimens or artifacts collected on the expedition," Dupin suggested.

"And in lying about his participation in the expedition, he preserved the right to keep that share?"

Dupin nodded. "Although I suspect he only realised this when arguing his right to sail away on the *Santa Theresa* with the ship's captain in Lima."

"From what we have heard and pieced together, Professor Renelle seems to be a man with an unpleasant temper who is accustomed to getting his own way." I turned back to Davey. "Thank you for your help. You're a good lad. We will do our best to secure justice for Jeremiah Mathews." I patted the boy on the shoulder, then turned to the formidable Mrs. Mermaid. "And thank you, madam. We appreciate your help."

"It was my pleasure," she said grandly.

Dupin stood and dipped his head to the lady. "Madame, the pleasure was entirely ours. Good day to you."

As we turned to go, Davey's voice piped up. "Do you know if the lady in England received Jeremiah's book with his drawings?"

"She did, Davey, and she is very grateful," I assured him.

The boy smiled. "Jeremiah would be pleased at that."

I did not tell him that Miss Loddiges was held captive by the man who, in all probability, had Jeremiah Mathews killed.

35

All above us was cerulean, like some exotic sea, with the buildings of Philadelphia set out in stark relief against that tranquil
expanse. Dupin, Sissy and I were walking down Seventh Street,
each silently enjoying the pure beauty of that fantastical hour
just after sunset when the veil between earth and heaven seems
at its most fragile. I felt Sissy jump, as did I, when a dark cloud
burst up from the horizon and swarmed across the glowing
blue. At first I thought it to be a flock of night birds, then realized from the creatures' strange darting and wheeling that it
was in fact a colony of bats.

"*Eptesicus fuscus*, I believe," Dupin said as if in response to my
silent query. "Large brown bats." Sissy gave a small huff of
disgust, which amused him. "Useful creatures, these bats. They
consume insects that destroy food crops."

"I fear I can only perceive them as birds with teeth," Sissy
muttered.

"In truth, bats are mammals, not birds," Dupin began.

"And, in truth, that does not comfort me at all," my wife
countered as we turned onto Chestnut Street. "Let us think of
more palatable things, please. For example, we are approaching
some of the most important buildings in Philadelphia. I

presume you and Eddy did not take the time to admire them during your first visit to the Philosophical Hall?"

"You are quite correct," Dupin said with a faint smile.

Moments later, Sissy came to a halt and indicated an imposing rectangular brick building with a tall clock tower and a smaller building with arched windows and a stately cupola. "Independence Hall and City Hall. While gaslight lends a certain romantic charm to our surroundings, it is more rewarding to visit by daylight," she added. It seemed she did not recall the tales I had told her of Dupin's predilection for nocturnal wanderings through his home city.

"I hope I will have time to see the city as a tourist might once Miss Loddiges is safe," Dupin said.

"Then let us do our best to secure an invitation to Professor Renelle's residence." I turned to continue our journey to the Philosophical Hall, but Dupin raised a hand to halt me.

"May I suggest that you and your wife enter the lecture hall first and that I follow separately? I believe it would be to our advantage to pretend we are not acquainted. I will conceal myself at the back. Once the lecture has concluded, let us rendezvous at your home."

"Yes, fine. And I will do my utmost to arrange a meeting with Professor Renelle."

"The sooner the better." Dupin retrieved his meerschaum from his pocket and lit it, then turned away to examine the grand buildings before him, as the last tint of cerulean turned to black.

Sissy and I made our way around the corner to Fifth Street and found ourselves amongst a group of people waiting to enter the Philosophical Hall. The mood of the crowd was convivial and I overheard remarks about Professor Renelle's great courage, intellect and expertise in all to do with the exploration of South America.

Once inside, we made our way upstairs, where we passed by a table at which Mr. Blackwell was stationed, collecting what was essentially an admission fee but which he deemed a small contribution to help finance Professor Renelle's next wondrous expedition.

"Good evening, sir," Mr. Blackwell said, when we arrived at the table. "I hope you will enjoy the presentation and look forward to hearing your opinion."

"I will certainly let you know what I think," I replied, handing him the entry fee.

Sissy and I entered the spacious lecture room and made our way to the front, where there was a table arranged with what I presumed were Peruvian artifacts: pottery, some jewelry made with exotic plumage, brightly colored textiles and a few ornaments in the shape of indigenous animals fashioned in gold and silver.

"Do you think that is a chieftain's necklace?" Sissy wondered, indicating an odd, woven piece with a cascade of strings tied with knots that formed a pattern.

"I would imagine this is more likely to be worn by a chieftain." I indicated a golden bird of prey that was about five inches across with its wings outstretched, suspended by a collar of that same precious metal. "Perhaps this one is a quipu, if you recall the woven object described in Fernández's book."

Sissy nodded. "It does seem to resemble his description. I suppose we will soon know," she said, smiling.

We took seats in the second row and the chairs around us quickly filled with chattering people. It was clear that Professor Renelle's presentation was highly anticipated and as I eavesdropped on my fellow audience members, I learned that he was considered a noteworthy speaker and there was no shortage of interest in the next expedition he wished to undertake.

At a few minutes before seven o'clock, the professor himself entered the room, exuding an air of supreme confidence, and made his way up the path through the audience, tapping the floorboards firmly with his walking stick as if to direct everyone's attention to him. Mr. Blackwell trotted after him and a third man pushed a wooden trolley, on which was situated a very handsome magic lantern. Professor Renelle indicated that it should be placed to the left of the table, facing the white wall in front of the audience. Mr. Blackwell fussed until all was to the professor's liking, then cleared his throat pointedly.

"Good evening, ladies and gentlemen. Welcome to the American Philosophical Society, the first learned society in our nation," Mr. Blackwell announced with a flourish, which was duly met with enthusiastic applause. "We are delighted to have with us tonight Professor Frederic Renelle, scholar of the ancient civilizations of South America, expedition leader and collector of antiquities. Professor Renelle has traveled extensively through Mexico and Peru, along the great Amazon River and into remote mountain regions. Tonight he will present a lecture on his travels through the Chachapoyas region of Peru in pursuit of the lost cities of the Cloud Warriors." Mr. Blackwell took a step to the side, raising his hands to applaud Professor Renelle, and we followed his lead.

But before the professor could begin his presentation, the door at the back of the hall opened and, with a dramatic rustling of skirts, a lady made her entrance, which was met by low gasps of surprise.

"It's Mrs. Reynolds!" my wife whispered, and I heard others sitting around us echo the same hushed exclamation.

I watched as the actress scanned the room, pausing to soak up the adulation. She was dressed in a velvet frock the color of lilacs, decorated with flurries of lace and heavily embellished with white silk embroidered blossoms. Violet plumes adorned her hair, and her pale face had clearly been enameled by the enterprising Mrs. Laird for the occasion.

"I am sorry we were delayed, Professor Renelle," she announced, her voice reaching every corner of the room as if it were a theater.

Professor Renelle glared at the lady, before forcing his lips into a false smile "I am sure your delay was unavoidable," he said with just enough sarcasm that the actress's eyes narrowed. "Please, we have seats reserved for you."

Mr. Blackwell rushed to escort Mrs. Reynolds to her chair, and as she stepped further into the room my heart dropped, for she was followed by the man I had hoped never to see again, scrivener turned playwright, Mr. George Reynolds, who wished me nothing but bad fortune. Worse still, Mr. Blackwell was leading the couple toward the two empty chairs at the center of the row in front of us, and there seemed little chance of George Reynolds missing my presence. All waited patiently as the actress settled in, pleased to be in such close proximity to the "Undisputed Queen of the Theater Boards", as she was known on the playbills, while I fervently wished I had selected seats at the back of the room.

My wife perceived my tension, for she gently squeezed my hand and murmured, "Let us focus on our task, my dear."

I nodded my agreement and did my best to comply with her wise advice.

"Now that we are all settled," the professor announced in a sonorous voice made less pleasant by its nuance of self-entitlement, "thank you for coming to my presentation." His gaze was fierce and aimed at the crowd, yet did not seem to attach itself to any individual—it was as if he were a lion surveying his kingdom.

As Professor Renelle pronounced the usual platitudes to ingratiate himself with his audience, I focused on the man's appearance rather than his words, determined to memorize every detail of him. His features were unremarkable, but his expression was haughty. He was very well dressed in a black suit, elegant white shirt and an expensive waistcoat that was overly showy, with vivid stripes of cobalt, lavender and gold. A very large diamond pin glinted from his neckcloth, his shoes were buffed to a mirror finish, and he wore a ring on the smallest finger of his right hand with a large dark-blue cabochon stone—perhaps lapis lazuli.

My scrutiny was interrupted when Professor Renelle turned his attention to the magic lantern, lighting its Argand lamp, then raising his hand to someone at the back of the room. The illumination from the chandelier was extinguished, leaving us in momentary shadow.

"The land of Peru is untamed and hostile and our small troop relied on native guides to take us along pathways few had dared to traverse. The journey was arduous but to explore the unexplored in the name of science made it worthwhile."

Moments later an image appeared on the wall in front of us, a scene that might have been taken from *Las Costumbres de la Gente de las Nubes*. In the foreground was a small troop of explorers, those riding mules following others with machetes in hand, and in the background were the tall Chachapoyan mountains, luminous green in color, surrounded by a bright blue sky. The picture was skillfully drawn and so beautifully tinted it appeared that we were looking through a window into that very world.

"And yet, despite the dangers battled, I observed flora and fauna of astonishing beauty and encountered species hitherto unknown to science. Some we merely recorded, but we also brought back numerous plant and bird samples for scientists to study and for the public to examine in our museums."

The audience burst into spontaneous applause as exotic flowers bloomed upon the wall: brightly colored orchids that were beautiful and strange, some resembling insects and one with the face of a monkey. There were peculiar blossoms shaped like lobster claws in vibrant sunset colors, torch gingers with showy magenta petals and graceful ferns in soothing green.

When the first bird appeared on the wall, it seemed that it had flown from the lantern itself to open sky before us. Sissy and I both gasped, for not only was the emerald and topaz hummingbird, exquisite and seemingly alive, it was identical to one of the birds depicted so beautifully by Andrew Mathews on a page from his journal. The audience echoed our gasp of surprise as Renelle managed, with some trickery of the lantern, to make it appear that the hummingbird was rapidly flittering its wings. Several other gem-colored hummingbirds appeared before us, flying above verdant foliage or sipping nectar from luminous flowers. These were followed by birds we had seen on display at the Academy of Natural Sciences—a pair of vibrant trogons, a charm of finches, a parrot, the strange tangerine-and-black cock-of-the-rocks, a soaring condor—and somehow they seemed far more real than any taxidermied specimens due to Renelle's wizardry with the magic lantern and the artistry of Andrew Mathews's ornithological drawings transferred onto glass. It was a magical display and Professor Renelle knew his audience well, for all were utterly engaged as he spoke.

"But there is much more to find in the wild mountains of Peru, not just strange new birds and flowers, but something even more startling. Civilized man had not ventured into this terrain in three centuries and imagine my wonderment when I discovered a lost city high up in the Chachapoyas."

The next image could have been plucked from my own fantasy, for it was of eight peculiar sarcophagi with enormous heads and dark, empty eyes stationed on a vertiginous clifftop. A chill went through me, so unearthly were the creatures suspended before us, and my disquiet was shared by those around me, as the audience murmured and shuffled with unease.

"This is the final refuge of the Cloud Warriors, a war-like race feared by the other natives of the region. Consider our astonishment when we came upon these." Renelle pointed at the monstrous-looking creatures. "The Cloud Warriors constructed these idols—these immense clay statues of their gods—upon an almost inaccessible cliff face, to terrify their enemies and keep their people safe." Renelle paused for a moment and gazed at the crowd before him. "But they failed. The Cloud Warriors are no more, defeated by the Spanish conquistadors and the Peruvian Inca tribe three hundred years ago."

Professor Renelle let his audience absorb this, and then a new image appeared, a masterly portrait of a fair-skinned man with blue eyes and long, straight black hair. Upon his head was a golden crown shaped from two emerald-studded serpents that faced each other, jaws agape to hold between them an emerald the size of a turkey egg. A life-sized golden humming-bird in flight was mounted above the emerald, as if perched upon it.

"This is a reproduction of a drawing of the last king of the Cloud Warriors by a sixteenth-century Spanish priest. The Spaniards came across this very city soon after it was abandoned and found valuable artifacts within a chamber behind these statues. They heard a legend told amongst the natives of the region that the Cloud Warrior king was buried in a tomb filled with treasure, including his crown, which was set with an enormous, magical emerald—the jewel of Peru. It was also said that the Cloud Warriors made a map—a *derrotero*—that revealed the secret location of the king's tomb with its treasure." Professor Renelle paused dramatically, and moments

later a new image appeared on the wall that made the entire
audience cry out, for it was a hideous depiction of a skull that
appeared to be screaming, its hands held up in horror by its
face.

"I mentioned that the idols of the Cloud Warriors were built
upon an almost inaccessible cliff—*almost* inaccessible. We
managed to scale that cliff and behind the idols there was a cave
with strange primitive paintings upon the wall, the same cave in
which the Spaniards found silver, gold and emeralds a few
hundred years ago. I hoped that we might find the king's tomb
there, but instead we discovered mummified Cloud Warriors.
This particular warrior," he said, indicating the screaming skull,
"had numerous objects around him in his burial alcove." He
signaled and the chandelier glowed again, bathing the room in
light while the professor extinguished the magic lantern, sending the ghastly, glowing skull back to the netherworld. Professor
Renelle then indicated the objects on the table. "This is but a
small selection of the goods we found with him—everyday
objects intended for his use in the afterlife, gold and silver ornaments, feathered necklaces and armbands, and this." Renelle
held up the strange woven object Sissy and I had discussed.
"Native Peruvians call it a 'quipu'. It is constructed from fibers
made from alpaca or llama hair and often dyed like this." He
indicated the red coloring and how some of the strings were
knotted. "Such objects are quite rare and burial with a quipu
suggests that the mummy was a person of considerable standing, perhaps royalty." Professor Renelle returned the quipu to
the table.

"And so, ladies and gentlemen, I trust you understand why it
is of great scientific interest for me to return to the Chachapoyas
in Peru, not only to gather further specimens of creatures not
found in these climes, but also in hopes of locating this great
hoard of antiquities and the remains of the king of the Cloud

Warriors. If you have enjoyed this presentation and support the quest for new knowledge, please take the opportunity to make a contribution to our next great expedition. Any amount will bring us nearer to our goal, but those who contribute twenty-five dollars or more will receive a set of ten magic lantern copper-plate slides such as those you saw tonight, either a selection of ten birds or ten exotic Peruvian flowers, or five of each. Please see Mr. Blackwell at the table in the hallway should you wish to make a contribution. Many thanks for your kind attention." Professor Renelle bowed and the audience applauded loudly.

My wife leaned toward me and whispered, "I'm going to say hello to Mrs. Reynolds before she is surrounded by admirers."

I had no desire to talk to the lady and even less interest in exchanging mock pleasantries with her husband, or, worse still, introducing him to Sissy.

"Truly we need to speak with Professor Renelle and try to secure an invitation to his home." As I glanced at the professor, I saw that he was staring at someone at the back of the room and I followed his gaze. I was startled to catch sight of Jeremiah Mathews—or a man who looked so similar as to be his doppelgänger. The man seemed to notice Renelle's gaze upon him and quickly exited the room. At first I thought the professor would follow, but an audience member intercepted him at the very moment I was cornered by my nemesis.

"Mr. Poe, Rowena said that we might meet again and, as usual, she was correct." George Reynolds stood in front of me, his arm linked through his wife's. She smiled at Sissy with what appeared to be genuine pleasure.

"Mrs. Poe, how delightful to see you again," the actress said. "And you, Mr. Poe," she added, acknowledging me as royalty might a commoner.

"It is fully my pleasure to see you," Sissy replied. "Did you enjoy the magic lantern show? I thought it marvelous."

"I did," Mrs. Reynolds said with apparent surprise. "Professor Renelle pestered me to attend and truly I had no desire to waste a free evening sitting through a dull lecture."

"Rowena had her fill of interminable literary recitations in London," George Reynolds smirked.

"Oh, hush, George," the lady murmured, giving him a fierce glare before turning back to Sissy. "We are often invited to tedious events by those who hope to use our attendance to pull in a crowd, and that was indeed the professor's game." She glanced toward Renelle then blinked her eyes in theatrical exasperation. "The man is such a bore. He is surrounded by people who might very well invest in his next foolhardy adventure, but he watches us and waits to pounce like a jaguar from a Peruvian jungle." She laughed then added, "But his performance did surprise me. He has picked up some skills from his years of being a patron to the theater. And the images were divine. I was transported to the mountains of Peru."

"Yes," Sissy agreed. "It was magical. I am so glad we came." Her warm smile at Mrs. Reynolds faltered when Reynolds pressed closer to his wife, directing his wolfish gaze at Sissy in such a way that it was impossible for her to escape it.

"I don't know why, Poe, but I have the sense that you do not wish to introduce me to your wife. Rowena has had the pleasure and was enchanted. You and I must surely agree—you do not deserve her."

"George, please," his wife said, her impatience clear.

"Indeed, you are correct," I said. "Such are the trials of men like us who marry women that exceed them in every way. We must agree on that too, Mr. *Reynolds*." I could not help but raise my brows as I said his name and he glared at my impertinence.

"And who could ever come close to Mrs. Reynolds in talent or beauty?" Professor Renelle pushed his way into our circle and glanced from Reynolds to me. His expression made it clear that he had witnessed our sparring match.

"Well done, Professor Renelle. It was quite the show. I will strongly encourage my friends to attend your next presentation," Mrs. Reynolds said.

"Please do. Let me take you to the magic lantern slides. Should you care to lend your support to our next expedition, I would be happy to present you with a full set of slides."

"Darling, we must hurry," Reynolds said to his wife. "We are late already."

"I am sorry to disappoint, Professor Reynolds. Farewell, Mr. and Mrs. Poe. Always a delight." She nodded at us and made her way to the door with surprising speed.

"A pleasure to finally make your acquaintance, Mrs. Poe," Reynolds said to Sissy with a malevolent expression he did not bother to hide. "Goodbye, Poe. You are a lucky man." His tone left little doubt that he was referring to his reluctant pledge to forget the history between our families. Reynolds strode after his wife, leaving us with a disgruntled Professor Renelle, whose eyes followed the Reynolds as they tried to exit the room, waylaid at each step by well-wishers.

"Sir, let me extend our congratulations. We were mightily impressed with your fascinating presentation. I am Edgar Poe and this is my wife."

Renelle's attention returned to us. "Mr. Poe the writer? I have read your stories, of course. How wonderful to meet you in the flesh," the professor said in a way that unsettled me. Was it mere flattery in hopes of a contribution to his next expedition or was he suspicious of our attendance? I hoped the man's excessive self-belief would make him presume that any person with an interest in the arts and sciences would wish to attend his lectures.

"I was amazed by the magic lantern show," Sissy added. "It takes enormous skill to make your audience feel as if they were on the expedition with you."

Sissy's flattering words captured the professor's attention. "I am glad you perceived the skill required. Not many do," he said, smiling like a fox. I understood why Dupin had suggested that Sissy attend the lecture—he had accurately assessed Renelle as a rake.

"The skeleton was more than gruesome," she shuddered, "but the tale of the king's tomb and the *derrotero* was fascinating."

"I had a thought regarding that," I said quickly. "I have a great passion for ciphers, conundrums and the like, and have something of a reputation for unraveling such puzzles. The quipu and its construction is most intriguing. Have you considered that it may be more than a mere ornament?"

"How so?" Professor Renelle frowned.

"The way it is dyed and the pattern of the knots may be more than decorative. Might the quipu harbor some hidden message? You said that it was buried with a person of high rank in the Cloud Warrior community. If that person were of royal blood, might the quipu actually be the missing *derrotero*?"

A glint came into Professor Renelle's eyes at my suggestion. "An intriguing notion. There are old tales that quipu were used by the Indians to relay messages."

"Well, there we have it. Perhaps the quipu conceals valuable information regarding the location of the king's tomb. I would be honored to examine it for you to see if I might unravel some meaning within it."

"It might be helpful if you studied the quipu in conjunction with the other objects Professor Renelle gathered at the site," my wife said. "It might spark an idea. And I would very much like to see more of your collection, professor. Your lecture tonight ignited a great curiosity within me. I do hope I can persuade you."

Renelle puffed up like a rooster—it seemed that my wife's flattery was successful. The professor was a man who thrived on an audience and adulation.

"Madam, I would be delighted to show you the collection. When would you like to visit?"

"Tomorrow would be perfect if that is at all possible. I have engagements all next week," she added.

The professor reached into his coat pocket and retrieved a silver case from which he took a printed calling card. "My address is here. Shall we say noon?"

Sissy took the card and bestowed a radiant smile upon him. "Noon is perfect, Professor Renelle. And rest assured, if anyone can decipher the quipu, it is my husband. You may soon know the location of the king's tomb and his treasure."

"That would be wonderful indeed," Professor Renelle said.

"I will do my best," I said. "Goodnight, sir, and thank you for a most informative evening."

"My pleasure," Renelle said with a smile fattened by greed.

36

When we returned home, the parlor fire was burning merrily and my mother-in-law was in her chair, knitting. Catterina was perched next to her, mesmerized by the tips of the knitting needles darting in and out of the wool. Once we were settled, Muddy made us cups of hot chocolate, then excused herself and retreated to bed. Catterina eyed Dupin's lap, but he quickly contorted himself in such a way that she reluctantly chose to curl up on me instead. When we began to discuss all that had occurred at the Philosophical Hall, it was clear that our appreciation of Professor Renelle's lecture was not shared by Dupin.

"His strategy of inviting the actress and her husband was a vulgar trick," he complained. "One that confirms to me that he is merely a treasure seeker with little true interest in the history or culture of the Cloud People."

"The trick did result in a full house. I have been to other talks at the Philosophical Hall that had half as many in the audience."

"And his magic lantern show genuinely pleased the crowd," Sissy added. "Mrs. Reynolds herself was grudgingly impressed."

"I wonder how she is acquainted with Renelle," Dupin murmured, his gaze directed at me.

"He seems to be associated with Philadelphia's theaters. We saw him try to ingratiate himself with the lady back in January at the Walnut Street Theater, but she ignored him. I do not believe they are friends."

"Certainly not. She was barely civil to Professor Renelle, just as her husband was only superficially polite to you," Sissy observed. She looked from Dupin to me and back to Dupin. "Were you aware of the enmity between Mr. Reynolds's family and my husband's?"

Dupin paused for a moment, then said carefully, "Mr. Williams, as he was known in London, did seem to hold unwarranted animosity toward your husband. There was little rhyme or reason to it that I could fathom, as your husband had done nothing to earn such ill will. But it seems that Mrs. Fontaine—or Mrs. Reynolds as she now calls herself—has extended an olive branch?"

"Correct, Dupin. I can only hope the lady has persuaded her husband of his folly, as she promised."

Dupin's expression indicated his doubts regarding this, but he kept his opinion to himself and said dryly, "Mrs. Reynolds is quite the toast of Philadelphia. Her extraordinary performances in London were the perfect training for her profession."

A thought then occurred to me that I hoped would divert the discussion from those unpleasant memories. "Did you notice a dark-haired man, small of stature, dressed in a black suit, who was seated in the back row and left immediately after the presentation? He wore a peculiar hat, wide of brim and with a tall, rounded crown." When Dupin frowned at my description, I added, "He had more than a passing resemblance to Jeremiah Mathews, and when Professor Renelle noticed him, the man hurried from the room."

"You think he might be a Peruvian?"

"Indeed."

"Unfortunately I was too focused on Renelle and the potential drama between you and the Reynolds to notice him." Dupin appeared to ponder what I had just revealed, but said nothing more on the subject. Instead he asked: "And so you succeeded in securing an invitation to Professor Renelle's home. When are you expected?"

"Tomorrow at noon," my wife said with much satisfaction.

"That gives us little time to formulate a plan," he frowned.

"As you said previously, the longer Helena is with her captor, the more rapidly our chance to rescue her diminishes," Sissy countered. "We must discover as soon as we can if she is held at Professor Renelle's house, and if she is not . . ." Her words trailed away at the dark possibility of that scenario.

"I feel certain that Miss Loddiges is there," I said quickly to reassure her. "Professor Renelle abducted her in hopes of securing Jeremiah Mathews's journal, as he believes it has a map that will lead him to the treasure of the Cloud People. We have witnessed how single-minded he is in pursuit of the treasure."

"I agree," Dupin said. "And Miss Loddiges's disappearance seems less mysterious now that we are aware of Father Nolan's alliance with Professor Renelle. If Father Keane mentioned the excursion to see the passenger pigeons, which is very likely as he borrowed the church wagon to travel there, Father Nolan would have told the professor where they would be—the perfect spot to abduct a lady."

"But if Helena no longer has the journal, why would Renelle continue to hold her hostage?" Sissy asked.

"We must put our worries aside and make our plan," Dupin said firmly. "And we must play our roles with confidence tomorrow. I believe that if I can find a way to surreptitiously examine the house and make note of its inhabitants while you have Professor Renelle engaged, we will be able to unearth enough to decide the best way to rescue your friend. What was your pretext to secure an invitation, Poe?"

"I suggested to Professor Renelle that the quipu might contain a concealed message, that it might actually be the *derrotero* he seeks."

As Dupin considered this notion, a light came into his eye. "Interesting idea. There may be something in it. Your discussion should certainly keep the professor occupied for a good amount of time. And if Renelle is in any way suspicious about your motives for wishing to come to his home, the very real possibility that you might work out the location of the treasure by deciphering the quipu should be enough to guarantee your safety."

"And what of you, Dupin?" I asked. "How shall we secure you access to Renelle's home?"

"I have been thinking about your role, Monsieur Dupin," Sissy ventured. "If you were to play our horse groom and coachman, we would of course need to have you with us at Renelle Mansion. In this weather, we could politely insist that you were permitted to wait for us in the warmth of the kitchen."

I had pretended to be Dupin's brother when in London, but the thought of him playing our servant amused me much more.

"I think Dupin will make a thoroughly convincing groom— he has quite a way with animals, doesn't he, Catterina?" I rubbed her head and she opened one eye to glance at me, then retreated back to sleep.

"I know enough about horses to play the role," Dupin said evenly.

"We will have to borrow or rent a carriage, but Professor Renelle won't know that," I added. "And if you pretend to understand very little English, Renelle's servants might speak more freely around you."

Dupin nodded, but Sissy quickly saw that his dignity was injured by my little jest.

"Of course that is just a suggestion. If anyone has a better plan?" She waited patiently for Dupin to suggest an alternative course of action, but he just shook his head. "We will have to assemble a convincing costume for you—some of Eddy's walking clothes will do, I think. From what we know of Professor Renelle, I feel he will not pay much attention to someone he believes is a servant."

This thought seemed to inspire Dupin. "What you say is very true. I may be able to exploit the disguise to good advantage so long as his servants don't see through my pretense."

Before I could make another jibe, my wife asked, "And do you have any advice for me, Monsieur Dupin? I am rather nervous about my role in this masquerade."

He considered her question for a moment, then said, "Renelle's braggadocio will give us some advantage. Ask questions and use flattery. He will happily dwell on himself rather than interrogate you."

I did not much like the idea of using my wife as a distraction, but she was sanguine about the tactic.

"While I find the man repellent, I will flatter him ruthlessly if doing so will help us to rescue dear Helena."

"And I will play a witless horse groom and observe all that I can about the house and its inhabitants."

"I will do my best to distract Renelle with theories regarding the quipu for a long as possible without raising his suspicions," I said. "Perhaps I shall even manage to decipher it, for I do believe it contains some kind of message."

"And if the quipu proves to be a *derrotero* showing where the treasure is hidden, will you reveal its location to Professor Renelle or will we take the next ship to Peru?" my wife said with a smile.

"Dupin will go in our stead—he knows the terrain—and when the jewel of Peru and the treasure in the king's tomb is ours, we will live for Art and never be Mammon's slave again."

My voice was jocular and Sissy laughed, but I did fleetingly wonder how our lives might change if the quipu were the legendary map. What a fine thing that would be!

37

THURSDAY, 21 MARCH 1844

The air was kissed by spring and lively with birdsong—it was the perfect weather for an excursion to the countryside. Dupin disappeared before breakfast and arrived back at our house with a one-horse brougham carriage he had hired. He had also purchased a worker's cap at the market, which completed the disguise we had assembled for him—my oldest coat, trousers and boots, items fit only for rambles through the forest. A knitted muffler and gloves contributed by Muddy completed the transformation.

"What a fine horse groom you make, Dupin. I would hire you without hesitation."

Dupin scowled. "Do not presume I would accept employment with you."

"Now, now. That's enough from you, sir, if you wish to keep your position. And we best make haste if we are to reach Germantown by noon."

"Shouldn't you remove your *chevalière?*" Sissy asked Dupin. "A man like Professor Renelle will notice such a ring," she added.

"You are correct, Mrs. Poe. Thank you."

"Take this with you," Muddy said, handing Dupin her heavy, wooden walking stick. "I don't know what you three are planning, but you will keep my daughter safe, won't you?"

"I give you my word, madame." Dupin darted from the kitchen and came back with his cobra-headed walking stick. "I do not think we will require weapons, but it is far better to be prepared, as your very wise mother has suggested." He handed it to me and nodded, encouraging me to test it. I held the stick in both hands and revealed the rapier hidden inside. Muddy's eyes widened, and then she smiled at Dupin.

* * *

A half an hour later, Dupin was perched on a box seat, horse's reins in hand, and Sissy and I sat in the enclosed carriage behind him. The morning light dappled pleasantly through the trees, illuminating the fresh green of young leaves and newly emerged woodland plants, while the birds flitted through the trees and the squirrels raced up and down them. Sissy was entranced with the bucolic landscape, and I was glad to see the expression of joy on her face, for I had missed it terribly during the long winter months, when every cough or hint of her poorliness filled me with dread.

"It truly is a relief to escape the city." Sissy breathed in, then smiled radiantly. "The air is so fresh and the colors seem stronger, brighter—the sky, the grass, the leaves."

I vowed to myself that I would find some way to secure a home for us, with a garden, away from the bustle and grime of the city. It mattered not to me where we lived if we found a place that brought her good health.

When we reached Germantown, we stopped at the train station to ask directions to Professor Renelle's home and learned that it was roughly half a mile away. The station master drew us a map and seemed surprised that we were unaware of Renelle Mansion's location.

"It's well known in Germantown," he explained. "It was one of the first grand houses built here, and Professor Renelle's father gave employment to many in the area when he ran the quarries."

We carried on toward our destination, and it was clear that this was an enclave for the wealthy, as we passed several imposing properties. When Dupin turned the brougham into a gravel-strewn lane that was guarded by two large stone lions, I could not help but picture Renelle with his mane of tawny hair. The drive disappeared into a woodland thick enough to obscure whatever lay at the end of the track, and Dupin brought the carriage to a stop and came back to speak with us.

"I believe this is it," he said.

"It must be very dark here at night," Sissy noted. "No street lamps, all these trees surrounding the house."

"Quite the perfect location to bring Miss Loddiges against her will," I said. "No one would hear her cry out."

"Except Professor Renelle's servants. We should therefore presume they are guilty of colluding with Renelle, if he did abduct the lady, and must trust no one who resides at the mansion," Dupin cautioned. "Our questions must be subtle enough to obscure our motive."

"Yes, of course," Sissy responded, her voice betraying—to me at least—that she believed Dupin's warning to be more than obvious.

"You may have the greatest success in gathering information from Professor Renelle and his servants, Mrs. Poe," Dupin continued. "I believe he will underestimate your intelligence and that is to our advantage."

Sissy's eyes widened at his unexpected compliment. She beamed and said, "I will play the naive wife to full effect and pelt him with questions. I do find that men very much admire a good listener who encourages them to talk only of themselves and their accomplishments."

I nodded at Sissy's words until a gurgle of mirth and a sardonic look from Dupin brought me up short. I felt an unwelcome flush rise up to my face.

"I was not referring to you, dearest, but some of your acquaintances are most tiresome."

It was Dupin's turn to redden, which pleased me greatly.

"Mr. Griswold springs to mind," Sissy continued. "A terribly dull man. And there are several others who call themselves writers and have some wit in conversation, but spend far too much time in the tavern." She smiled mischievously, then closed her eyes and took a deep breath. *"Bon courage,"* she murmured to herself. She then opened her eyes, straightened in her seat and said firmly, "Shall we carry on?"

Dupin nodded and climbed back onto the box seat. Soon we were moving again up the carriage drive, which proved to be well over a quarter of a mile long. It was meticulously raked and lined with large rhododendron bushes. Indeed, they were so tall that they screened the house from the drive until we veered to the left, then right again, and there it was.

"Oh, how magnificent!" Sissy gasped as Renelle Mansion came into sight. Mansion was not an exaggeration—Renelle's home was immense and impressive. It was fashioned from gray Wissahickon schist and the mica that was shot through it glimmered in the sunlight. The house was Gothic in style with a steeply-pitched roof, a large turret and a grand buttermilk-yellow porch with contrasting maroon decorative trim that matched the large door. The downstairs windows were very tall and diamond-paned, while the upstairs windows were smaller, four of them directly above the porch roof. The turret at the far left side of the house had two long, narrow windows.

We climbed down from the carriage and Dupin took his time soothing the horse and attending to the carriage while taking in his surroundings.

"Look at the gazebo," he said in a low voice. It was a lovely structure and had a dovecot on top of it, complete with noisy inhabitants. "A highly useful way to send and receive messages when living out here." Dupin paused for a moment and surreptitiously studied the house. "I would presume that Miss Loddiges is imprisoned in the turret or the cellar."

"I hope the turret or truly the man is a barbarian," my wife said. "Notice that the curtains in the turret are drawn. One would think there would be little need for curtains in such a space and certainly no reason to have the curtains closed during the day, unless attempting to hide someone away."

Dupin nodded. "And the turret windows do not allow access to the roof, which makes both escape and rescue difficult. We will either need a very long ladder or to gain entry from inside the house to release her."

"But surely if Miss Loddiges is in the turret, she would have signaled to us from the window after hearing our approach," I said.

"Not if someone else is in the room with her to prevent that," my wife countered.

"Or she is gagged and bound," Dupin added.

"The beast," Sissy muttered.

"Shall we?" Dupin said.

Sissy and I advanced to the house before him and I let the knocker fall twice. Moments later the front door opened.

"Welcome, Professor Renelle is expecting you." A formidable-looking woman stood in the doorway and her bulk filled most of it. Her face was broad and plain, framed with iron-gray hair that was mostly tucked under a white cap. Her ill-fitting dress was black with a lace collar that gave the housekeeper the look of an early Puritan settler. She stared at us awkwardly for a moment, then turned and led the way inside, her heavy shoes thudding on the floor like clumps of soft bread dough slapped on a tabletop.

The foyer was beautifully illuminated by light strewn from the diamond-paned windows, which softened the gloom emanating from the portraits of Renelle's stern, squinting ancestors congregated upon the walls. A grand Italianate chandelier was suspended from the vaulted ceiling and the floor was an extraordinary mosaic that featured an unusual selection of birds in flight and repose. As the light danced across its surface, it was as if the birds themselves were in motion—the floor was a true thing of beauty. The staircase to the upper floors was directly in front of us and the upstairs hallway was open except for an elegant balustrade where one might stand and gaze down into the foyer or through the large windows on either side of the door.

A hallway to the right of the staircase ran to the back of the house and, presumably, the kitchen. The parlor was directly right of the foyer and visible through an open door. It was elegantly furnished, albeit in a style fashionable at the turn of the century. Professor Renelle's mother—or perhaps grandmother—had possessed a good eye and had spared no expense. To the left was the dining room with an immense table and another very grand chandelier hanging above it. The room was dominated by a still life in a gilded frame that was mounted above the marble fireplace. It was a banquet piece in the style of a Dutch master and featured a cornucopia of fruit in sumptuous colors arranged around a peacock and a peahen entwined in death, the male's glorious feathers drooping over the table edge and shimmering under candlelight that failed to hold back the encroaching shadows. It was a melancholic scene to dine by.

I was jarred from my contemplations by the housekeeper's voice. "Professor Renelle will be ready for you shortly. Would you like some coffee or tea?" She looked at each of us, but her gaze lingered on Dupin's clothing and a slight frown knit her brows.

"Tea would be much appreciated. And is there somewhere our coachman might wait? The kitchen perhaps?" I asked.

The housekeeper half-nodded, as if my comment answered her unspoken question of Dupin's identity. "Yes, certainly."

"Madame?" Dupin said to the lady, indicating the boots he had purposefully dirtied that morning.

"Is there an entrance directly into the kitchen from outdoors?" Sissy asked. "He worries about his boots on your immaculate floors."

The housekeeper's relief was palpable. "Turn left from the front entrance and walk to the very back of the house. I will let you in through the kitchen door," she told Dupin in a louder voice, supplementing her explanation with the exaggerated gestures of a bad actor.

He stared at her, feigning a lack of comprehension.

"Unfortunately he is dim-witted and speaks very little English," I said. "But we have an appointment to look at carriage horses this afternoon and he does have a way with the creatures." I made a show of repeating the housekeeper's words to Dupin in French, then directed the gaping jaws of Dupin's cobra-headed walking stick at the door with a commanding flourish.

Dupin scowled, quite genuinely, and exited. I caught sight of him through the parlor window, and I waved his own walking stick at him again as if to hurry him along. He favored me with another scowl.

"Such a lazy fellow," I said, shaking my head. "If there is a chair near the fire, he is likely to fall asleep, and we will be fortunate to rouse him."

"Do not be so hard on him," my wife said. "He is extremely good with horses and is an honest if uncultivated man."

"Rest assured, he will be no trouble to you," I told the housekeeper.

She nodded and started to turn toward the kitchen, but Sissy intervened. "I am certain you have a great deal to manage in running a house so grand. How do you keep this chandelier so sparkling?"

"Yes, it is remarkable. I have seen ostrich feather dusters used." I struggled to think what else I might say to engage the housekeeper long enough for Dupin to learn as much as possible about ways to surreptitiously enter the house, but a booming voice made us all jump.

"Mr. Poe! And the delightful Mrs. Poe. Greetings and welcome."

Professor Renelle looked down at us from over the balustrade to the left of the staircase, the direction in which the entrance to the turret must be. "Please, come upstairs to my study." He turned his gaze to his housekeeper. "We will take refreshments later rather than now, Miss Thomassen."

"Yes, sir," she said and ambled to the kitchen with the rolling gait of a giantess from some old fairy tale.

"I'm sure you understand," he said. "It is better not to have liquids near the artifacts."

"Yes, of course."

"Well, do come up."

Sissy and I ascended the stairs, which were wide enough to accommodate both of us side by side. Professor Renelle waited, and bowed graciously when we reached the landing.

"Again, welcome. Thank you for journeying out to my eyrie."

"Your home is magnificent," my wife said. "I do not wonder that you have made it your place of study."

"Thank you, madam. Of course the building is from my grandfather's imagination and my grandmother and mother were responsible for the furnishings. My modest contribution is the mosaic floor."

"It is glorious. I've never seen a floor as lovely," Sissy declared.

"You must view it from here." Professor Renelle offered us space to look over the balustrade. We both peered down at the foyer floor. The gas-lit chandelier, which was just above eye level, filled the space with a warm glow, while the diamond-paned windows let in a rush of crystal daylight, and the effect was incredible, as if one were observing a living kingdom of birds from Heaven itself. Sissy gasped at the sight of it, and Professor Renelle smiled with pride. As I gazed at that master-piece of craftsmanship, a thought came to me.

"Is there a legend behind the scene depicted, professor? I notice that various ornithological species which might never meet seem to reside in one kingdom on your floor. The toucan, passenger pigeon, flamingo, an ivory-billed woodpecker, a bald eagle, hummingbirds from both the northern and southern American hemispheres," I said, pointing at each.

"Well observed, Mr. Poe. The birds depicted are indeed from North, Central and South America and the story hidden within the floor is simple—each is a bird I have collected during my expeditions."

"How fascinating," my wife said. "A record of your adventures."

"I am very proud of the floor, but it is nothing compared to the artifacts I will show you. Come."

As we walked I noticed that all the doors to the rooms along the hallway were closed but for one at its far end: Professor Renelle's study. This struck me as rather odd. Was this chance or had he guessed our true agenda and this was a strategy to hide where he might have imprisoned Miss Loddiges? I peered over my shoulder—the other end of the hallway finished with a short staircase that led to a closed door, which was presumably the entrance to the turret. From the building's exterior, this seemed the obvious place to imprison Miss Loddiges, as it was the most difficult room to escape from. Sissy's eyes met mine and I knew that our thoughts were in alignment.

When we entered the study, the differences between it and the rest of the house were immediately apparent. An immense oak desk faced the door and held the accoutrements of a scholar: writing implements, an Argand lamp and a green glass paperweight. A large globe stood on the floor next to the desk. Shelves with cabinets covered the walls and were filled with books and an array of artifacts, from tribal masks, peculiar figurines, primitive tools and weapons to immense seashells, taxidermied birds and small mammals. It was difficult to know where to look first, the shelves were so crowded with unusual objects, a veritable museum dedicated primarily to Southern America. A map of Peru was mounted on a board and stood like a painting upon an easel. It was marked with various lines and notations that I presumed referenced Professor Renelle's expeditions.

"Sit, please." He indicated two small armchairs that had been placed before his desk and eased into his own imposing leather chair. As I sat down, the paperweight caught my eye again; it was about two inches in diameter and shaped like a small turtle.

"Yes, it is an emerald," Renelle said, his eyes fixed on mine. Had he guessed how my thoughts had drifted to the legendary jewels Fernández had described? "During my first expedition to the Chachapoyas I discovered it inside a pottery jar with some smaller emeralds, entombed with a mummy, very like the one I had showed in my presentation."

"Goodness," Sissy muttered, her amazement at the emerald tempered by where it had been found. "Why do you think the jewels were entombed with the mummy? Was he of Chachapoyan royalty?"

"It is difficult to say. Royalty, perhaps, or a pagan priest. Oddly, there was nothing to distinguish that particular mummy from the others buried there, beyond the jar of emeralds. Each mummy was arranged in the same position, curled on its side, knees drawn up with arms wrapped around them and head tucked down. There were no ornaments on any of the mummies and all the wrappings were the same. The Peruvian natives who accompanied us were spooked by the burial chamber and how the mummies were placed in open alcoves without any sort of sarcophagus enclosing them. They feared the mummies were animated by moonlight and would exact revenge upon us for disturbing their tomb." Renelle laughed at this, but I could easily imagine this scenario and, from her expression, so could my wife.

"In your presentation, you mentioned that the Cloud Warriors were defeated by the Spaniards and the Incas—do they still exist as a people?" I asked.

"The accounts of Spaniards who witnessed those battles state that the Cloud Warriors were destroyed as a race, but there are rumors amongst the natives of the area that a small group of Cloud Warriors fled into the forest and made their way to another city higher still in the mountains. The location of this sanctuary remains a mystery."

"Imagine," Sissy murmured. "A city on the doorstep of the heavens where one might see for hundreds of miles."

Professor Renelle grinned wolfishly. "Not only can I imagine it, madam, I wish to discover it. Untold treasures are hidden in the Chachapoyas, waiting to be found by the most intrepid explorers. Once I finance this next expedition," he said, banging his fist on his desk, "I will bring back marvels that will astound both antiquarians and ordinary folk." Renelle's eyes gleamed with the thought of what he might achieve and his fervor was unsettling. Hoping to redirect the subject to calmer waters, I pointed at a trio of demons leering over his shoulder.

"The masks on the shelf behind you, are they artifacts from the Chachapoyas?"

"No, those were made by the Aztec, a blood-thirsty people from Mexico. We did not find any masks at the Chachapoyan site, just the strange statues I showed during my presentation."

"They had very somber visages, like judges staring down on the world," Sissy offered. "You believe they were idols worshipped by the Cloud Warriors—their gods?"

"Yes, for certainly they are not things of beauty. But let me show you the quipu. I am intrigued by your notion that it might be a *derrotero*." Renelle turned, unlocked a cabinet door in the bookcase and drew out the quipu he had displayed at his lecture. It was pinned to a board, its thick string tied into a circle as if fastened around a person's neck, and the numerous strands hanging from it were stretched out like sun rays. He placed it on the desk so that we might see it better.

"It is a strange thing, but quite lovely." Sissy leaned in to look at it more closely. "You said it is made from llama wool?"

"Yes, colored with dyes made from local plants, or so I was told."

"So many shades and so subtle—it was difficult to see the different colors in the lecture," Sissy added. "Perhaps each has a meaning." She glanced at me to interject.

"That seems likely indeed if the quipu was devised to contain a message," I said. "Are they still in use today, Professor Renelle?"

"I have seen very primitive quipus in use, primarily as a way of recording the number of livestock, but this is far more complex." Renelle fixed his eyes back on me and waited for my interpretation of the quipu. I knew it was a test, and if I failed to convince him I risked exposing the charade we were putting on.

I stared quietly at the strange and beautiful object, taking in the shape of it, its colors, the knots, and immediately I saw a simple pattern—there were four strings of the same length dyed red that divided the quipu strings into quadrants. Four strings of orange were evenly placed between the red strings. It reminded me of the points of a compass. In addition, there were eight green strings and twenty-four yellow ones. Again, the pattern was simple: two green strings were placed equidistant between the red strings and two yellow strings divided the twelve sections created by the green and red strings. There were a quantity of oatmeal-colored strings and I quickly counted those in the first quadrant and found there were eighty, which supported what I had intuited.

"I presume you noticed that the quipu has three hundred and sixty strings?" I said to Professor Renelle. "Like the degrees of a compass?"

Professor Renelle's face indicated that he had not. "Like a compass," he muttered, staring at the strings.

"The red strings would appear to represent the cardinal directions and the orange strings the intermediate directions."

"And what of these?" Sissy asked. "The green and yellow strings?"

"The green strings divide the quadrants formed by the red strings into sections—of thirty degrees if we think again of a compass."

"And the yellow strings divide each of those sections into ten degrees," Renelle murmured.

"Which leaves the oatmeal-colored strings, which mark out the rest of the degrees on the compass," I concluded.

Professor Renelle stared at the quipu, both intrigued by what we had perceived and irritated that he had not seen the obvious pattern himself.

"That is all very interesting," he said crossly. "But I don't see how it might be a map."

"I believe it is something to do with the knots tied in the strings," I said. "They appear to be decorative, but perhaps they form a message."

"Well? Illuminate me," Professor Renelle snapped.

In truth, I did believe a message was concealed within the quipu, but I would need more than an afternoon to work it out. Silent, focused pondering was not going to help keep Professor Renelle occupied for long, so I decided to extemporize as best I could in order that Dupin could learn as much as possible.

"See these seven oatmeal-colored threads? Each has a knot tied in exactly the same manner. Seven is quite a special number. There are seven days in a week, seven heavenly bodies known to the ancients. Perhaps the quipu gives points on a compass and also refers to the heavens—a star map of some kind."

"All very interesting, but I still do not see how this might be the *derrotero*. How might the knots in the quipu reveal the location of the king's tomb?" Renelle demanded.

"It is complex, I admit. I would need more time to study it, I'm afraid."

"Clearly the quipu is a masterly puzzle or you would have deciphered its secrets already," Sissy added.

Renelle nodded at this. "I will have to continue the task at my leisure then, as it seems we will get no further in unraveling the mystery today. Let me offer you some refreshments before you are on your way." The professor pulled a cord behind him, which I presumed rang a bell in the kitchen to alert his housekeeper. It would be a useful alert to Dupin as well if he were somewhere he shouldn't be.

Professor Renelle led us downstairs and into the elegant parlor, which had pistachio-colored walls and white trim, a thick oriental carpet in peacock-feather tones and silvery draperies framing the windows. The chandelier bloomed from a decorative white ceiling festooned with what looked to be angel wings, and the furniture was a muted rose velvet. Despite the ostentatiousness of the decor, the room was surprisingly tranquil and pleasing to the senses. Renelle indicated that Sissy and I should take the sofa while he arranged himself in a plump armchair. Moments later, Miss Thomassen lumbered in carrying a large tea tray, which she placed on the table in front of us.

"You asked me to remind you about this, sir." Miss Thomassen retrieved an envelope from her apron pocket and handed it to Professor Renelle.

"Ah, yes. Thank you, Miss Thomassen."

She nodded and poured us each a cup of tea.

"I am a Friend of the Chestnut Street Theater and that pleasant euphemism means that I receive tickets to their theatricals. I cannot attend the performance tonight as I am traveling to New York early tomorrow morning to deliver several lectures at Columbia University." He removed two tickets from the envelope and handed them to my wife. "But I hope you might enjoy seeing the play, Mrs. Poe. I could not help but notice last night that you are acquainted with Mrs. Reynolds."

This remark did not sit well with me, but Sissy beamed. "Thank you, Professor Renelle. I do so admire her. She is the most gifted performer."

My heart sank at the thought of sitting through another of George Reynolds's theatricals, but the news of Renelle's imminent travels was promising.

"I am sorry not to see the lady perform again," the professor said, before turning to me. "Are you an admirer of her work also, Mr. Poe?" His smirk suggested he had observed my lack of enthusiasm.

"She is quite the actress," I said carefully. "And she does the best with the material she has to work with."

Professor Renelle laughed. "I see. Well, perhaps you should pen something for the lady."

"I am not a playwright, sir, but perhaps I should try."

"What a lovely painting that is over the fireplace," Sissy interrupted before I could say anything overtly negative about George Reynolds's writing skills. "Am I correct in thinking I see a family resemblance?"

"You are indeed. It is my mother and my father."

The woman depicted was very handsome, with abundant coppery locks piled in an extravagant hairstyle and a formidable expression that was surprising as she looked to be no more than eighteen years of age. In contrast, *père* Renelle appeared a good twenty-five years older than his wife, with saturnine features and a dour expression.

"She is very beautiful. You resemble her greatly," my wife said.

"You flatter me, Mrs. Poe. My mother was both beautiful and a strong character. I was saddened to lose her when I was still a child. She entirely redecorated Renelle Mansion, making it one of Philadelphia's most admired homes, and my father enjoyed bringing her ideas to fruition, no matter what the cost. I do my best to keep the house and property in good condition, as they would have wished."

"And you have succeeded admirably," Sissy replied.

"It is my duty," he said, "but also my pleasure. My grandfather made a fortune in France through trade with Senegal and my father made a second fortune here, mining for stone, as he put it."

Senegal? I remembered the bird clues left by Andrew Mathews—the two birds from Senegal. I wondered if the trade with Senegal that Renelle's grandfather had profited so handsomely from was the slave trade.

"I find there is symmetry in the fact that my father provided the basic materials to help build a city and that my vocation is to search for lost civilizations, ancient and mysterious cities overtaken by nature and forgotten," Renelle added.

And treasure, I thought, but did not say.

"It is an honor to present my discoveries to audiences who will never venture to the places I have dared to visit and to expand the canon of knowledge," Renelle pronounced, as if he had just been given an award by a learned society.

I wondered how he would explain away his lies about trekking to the lost city a second time when in truth he had been confined to his sick bed, and how he would rationalize his involvement in the murder of three men and the abduction of a determined young woman during his quest for treasure when he was finally called to account for his actions.

38

The journey back from Germantown seemed to take twice as long as the journey out. Sissy and I were desperate to learn what Dupin had been able to find out at the mansion. When the carriage stopped at last, I was surprised to see that we were outside the undertaker's premises on Coates Street. Dupin, in enterprising spirit, had hired the horse and brougham from there.

"How ever did you know of Helverson's?" I asked him, as we began walking west toward home.

Dupin looked as baffled as I felt. "You wrote to me about the undertaker and his coffin business when you were residing on Coates Street—it inspired an idea for a tale."

"Of course, that's right,' I replied, though I had no recollection of telling Dupin. I marveled again at his uncanny memory and hoped it would lead us to success in our bold adventure.

"I am anxious to hear what you observed at Renelle Mansion," my wife said to him. "I certainly found it an illuminating visit. The house means a great deal to Professor Renelle, and it would not surprise me if his greed springs in part from the need to pay for its upkeep, which must be considerable as the house and its grounds are enormous. We met Miss Thomassen, his house-keeper, but surely he has many more servants."

"Were there any additional servants in the kitchen, Dupin? A horse groom such as yourself?"

"There is indeed a horse groom, a gardener, a general repairman and a pigeon keeper," Dupin replied, ignoring my little joke. "But they are all one and the same person: a man called Jimmerson. He has his own cottage in the grounds directly behind the house, but came to the kitchen for his dinner. He looks to be in his mid-thirties and, from his actions, seems to believe himself to be superior to Miss Thomassen—perhaps his parents also worked for the Renelles. I did not see any evidence of other servants."

"Which suggests Renelle cannot afford them, for surely, given his high self-regard, he would have a veritable army of them to tend to his whims."

Dupin guffawed at this. "I do believe you are correct, Poe, but Miss Thomassen seems to do all his domestic chores, including preparing his meals and those of his guests. Or *unwilling* guests in this instance."

"You saw Helena?" Sissy asked, her face full of hope.

"I'm afraid not, but I did observe two things that make me confident she is at Renelle Mansion. First, there were a number of coats hanging on pegs near the kitchen door. There was a bright blue cloak with yellow trim amongst them. If I remember correctly, you told me that Miss Loddiges has such a garment?"

"Yes! That is Helena's cloak. It's very specific," my wife said. "And her bonnet is the same blue and of silk, decorated with flowers and hummingbirds."

Dupin nodded. "Also very specific. I think Miss Thomassen rather coveted both items. When she went to fetch Jimmerson for his dinner, she put on the cloak, and then I discovered something highly useful." He looked at each of us and swung his cane jauntily as he walked, leading us down Second Street.

"Well, go on, Dupin," I said impatiently.

"Rather than exit through the kitchen door as I expected, Miss Thomassen opened a pantry door, revealing a passageway at the back of it. She took a lantern and went down it. I presume the tunnel leads to the springhouse that is visible through the kitchen window, positioned close to Jimmerson's cottage. She returned with eggs and Jimmerson arrived for his dinner a few minutes later."

"You think the spring house tunnel might offer a way into the kitchen at night?" Sissy asked.

"Indeed. And I should mention that after Miss Thomassen and Mr. Jimmerson finished their dinners in the kitchen, he returned to his duties outdoors, and she prepared a tray with soup and bread, which she carried from the kitchen. I crept after her and watched as Miss Thomassen ascended the stairs and walked in the direction of the turret room."

"Excellent. We will know where to search for her tomorrow evening," I said.

Dupin raised his brows and simply waited for me to explain myself.

"Renelle will be traveling to New York early tomorrow and will not return until next week. He bestowed two theater tickets on Sissy for Mrs. Reynolds's performance at the Chestnut Street Theater tonight as he cannot attend."

Sissy's face suddenly fell. "Two tickets. You must take Monsieur Dupin. It may be his only chance to see Mrs. Reynolds on stage."

"You forget that I saw the lady perform several times in London, so there is no need for me to attend this theatrical." When Sissy hesitated he added, "It would offend me terribly if you did not take the opportunity to use the tickets with your husband."

The happiness was perfectly clear on Sissy's face, whereas self-pity was equally visible on mine.

"Fear not, Poe," Dupin said with a mocking smile directed at me. "The lady's talent is sure to make up for the deficits of the play itself."

"Would you care to make a wager regarding that?" I muttered.

"Be kind, Eddy," Sissy interjected. "One might think you were envious of Mr. Reynolds's success."

Dupin barked with mirth. "Quite right, Poe. And that would please him enormously. Do you wish to give Reynolds that satisfaction?"

"Certainly not. I will give him a fair and honest appraisal of his work should the opportunity arise."

"You will not play the critic tonight," my wife instructed. "I wish to enjoy myself without your huffings and puffings."

"Fine. I will suffer the spectacle in silence and will improvise my own audacious fiction if we meet the actress and her husband."

"Thank you," my wife said cheerily, pretending not to hear my discontentment.

Dupin's eyes crinkled in mirth. I had never witnessed such a surfeit of good humor in him before and was not pleased that it was at my expense.

"That is settled then," he said as we turned right into Spring Garden Street and began our way down that pleasant thoroughfare. "Did you learn anything more about Renelle's motivation for abducting Miss Loddiges? Or what he thinks he might gain from Jeremiah Mathews's journal?"

"There was no way to ask him directly of course, but when examining the mummies in the burial chamber, he came across an earthenware jar placed with a mummy that proved to hold several emeralds, including a sizable one shaped like a turtle. I suspect he sold the smaller emeralds, but the turtle is used as a paperweight on his desk—clearly it has whetted his appetite for finding more treasure. From his remarks, he has read

Fernández's book and the tale of the huge emerald. He must believe that Jeremiah found the jewel and perhaps the location of the king's burial chamber. Certainly he hoped the quipu would reveal that location, but he was not impressed with my efforts to decipher it."

"Did you notice anything of interest?" Dupin asked. "I would relish the chance to examine the quipu properly."

"There is certainly a message hidden within it—I wondered if it could be a sort of sky map."

"But our objective is to rescue Helena, not to play at ciphers and hope they are treasure maps," my wife said tartly. "We must make a plan for tomorrow night."

"Quite right, my dear. This is what I suggest. Dupin and I will make our way to Renelle Mansion so we arrive after midnight in hopes that Miss Thomassen and Mr. Jimmerson are asleep. We will attempt to enter the house through the passageway from the springhouse that Dupin observed Miss Thomassen use. If that endeavor fails, Dupin may need to use his considerable lock-picking skills on the kitchen door. We will then make our way to the turret room and rescue Miss Loddiges without waking Miss Thomassen, bring her back home and, when Miss Loddiges is ready to testify to his crimes, report Professor Renellle to the officers of the police."

"You mention the officers of the police—might it not be more sensible to send *them* to free Miss Loddiges?" Sissy asked.

"You would not suggest that if you had met Lieutenant Webster and Captain Johnson. Remember that Father Keane and I reported Miss Loddiges's abduction and they did not seem to believe our story. They certainly made no effort to find our friend. We would have to explain everything to an officer of the police in Germantown. Given that the Renelles are a prestigious local family, I do not believe it would be possible to persuade an officer to search the mansion to see whether he is holding a lady prisoner."

"And if an officer of the police should reveal our accusations to Professor Renelle," Dupin said, "he would certainly move the lady to another location or, perhaps, dispose of her if she is of no further value to him."

Sissy shivered at his words. "What will my task be?"

"If we do not return before dawn, you must summon the night watch," I said.

"You mean I am to sit and do nothing?" Sissy complained. "Surely I can help in some way, as I did today."

"Mrs. Poe, your courage and loyalty are admirable, but if the three of us enter Renelle Mansion and our plan goes awry, four lives will be in danger," Dupin said. "Truly, we need you to remain vigilant at home, prepared to send help if we do not return by dawn."

Sissy was not happy with our little plot, but before she could further argue its logic, we heard shouting.

"Save the Bible!"

"Go home, papists—leave these shores!"

A gang of brawling men tumbled from a side street, exchanging blows with fists and feet and loathsome words.

"This does not look good," Sissy murmured.

Dupin's eyes narrowed as he watched the altercation, trying, as I was, to gauge its tenor.

"On, on, Americans, *native* Americans!"

Three of the melee were priests, who did their best to avoid the blows of their aggressors, but when the most elderly of the trio was shoved to his knees, a different cry went up.

"Leave him be, you brutes."

"A man of God—shame!"

Both men and women from the street went to the aid of the priest, which only served to enflame the Nativist gang further.

"Foreigners out!"

"Irish thieves plundering our work!"

Sissy clutched my hand and I stood ready to shield her, glad to have Muddy's stout, wooden walking stick in hand. Dupin had his cane gripped in both hands, the golden cobra glaring at the crowd with its ruby eyes. He stepped forward and positioned himself in front of the two of us.

It was difficult to know who first employed a weapon, but suddenly we were in the midst of full warfare, with fists and sticks and rocks hurled, and words of hatred flung in every direction. And then there were more men, with cudgels and shillelaghs that crashed into flesh and bone most hideously, sending victims earthward with a groan.

My wife trembled like a deer surrounded by wolves, her frightened eyes flitting in every direction, her breath overly fast. She cried out as a missile sailed over our heads and a bottle broke at our feet.

"On, on, Americans, native Americans!"

"By the Holy Virgin, send every heretic to burn!"

There was a loud *crack*. I feared gunfire and so, it seemed, did Dupin, for he released the rapier concealed within his walking stick and thrust it at the first brute that approached us, a brick gripped in his paw and growling the challenge: "Are you native or foreign?"

Dupin's rapier lashed through the air and bit the man on his wrist so fiercely he dropped his missile with a shriek. "Prejudice is what fools use for reason," Dupin snapped. And he drove his way onward, rapier slashing, disarming the most brutal stick-fighter. Sissy and I dashed along in the wake of his charge until we were free of the mob that wished any person of a different origin or faith either gone or dead.

39

The playwright who called himself George Reynolds was undoubtedly pleased, for the opening night of his drama at the Chestnut Street Theater looked to have a full house and the audience was loud in its appreciation of the dubious work entitled *The Lovers' Escape*. I was more interested in the theater than the terrible play, as my mother had performed there when she was but a girl, just after the death of her own mother. It gave me enormous pleasure to think that she had graced that stage and pleased an audience as large as this one. In truth the theater had been rebuilt since my mother's performances there, for it had burned to the ground in 1820. William Strickland had designed the new structure, which was most grand, with space for two thousand theatergoers, the seats arranged in a horseshoe shape, with a triple tier of boxes. Despite all that, I could feel my mother's spirit within the place and her success there gave me the courage to sit through Reynolds's latest travesty.

"Mr. Reynolds must be pleased," Sissy whispered. "I cannot see an empty seat."

"Indeed," I said. "It is surprising given—"

"Eddy, please."

I let my words dissolve in my mouth and turned my gaze

back to Mrs. Reynolds, who stood alone in the glow of the gaslights, pining interminably for her lost lover, or that is what I gathered.

"She is indeed talented," I whispered to Sissy. "To remember such a long and tepid speech would be beyond the skills of most."

Sissy put her finger to her lips and frowned. What felt like hours later, Mrs. Reynolds drooped her head, tormented by the absence of her true love, and on cue the lights dimmed until the stage was in darkness. A noise like thunder rumbled up from all around us as the crowd applauded vigorously.

"Let's take some air. The intermission is likely to be lengthy and I need to revive myself," I murmured to Sissy.

My wife shook her head. "I am fine here—it's far warmer than outside."

I leaned to kiss her cheek and made my way toward the foyer. As I neared the door, a voice called out, "Mr. Poe! A message for Mr. Poe!" A young man dressed neatly in black stood in the aisle, his hand in the air to call attention to his location. "Mr. Poe, please!"

"Here, sir," I called out, waving back at him.

"A message from Mrs. Reynolds," he said, beckoning me toward him. "She would like to meet you upstairs. There isn't much time. Come, I will show you the way." The young man turned heel and I followed him. I wondered what was so urgent that it could not wait until after the show, then I remembered how her admirers had surrounded her at the play's end. The young man I was following paused and pointed at a set of stairs. "This way, sir. She is waiting for you in her visiting room."

"Thank you."

But he was gone, disappeared into the crowd of people filling the foyer. I climbed the thickly carpeted stairs, racking my mind for some platitude to bestow that the astute lady might accept

without accusing me of insincerity. I was halfway up the staircase when a woman's scream rang out. Instantly I dashed up
the remaining stairs, then through the door at the top. The
room was dimly lit by a flickering gaslight, and I saw a monstrous
shadow grappling with a ghostly woman. She emitted a stran-
gled scream, a horrid gagging noise, and there was a terrible
thud as she banged against the wall, struggling to get loose
from her assailant's grip.

"Stand back!" I shouted at the brute as I ran toward him, but
it was as if I were transported into a terrible nightmare, each
moment slowed, every sound distorted and far too loud. Before
I could reach him, the devil gave the lady a mighty push, and I
was horrified to see her slam into the open window, which
engulfed her like a gaping mouth.

"No!" The word came up from my very soul. I threw myself
toward her, hoping to catch her skirts and halt the inevitable,
but the villain knocked me off course as he barreled from the
room. There was a terrible swish of silk along the window sill,
a *thunk* as her foot hit the window ledge, and the lady disappeared gracefully into the darkness, one dainty slipper drop-
ping gently to the floor like a lost memory. I crashed down
empty-handed and saw that both victim and assailant had
vanished. Horror struck, I dragged myself to my feet and
staggered to the window, ill at the thought of what I might
see, yet with the ridiculous hope that the lady had managed to
grasp some part of the building, that she was clinging to for
her very life and I might still rescue her. But when I looked
out, all hope fizzled away, for there, far below in the street, lay
the sprawled figure of Rowena Reynolds, broken like a china
doll. I reeled back from the macabre scene and saw the young
man who had showed me to the room standing in the doorway, mouth agape.

"Fetch a doctor," I shouted as I ran past him and down the

stairs, then pushed my way through panicked theatergoers to the exterior of the theater, where a circle of people had gathered around the actress. A man was crouched by her side, checking for signs of life, but it was amply clear from the nimbus of blood about her head that she would not be revived. Moments later, a night watchman arrived at the scene, led by a member of the public. He was a young man, perhaps new to the job, but full of bluster, and his gait suggested he had fortified himself against the cold night air with a bottle of something strong.

"Where is she?" he demanded, but when he saw Mrs. Reynolds, he staggered and pressed his hand to his mouth. "Is she dead?" he asked, betraying his lack of experience.

"I am afraid she is," the man crouched near her said. "I'm Dr. Green," he added. "I saw what happened but there was no way to save her."

"Did she jump?" the watchman asked.

"She fell backwards through the window, so it seems unlikely," the doctor said.

And suddenly my heart ceased its beating—where was Sissy? I had left her alone in the theater! I dashed for the entrance, struggling through the gawping crowd, and heard my name called out. When I saw her face frozen in shock, I knew my wife had seen Mrs. Reynolds lying on the ground. I rushed to her and she threw her arms around me.

"Did you see it happen?" she whispered.

"Yes, my love. A man pushed her. I tried to save her, but could not." I gently stroked her cheek. "Forgive me for leaving you alone. I am relieved you are safe."

"There he is!" a voice rang out.

I looked up to see the young man who had invited me to meet with Mrs Reynolds. He was in the company of the watchman. I felt a chill. This could not be mere coincidence.

"That is the man who pushed her," he said, pointing at me.

The watchman strode toward me and a small gang of men from the crowd followed him. "We have witnesses that say you pushed Mrs. Reynolds—that you pushed her to her death." He leaned toward me in a threatening manner and I could smell the heavy perfume of whiskey.

"No! I tried to save her. There was another man fighting with her when I walked into the room. He pushed her and she fell through the window. There was nothing I could do, it happened so quickly."

"And what did the man look like?" the watchman asked.

"I . . . it was dark. I'm not certain. Very tall and exceedingly strong. His face was concealed. He was wearing his coat and a hat and he shoved me to the ground before running from the room." It was not the solid truth, as I could not recall with certainty if I had tripped in my efforts to save the lady or the villain had pushed me.

The young watchman looked at me, unsure, but the crowd did not believe me.

"He's lying!"

"Take him in!"

"It was not me—there was another man! You must have seen him," I said to my accuser.

"I saw no one but you," the young man said.

"What is your name?" the watchman asked, with steel in his voice.

"Edgar Poe. But honestly I tried to save Mrs. Reynolds."

"My husband most certainly did," my wife said firmly, but she was interrupted before she could say more.

"There's something in her mouth," the doctor called out. "Shall I remove it?"

The watchman hesitated for a moment, but the crowd was far more decisive and he echoed their demands. "Yes," he agreed.

The doctor tugged and pulled a piece of cloth from the lady's mouth like he was executing a conjurer's macabre trick. I thought back to the struggle I had witnessed and wondered if the villain had subdued Mrs. Reynolds with a hanky soaked in ether. Certainly it explained the terrible silence as she fell to her death.

"There is something inside the handkerchief," the doctor said. He extracted a square of paper from the folds. "Shall I open it?"

"Yes. And tell us what it says." The watchman gestured for a lamp and the doctor held the paper in the light.

" 'Ah, broken is the golden bowl,' " he read aloud, " 'the spirit flown forever.' " In my mind, I joined in with him as he spoke the words that followed. " 'Let the bell toll—a saintly soul floats on the Stygian river.' "

"Your poem, Eddy. Why was your poem in her mouth?" Sissy whispered.

"I do not know, my dear,' I said softly.

"Sounds like a threat," a voice said grimly from behind us. I turned and was face to face with my old enemy, whose brown eyes were filled with fury, despite the trails of tears upon his cheeks. "Arrest him now, for surely this man murdered my wife."

"No! That is preposterous," I protested. "I did my best to save her."

"He was seen at the window from which she fell," he continued. "And those are the opening lines from a poem he wrote. A poem about the death of a beautiful woman; a sentiment he has clearly put into action."

"You know that is not true!"

But George Williams, the man who now called himself George Reynolds the playwright, stared into my eyes, his gaze radiating hatred, and pronounced: "He is guilty." Then he crouched down by his wife and began to sob, which set the crowd muttering sympathetically.

The watchman took me roughly by the arm and said, "Come with me. I am placing you under arrest."

"But I've done nothing wrong!"

"Stop your arguing," he said gruffly. "And cause no trouble or it won't go well for you. If you are telling the truth, then you have nothing to fear. And if you're a fabricator—well, then justice will be served."

And with that he began to march me away from the theater and the crowd, fingers firmly clutching my arm. I could hear my wife trying to catch up with us, arguing my innocence, but her words fell upon deaf ears.

"Tell Dupin," I shouted back to Sissy. And then the noise of the crowd rose up like the sound of swarming bees and consumed her reply. Dread took hold of me with an implacable grip.

40

FRIDAY, 22 MARCH 1844

Time became thick and unwieldy, a dark and ill-natured thing that would not shift as I lay on a hard pallet, tormented by demonic noises in darkness so deep the sun feared it. When at last dawn came, it was gray and recalcitrant, and I found that my lips were sealed with wax, my tongue swollen to fill my mouth. There was a tin cup on the floor, and I tried to sip some water to ease the tickling aridity of my throat, only to find that something was lodged under my tongue. I irrigated my mouth and spat it onto the floor, expelling a feather that was bright red, like blood. And then I retched, knowing that the thing could not have got there on its own.

I pulled the scratchy, thin blanket up to my ears and tried to suppress the dreadful sounds that had plagued me all night— moans of pain, shrieks of terror, mutterings of diseased minds. All of any value had been taken from me, and I was locked into my cell, a small empty room with a tiny window that was too high to reach. Minutes, then hours, ticked away and still no one came. I feared I would never leave that nightmare, that my family was lost to me.

When at last I heard footsteps echoing in the cavernous hall-way, I rushed to the barred wall.

"Hello! There has been an error—I should not be here."

From the shadows a specter emerged, tall and stern with a long saturnine face. I wondered if he were the Devil himself.

"I should not be here. The true murderer has escaped," I pleaded.

The man looked at me through the bars as if examining a dangerous creature that he had whipped into submission and would destroy without a second thought.

"You must believe me. A man was with Mrs. Reynolds in that room. He stuffed the handkerchief into her mouth and pushed her from the window."

At last he opened my cell door. "Follow me," he instructed as he began to walk down a long corridor that seemed to stretch into infinity. Our footsteps echoed against the cold, stone floor, but not as loudly as the laughter from the villains we walked past, each recidivist pressing his face up against the bars of his cell, which distorted his features into those of a cackling demon, shouting out words I could not understand, curses and incantations from the depths of Hell itself. Some thrust their hands through the bars, grabbed at my clothing, pulled and tugged so that I stumbled from one side of the corridor to the other, tortured by their pinching fingers, the ragged edges of their nails digging into my flesh. Was this the corridor that led to Hell itself?

"Where are we going?" I cried out to my jailer.

"You shall see," he growled, without turning to look at me.

"You shall see!" cackled the inmates from their cages. "You shall see!"

And moments later, I did. At the end of the interminable corridor was a room like a small theater. On the stage was a scaffold, a noose that seemed to glow in the darkness and a masked and hooded hangman, wide of girth and all in black, who stood silently next to the deadly contraption. And when I turned from that instrument of death to the theater benches, I saw that they were filled with convicts dressed in gray uniforms, their faces hideously eager.

"We are ready," my jailer said to the hangman, who stepped forward and grabbed me, his hand so monstrously large that it encircled my arm like it was but a thin spindle of wood. He wrenched me into place and pulled the noose over my head in one fluid movement. The audience burst into rapturous applause, their raspy voices ululating, feet stamping in terrible rhythm.

"Now," the jailer commanded before I could scream out, and then I was plummeting inexorably down into utter blackness, so fast that all breath whistled from my lungs. I grasped at the rope around my neck, amazed that my hands had not been secured, and kicked and flailed, trying to halt my descent, to stop that inevitable wrench of rope on neck. Until all went black.

* * *

Metal clanged on metal, driving a spike of fear into my heart. I felt the itch of rope around my throat, tugging, pulling, choking me. And then, a voice.

"Up, do you hear me? Rise up."

Another clang. A set of keys against the bars. I opened my eyes. Peering through my cell bars was a specter—tall, stern, long saturnine face—the Devil's now familiar face.

"Wake, sir, wake!" he intoned.

And yet I could not, for surely I had died. I rubbed at my eyes, hoping the apparition before me would disappear, that I would be returned home, delivered from my nightmare, but it was soon clear that only part of my nightmare had been a dream.

"Here is your situation," my jailer told me. "Have someone bring me the journal you have stolen if you wish this to end."

I was stupefied by his pronouncement. "What journal?" I whispered, appalled that the jailer at Moyamensing Prison was, it seemed, in league with Frederic Renelle.

"Don't play stupid, Mr. Poe." He handed me a sheet of paper and a mechanical pencil through the bars. "Write a note stating you need the journal for evidence to prove your innocence and to secure your release. If it is delivered, we will make it so."

Thoughts crowded my mind as I considered his words. How many false witnesses were there to my supposed guilt? And what would happen to me in this terrible place before Dupin managed to secure my freedom?

"Your employer seems to have taken Miss Loddiges hostage," I said. "The lady whose disappearance was reported to the officers of the police. Will he release her if he receives the journal?"

"If he has the lady, no doubt he will," the jailer said.

I could see no other option but to write the letter he had demanded. I then folded the note and handed it to my jailer. He put it into his pocket and disappeared down the dark corridor. I returned to my pallet to pray that when Renelle at last had the journal he would indeed release Miss Loddiges and myself. And yet I knew that he might more easily hide his crimes from the world if he murdered us both.

41

SATURDAY, 23 MARCH 1844

The sunlight seemed sharper than usual, as did the noises of the street when I stepped out into the glare of morning. I paused for a moment to close my eyes and breathe in the scent of spring and freedom. When I opened them again, Dupin was before me, as if summoned from the air itself, and without exchanging a word, we began to walk in step away from the formidable marble facade and Gothic towers and battlements of Moyamensing Prison.

"Shall I find us a carriage?" Dupin said after a while.

"I'd like to walk further. The air will help clear my head."

Dupin nodded. "I am sorry for what happened, Poe. I should have guessed that Renelle had something planned when he gave you the tickets."

"How could you have? The man's skills as an actor are comparable to those of Mrs. Reynolds. I did my best to save her, truly I did, and my failure will haunt me."

"You could not have succeeded and must not castigate yourself. I went through every detail of what occurred with your wife, who has an acute sense of observation and excellent memory. I then examined the theater in general and the room in which the murder took place, measuring each area most carefully. As the villain had already forced Mrs. Reynolds to the window when you came through the door, which is sixteen feet away, it was inconceivable that any human might reach her in time to prevent her death."

I did not bother to tell Dupin that he had not envisaged the scenario exactly as it had happened, for it was kind of him to endeavor to salve my conscience. Despite what he might say or Sissy might think or I might wish, the vision of the actress's murder would never leave my mind—the silk of her dress slipping through the wood, her foot on the window frame as she fell through its gaping mouth, her dainty satin slipper huddled upon the floor.

We walked along Passyunk Avenue until we came to Seventh Street, and then continued north in silence as I watched all around me, absorbing the life of the city, quietly rejoicing in it.

"I wonder if Renelle truly had the means to keep me imprisoned if we did not deliver the journal."

Dupin was silent for a time, then answered carefully, "It is always surprising what people will do for money. I am certain justice would have prevailed, but it was not possible to ensure your safety while imprisoned amongst enemies. In any case, it is not important that he has the journal now. If there are clues regarding the location of the jewel he seeks or the king's tomb, they must be in the pages drawn by Andrew Mathews in 1841, and of course we did not deliver those."

"Truly?" I asked, my heart lifting.

"Why would we when only we know of their existence?"

"And has he freed Miss Loddiges?" I asked hopefully.

"No, but we did not expect him to. Miss Loddiges's captor is both arrogant and dangerous, but I will free her tonight."

"I will be with you."

Dupin frowned slightly, surprised by my words. "Are you certain? I presumed you would wish to remain with your wife."

"Of course that is what I wish, but it is not what I will do. Sissy fervently hopes for Miss Loddiges's safety and will understand that it is best if we undertake our plan together, for we cannot presume that Renelle has actually gone to New York if he has been masterminding this infernal scheme to get the journal."

"True," Dupin agreed.

"And he is less likely to anticipate trouble tonight, after all that has befallen me."

"If you genuinely believe yourself recovered enough, it is of course the best plan."

"The thought of bringing Renelle to justice tonight is a true tonic," I said grimly. "How he uncovered the history between Reynolds's family and mine I cannot fathom and what he did—for surely it was Renelle who murdered her—is the work of the Devil himself."

"Do not read too much into it. I would be surprised if Renelle knew anything of your history with George Reynolds. I believe he simply observed after his presentation that you and Reynolds deeply dislike each other, and his anger at Mrs. Reynolds for making him look the fool made him more than happy to sacrifice her to get to you."

Accurate as it no doubt was, Dupin's logical dissection of what had occurred offered little comfort. Four years previously I might have appreciated any retribution meted out to the woman who had tried, with her paramour, to destroy me, but today I felt only guilt and grief.

"Success and a new identity has not changed my nemesis," I said. "But I think it improved his wife. Sissy liked her very much and she can sense a wicked heart in an instant. Despite all the ways that Mrs. Reynolds made me suffer in London without cause, I felt that I could forgive her when I observed how she spoke with Sissy. And I believe she tried to end the bad blood between her husband and me. All that she did to hurt me in the past was because she loved George Reynolds. I cannot understand her love for such a man, but I could see that their love was true. And I will be forever sorry that she died because we crossed paths again."

Dupin nodded, but said nothing more. We walked on until my home came into view. Sissy and Muddy must have been stationed by the window in vigil, for the door flew open and my wife ran up the path and threw her arms around me. We stood quietly on the footpath, her face buried in my coat, her shoulders juddering. Muddy approached after a time and gently ushered us to the door.

"Come into the warm," she said. "Come into the warm, dear boy."

42

We took the last train to Germantown and waited in a tavern until it closed, just after midnight, then set off for Renelle Mansion on foot. The waxing moon was near halfway to full and spilled enough light to help us to make our way through the woodland that surrounded the house. We had avoided the long private drive, hoping to keep our arrival concealed, but the journey through the trees was not easy as there were innumerable low branches to catch at one's clothing or deliver a stinging blow to the face. The distance we had to travel was no more than four hundred yards, but it felt as if we had walked a mile by the time we reached the woodland's perimeter at the back of the mansion. We both scanned the house—all the windows were dark, which was promising.

"Thick draperies may be concealing candlelight, so we must proceed with caution," Dupin said in a low voice. "I will make my way past the caretaker's cottage to the springhouse to ensure it is safe for us to enter it and that there is access to a passageway to the kitchen. Should someone give chase or apprehend me, run in the opposite direction and, if you are able, make a diversion."

He scurried, bent low, toward the springhouse, and I tracked him with my eyes until his movements were lost to the darkness. As I waited anxiously, the sounds around me seemed to amplify—the unexpected crack of a twig, the rustling of leaves overhead and across the ground. I felt a blast of air across my shoulders and crouched to avoid a blow, but it was an owl on the wing, which swooped to the ground and glided back into the night sky with a field mouse grasped in its talons.

Dupin materialized moments later. "It appears safe. The cottage is dark. I saw no one," he said in a low voice. "The springhouse door is unlocked."

"And the tunnel?"

I caught a flash of white as Dupin grinned. "It is as I suspected. There is a door inside and a tunnel leading towards the mansion. Come."

Dupin retraced his steps at a trot and I followed, crouching low as he did. He opened the springhouse door, and I flinched as it creaked. We slipped inside and cautiously made our way down four steps. A lucifer match rasped and the glow of Dupin's candle dappled the springhouse walls and floor with gold. Where the two met there was a shallow trench filled with water in which perishable foodstuffs were placed to stay cool. A spring bubbled up somewhere at the far end of the structure. In the heavy gloom the place had the grim atmosphere of a dungeon.

Dupin lit a candle for me, and we made our way into the tunnel, the light bouncing off greenish walls, the smell of damp hanging in the air like death. The thirsty darkness seemed to drink up the light, but we kept going until we came to another door. It appeared very solid, and I prayed that it wasn't locked. Dupin handed his candle to me, reached for the latch and pushed. Nothing. He tried again, heaving against the wood with his shoulder. It creaked under his assault, then slowly the door swung into the kitchen and my heart fluttered with fear that an adversary might be waiting on the other side, pistol drawn. More shadow greeted us, and we cautiously made our way forward, Dupin leading. Only the faint red glow of dying embers in the fireplace lit the kitchen, which suggested that the housekeeper and caretaker had retired a good hour or more ago. I started to feel cautiously optimistic that we would achieve our mission. We came to the hallway and Dupin gestured that we should climb the stairs. The light from our candles illuminated the portraits of Renelle's forebears, who glowered as we passed them. The hallway ran to the left and the right, and we had calculated from the size of the house that there were perhaps seven bedrooms, Renelle's study and one other room up in the turret. We had initially presumed that Miss Loddiges was imprisoned there, but Dupin wondered if that were too obvious and Renelle might be sleeping there himself. Despite his concerns, I impetuously made my way to the turret stairs and when halfway up I noticed a glow under the door. Someone was surely inside. Dupin tugged upon my sleeve to halt my ascension.

"Do not be hasty. It may be a trap," he whispered.

Dupin was correct to be cautious, for what excuse might we offer if the night watch were summoned? And yet, what choice did we have but to play housebreaker? Miss Loddiges had been missing for eleven days. Her friend had been murdered, as had his father. I felt in every fiber of my being that she was still alive, but might not remain so for long.

I crept up further, gave Dupin my candle, then knelt down so I could peer through the gap beneath the door. The room seemed well-enough lit, presumably by an Argand lamp. The floorboards were bare and to the left I saw the iron legs of a bed. Thick curtains fell to the floor on the opposite wall, and a fire burned brightly in the hearth to the right. There in front of the fire was a chair and, to my relief, a woman's long skirts. But a less reassuring thought came to me—was it Miss Loddiges or the housekeeper? I raised myself to my knees and Dupin held the candles so that they briefly illuminated the keyhole, which I immediately peered through. I had a good view of the window, a glimpse of the bed, and could just discern the back of the chair, but nothing useful about its occupant. It came to me then that there was only one course of action in the limited time we had. I knocked as softly as I could upon the door, then turned to Dupin with my finger held to my lips. He nodded. I heard the rustling of skirts but nothing more, and crouched again to peer through the keyhole. My view of the chair's occupant was still obscured. I knocked again, a bit more firmly, but not loudly enough, I hoped, to disturb anyone in the bedrooms.

"What is it?"

My heart leaped—Miss Loddiges! It was her voice.

"Miss Loddiges, it is I—Poe," I said softly. "Do you know where the key is?"

I peered through the keyhole and moments later my view was blocked by her eye peering back at me. I leaned back from the door and Dupin let the glow of the candle fall upon my face. I heard a gasp.

"Mr. Poe!" she whispered. "Has he been arrested?"

"No. So we must hurry. Do you know where the key is?"

"His study, perhaps. The housekeeper has a key, but I believe she keeps them with her."

"Where is her room?" I whispered.

"The first bedroom to the right of the staircase as you ascend."

"Here, Poe. Let me try." Dupin gestured that I should let him near the keyhole. He withdrew a ring of keys from his pocket. "Please." He indicated that I should hold both candles to illuminate the keyhole and selected one of the keys. He tried it, then another; the third key turned and there was a satisfying click. He quickly opened the door and we were inside, where Miss Loddiges waited, her hands held anxiously in front of her mouth. She was wearing a very plain rough-spun dress, much of the type a servant might wear, and house slippers.

"Truly I thought I would perish here." She threw her arms around me as a small child might, then pulled away and fluttered her hands about her eyes, blotting tears. She took a breath and her face set into a calmer, more English demeanor.

"Did he confess why he has acted so treacherously?" I asked as softly as I could.

"We must go," Dupin said in a low voice. "All will be in vain if the housekeeper wakes or Renelle finds us."

"He has taken my coat, my boots, my bonnet," Miss Loddiges said.

"No matter. I will give you my coat. The slippers will have to suffice, I'm afraid. Now let us escape this place as quietly as we can."

Miss Loddiges picked up the Argand lamp, but I shook my head and handed her my candle. We made our way from her prison, creeping down the stairs before her so we might shield her if confronted. On the landing, Dupin paused to listen and all was reassuringly quiet. He began to descend the grand staircase and I took several steps after him until I noticed that Miss Loddiges was no longer dogging my footsteps. She had vanished. The housekeeper's door was still closed and I heard no sound from within it. The door to the turret room was closed. And then I noticed a faint flickering glow emerging from Renelle's study—I could only think that Miss Loddiges knew of evidence that would implicate Renelle in Jeremiah Mathews's murder, but truly it was not the time to search for it. I hurried after her, and moments later candlelight glinted upon the wall and I knew that Dupin was on my heels. We entered Renelle's study and found the door to an adjoining room ajar. I crept to its threshold and witnessed a peculiar tableau. Miss Loddiges had wedged her candle into a holder on the mantelpiece and had placed a small birdcage on a table. With visibly shaking hands, she was trying to unlock the door to an extremely large cage that appeared to be empty. Then a flittering motion caught my eye and shadows swarmed over the walls behind what looked to be a large white hawk-moth.

"Miss Loddiges, there is no time!"

"If I don't take her now, he will murder her," she said stubbornly.

I was confounded by the lady's eccentricity. "I don't think— "

"She is the reason he has kept me prisoner."

Dupin held his candle closer to the cage and gave a soft gasp.

"*Loddigesia mirabilis*—your father's namesake—and an albino," he muttered. "It is a most elusive species, but this bird—she is exceptional."

I peered more closely and realized that what I had taken to be a large, pale moth was actually a hummingbird with a peculiar tail. The bird was exquisite, her white feathers glimmered under the candlelight like freshly fallen snow. Two, long wispy strands tipped with oval feathers sprang from either side of the bird's tail feathers and bobbed in the air. It was like a creature from a fairy tale.

Miss Loddiges succeeded in capturing the tiny white bird in her hands and transferred it into the smaller cage.

"The jewel," Dupin said, a mixture of wonder and annoyance in his voice. "How did I not fathom it?"

"This is the jewel?" And then I remembered the Cloud Warrior crown with its hummingbird and Andrew Mathews's seemingly unfinished drawing of the spatuletail hummingbird in his strange picture of the birds in the tree.

Dupin nodded. "This is the specimen referred to in Jeremiah Mathews's log of the birds he collected: '*Mathewsii nubes*, live'. It is the jewel he kept hidden in his ship cabin—Jeremiah

Mathews captured the rarest example of an elusive hummingbird species."

"And that hummingbird is mine."

I spun round to see Professor Renelle standing in the doorway, pistol leveled at us.

Dupin turned slowly. He appeared unsurprised by Renelle's
presence. "The speaking engagement was a hoax?" he asked
genially.

"Naturally," Renelle said, as he haphazardly aimed the pistol
at each of us.

"Please put away the gun, professor," I said in my most
reasonable voice. "Murder is not a result that any of us would
wish for."

"I believe the law will be on my side when I report that I fired
on intruders who broke into my home."

"It is clear you are not averse to murder," Dupin said, as if
making pleasant small talk. "What provoked you to kill Andrew
Mathews?"

"He fell victim to an accident—I did not kill him."

"Oh? What happened?" Dupin asked.

"The man refused to divulge what he found on my expedition. He tried to prevent me from collecting artifacts in the
burial chamber. He was belligerent and threatening and careless," Renelle said. "When climbing a ladder up to the cave, he
slipped and fell."

Dupin nodded as if Renelle's explanation was perfectly plausible. "And did you come to know what Andrew Mathews
found?"

"I believe he found the *derrotero*," Renelle said impatiently.
"The map that shows where the king's tomb is. He was inside
the burial chamber when I was not there, he and that guide.
They were in collusion. But Mathews died before he could find
the king's tomb."

"So what happened to the *derrotero?*" Dupin asked.

"He must have hidden it in his bird collecting journal, which disappeared. It was my property, but someone took it. When Loddiges sent Andrew Mathews's son to collect birds on my last expedition, I was suspicious. When he poisoned my water so that I could not travel and went on to the lost city by himself, I knew young Mathews had the map."

Renelle's fury was tangible. I began to fear that Dupin was making the situation worse, that his need to fully unravel the mystery might result in our murders. And then I noticed that he was inching slowly and carefully toward Renelle, doing his best to keep the professor focused on airing his grievances.

"So you presumed that Jeremiah Mathews had found the legendary jewel and hidden it in his cabin," I said, hoping to divert Renelle's attention from Dupin. "And when you were refused permission to board the *Bounteous* at the Lazaretto, you hired the Schuylkill rangers to loot his cabin. Jeremiah Mathews tried to stop the thieves and was drowned, and so you ended up with the true jewel of the Chachapoyas, but did not know that at the time."

Renelle scowled at me, making it clear my supposition was correct. Dupin quickly edged closer to the professor.

"You didn't find the emerald or treasure map you were seeking in Jeremiah Mathews's cabin, but you still believed that he and his father had made discoveries about the king's tomb they were hiding from you," I continued.

"Recorded in those infernal notebooks they were continually scribbling in," Renelle snapped, waving the pistol again.

"It must have been very disappointing to learn that Miss Loddiges had passed the journal into the care of Mr. Poe," Dupin said.

Renelle couldn't help taking on the stance of a rooster, chest puffed out with pride. "Not especially. Miss Loddiges had far more to offer me than simply the journal, you see. I had every intention of using her to progress my negotiations more quickly."

"The hummingbird," Miss Loddiges interjected. "He wrote to my father about the spatuletail, claiming he found it on the expedition. He took daguerreotypes of the bird and sent some as proof of its existence. He believed my father would pay a very high price for such a rarity," she added bitterly. "But my father refused to offer him the fee he desired for the spatuletail alive, so Professor Renelle wanted me to kill and preserve the bird in order to sell it to another collector."

"And the stupid girl refused. It is the most rare and exquisite hummingbird known to man and should be preserved forever while it is in peak condition. Her recalcitrance is unforgivable."

"I will not kill such a rare and sublime creature. I simply will not."

Renelle shook his head with exaggerated disappointment. "I truly wished for you to stuff the bird, Miss Loddiges, as you have immense skill. I had hoped you would kill the creature in such a way that the body would remain perfect, but if I must shoot it myself and get someone else to preserve it, then so I shall." Renelle aimed his pistol at the tiny bird. There was a click as he pulled back the hammer.

"No!" Miss Loddiges gasped.

As if in answer to her shouted prayer, Renelle suddenly collapsed forward and the gun skittered across the floorboards out of reach. Then a man dressed all in black was roping him up like a steer. When he was finished, he hauled Renelle over and got to his feet.

Renelle, dazed, looked up at his aggressor and growled, "You."

"Yes." The man had a deep voice, and when candlelight illuminated his features, the doppelgänger of Jeremiah Mathews was before us. Miss Loddiges was frozen with wonder. He left Renelle in his ignominious position on the floor and approached the bird cage. A beatific smile illuminated his solemn countenance as he studied the hummingbird. He muttered something, perhaps a prayer.

"Was it you who went into the glasshouse with our hummingbird?" Miss Loddiges asked in a voice that faltered with emotion. "And did you move the birds displayed in my sitting room?" She stared at the man as if examining his every feature, then whispered, "Was it you in my room that night?"

"Yes," he said quietly. "I am sorry if I frightened you. I was searching for *la Joya*." His words were inflected with a Spanish accent and his sentiment sounded genuine.

"I was not frightened. I just . . . hoped you were someone else." Miss Loddiges looked as though her heart would break.

"From Professor Renelle's reaction, I presume you were on the first expedition with him and that you were a friend to Andrew Mathews. May I ask who you are?" Dupin's polite inquiry was all the more strange given the circumstances we found ourselves in.

The man scrutinized Dupin for a moment, then said, "Andrew Mathews and I were friends. I was on the 1841 expedition as a guide and translator—my people come from the Chachapoyan mountains. This one," he said, tapping Renelle's foot with his own, "endangered everyone on the expedition with his reckless behavior. Two of my people died and he wanted to leave their bodies where they fell." The man said the words as if they hurt his mouth. "Because Andrew was hired by the lady's father to collect birds, he went where he wanted to go, which made this one angrier. He warned Andrew not to try to hide anything from him."

"So Andrew Mathews put clues in his journal?" Dupin asked.

The man shrugged. "Perhaps. He asked me to make sure his son received the journal if he met the same fate as my friends. I agreed because he was a man of honor. When Andrew discovered *la Joya* and I told him the legend of this bird—how she is sacred to us—he let her remain in her home."

"Ridiculous," Renelle growled. "The hummingbird is a rarity that must be studied by scientists, not kept in confinement or eaten by savages."

The Chachapoyan's expression suggested that he might like to murder Renelle.

"You made the bird call to warn us about the lockpick," Dupin said. "And you released the pigeon into the house."

"Yes."

"So that we might find Renelle and make it easier for you to take the bird?"

The man did not confirm Dupin's theory, nor did he contradict him. He turned instead to Miss Loddiges, whose eyes were still fixed on him in wonderment. "*La Joya* embodies the spirit of the Cloud People. She must be returned to her home."

"Did you know Jeremiah?" she asked softly. "Were you on the expedition with him?"

The man shook his head. "I was working in the Chincha Islands. I could not protect *la Joya* or inform Andrew's son of his error. I believe he would have understood, as his father did, that we need *la Joya* for our people to rise again."

"Pure nonsense. The Cloud People are finished. The Spaniards and the Incas saw to that centuries ago," Renelle grunted from the floor. "Will you truly let this heathen take one of the rarest and most elusive birds in all of creation away with him?"

Dupin's face creased with disdain. "It is not my decision."

"Miss Loddiges must make that choice," I said. "It was her friend who captured the hummingbird for her father and who died trying to bring the creature to its new home."

Miss Loddiges peered through the bars of the cage at the miniature bird, which was in calm repose on its tiny perch. "So beautiful," she whispered. "So very beautiful." A moment later she gathered herself and announced in a clear voice, "I would like to have all the daguerreotypes of the spatuletail Professor Renelle kept for himself."

"No!" Renelle shouted. "Absolutely not."

"I believe I have the right," Miss Loddiges said coldly. "You are nothing more than a thief and a cold-blooded killer. Furthermore, Jeremiah's journal must be returned to me and *la Joya* must go back to the Chachapoyas. It is the just thing to do."

The Chachapoyan nodded, his expression solemn.

Miss Loddiges's face was full of sorrow as she gazed at the tiny bird. "You will get her back safely, won't you?" she said quietly.

"I believe that I will," he replied. "It is the destiny of *la Joya* to go home."

Miss Loddiges nodded and wrapped a heavy cover around the bird cage. "Will you tell me your name?" she asked the Chachapoyan as she held the cage toward him.

He took it and said, "I am Colibrí."

"Colibrí. Very good," she said with the faintest smile. "I am Helena."

"Helena," he echoed softly, then turned to leave.

"I believe you know where Bartram's estate is," she called out hurriedly as he reached the door. The Chachapoyan stopped and faced her, but said nothing. "I thought I saw Jeremiah there one night, but I suppose it was you." Miss Loddiges looked as if she might weep, but gathered herself and said, "I worry for the spatuletail. She is so delicate and Peru is so very far away." She waved a trembling hand at the covered bird cage. "Come to Bartram's estate tomorrow. I cannot bear the thought that she might die." It was clear from the Chachapoyan's expression that he was mistrustful of Miss Loddiges's intentions, which she quickly perceived. "I give you my word that we will assist you in returning the spatuletail—the jewel or *la Joya* as you say—to your homeland. I will pay for your passage to Peru if you will come to Bartram's tomorrow afternoon," she added. When Colibrí remained silent, she said with more than a little desperation, "My friend was murdered trying to bring the bird to our nursery in Paradise Fields so it might live within our glasshouses there. I see now that he was in error, but he did not deserve to lose his life. Mrs. Carr is my friend, and I pledge to you that she and her husband will assist you." Miss Loddiges stared at the Chachapoyan, who held her gaze for such a long time it seemed that he was examining her very soul.

"Perhaps," he finally said. Then he slipped away with the ghostly hummingbird like a phantom from an exotic dream.

43

Candlelight scuttled along the walls, enlarging our shadows into grotesque monsters. Miss Loddiges preceded me down the hallway, despite my attempts to overtake her. We had left Dupin to watch over Renelle, who was secured in his study, and had taken the devil's pistol and keys so we might disarm his housekeeper and caretaker. I held the gun clumsily and was not certain that my aim would prove true, should I be required to use it—I dearly hoped that would not be the case.

When we reached the housekeeper's door, some of my anxiousness abated as a reverberating snore was audible. While my own mother-in-law disrupted our sleep on occasion with the clacking of her breathing, this was very loud indeed and there was no doubt that the sleeper was immersed in her dreams. Miss Loddiges boldly threw open the door before I could stop her and there lay the housekeeper, her noisy emanations obscuring all other sounds. It was impossible that she might have heard the earlier scuffle. Miss Loddiges shook the slumbering lady until she emerged to wakefulness and let out a wail of pure terror. She pulled the quilt right up to her nose, so only her eyes peered out from the gap between it and her large nightcap.

"Hush now, Miss Thomassen. There is no point in making a fuss," Miss Loddiges instructed sternly. "We have Professor Renelle in custody and the night watch will arrive soon. You will be locked in your room until they question you."

Miss Thomassen immediately burst into noisy tears. "But I am innocent!" she sniffled, gulping air like a land-anchored fish. "I did nothing wrong!"

"You most certainly did. You are an accomplice to Professor Renelle's crime," I said.

"No! That was Jimmerson. He helped take the lady."

"And you did nothing to address what you knew to be a crime," I retorted. "It was your duty to inform the police and if you fail in that tonight, things will go very badly for you indeed." It was something of an idle threat given that I had no way of knowing what influence Renelle might have over the local officers of the law, but I hoped it might deter the housekeeper from corroborating any untruths he might tell. A gasp from Miss Loddiges interrupted my thoughts, and I saw that she was staring at a pair of very small boots on top of the dresser, like a religious artifact upon an altar.

"My boots." She grabbed them and sat in a rocking chair to pull them on.

Miss Thomassen's weeping increased in volume, whether at the loss of the boots or fear of prison was not clear. She curled up into a ball like a small child and sniveled, "It's not my fault. I did nothing wrong. It's not my fault!"

"You will have to prove that," Miss Loddiges said, adding her own threat to mine.

"Now where is Jimmerson?" I said. "Is he in the house?"

"The cottage. Or he should be. He retired before I did," she whimpered.

"Thank you kindly," Miss Loddiges said coldly and marched from the room.

"Remember, tell the truth and things will go more easily for you," I advised, taking the key from the inside of the door and pulling it shut. I hurriedly locked the housekeeper in and ran after the determined young taxidermist, fearful that she might try to confront Jimmerson on her own. I reached her side just as she was approaching the front door.

"This way," I said, indicating the hall leading to the kitchen. "There is a tunnel connecting the kitchen and the springhouse, which will provide an element of surprise."

"For what purpose?" Miss Loddiges said. "You have Renelle's pistol."

"What if the caretaker has a hunting rifle or some other firearm? I've no wish to duel with the fellow." I did not reveal my lack of confidence in hitting a moving target or out-shooting someone intent on killing us. "If Jimmerson heard the scuffle with Renelle, he will be expecting me to approach the cottage from the side of the house and will have an unimpeded shot as I cross the lawn. But if I emerge from the springhouse, he will not be able to see me from the window, thus providing me a chance to capture him unawares."

"I am going with you," Miss Loddiges said.

"Certainly not. I cannot in good conscience put you in harm's way again."

Miss Loddiges picked up the poker from the fireplace. "Two against one gives us better odds, and you will not keep me imprisoned in the kitchen. The man wronged me, and I will not stand by and do nothing." Her words sounded all the more fierce when expounded in her small, angry voice.

"I disagree with your decision, but time is too short to argue. Stay behind me, please. If I am to be thought a cad after this folly, at least allow me to shield you as best I can."

She nodded, and I opened the door that appeared to lead to a cupboard and descended down the stone steps, Miss Loddiges at my heels. We both inhaled sharply as a rush of cold air near swallowed the candle flames, but they recovered and we continued through the dank tunnel. I cautiously pushed open the door that led into the springhouse. There was a scurry of feet and a mouse or something larger disappeared into its lair. Thankfully the springhouse was otherwise empty.

"The moon is bright enough to make our way without the candles," I said.

Miss Loddiges nodded and blew out the flame she carried.

"But please wait here," I pleaded. "It would be infinitely safer."

"I will not. I am not afraid, and I wish to know if Jimmerson had anything to do with Jeremiah's death. Now let us capture the villain before he escapes." She pushed open the door, so I had no choice but to extinguish my candle flame and step out into the thin moonlight with her. We scuttled across the lawn like night creatures and waited at the side of the cottage, listening for any movement inside. All was quiet. I put my hand to the pistol and felt the reassuring cool of its metal barrel and its wooden handle. I ardently hoped I would not have to use it, but knew that I must make the caretaker think that I would. Taking a deep breath, I threw open the cottage door.

"Mr. Jimmerson, sit up and show me your hands!" I shouted.

There was a groan, a thrashing of bedclothes, and the caretaker sat up. I moved swiftly toward him, clutching my pistol.

"Hands up — now!"

I could not truly see what Jimmerson was doing until a faint light bled into the gloom. Miss Loddiges had lit the lantern that was on the small table, and I was at once glad of her presence. Jimmerson's face was the picture of terror, eyes darting from the pistol in my hand to the fire poker Miss Loddiges brandished.

"What do you want?" he stuttered. "I have nothing to steal."

"Do not play the innocent," Miss Loddiges said sharply. "You know very well who I am. Your victim has escaped and will bring you to justice. Now put on your trousers and coat. You must come with us."

"Where?"

"The police will wish to speak with you," I said. "We have captured your employer and you must testify against him."

"And confess your crimes," Miss Loddiges added.

"But I did nothing," he declared. "I am innocent."

"Do not lie. You were Renelle's accomplice when he kidnapped me. You carried me to the coach!" Miss Loddiges protested indignantly.

Shame-faced, the man said nothing more as he climbed cautiously out of bed and pulled on his trousers, then put on a coat over his nightshirt. He took his time lacing his boots until Miss Loddiges shook the poker at him.

"Do not believe that I am afraid to use this weapon," she said.

Jimmerson got quickly to his feet and walked outside with his hands on his head, while I followed behind him, my pistol directed at his back. Jimmerson whined and whimpered the entire walk toward the house, but he was not fully moronic for he had judged my character accurately. When we were about ten yards from the door, he took to his heels, leaving me with the option of shooting him in the back.

"Fire before he reaches the woodland!" Miss Loddiges cried out.

I do not know if she truly meant what she said or was merely trying to frighten the man, but the caretaker's speed doubled and he disappeared into the trees.

"You had a clear shot," she snapped, wheeling to face me, pure anger on her face.

"A clear shot at murder and I am in no hurry to commit such an act."

"He deserved it!" she shouted, hurling the poker as if it were a spear.

"No, he did not," I said quietly. "He was but a pawn. Now, let us go find a night watchman and inform him of Renelle's treachery."

"Fine," Miss Loddiges muttered. "But I would not have hesitated in your position."

I was aghast at the lady's vehemence and very glad she did not have her own pistol. Through her work she had become inured to the sight of dead creatures, and I wondered if that made her equally inured to the thought of murder.

44

The long walk to the night watchman's station house in Germantown was made in relative silence as my attempts at conversation were met with monosyllabic answers. Miss Loddiges's tangible fury at my failure to shoot the caretaker was most disconcerting. When we found the watchman, she described all that had happened in precise detail, and when the watchman roused an officer of the police, she repeated her story; the officer immediately agreed to make his way to Renelle Mansion to apprehend her abductor.

The night watchman secured us a carriage to take us back home, and we arrived to a worried but joyful Sissy, who threw her arms around each of us before ushering us to the parlor fire. Muddy brought in cups of steaming broth, which improved Miss Loddiges's humor greatly, and she recounted her abduction to Sissy when gently pressed.

"It was incredible," she told my wife. "I had never imagined that such a thing might occur in nature, that number of birds in one place. And the pigeons themselves are exquisite. The delicate colors, the elegant shape of them, and so unafraid of humans. Which will be their downfall," she said darkly. "When the men appeared amongst the trees and began to fire their guns, truly it was a massacre. I could not believe that anyone might be so cruel as to slaughter such magnificent creatures, but to the hunters, it was great sport."

"It was a terrible thing to see," I said. "Forgive me for taking you there."

"No, no," Miss Loddiges said, shaking her head. "I needed to witness it. It made me question everything—my father's collection, my taxidermy work and, dare I say, humanity. Must we extinguish the lives of these wondrous creatures with the aim of fashioning a facsimile? Surely a drawing of the bird alive in its own habitat is preferable to a dead bird used to ornament our parlors. And as these thoughts ran through my mind, I understood that Jeremiah had come to a similar conclusion, that he had found a hummingbird so extraordinary he had wished to bring it back to us alive—that he hadn't killed and skinned it. And just as that thought came into my mind, someone grabbed me and stuffed a handkerchief into my mouth so that I nearly choked. He then hoisted me up and his accomplice—the caretaker—held my feet. As they carried me through the woodland, I tried to struggle and could not believe that no one seemed to notice what was happening to me, all were so focused on shooting the birds. I managed to drop my gloves on the path and then a hummingbird ornament, which I thought would be clues that I had been abducted if you managed to find them."

"My word," my mother-in-law mumbled.

"Excellent clues indeed," I said. "We searched every inch of the ground, but it was only when we came across your gloves and the bird that we had any notion of what might have happened to you and the direction in which your abductor had taken you."

"When we arrived at Renelle Mansion, the professor pretended that my father had sent him. Quite why he thought I would believe that my father would want me hoisted over a man's shoulder, bundled into a carriage and locked in a room before I was escorted home is a mystery to me."

"He made quite a mistake in presuming that you are lacking in intelligence," Sissy declared. "Truly, it is a trial to be continually underestimated."

"Indeed," Miss Loddiges said. "Although in this instance it was, perhaps, an advantage. As much as it pained me to play the imbecile, I thought doing so might provide an opportunity to escape, but my plan did not succeed."

"You cannot imagine how sorry I am that we did not discover where you were more quickly," I said, brimming with guilt.

"That was nearly impossible," Miss Loddiges replied with great magnanimity. "I myself knew nothing of my father's dealings with Professor Renelle until I met the man, and it is to my infinite shame that I now perceive the lengths men will go to in order to claim a prize in the name of science, when truly they wish to aggrandize their reputation and profit from it."

It was then that Dupin arrived at our door with the news that Renelle had been safely escorted to Moyamensing Prison. I felt great pleasure in hearing that.

"I warned the officer of the police that Renelle has a prison guard in his pay, and he pledged to spend the night there to ensure the professor remains locked up. He is not as admired in Germantown as he or we presumed," said Dupin with a smile. "You will need to identify the guard in the morning if the man has the audacity to return to the prison, or provide a description of him if he is not there."

"I should be only too glad to. I will go at the crack of dawn."

Dupin then produced a bottle of very fine brandy, which he had mysteriously procured, presumably from Renelle Mansion, and handed Jeremiah Mathews's journal to Miss Loddiges.

She gasped and held it close to her heart. "Thank you," she said. "I thought I would never see it again, and that pained me more than I can describe."

Sissy fetched five glasses, which Dupin filled with brandy. "Let us toast Miss Loddiges's liberty," he said.

We raised our glasses then drank deeply from them.

"Please, continue your story," he added.

Miss Loddiges took another large gulp of brandy, then said, "Initially, Professor Renelle treated me well enough. As I explained earlier, he pretended that my father had hired him to bring me back to England. That was almost credible, although I could not believe my father would sanction such rough treatment no matter how angry he was with me."

"Of course not," Sissy murmured.

"The professor told me he had booked passage back to England and that I would be his guest until we sailed, for he would accompany me. In the meantime, he had some work that my father wished me to undertake. When he showed me the spatuletail and claimed he found it on the expedition, I knew he was lying, for it had to be the *Mathewsii nubes* noted in the inventory of birds Jeremiah had collected—the 'live' *Mathewsii nubes*. He must have named it to honor his father. Of course, I had not found the pages from his father's journal that you say were hidden inside the binding."

"They are here." I picked up the collection of drawings that was wrapped in a protective envelope of paper and handed it to Miss Loddiges.

"They hold vital clues that Andrew Mathews knew his son would spot," Dupin said. "Birds that are not endemic to Peru. The first letter of each bird spelled out 'Renelle'."

"How exquisite," she murmured when she saw the first sketch from Andrew Mathew's journal. "Jeremiah's father had such skill in bringing the birds to life on the page." She leafed through the beautiful drawings, intently studying each one. The silence was bruised by her pain, but none of us wished to interrupt it with some unworthy platitude. "How alone Jeremiah must have felt, traveling such a distance with the man who took his father's life," she finally said. "It will be difficult for me to forgive my own father for financing the expeditions of the dissembler responsible for our friends' deaths."

"Your father will have invested in Renelle's expeditions in good faith, for the professor is charismatic and more than charming when it suits him," I said. "And he does have an impressive reputation as an adventuring scholar, as we witnessed at the Philosophical Hall. But Renelle must have revealed his true colors to Andrew Mathews in Peru. Indeed, he made Mr. Mathews fear for his life enough to leave the hidden message in his journal."

"And he was proved right," Miss Loddiges murmured.

"We didn't put together the clues until we came to know of Professor Renelle's role in the expedition," I continued, "but I believe your friend quickly spotted the rogue birds and worked out Renelle's name, which he took as a warning. He told the professor nothing and was very guarded in his own journal, writing only of the birds and plants he saw, but no specifics regarding the lost city or his discovery of *la Joya*."

"Renelle is an obsessive and dangerous man," said Dupin. "So convinced was he that Andrew Mathews had found the legendary treasure, that he took Jeremiah's involvement in the 1843 expedition as confirmation that his father had sent him a map before he died."

"And he was not entirely wrong." Sissy indicated the drawing of the tree full of birds. "This might not be the fantastical picture it initially appears. There are elements in it that correspond with descriptions in Diego Fernández's book of the chamber where the Spaniards saw the enormous emerald. We wonder if this Peruvian pepper tree subsequently grew in the chamber and Andrew Mathews searched for the emerald here, but found what was in his eyes a more extraordinary treasure." She drew a circle around the hummingbird with her finger.

"And Jeremiah used this drawing to locate the chamber and took the white spatuletail to honor his father," Miss Loddiges murmured.

"And you," Sissy added.

Miss Loddiges nodded slowly, absorbing all we had told her. "What of the emerald and the king's treasure Professor Renelle was searching for. Is it truly there?"

"There was nothing in Jeremiah's journal to suggest he found it, or in the pages we have seen from his father's journal, so it is impossible to know without traveling to the Chachapoyas and finding our way to the lost city," Dupin said, his expression leading me to think that he might try that very thing some day. "But I would not be surprised to learn that the last king of the Cloud People is buried in a hidden chamber beneath the roots of the *Schinus molle*, as Mrs. Poe wisely suggested."

"Surrounded by baskets full of silver and gold and emeralds, and watched over from above by ghostly hummingbirds," my wife said.

Miss Loddiges tried to smile, but her lips trembled and her eyes began to brim. "So both Andrew and Jeremiah died for what might merely be a dream, a vision of a king's treasure that truly must be cursed if it exists at all."

My wife reached out and embraced her. Miss Loddiges hid her face as her grief turned into tears.

45

SUNDAY, 24 MARCH 1844

We were huddled around the kitchen table, warming ourselves with coffee, waiting for Miss Loddiges to eat the poached eggs Muddy had insisted on feeding her. I had been to Moyamensing prison to identify the guard in Renelle's employ, but he was nowhere to be seen. The description I had prepared of the fellow was read with knowing glances. I doubted that the man would be called to account for his actions, but equally I did not think he would return to his position at Moyamensing to assist Professor Renelle in any way.

"Helena has been a prisoner for two weeks. She needs sustenance," Muddy declared when she saw me glance at my pocket watch. I knew from her tone that nothing I could say would persuade her that Renelle had fed the lady on anything but bread and water. I sighed, poured myself more coffee and settled back to watch as Miss Loddiges mopped up every bit of egg with her bread and finished a second cup of coffee.

"That was delicious. I thank you with all my heart for your kindness," she said to Muddy, which pleased her enormously. "And I have not slept so well since I arrived in Philadelphia," she added. Muddy had done her best to make up a comfortable bed for Miss Loddiges on the sofa, relinquishing her own pillow.

"My dear, I am relieved you are safe and sound," my mother-in-law said. "If Virginia had been in your position my heart would ache with worry."

"As would mine, knowing how distressed you would be," my wife said, stroking her mother's arm. "But we must press on. We will have to leave here at half past eleven for Bartram's estate if we are to arrive in time for the assignation with the mysterious doppelgänger."

Before retiring for the night, Miss Loddiges had penned a letter to the Carrs to inform them that she was out of harm's way and to suggest that Colonel Carr might help to modify a Wardian case for the Chachapoyan to transport the ghostly hummingbird. Early that morning, on my way to the prison, I had taken her missive to an old man with a decent horse who could be relied upon to courier urgent letters and wait for the response. True to his promise, he brought back a note from Mrs. Carr, who was relieved to hear that Miss Loddiges was safe and promised to assist.

Dupin looked at his pocket watch for the third time with ill-disguised impatience. "It is nine o'clock. We should make our way to the officers of the police now to report the activities of Renelle's accomplices. If Father Nolan learns of Renelle's capture he might find a way to disappear, as might the two priests in his command who may have had a hand in Jeremiah Mathews's murder."

Dupin's words had the intended effect on Miss Loddiges. She leapt to her feet and immediately made her way to the hall, where her outerwear, which we had recovered from Renelle Mansion, was hanging up. She put on her bright blue cape and bonnet, and with her determined expression and commanding posture transformed into the image of an exotic adventuress, quite in contrast to the delicate English eccentric I had met almost four years previously.

Fifteen minutes later, we entered the office of the police. Lieutenant Webster and Captain Johnson looked as if they hadn't moved since Father Keane and I had first reported Miss Loddiges's abduction.

"Good morning, sirs," I said. "I am Edgar Poe, this is C. Auguste Dupin, and this is Miss Helena Loddiges, the lady I reported missing two weeks ago."

"Well, it appears she's been found, doesn't it?" Lieutenant Webster shrugged.

With no assistance from you, I wanted to add, but instead answered, "Yes, that was accomplished last night and Professor Frederic Renelle is now in Moyamensing Prison charged with her abduction and accused of Andrew Mathews's murder. We are here now to ask that you apprehend his accomplice, Father Nolan of St. Augustine Church, on suspicion of the murder of Father Michael Keane and for the theft of valuable treasure books from St. Augustine's library."

Lieutenant Webster and Captain Johnson stared at me as if I were a madman escaped from Old Blockley.

"Here is a signed statement that summarizes in detail what Mr. Poe just outlined," Dupin interjected, placing it in front of Webster. "I was with Mr. Poe at the Philosophical Hall on the nineteenth of March when we witnessed Father Nolan selling stolen treasure books to Professor Frederic Renelle. Evidence we have gathered during our efforts to rescue Miss Loddiges strongly suggests that Nolan was responsible for the murder of Father Michael Keane in St. Augustine's library, where he was found dead on the morning of the fifteenth of March. He may have committed the act himself or instructed his two known accomplices, Fathers Carroll and Healey, to murder their colleague after Father Keane discovered their illegal activities at St. Augustine's. We fear the priest may abscond when he learns that Renelle is in prison."

"A thieving, murdering priest at St. Augustine's?" Lieutenant Webster said with interest.

"I too have written a statement that explains in detail what I reported to an officer of the police in Germantown last night," Miss Loddiges announced. "In addition to all that Mr. Dupin has just told you, it is likely that Father Nolan, together with Professor Renelle, was involved in the murder of my friend, Jeremiah Mathews, on the twenty-sixth of October 1843 while he was on a ship anchored at the Lazaretto in Philadelphia." She placed several ink-filled pages before Lieutenant Webster. "I want justice for my friend," she said fiercely.

"More murders by the priest, Johnson," Webster said with raised eyebrows.

"I heard that, sir," Johnson replied.

"A dangerous place that St. Augustine's."

"A regular hornet's nest," agreed Johnson.

"Then you must act," Miss Loddiges said, as if speaking to someone feeble-minded.

"Oh, we will," Webster said with a smirk to Johnson.

"Good, then that is settled. Now, I would like my gloves back—they are yellow. Mr. Poe gave them to you as evidence of my abduction. Along with a hummingbird ornament for my hat."

"Johnson, do we have yellow gloves and a bird ornament? Delivered two weeks ago by Mr. Poe?"

Johnson gazed up at the shelf with thirty pigeonholes mounted on the wall and reached into the space labelled "P". He pulled out a small parcel of brown paper and unwrapped it in front of Miss Loddiges, revealing the hummingbird nestled on the dainty yellow gloves. "These them?"

"Thank you." She pulled on the gloves and attached the ornament to her bonnet as if returning a bird to its nest, then fixed her gaze on the two officers. "Shall we go to St. Augustine's, gentlemen?"

It was not truly a question. Miss Loddiges swept from the building. Lieutenant Webster collected a billy club and got to his feet.

"Let's get the wagon and go catch us a priest, Johnson," he said with unconcealed satisfaction.

Johnson stood up, his own billy club in hand. "With pleasure, sir. With pleasure."

* * *

We went straight to the library without invitation and my eyes were drawn to the words *Tolle Lege* written on the marble plaque facing the library's entrance. As if following that order, most seats in the library were filled with students quietly at work. Father Nolan was at his desk, immersed in a book, and I led Webster and Johnson to him. Miss Loddiges trotted after us and Dupin followed behind her.

"This is Father Nolan," I said.

The priest looked up, startled at hearing my voice, and his eyes widened with surprise at seeing our small band.

"Mr. Nolan, you are accused of the murder of Michael Keane, of the theft and sale of valuable books, of being in collusion with Frederic Renelle, recently arrested, and of being involved in the murder of Jeremiah Mathews at the Lazaretto. It will be my great pleasure to escort you to Moyamensing Prison, where your accomplice is already incarcerated," Lieutenant Webster announced.

"I haven't the faintest idea what you mean," Father Nolan said, with such a perfectly blank expression I almost believed him.

"Do not compound your crimes with falsehoods. Rise up, sir." Dupin gestured with his cobra-headed walking stick—the snake seemed almost alive as the light caught its glaring red eyes.

For some unfathomable reason, Father Nolan decided to run. Lieutenant Webster neatly smashed him in the knees with his billy club so that the priest tumbled over, and Dupin pulled his rapier from his walking stick and pinned Nolan to the ground. There was a collective gasp, and I looked behind me to find that all the students were staring at us. Johnson took a short length of rope from his pocket and neatly tied up Father Nolan's hands. Someone must have fetched Father Moriarty when we arrived, for he suddenly entered the room.

"What is going on here?" he demanded.

"Taking a thief and murderer to prison," Webster said matter-of-factly.

"Father Nolan has been stealing treasure books from the library and selling them," I said. "And we believe he had a hand in Father Keane's murder."

"Surely this is nonsense," Father Moriarty said with bewilderment. "Why would he do such things? He is a man of God."

"Greed and a lust for power," Dupin said.

"Deadly sins," Webster smirked.

"We intercepted a note Professor Frederic Renelle sent by carrier pigeon to Father Nolan. It requested that he deliver two more treasure books to the professor for the purpose of selling them," I explained, telling close to the truth. "We spied on their assignation at the Philosophical Hall and witnessed Father Nolan giving Professor Renelle two treasure books that were undoubtedly from this library."

Father Moriarty looked stricken. "From this library?" he echoed.

"Let me ask you this, sir. Do you take an inventory of the treasure books kept here?" Dupin inquired.

"No, that is Father Nolan's job as librarian."

Dupin looked triumphant and Father Nolan's expression of outrage shifted to quiet fury. "Just as I thought. If you review the inventory list of treasure books, you will find that a number are missing," Dupin said.

Including, I thought, the exquisite copy of *La Langue des Oiseaux* that my friend had reclaimed.

"Father Nolan?" Father Moriarty stared at the priest, who remained belligerently silent.

"Based on my observations, it is my belief that Father Nolan stole treasure books to finance certain activities. He is a man who prefers violence to reasoned discussion," Dupin said rather cryptically.

I wondered what my friend was up to. When disentangling a mystery, Dupin had a tendency to make a host of observations and inferences in silence and then to abruptly present his conclusions. It was in this way he had earned a reputation in Paris for having miraculous powers, a notion he did little to discourage.

"Where might we find Fathers Carroll and Heaney?" Dupin continued. "It is urgent, for they are Father Nolan's accomplices."

"Dealing with a delivery of flour, I believe. I saw them in the gardens on my way here," Father Moriarty said.

"Near the pigeon houses?" Dupin asked.

"Yes. They were in the outbuildings where we store food, gardening implements and the like," Father Moriarty said. "Why?"

"I will show you in due course. Bring Father Nolan." And Dupin strode from the library, down the hall and through the door into the garden with the rest of us at his heels.

The two priests we were searching for were hard at work carrying large sacks of flour from a wagon into a storeroom built into the wall near the kitchen.

"Father Carroll, Father Healey, join us, please," Father Moriarty commanded.

The two men stopped in their tracks, each holding a sack. Their eyes darted from Father Moriarty to the trussed-up Nolan and then Officers Webster and Johnson, who made their identities clear enough by lazily tapping their billy clubs against their palms. As we formed a semi-circle round them, both priests quickly ascertained that running was futile and lowered their sacks of flour to the ground.

"These men spent time at your mission in Cuzco last autumn, correct?" Dupin asked Father Moriarty.

He frowned slightly. "We sent some volunteers—Father Nolan organized it—to spread the faith."

Dupin nodded, the picture of confidence. "These are the men who murdered Jeremiah Mathews last October at the Lazaretto," he told Lieutenant Webster. "Under the order of Father Nolan."

Of course we had no proof of this at all, but Dupin often said that most men were as transparent as window glass, their desires were that obvious, and he used this to find ways to seduce an opponent into error. Only by provoking a confession could we be sure that these villains would be sent to prison and remain there, and since Nolan was refusing to speak, Dupin must have sensed that his accomplices would quickly spill the truth if threatened.

Father Moriarty stared at Healey and Carroll with an intensity that made it clear why he commanded the position he did. "Is this true?" he asked, in a voice made all the more fearsome by its low tone.

"No!" Father Carroll protested.

"We did not kill him," Father Healey said.

"You must tell the entire truth," Dupin demanded. "For surely you understand that Father Nolan seeks to put all blame on you by remaining silent about his crimes?"

"We only did as he told us," Father Healey said.

"Let us start from the beginning then," Dupin said. "Father Nolan struck up an alliance with Professor Renelle when he came to the library seeking ancient texts on Peru, knowing that the Augustinians have had a presence in the country since the sixteenth century. They both read a volume that claimed a king's tomb full of treasure, including an enormous emerald, was hidden in the Peruvian mountains. Renelle hoped to find it."

I watched Father Nolan carefully as Dupin recounted his perception of all that had occurred and the priest's expression shifted from self-righteous anger to disquietude.

"Renelle failed to find the treasure during his 1841 expedition, so with Father Nolan's help, a second expedition was organized last autumn," Dupin continued. "Father Nolan decided that this time he needed his own men on the expedition to keep an eye on Professor Renelle, for while the two were in league, Nolan did not trust him. He sent you both under the pretense of taking supplies, or some such thing, to your missionaries in Cuzco, but your true assignment was to go on the expedition with Professor Renelle and Jeremiah Mathews. Renelle believed young Mathews had a map showing the location of the jewel and the king's tomb. Am I correct?" Dupin demanded.

"We did take the bibles to Cuzco," Father Carroll said fearfully to Father Moriarty. "It was not a lie."

Father Moriarty stared at the two priests as if they were strangers.

"You were instructed to stay with Jeremiah Mathews and, if he found the jewel, to confiscate it," Dupin went on. "It was you who gave Professor Renelle tainted water so he was forced to stay in Cuzco, leaving you free to follow Mathews to the lost city without him. You were fortunate that the man did not die of dysentery, for that would have been murder," he added.

"Father Nolan told us to do it," Healey cried out. "He said it would make him ill, not that it might kill him."

"That's true," Carroll agreed, looking to Father Moriarty as if in search of absolution.

Dupin raised his eyebrows and shook his head slightly as if pained, but I knew he was pleased that his strategy was working. "You kept an eye on Jeremiah Mathews, as Nolan instructed, and he collected birds and plants for his employer, which he recorded in the journal he always kept with him. On the journey back, he acted suspiciously and would not let anyone in his cabin. Renelle had made no secret of his search for treasure and rumor spread amongst the crew that Jeremiah Mathews was hiding something, perhaps the jewel Renelle had talked about. When he sent the Schuylkill rangers to raid Jeremiah Mathews's cabin, you forcibly removed him when he tried to defend the bird that was actually hidden there and pushed him overboard when he struggled."

"That is not true!" Father Carroll protested. "The rangers did it. The boy was stupid to fight them."

"But you did not help him," Miss Loddiges snapped. "Why didn't you dive in after him or throw him a rope or *something*?"

"We . . . could not," Healey muttered to his feet, unable to face her.

"Without being drowned yourself?" I asked and Healey nodded.

"Coward," Miss Loddiges said with vehemence.

"But why? Why would you do any of this?" Father Moriarty asked.

"Father Nolan said it was all to save the Church," Father Carroll said.

The pastor turned his gaze to Father Nolan, who remained silent and scowling. "Is this true?"

"I will show you," Dupin said matter-of-factly. He briefly cast his eyes around the storehouse. "Open this," he directed at Healey and Carroll, pointing to a door near where the wagon was tethered.

The two priests looked at one another and hesitated.

"Do as he says!" Father Moriarty thundered, causing us all to flinch.

Carroll, pale-faced and trembling, dug into his robes and pulled out a set of keys. He unlocked the door and stepped aside as Dupin entered the storeroom within, where I could see a number of large wooden crates. He removed the lid from one and looked inside. "As I suspected," he said with unmistakable satisfaction. He lifted out a musket and showed it to our shocked assembly. "Crates of munitions bought with a portion of the money from the treasure books to defend St. Augustine's against the Nativists. While it is undeniable that there has been violence against Catholics in the city of Philadelphia, it was not a Nativist who murdered Father Keane or pinned the inflamma-tory broadsheet to his chest," Dupin said. "This was merely a scenario constructed by Father Nolan to hide the fact that he killed him. Am I correct?" Dupin asked Fathers Healey and Carroll, who were struck dumb with terror.

"He will blame you for his crimes and let you rot in prison without a second thought," I told them. "You must speak the truth."

"Yes," Carroll muttered, and Healey nodded. "He said Father Keane would tell Father Moriarty, who would have us locked up, and all we had done to save St. Augustine's would be undone."

"I ask you again, is that the truth?" Father Moriarty demanded, but Nolan remained stony-faced and would not speak a word.

"I believe the night of the fourteenth of March went some-thing like this," Dupin said, staring at Father Nolan. "Renelle brought the cache of muskets, which Fathers Healey and Carroll transferred to the storehouse, while you talked with Professor Renelle about Jeremiah Mathews's journal, which he was determined to get at any cost. You had seen Father Keane examining a journal in the library and knew it was the one he sought. You promised to send Renelle a message with a pigeon as soon as you took it from Father Keane." Dupin paused so that his words might be absorbed by all.

"What Nolan did not realize," Dupin said, shifting his gaze to Father Moriarty, "was that Father Keane had been disturbed by the noise outside and had witnessed all that occurred. So he hid the journal and the treasure book in the church and wrote a note warning Mr. Poe, which he put in an envelope with a key to the treasure book cabinet. In that cabinet Father Keane had hidden clues that would lead Mr. Poe to the books and would warn him about Father Nolan. They were clues that Nolan himself would think nothing of if he came across them. Correct, sir?"

The priest remained resolutely silent, but he could not keep the anger from his face. Dupin continued, fixing Father Nolan with his stare.

"You found Father Keane when he was still in the library and quickly realized that he had overheard something that revealed you to be a thief. Frightened as he was, Father Keane could not believe you would stoop to murder, for he was convinced you were a good man at heart. Sadly he was wrong," Dupin said. "You killed him in cold blood and pinned the Nativist broadsheet to his cassock to insinuate outsiders were responsible for your crime. You found the warning letter he had written and destroyed it, but gave the envelope with the key to Poe so he would lead you to the treasure book and journal," Dupin concluded.

All were silent for a time, then Father Moriarty said, "This is how you would lead St. Augustine Church? Through theft and murder?"

I was surprised at how quickly he had come to presume Nolan's guilt, but sensed there was a history of conflict between the two men. Nolan stared at Father Moriarty, cold-blooded as a snake, and his apparent disregard for my friend's life made me angrier than anything that had been said.

"Father Keane was your friend," I said passionately. "You spent hours discussing the books you read, talking about all he observed on his walks, sharing a joke. He admired you greatly and thought you to be a man of principle and wisdom, as did I. And yet you murdered your friend, a man who thought of you as a brother."

Father Nolan turned his gaze to me and chose, at last, to speak. "Father Keane was my friend. And I believe he would have understood, in time, what we needed to do to protect St. Augustine's. But you decided his fate, Mr. Poe. You brought those dead birds and poppets to his office and got him reading about the Chachapoyas and asking questions. And then you brought the journal here so that he was prying into things he never would have looked at twice before." Father Nolan's eyes narrowed. "Do not be so self-righteous, Mr. Poe. If you had kept away from our library, my friend Michael Keane would still be alive." His intent was to twist a knife in my heart and he fully succeeded.

Father Moriarty pointed to the door in the wall that surrounded St. Augustine's and said to Lieutenant Webster, "Take them away. They have no place here."

Healey and Carroll gave wails of anguish but offered no resistance as Johnson tied up their hands and led them out.

"Let's go, priest," Lieutenant Webster said to Father Nolan. "Your chariot awaits thee outside." He chuckled at his own joke and led Nolan away from the sanctuary of St. Augustine Church.

46

The sun fell through the glass, splitting into hard, bright fragments that warmed the air to that of a summer's day. We were
a peculiar assembly, the amiable Colonel Carr doing his best to
modify a transportation case to suit the white spatuletail
hummingbird, while Miss Loddiges, Sissy, Mrs. Carr, Dupin
and I looked on. Of course we had no guarantee that Colibrí
would arrive with the magical hummingbird, but Miss
Loddiges was confident that he would; the Carrs were desperately keen to view the creature once they had heard Miss
Loddiges's tale and had offered to assist with the costs of
Colibrí's passage back to Peru. All they wished for in return
was the opportunity to sketch the ghostly hummingbird and to
take their own daguerrotypes with the camera they had set up
in the glasshouse.

The hummingbird transportation box was a large, modified
Wardian case with one wire mesh wall covered by a drape. Its
three glass pane walls were coated with white paint.

"It will allow in sufficient light," Colonel Carr explained,
"while obscuring the outside world, which is bound to frighten
the bird. We would not wish it to injure itself by flying into the
glass." A wooden perch was suspended across the enclosure

and a mound of fine straw covered the bottom of the cage. Colonel Carr attached a bottle of sugar water to the mesh wall with a spout that the hummingbird might sip from. "This will enable your friend to easily feed the bird and the curtain will protect the bird from drafts and visual disturbances. The cage should be sufficiently warm if kept in his cabin."

Dupin circled the makeshift hummingbird case solemnly, scrutinizing every aspect of it. "Most impressive," he said. "I would imagine that Jeremiah Mathews constructed something similar to transport the spatuletail on the arduous journey from Peru to Philadelphia."

"I would think so," Colonel Carr agreed. "Helena's father sent me some sketches of the case Andrew Mathews used to successfully transport his *Trochilus colubris* three years ago, and we might presume Jeremiah used the same design or improved upon it."

"Perhaps these successes will inspire ornithologists to collect live birds to study," Sissy ventured.

"It is something I would like to try," Miss Loddiges said. "To house exotic birds in our glasshouses in a facsimile of their habitat so visitors might appreciate the true beauty of them when alive."

"It is a worthy goal," I said. "I hope you will succeed in it."

Colonel Carr glanced at his pocket watch. "Half past three o'clock," he murmured with a despondency we all felt.

"Why don't we have a walk around the spring garden," Mrs. Carr suggested. "There is a wonderful array of daffodils and jonquils and so many purple crocuses they are like an exotic carpet. The forsythia is all ablaze too."

"Yes, that would be lovely." Sissy linked her arm through Miss Loddiges's. "Let's have a stroll, Helena. It may be some time before I manage to get back here for the early spring blooms."

"Very well," Miss Loddiges reluctantly agreed, and the three women made their way out into the brisk late afternoon while Dupin, Colonel Carr and I sat inside the glasshouse with the empty hummingbird case.

"Sunset is about half past six. I had rather hoped to see the bird by daylight," Colonel Carr said.

"I would not hope too much," Dupin said. "The Chachapoyan had utter faith in his destiny to return the bird to his homeland and is unlikely to take up the assistance offered. I fear he is being foolhardy, like so many men of faith, but perhaps luck will be with him."

Colonel Carr shook his head, more than disappointed.

"He believed it to be a mystical bird," Dupin added. "That *la Joya*, as he called it, was perhaps immortal. Of course, if there have been a number of white spatuletails recorded by his people over the centuries then it must be a species rather than a mere aberration—*Mathewsii nubes* as Jeremiah Mathews fittingly called it."

"We must suggest that a record of it is lodged with that name," I said.

"Indeed," Dupin nodded. "To address another point, I will travel back to Europe with Miss Loddiges. I would not like to trust anyone claiming to be sent by her father to accompany her unless Colonel Carr personally knows the man."

"Quite right," the colonel said. "Any notion when Renelle will be sentenced?"

"I'm afraid not," I replied. "But I am more than pleased that he has taken my place at Moyamensing Prison."

"Let us hope justice prevails and the rogue stays there," Dupin said.

A half an hour passed in pleasant conversation until we saw the ladies approaching. They were just at the door to the glasshouse, about to enter, when a dark shadow thudded with a *crack* against the glass pane directly above Sissy's head. She gave a little shriek and clasped her hands to her mouth as an object tumbled to the ground. I rushed outside, followed by Colonel Carr and Dupin.

"Ah, a bird," Colonel Carr said. "Unfortunately they sometimes fly into the glass. They don't see it, I presume."

Miss Loddiges was crouched down, tenderly stroking the red-feathered breast of a robin, while tears slid from my wife's eyes as she looked down at the dead bird, its normally cheery black eyes staring at oblivion.

"The poor darling thing," Sissy murmured and I enclosed her in my arms.

"I'm sorry you saw that, dearest. Come inside where it's warm."

My wife nodded and let me lead her into the glasshouse. Mrs. Carr went to ask her housekeeper to bring us tea and once we had consumed that, Sissy regained a modicum of cheer, especially when describing the spring blossoms they had viewed.

"What an idyllic place," she sighed. "Truly I would relish even the hardest labor digging in the dirt if the result were as glorious as your gardens, Mrs. Carr."

"If more thought like you, Mrs. Poe, the world would be full of grace and beauty," Dupin said.

"Hear, hear," Colonel Carr agreed.

When nightfall came and Colibrí did not, Dupin and Sissy climbed into our host's carriage, and I was just about to do the same when Miss Loddiges clutched my arm and gestured for me to lean closer.

"Beware the robin's song, Mr. Poe. I feel you must leave Philadelphia. It is not a good place for Virginia. You must leave and soon."

"The robin?" I said in a low voice. "A sign?"

She nodded. "You really must go from here. I feel it."

"Thank you for your warning." I climbed into the carriage and let the Carr's coachman ferry us away from Bartram's gardens, but Miss Loddiges's words left me with an itch born of fear that could not be salved by logic.

47

WEDNESDAY, 27 MARCH 1844

Seagulls cartwheeled through the air and skimmed the water, their raucous calls an unfortunate accompaniment to their exuberant dance with the elements. The ship, the *Martha*, was anchored in the harbor, stately and elegant, gangplank extended from the edge of Philadelphia to its decks, an invitation to her passengers. We were approaching the ship when a figure emerged from the crowd and ran directly at us. I felt Sissy's hand clutch my arm and knew she had the same fearful reaction. Was it someone in the employ of Renelle or Nolan bent on revenge? In the blink of an eye, Dupin's rapier was unsheathed from his walking stick and directed at the chest of their attacker. The boy stopped in his tracks, utterly frightened.

"Don't murder me, sir!"

I realized it was young Davey.

"Mr. Poe, sir, don't let him murder me, please. I have a message."

"From whom?" Dupin growled, rapier still directed at the boy's chest.

"Is this the lady, Mr. Poe?" Davey asked, thoroughly frightened but determined to remain on his mission, whatever that was. "Is this Helena?"

"Yes, I am Helena," Miss Loddiges told him gently. "How did you know my name?"

"Truly is it her, sir?" the boy asked me again.

"Yes, Davey, it is Miss Loddiges. Who has sent you?" I gestured for Dupin to lower his blade. "We met the boy, remember?"

"Of course I remember," Dupin snapped. "But I wish to know who sent him and for what purpose."

"Jeremiah," the boy cried out. "I have a message for Helena from Jeremiah."

"That is impossible. Jeremiah Mathews is dead, as you well know," Dupin said harshly.

"Yes, but he gave me this before he died, when we were moored at the Lazaretto." The boy reached into his coat pocket and only when he brought out a sealed-up letter did Dupin lower his blade. "He told me to give it to Helena and only Helena when we next sailed to London. Her address is written on it, see?" He pushed the letter to Miss Loddiges, who took it and gasped.

"It is Jeremiah's writing," she said.

"Why did you keep the letter from us when you knew we were helping Miss Loddiges?" I asked.

A stubborn look came onto the boy's face. "He made me swear that I would give the letter to no one but Helena. He was kind to me and I was very sorry that he drowned. And so I had to keep my word."

"Jeremiah would have been proud of you, Davey," Miss Loddiges said quietly.

The boy beamed and continued to stand there, clearly waiting for her to open the letter, as we all were, albeit rather more secretly. Miss Loddiges obliged us and broke the seal. As she scanned the page, her eyes became glassy with tears. She refolded the missive and tucked it carefully into the carpet bag she carried.

"He knew that he was being watched and feared that he might be murdered when Professor Renelle came to the Lazaretto and made threats," she said. "The only person he could trust on the ship was Davey." She smiled at the boy and placed a hand on his shoulder. "You have done me a great service. And Jeremiah. I will treasure this letter forever," she said. "And if you do sail to London, please come to visit me at Paradise Fields. You will be very welcome." Miss Loddiges then reached up into her peculiar bonnet and removed one of the hummingbirds. She handed it to the boy in cupped hands, as if the thing were still alive. "This is a *Heliothryx auritus*—a black-eared fairy hummingbird. It is from Peru. Perhaps it will help you to remember us."

The boy took the tiny bird in his own hands and examined its vibrant green wings and back, its white belly and black mask. "It looks alive, but it isn't, is it?"

"No, but if you look at it in a certain light it can seem so, and it might tell you things as it does me."

"Thank you, miss," the boy said, beaming.

"Farewell, Davey."

He grinned at her, then walked into the crowd, the little hummingbird nestling in his hands.

"It is time to board the ship, Miss Loddiges," Dupin said. "And time for me to say farewell. Thank you again for your hospitality, Mrs. Poe. I had feared that your husband's rapturous descriptions of you were exaggerations, but they have proved to be more than modest. Please know that I am at your service should you ever require assistance." He bowed as if to a queen and then turned to me. "I hope that I have helped you in some small way, my friend, for it is my greatest honor to do so—*Amicis semper fidelis*. Never hesitate to call upon me when in need of aid."

"And vice versa, of course." I reached out to shake his hand and hoped I would prove as true a friend as Dupin if he ever needed my assistance.

"And I will never forget what you've done for me," Miss Loddiges said to me. "Thank you, Mr. Poe." She turned to Sissy and the two embraced. "I have made a dear friend in you, Virginia, and Lord knows I have few of those. Be well and be safe," she said fiercely.

"I will expect many letters," my wife replied. "Safe journey."

Miss Loddiges gazed at us both as if memorizing our faces, then turned and walked with Dupin toward the *Martha*. They crossed the narrow bridge and when both had reached the safety of the deck, the two positioned themselves to gaze upon us. They were an odd pair, the tiny Miss Loddiges like an exotic bird in her bright blue embroidered cape, her hat secured to her head with a voluminous scarf, and Dupin dressed entirely in black as ever, his overcoat flapping in the breeze like stygian sails. They remained in that position when the ship weighed anchor and sailed from port, Miss Loddiges waving until the distance between us was too great to see her, whereas Dupin did not raise his hand in farewell at all—he simply remained silent and watchful by the lady's side as the *Martha* journeyed out to the Atlantic.

"It is a great credit to you to have such devout friends," my wife said when Dupin and Miss Loddiges were but shadowy forms upon the deck. "And I am happy to have met them, for I admire my husband all the more. Now let us go home." And she gently touched her lips to my cheek.

48

MONDAY, 1 APRIL 1844

A haze of green surrounded me, a tender verdant tone particular to spring that deepens with time or is scorched to brown by the sun's fierceness. Morning's gentle chorus hummed: leaves rustling like silk mixed with the songbirds' trills and the flow of the Schuylkill over its rocky bed. It glistened and splashed, then collected in dark, deep pools where I might swim in a few month's time when the water warmed under the sun. The early morning air still had the bite of winter, but all around me was unfurling with life and the world felt new and good.

"*Chick-a-dee-dee-dee*"—the warning call rang out above the other morning birdsong. I glanced in the direction of the sound and saw a black-capped chickadee hanging from a twig, watching my progress along the river path. Moments later, I spied the bird's mate peering out from the hollow of a white ash tree where the two had made their home. The male swooped from its roost, seizing an invisible insect, then flitted to the tree, delivering its prize to the female. I continued along the river, greatly cheered by all that I saw.

It was close to nine o'clock when I arrived home. The kitchen fire was reduced to embers and neither my wife nor Muddy were anywhere to be seen, which was more than unusual at that time of day. Moments later, the sound of my wife singing came to me from the parlor, and I made my way toward it, then stood for a moment in the hallway, relishing the pure beauty of her voice as she sang the popular ballad "Long, Long Ago". When the song concluded, I threw open the door and stepped inside, offering my applause.

"Bravo!"

My mother-in-law smiled in greeting and my wife flushed prettily as she dipped a mock curtsey. And then another pair of hands began to clap in unison with mine.

"Bravo, indeed. Thank you most kindly, Mrs. Poe, for your delightful recital. It has brought great cheer to my heart, despite the song's rather maudlin message."

My hands fluttered down to my sides like a wounded bird, for there, sitting in the armchair on the other side of the fireplace, was a man I had hoped never to see again.

"I am sorry if the ballad's sentiments caused you any pain, Mr. Reynolds," my wife said anxiously.

"Not at all. Rowena was terribly fond of the song. Indeed, she occasionally sang it herself on stage and was acquainted with Mr. Bayly, the song's author, back in London."

"Mr. Reynolds came to inform us that there will be a memorial concert for his wife at Christ Church this Friday evening, performed by her theater company to raise funds for a suitable memorial plaque for her at the Chestnut Street Theater."

"I see." I was unable to think of anything else that might hide my shock at finding my nemesis in my own home, particularly after his accusations at the theater had sent me to prison.

"I told him how terribly saddened we were by Mrs. Reynolds's demise," Sissy continued.

"Indeed," I muttered.

"I so admired your wife's talent and charm," Sissy continued. "I feel lucky to have conversed with her."

"Thank you, Mrs. Poe, that is very kind. Rowena was utterly charmed by you. We had talked about calling on you, but there is never enough time to enjoy life's small pleasures, and then, tragically, she was taken from me." His head drooped in sorrow and a solitary tear ran down his cheek. "And still the police claim not to know the identity of her murderer."

"We were terribly shaken by the false accusations against Eddy."

"But without doubt it was Frederic Renelle who murdered your wife, as I testified to the officers of the police. He had motive and I am certain her assailant was the same size and build."

"He denies it and there is no evidence to support your accusations," Reynolds said.

My wife shook her head in commiseration. "Professor Renelle's imprisonment must not be fully comforting for you, as it is for crimes other than your wife's murder. I pray in time you will receive justice," she said.

Reynolds's face hardened. "That I will, most assuredly, Mrs. Poe," he said, staring at me. "Rowena was no fool. She would not have accompanied a stranger to that room at the top of the theater. Her murderer was someone she did not fear. The culprit may believe he has escaped justice, but that will not be the case forever." His eyes, cold and as unforgiving as obsidian, held mine until I was forced to glance away. Triumphant, he turned to my disconcerted wife. His grim face eased into a false smile and he said: "But I dwell too much on my sorrows, so much that I am hardly able to put pen to paper to complete the last play my wife and I were composing together. It would give me great comfort if you would sing again, Mrs. Poe, for truly your voice is that of an angel. Perhaps you might perform 'The Little Turtledove' if you know it. The song was a favorite of my wife."

"Yes, of course. I know it well." And Virginia began to sing, her gaze fixed on some invisible point, her voice clear and pure as spring water:

> *Oh, can't you see yon little turtle dove,*
> *Sitting under the mulberry tree?*
> *See how that she doth mourn for her true love:*
> *And I shall mourn for thee, my dear,*
> *And I shall mourn for thee.*

Reynolds murmured the words tunelessly, tapping the rhythm on his knee:

> *You leave me here to lament, and well-a-day!*
> *My tears you will not see, my love,*
> *My tears you will not see.*

Reynolds's voice increased in volume, bringing an unpleasant harshness as his voice merged with Sissy's. My impatience and anger at his insolence grew until I stepped further into the room, prepared to interrupt the song and oust Reynolds from our home, but my anger was immediately forgotten when my wife's voice broke mid-note and she clutched at her throat.

"My darling!" I rushed to her, as did Muddy. Reynolds leapt to his feet.

Sissy tried to speak and, as she did, red bubbled from her lips and splashed onto the white bodice of her dress. She coughed and sputtered until I pressed my handkerchief to her mouth—vermilion bloomed through it like a rose. She fainted away and I caught her in my arms, gently lowered her into the armchair.

"Oh my Lord, oh my Lord," Muddy whimpered in repetitive prayer. She crouched down and stroked her daughter's hand, utterly distraught.

Reynolds took a large shawl that was draped over the sofa and offered it to cover her. "Fear not, I will fetch a doctor," he said, picking up his coat.

"Thank you, yes. I would be grateful." I was in a daze of shock and grief as I followed Reynolds to the door. When I opened it, a gust of cold air pushed its way inside like a malevolent spirit. "I am appreciative, sir, and am relieved that the animosity of the past has at last been resolved between us," I said, my words utterly heartfelt.

George Reynolds stepped out into the unforgiving glare of late morning, then looked back at me. "I gave my word to my wife that I would not pursue recompense for what your forbears did to mine, that it was time to allow the crimes of the dead to be buried with them. But the crimes of the living must be avenged one way or another. I will never forgive you for Rowena's murder, for I believe you to be culpable," he said with pure hatred on his face. "Now go attend to your wife, Poe," he said with a dismissive flick of his wrist. "For truly she is dying. You will know the pain I feel soon enough and that will give me deep satisfaction."

When he perceived that his pernicious words were lodged like daggers in my heart, George Reynolds turned his back to me and walked away, jauntily whistling the lament "The Little Turtledove".

49

Brennan Farm, New York
3 June 1844

My dear Dupin,

This morning at the river I spied a green heron picking its way elegantly through the shallows in search of
its breakfast. It half-froze for a moment, then quickly
grabbed a fish in its bill, a fish that was large enough to
be unwieldy. The heron carried it to the riverbank,
trying to maneuver it into a position that would make
it easier to swallow, but the fish wriggled, determined
to escape back into the water. Moments later, two
crows swooped down from the trees and pranced up
to the heron on either side, like two cutpurses intent
on robbing an innocent. Back and forth they went until
the poor heron gave up trying to swallow the fish and
scurried back into the water while the crows feasted
on his catch. Later in the afternoon, Sissy was
enchanted by a ruby-throated hummingbird in our
garden, which darted from blossom to blossom like a
radiant jewel of an insect and seemed to hover directly

in front of her as if to say hello. And of course we both wondered what Miss Loddiges would make of our visitations and thought of you both with affection and no small amount of guilt, as I have taken far too long to put pen to paper.

Much has happened since my last letter and indeed it seemed for a time as if Hell itself had ascended to Earth as the city of Philadelphia burned after the mob took to the streets, rioting, killing and setting the city alight. The skirmishes we experienced when you were with us in Philadelphia escalated terribly on the third of May after those who call themselves "native Americans" held a meeting in Nanny Goat Market in Kensington, claiming it was their right to publicly express their views as guaranteed by the Constitution of the United States. You will remember that the area is heavily populated by recently arrived Irish Catholics, and a crowd soon gathered that vehemently expressed disapproval of the speeches being made. What began as a verbal exchange quickly became physical, with much pushing and shoving followed by volleys of stones and bricks. Then musket shots rang out from both sides, which had the effect of dispersing the crowd, but a number of combatants were wounded. A youth who was but eighteen years old was hit in the chest, and despite the best efforts to save him, he expired, the first but not the last death in the affray.

Worse still, rabble-rousers fanned the violence. A torn American flag was put on display at Second and Franklin streets, with a printed notice: "This is the flag which was trampled upon by the Irish papists." Over the following days, incendiaries set bonfires and burnt the dwellings of innocent families, who ran from the inferno carrying what they could in small bundles, looking for refuge in vain. The only houses in the area that escaped deliberate destruction were those who put a sign, "Native American" in the window. Rumors that weapons were held in the Catholic churches convinced the mob that all such "strongholds" had to be destroyed. St. Michael's was set alight after darkness fell on the eighth of May and, despite efforts to protect it, St. Augustine's followed soon after, when a young boy sneaked into the guarded church and lit a fire in the vestibule. The entire building was quickly ablaze, masses of smoke curling from its windows, the flames creeping up to the very belfry until the entire steeple was shimmering, the elegant cupola with its clock and gilt cross consumed by fire. The steeple burned to its very bones and crashed to the ground, raining down a trail of gold like a meteor's tail. St. Augustine's was home to the Sister Bell, that twin of the famed Liberty Bell, but the conflagration broke it into fragments, a terrible omen for the city. Perhaps worst of all, the entire glorious library of St. Augustine's, all its priceless treasure books and singular tomes, were embraced by the insatiable flames and transformed one by one into silvery ash. By sunrise on the ninth of May, all that remained of St. Augustine's was the wall behind the altar, where charred gilt letters warned: "The Lord Seeth." One might only hope that it was a pledge from God himself.

Father Moriarty relayed the terrible news to me himself, bemoaning the fact that Father Nolan's theft of the treasure books had been revealed only for the entire library to be destroyed by fire a few weeks later. I share his sorrow in the loss of such a precious collection and wonder if we might have done more to prevent the destruction of St. Augustine's. I suspect you will tell me that reason would have done little to change what happened—the mob is a beast unto itself, rabid, illogical and purely malevolent.

You will have fathomed by now that we are no longer resident in the city of brotherly love. I acted on the warning from Miss Loddiges and left Philadelphia in early April We now reside in a bucolic spot in New York, where Sissy, Muddy and your friend Catterina are more than happy. The dwelling is two-storied, double-framed and on a farm of over two hundred acres. It is owned by Patrick Brennan and, happily, his wife agreed to take us in as boarders. While I miss my swims in the Schuylkill, the Hudson is quite a wonderful alternative. The Brennans themselves are amiable people, very fond of Sissy, and their children are well-mannered and pleasant company when I go walking. One of the girls has developed a keen interest in watching me at work, determined to catch sight of the Muse when she bestows her inspiration. So far the girl has been disappointed in her quest and wonders if my work is any good, if that mysterious phantom has avoided my company. On occasion I admittedly have the same concerns. Sissy assures the child that writing requires hard labor more than oft-fleeting inspiration, hence the long and, as the child puts it, dull hours I spend at my desk. Thinking back to our debate in London, I continue to hold fast to my belief that my wife and our future children will be my more constant Muse, inspiring rather than reducing my literary oeuvre.

But I am certain you have guessed that it was more than Miss Loddiges's premonition that persuaded me to make such a sudden move to an entirely new city, and the answer is very simple: the return of my nemesis. With immense guile, George Reynolds, criminal turned playwright, weaseled his way into my home when I was out and persuaded my wife to sing, which caused a blood vessel to burst in her throat. The monster then gloated. Reynolds may have promised his dead wife that he would not seek revenge against me, yet it is more than clear he will not hesitate to destroy those I hold dearest.

But I must not bring my letter to a close on such a tenebrous note, as I feel New York will bring many improvements for us. Enclosed for your amusement is an article inspired by the French aeronaut we met in London, which was published in the thirteenth of April edition of the *New York Sun*. The newspaper's offices were besieged by those who wished to read about the traversing of the Atlantic by balloon, and I was fortunate to procure a copy myself. The effect of my little hoax has been most gratifying. I am working on several poems, one of which Miss Loddiges is certain to appreciate as there is a touch of ornithomancy about it. I suspect it will remind you of that afternoon in Mr. Dickens's library, although the tone is not in the least comical.

Please do send your news, my dear Dupin, and accept fond good wishes from Sissy, cautious regards from my mother-in-law and undying affection from Catterina, who quite pines for you.

With greatest respect from your sincere friend,
Edgar A. Poe

ACKNOWLEDGEMENTS

Heartfelt thanks, as always, to my superb agent Oli Munson and the fantastic team at A.M. Heath. I am very lucky.

I'm grateful to my editor, the wonderful Jenny Parrott, and all at Oneworld Publications—you are brilliant and such a joy to work with.

Appreciative thanks to Claiborne Hancock and the excellent team at my U.S. publisher Pegasus Books; it's been a true pleasure.

I am also thankful for the forensic mind of Helen Szirtes, copy-editor extraordinaire, and for the invaluable feedback from my writer/ reader friends: Alice Bowen, Shauna Gilligan, Sally Griffiths. Technical advice was much appreciated from Dmitry Starkov and from Santiago Herrero, gone too soon and deeply missed. The endless support from faraway friends and family was gratefully received through the ether and thanks, especially, to Darren Hill and Ziggy, as always.